STORY AND ART BY
NORIYUKI KONISHI

ORIGINAL CONCEPT AND SUPERVISED BY LEVEL-5 INC.

YO-KAI WATCH™
Volume 6
JIBANYAN EVOLVES
Perfect Square Edition

Story and Art by Noriyuki Konishi
Original Concept and Supervised by LEVEL-5 Inc.

Translation/Tetsuichiro Miyaki
English Adaptation/Aubrey Sitterson
Lettering/William F. Schuch, Zack Turner & Paolo Gattone
Design/Izumi Evers
Editor/Joel Enos

YO-KAI WATCH Vol. 6
by Noriyuki KONISHI
© 2013 Noriyuki KONISHI
©LEVEL-5 Inc.
Original Concept and Supervised by LEVEL-5 Inc.
All rights reserved.
Original Japanese edition published by SHOGAKUKAN.
English translation rights in the United States of America and
Canada arranged with SHOGAKUKAN.

Printed in the U.S.A

Published by VIZ Media, LLC
P.O. Box 77010
San Francisco, CA 94107

10 9 8 7 6 5 4 3 2 1
First printing, December 2016

www.perfectsquare.com

www.viz.com

PARENTAL ADVISORY
YO-KAI WATCH is rated A
and is suitable for readers
of all ages.
ratings.viz.com

YO-KAI WATCH™

6

STORY AND ART BY
NORIYUKI KONISHI

ORIGINAL CONCEPT AND SUPERVISED BY LEVEL-5 INC.

CHARACTER INTRODUCTION

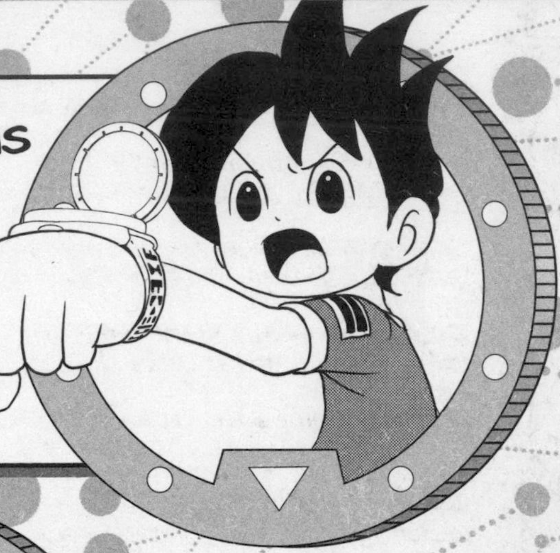

NATHAN ADAMS

AN ORDINARY ELEMENTARY SCHOOL STUDENT. WHISPER GAVE HIM THE YO-KAI WATCH, AND THEY HAVE SINCE BECOME FRIENDS.

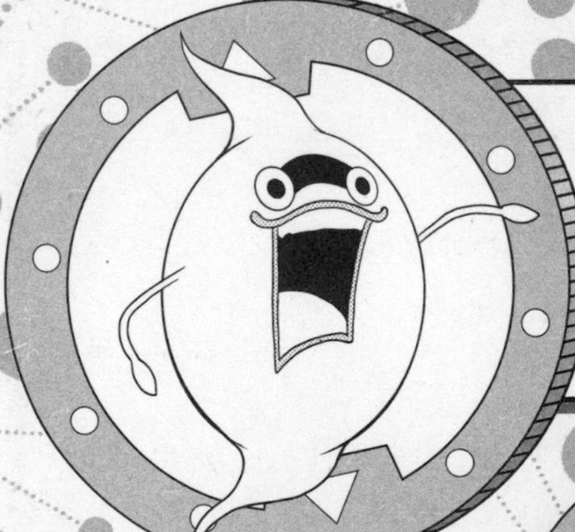

WHISPER

A YO-KAI BUTLER FREED BY NATE, WHISPER HELPS HIM BY USING HIS EXTENSIVE KNOWLEDGE OF OTHER YO-KAI.

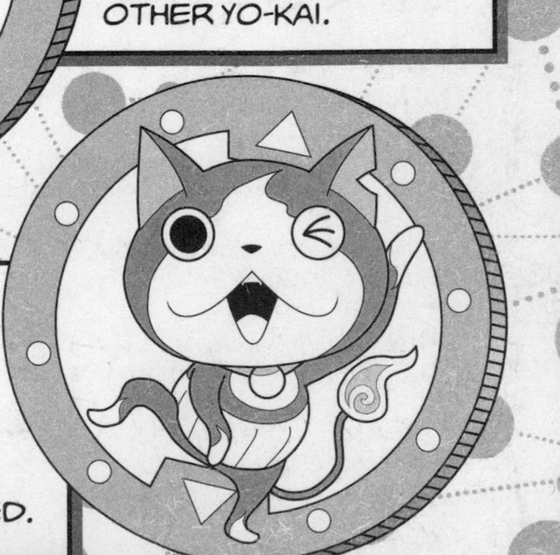

JIBANYAN

A CAT WHO BECAME A YO-KAI WHEN HE PASSED AWAY. HE IS FRIENDLY, CAREFREE AND THE FIRST YO-KAI THAT NATE BEFRIENDED.

TABLE OF CONTENTS

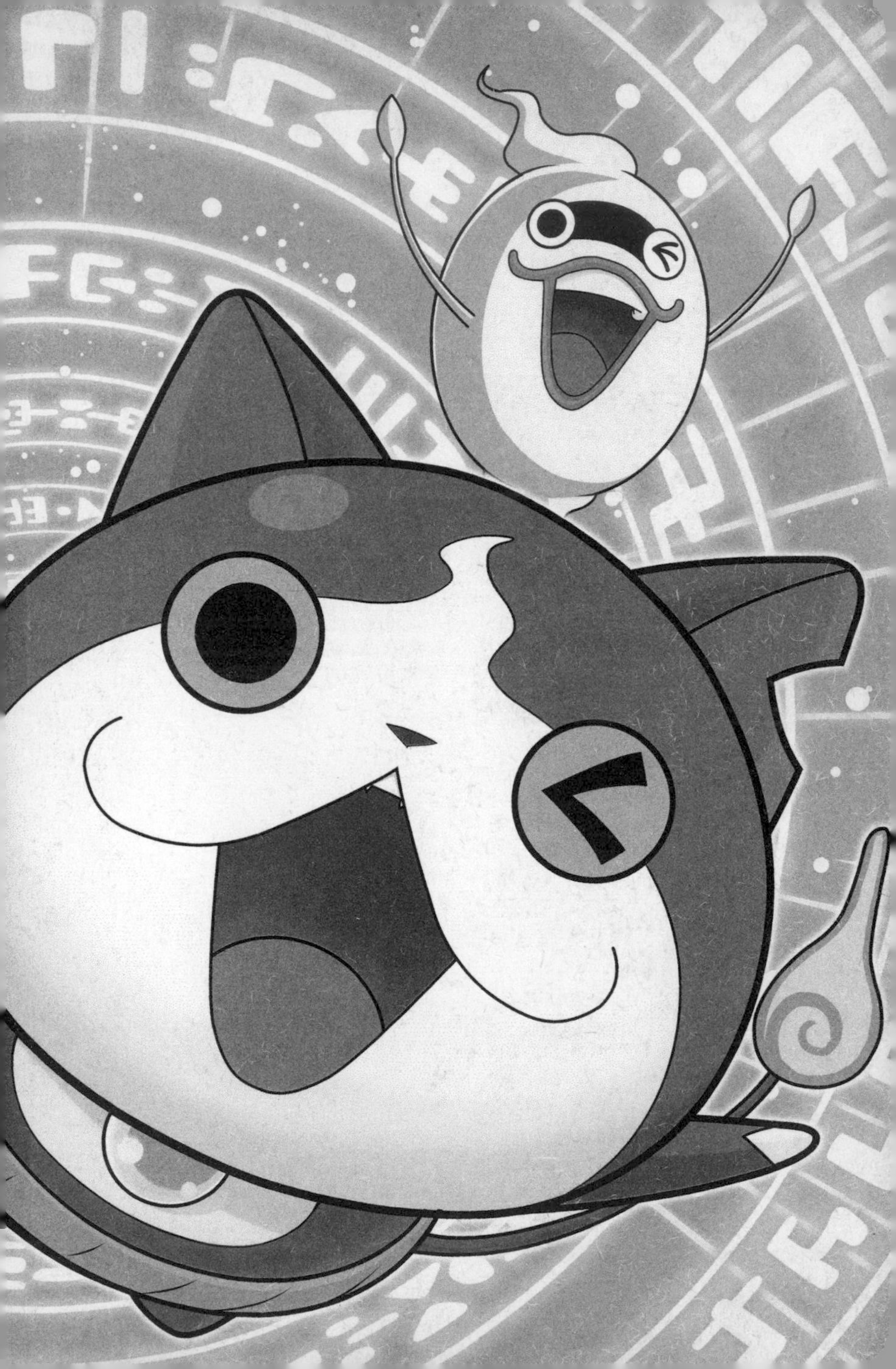

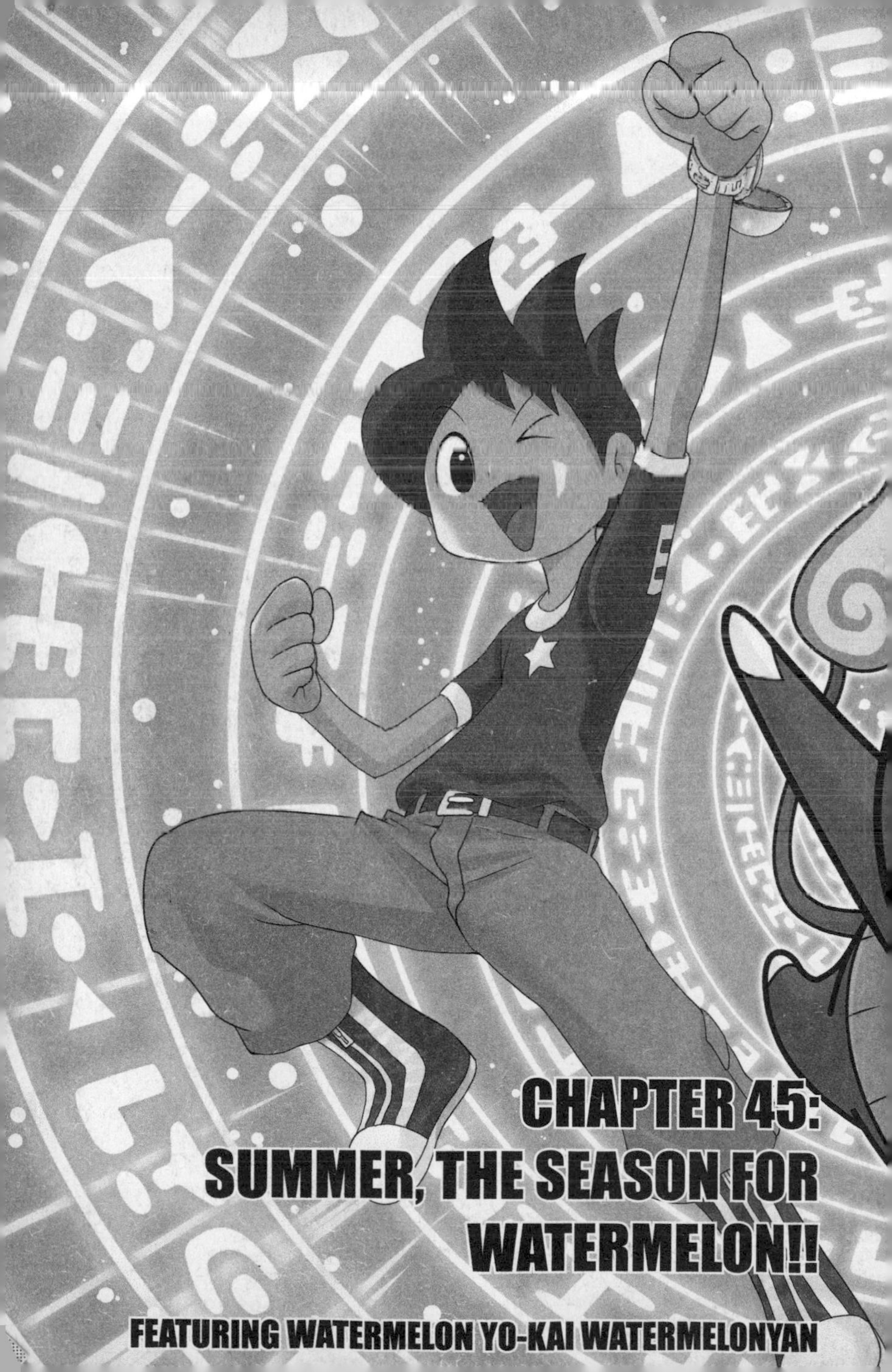

CHAPTER 45: SUMMER, THE SEASON FOR WATERMELON!!

FEATURING WATERMELON YO-KAI WATERMELONYAN

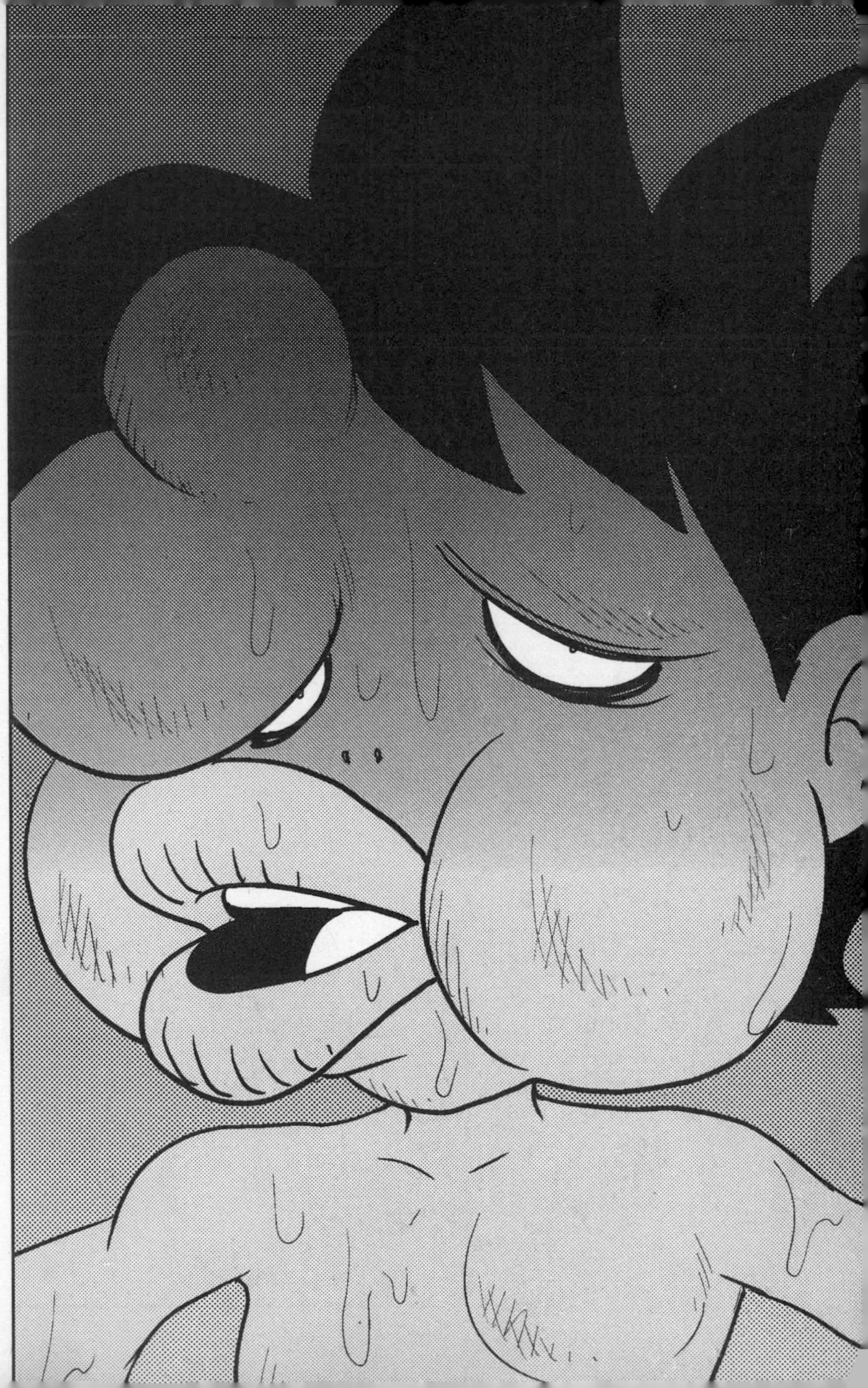

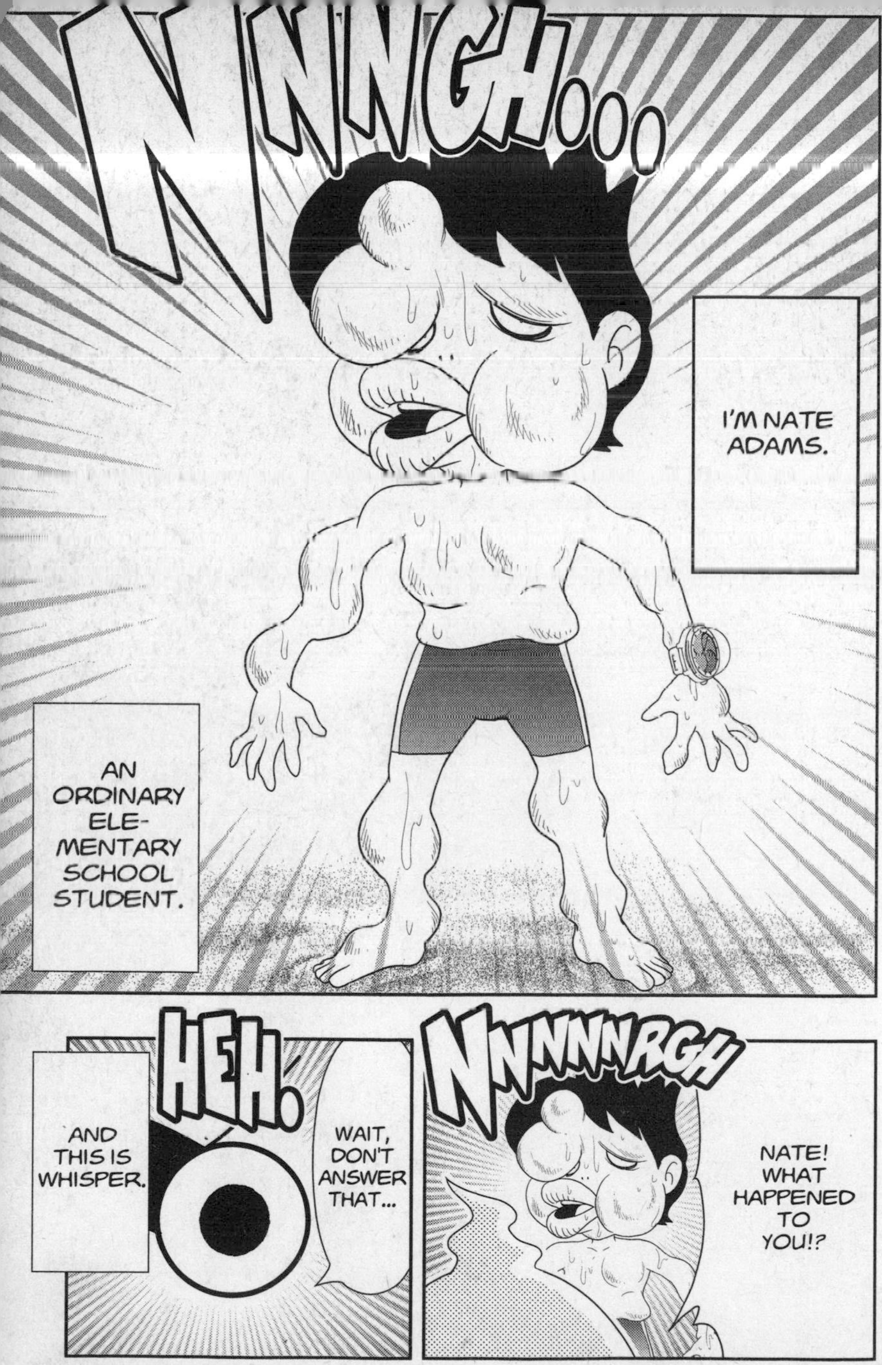
NNNGH...
I'M NATE ADAMS.
AN ORDINARY ELE-MENTARY SCHOOL STUDENT.
NNNNNRGH
NATE! WHAT HAPPENED TO YOU!?
HEH.
WAIT, DON'T ANSWER THAT...
AND THIS IS WHISPER.

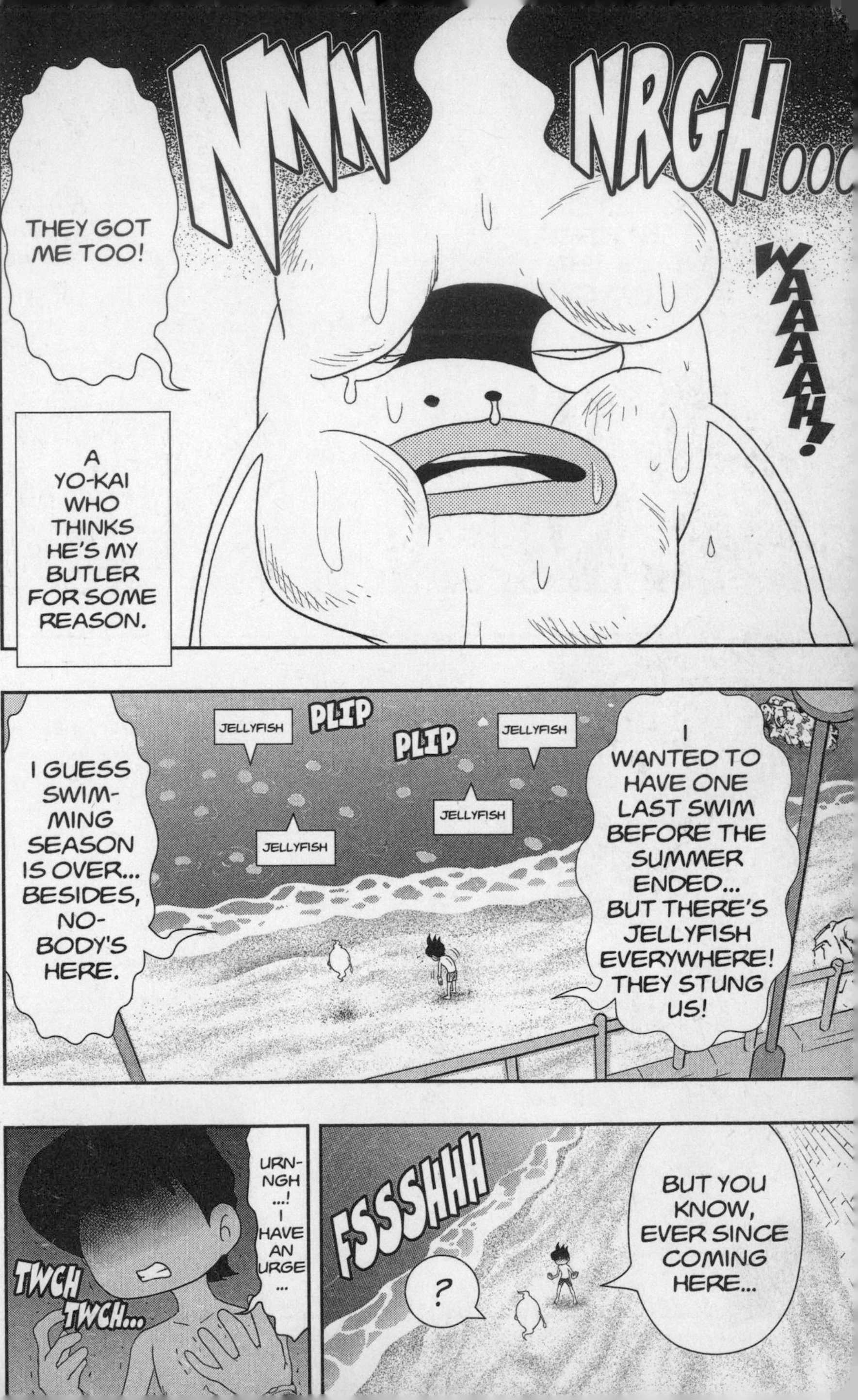
NRGH...
NNNN
WAAAAH!
THEY GOT ME TOO!
A YO-KAI WHO THINKS HE'S MY BUTLER FOR SOME REASON.
I WANTED TO HAVE ONE LAST SWIM BEFORE THE SUMMER ENDED... BUT THERE'S JELLYFISH EVERYWHERE! THEY STUNG US!
JELLYFISH
PLIP
PLIP
JELLYFISH
JELLYFISH
JELLYFISH
I GUESS SWIMMING SEASON IS OVER... BESIDES, NOBODY'S HERE.
BUT YOU KNOW, EVER SINCE COMING HERE...
FSSSHHH
?
URNNGH...! I HAVE AN URGE...
TWCH TWCH...

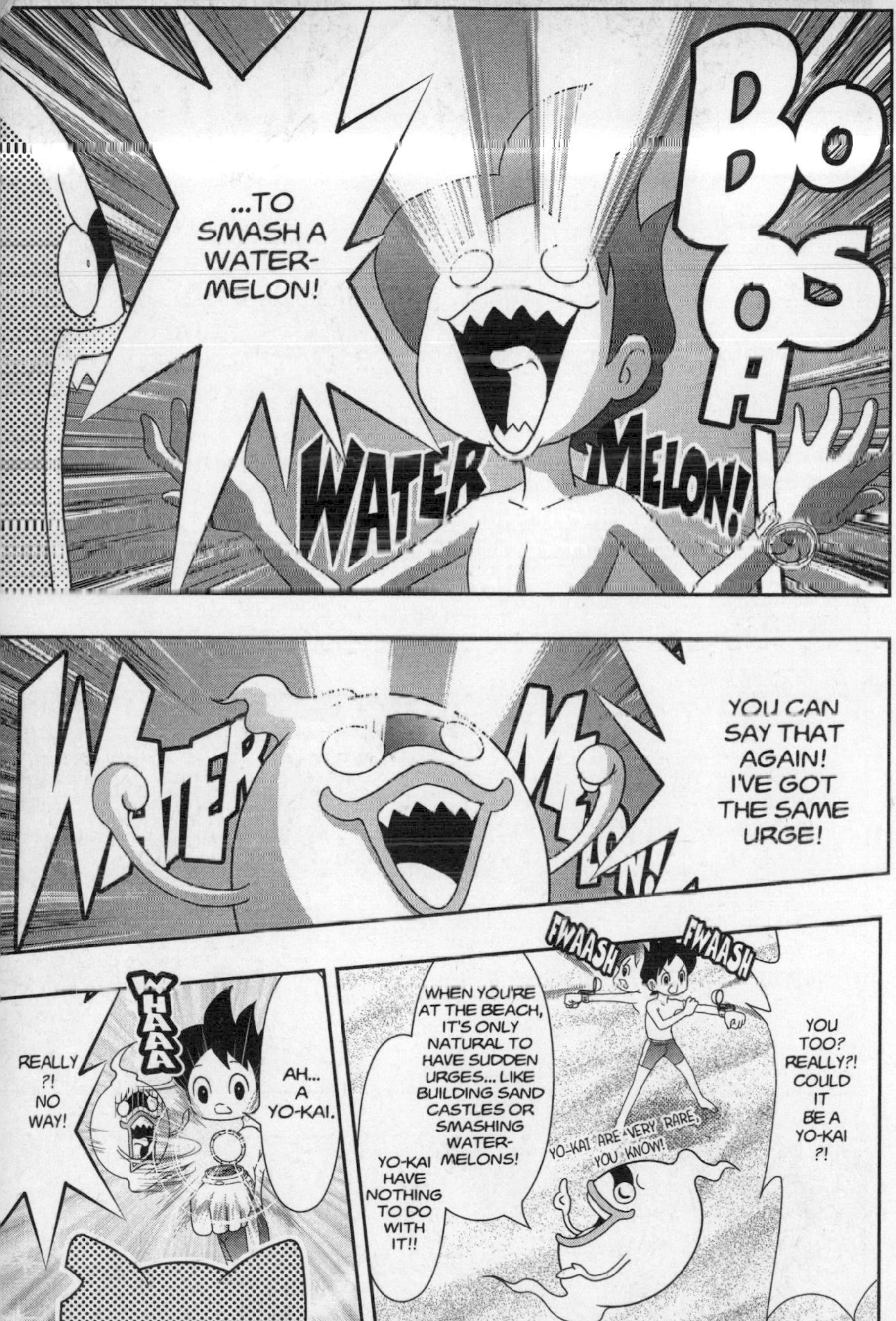
BOOSA!
WATERMELON!
...TO SMASH A WATER-MELON!
YOU CAN SAY THAT AGAIN! I'VE GOT THE SAME URGE!
WATERMELON!
YOU TOO? REALLY?! COULD IT BE A YO-KAI?!
FWAASH
FWAASH
YO-KAI ARE VERY RARE, YOU KNOW!
WHEN YOU'RE AT THE BEACH, IT'S ONLY NATURAL TO HAVE SUDDEN URGES... LIKE BUILDING SAND CASTLES OR SMASHING WATER-MELONS!
YO-KAI HAVE NOTHING TO DO WITH IT!!
AH... A YO-KAI.
WHAAA
REALLY?! NO WAY!

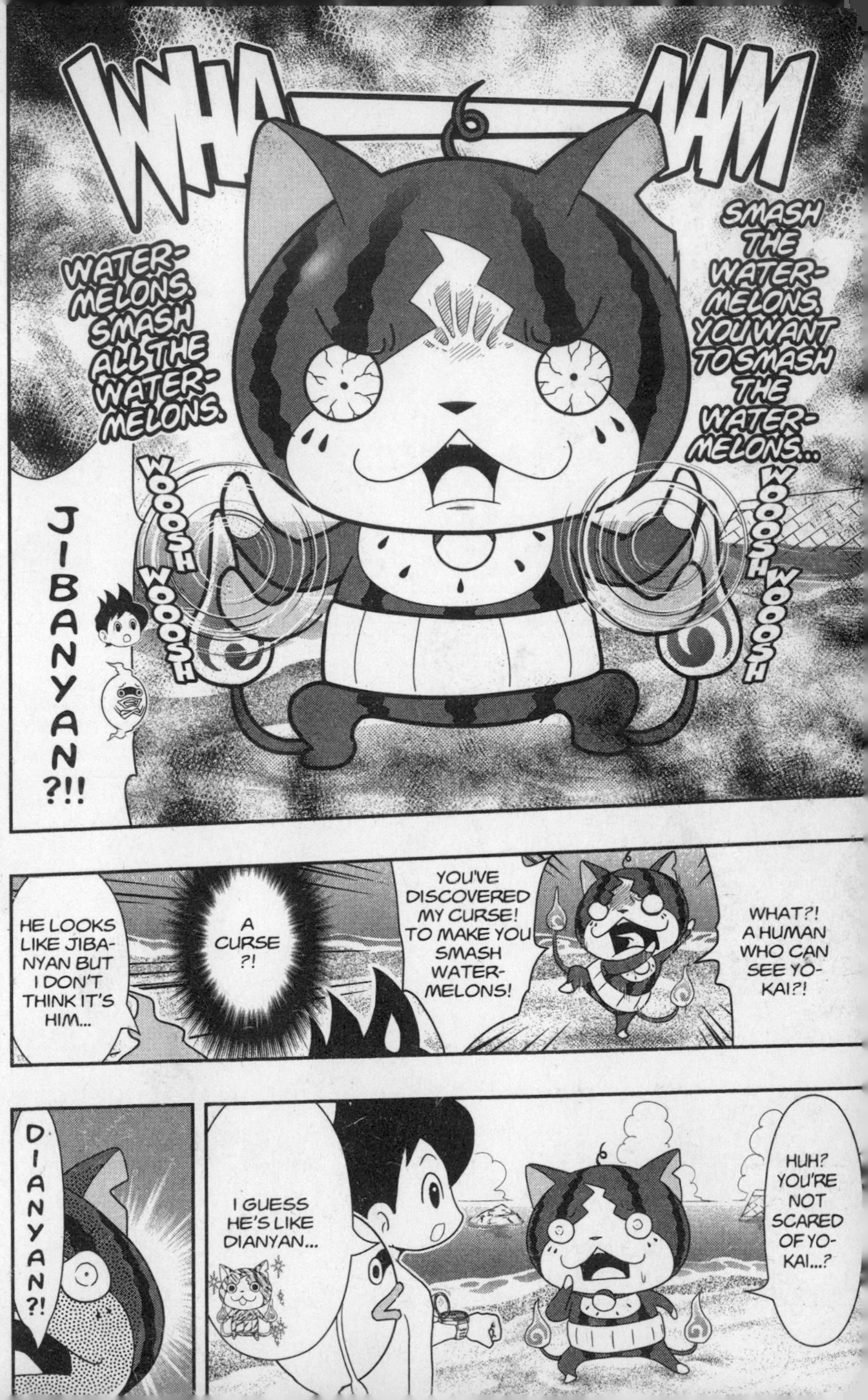
WHAAM
SMASH THE WATERMELONS. YOU WANT TO SMASH THE WATERMELONS...
WATERMELONS. SMASH ALL THE WATERMELONS.
WOOOSH WOOOSH
WOOOSH WOOOSH
JIBANYAN?!!
WHAT?! A HUMAN WHO CAN SEE YOKAI?!
YOU'VE DISCOVERED MY CURSE! TO MAKE YOU SMASH WATERMELONS!
A CURSE?!
HE LOOKS LIKE JIBANYAN BUT I DON'T THINK IT'S HIM...
HUH? YOU'RE NOT SCARED OF YOKAI...?
I GUESS HE'S LIKE DIANYAN...
DIANYAN?!

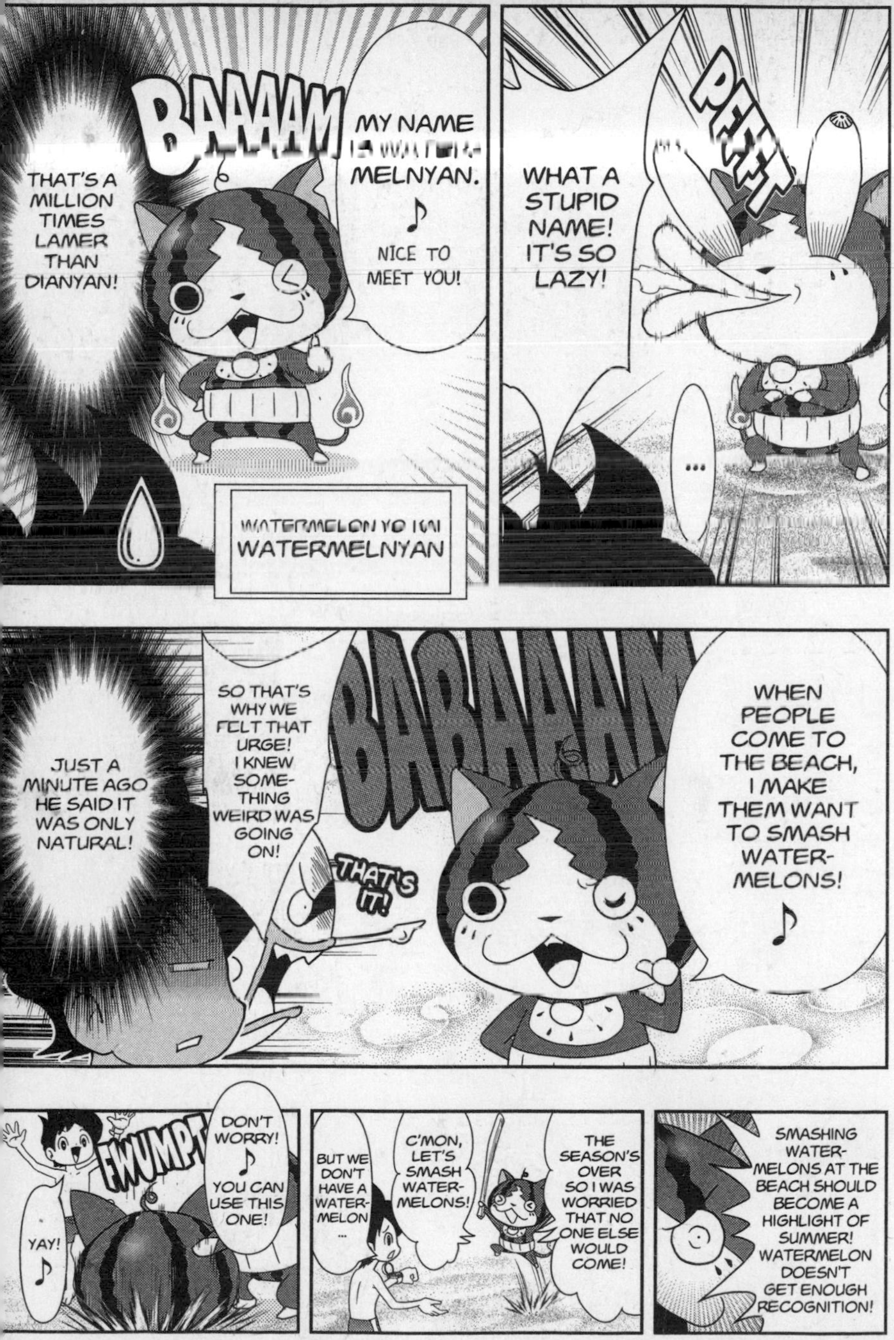
PEFFT
WHAT A STUPID NAME! IT'S SO LAZY!
...
MY NAME IS WATERMELNYAN. ♪
NICE TO MEET YOU!
BAAAAM
THAT'S A MILLION TIMES LAMER THAN DIANYAN!
WATERMELON YO-KAI WATERMELNYAN
WHEN PEOPLE COME TO THE BEACH, I MAKE THEM WANT TO SMASH WATERMELONS! ♪
BABAAAM
SO THAT'S WHY WE FELT THAT URGE! I KNEW SOMETHING WEIRD WAS GOING ON!
THAT'S IT!
JUST A MINUTE AGO HE SAID IT WAS ONLY NATURAL!
SMASHING WATERMELONS AT THE BEACH SHOULD BECOME A HIGHLIGHT OF SUMMER! WATERMELON DOESN'T GET ENOUGH RECOGNITION!
THE SEASON'S OVER SO I WAS WORRIED THAT NO ONE ELSE WOULD COME!
C'MON, LET'S SMASH WATERMELONS!
BUT WE DON'T HAVE A WATERMELON ...
DON'T WORRY! ♪ YOU CAN USE THIS ONE!
FWUMP
YAY! ♪

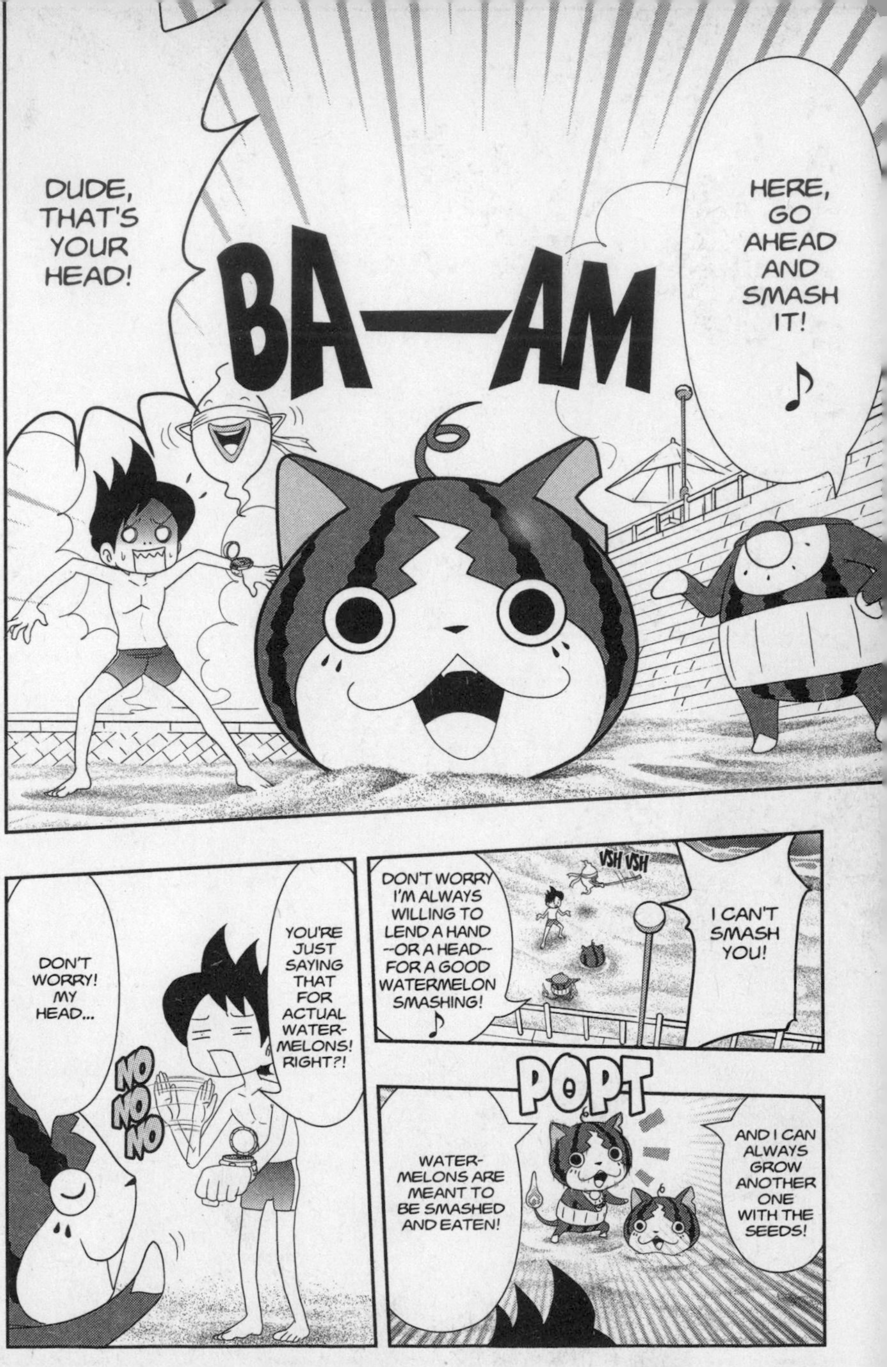
HERE, GO AHEAD AND SMASH IT! ♪
BA—AM
DUDE, THAT'S YOUR HEAD!
I CAN'T SMASH YOU!
VSH VSH
DON'T WORRY I'M ALWAYS WILLING TO LEND A HAND --OR A HEAD-- FOR A GOOD WATERMELON SMASHING! ♪
POPT
AND I CAN ALWAYS GROW ANOTHER ONE WITH THE SEEDS!
WATER-MELONS ARE MEANT TO BE SMASHED AND EATEN!
YOU'RE JUST SAYING THAT FOR ACTUAL WATER-MELONS! RIGHT?!
NO NO NO
DON'T WORRY! MY HEAD...

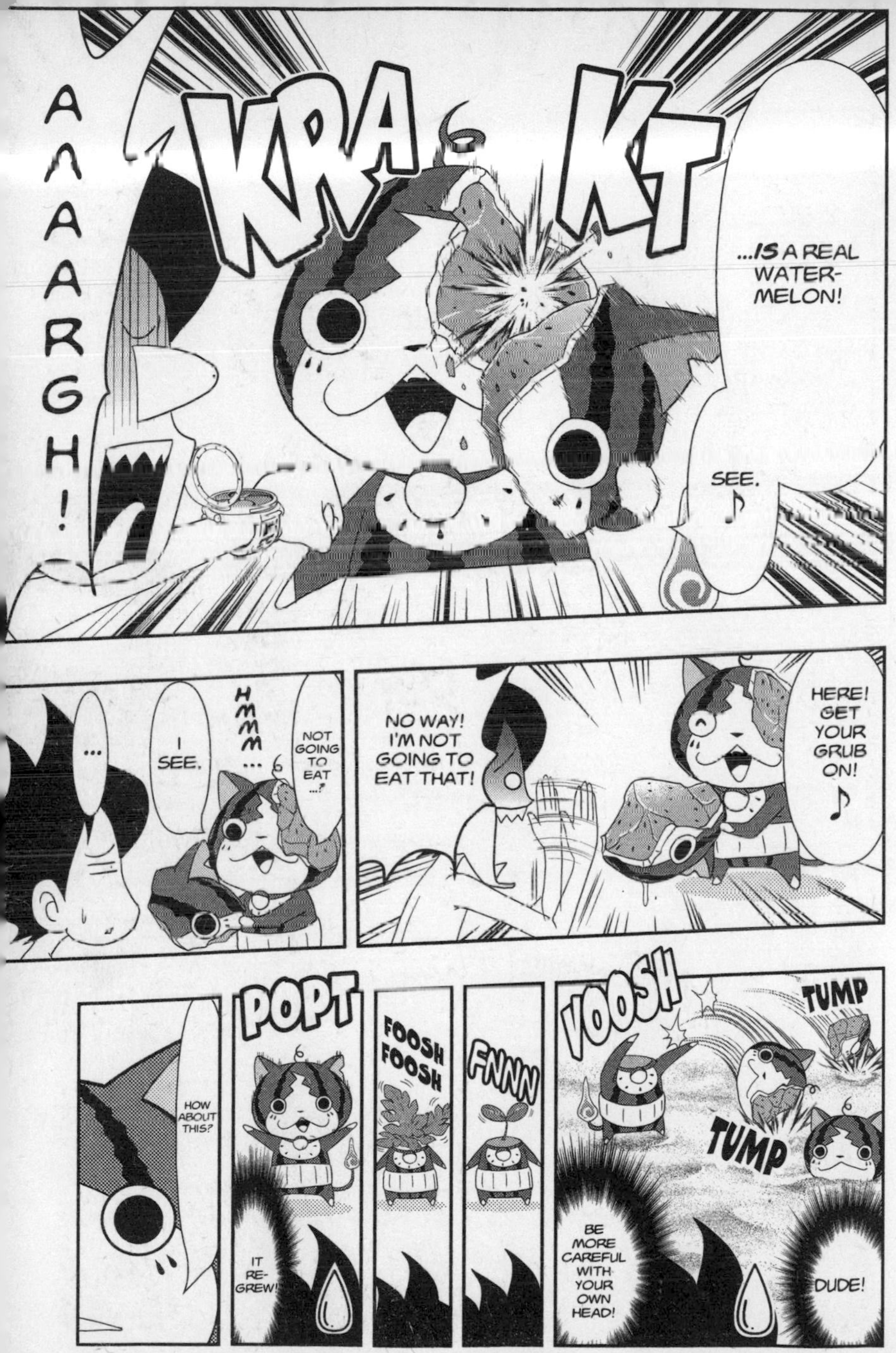

...IS A REAL WATER-MELON!
KRA-KT
SEE. ♪
AAAARGH!
HERE! GET YOUR GRUB ON! ♪
NO WAY! I'M NOT GOING TO EAT THAT!
NOT GOING TO EAT ...?
HMMM ...
I SEE.
...
TUMP
VOOSH
TUMP
DUDE!
BE MORE CAREFUL WITH YOUR OWN HEAD!
FNNN
FOOSH FOOSH
POPT
IT RE-GREW!
HOW ABOUT THIS?

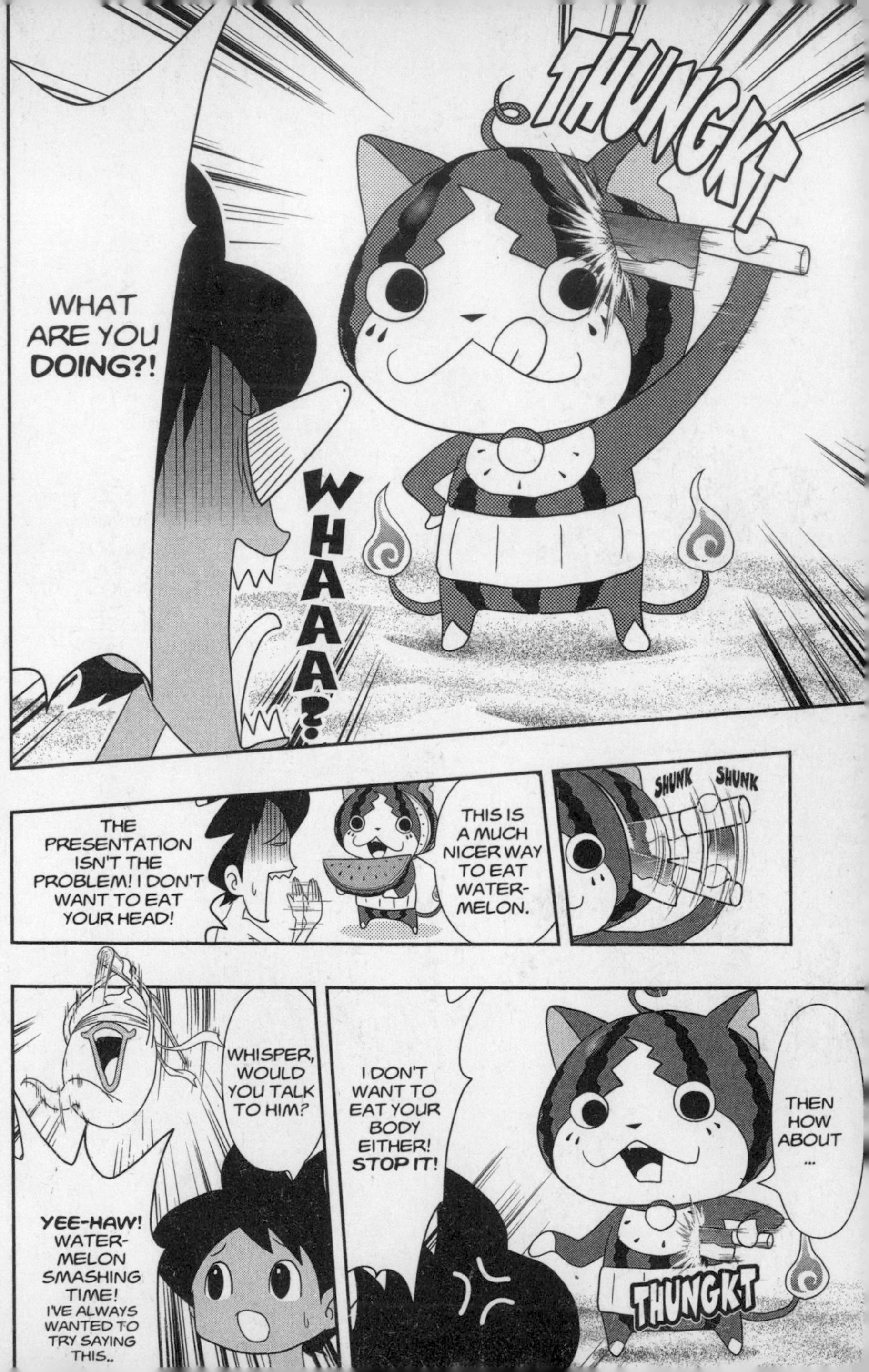
THUNGKT
WHAAAA?!
WHAT ARE YOU DOING?!
SHUNK SHUNK
THIS IS A MUCH NICER WAY TO EAT WATER-MELON.
THE PRESENTATION ISN'T THE PROBLEM! I DON'T WANT TO EAT YOUR HEAD!
THEN HOW ABOUT ...
THUNGKT
I DON'T WANT TO EAT YOUR BODY EITHER! STOP IT!
WHISPER, WOULD YOU TALK TO HIM?
YEE-HAW! WATER-MELON SMASHING TIME! I'VE ALWAYS WANTED TO TRY SAYING THIS..

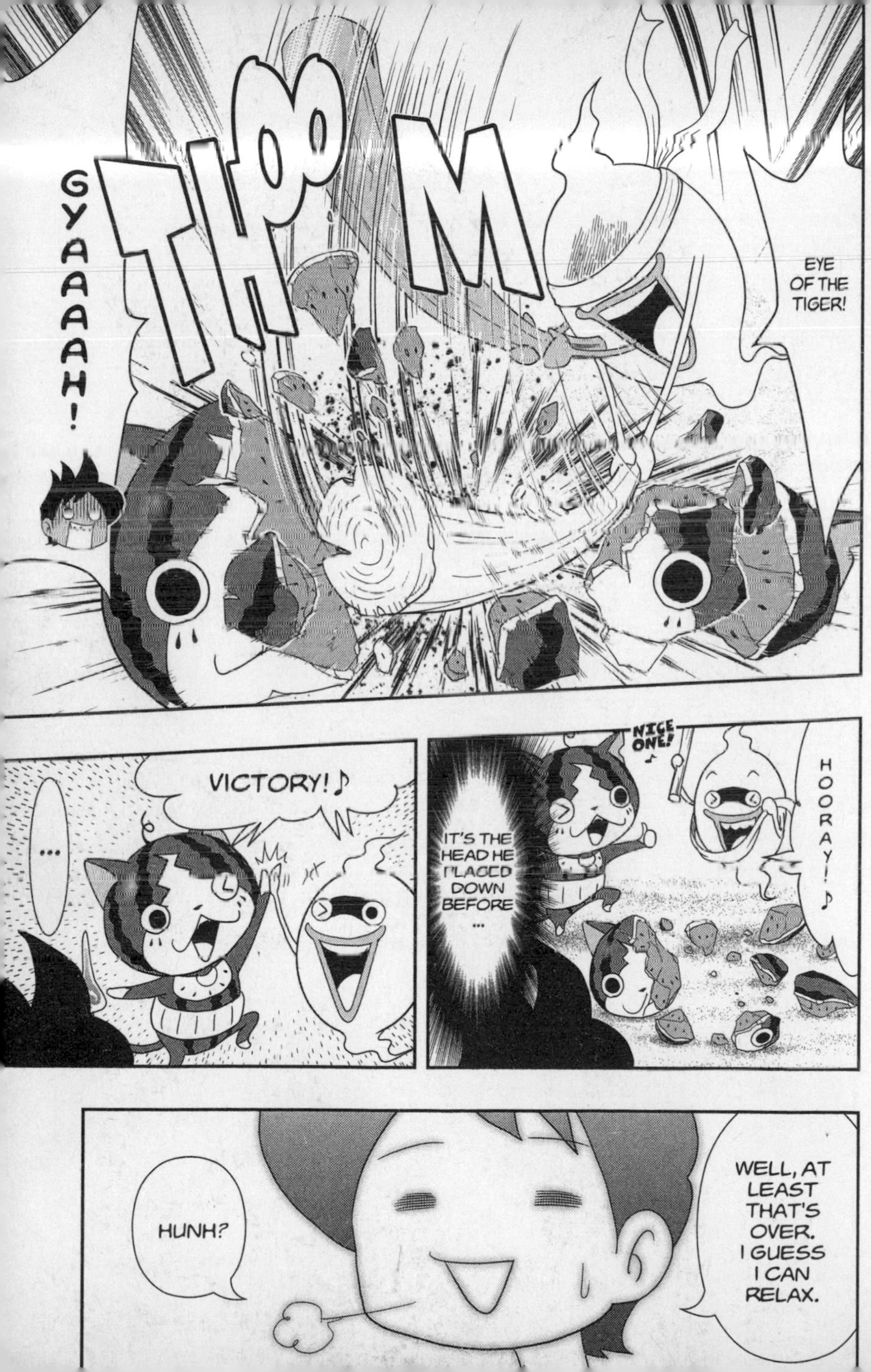
EYE OF THE TIGER!
THOOM
GYAAAAAH!
HOORAY! ♪
NICE ONE! ♪
IT'S THE HEAD HE PLACED DOWN BEFORE ...
VICTORY! ♪
...
WELL, AT LEAST THAT'S OVER. I GUESS I CAN RELAX.
HUNH?

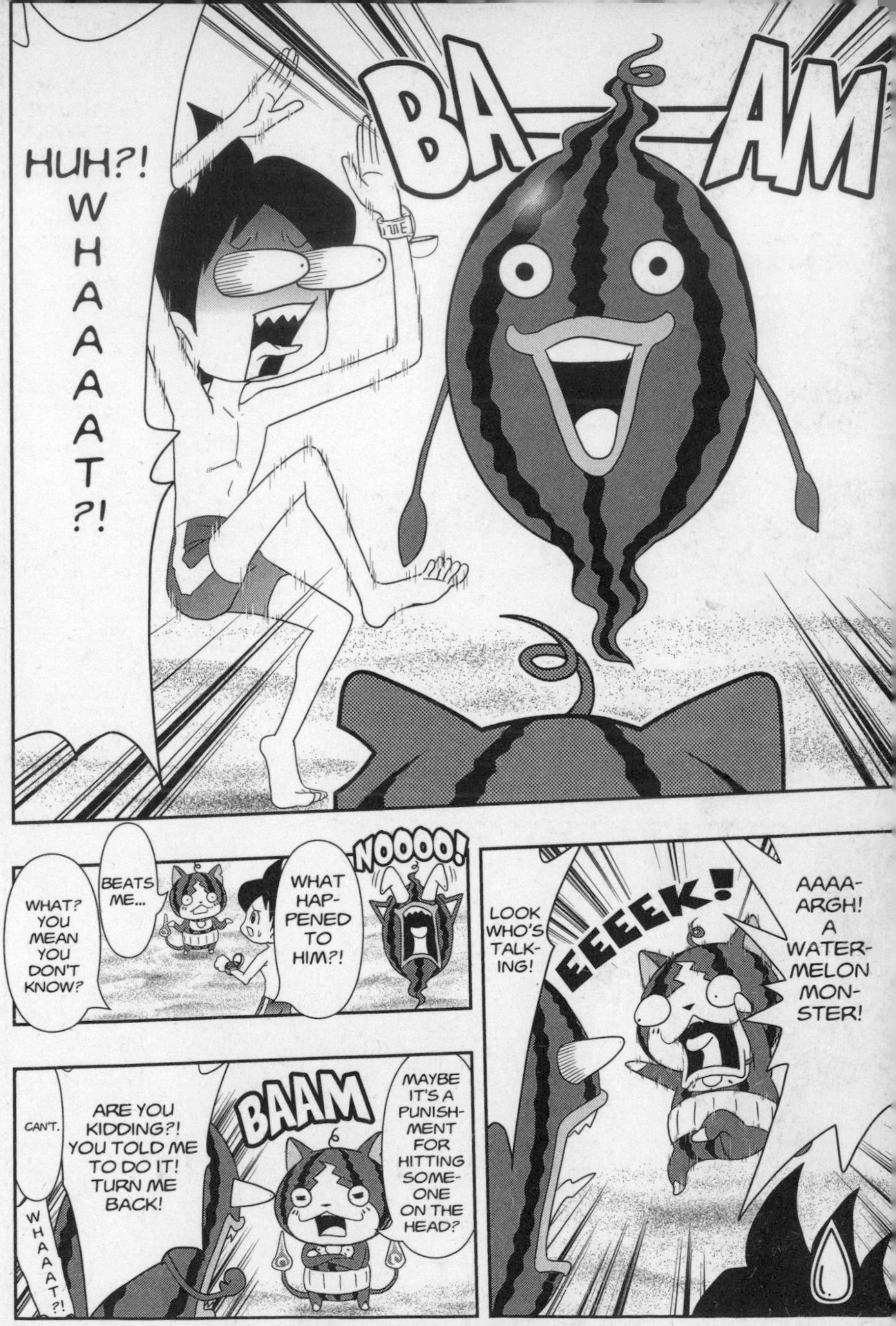
BA-AM
HUH?! WHHAAAAAT?!
EEEEK!
AAAA-ARGH! A WATER-MELON MON-STER!
LOOK WHO'S TALK-ING!
NOOOO!
WHAT HAP-PENED TO HIM?!
BEATS ME...
WHAT? YOU MEAN YOU DON'T KNOW?
BAAM
MAYBE IT'S A PUNISH-MENT FOR HITTING SOME-ONE ON THE HEAD?
ARE YOU KIDDING?! YOU TOLD ME TO DO IT! TURN ME BACK!
CAN'T.
WHAAAT?!

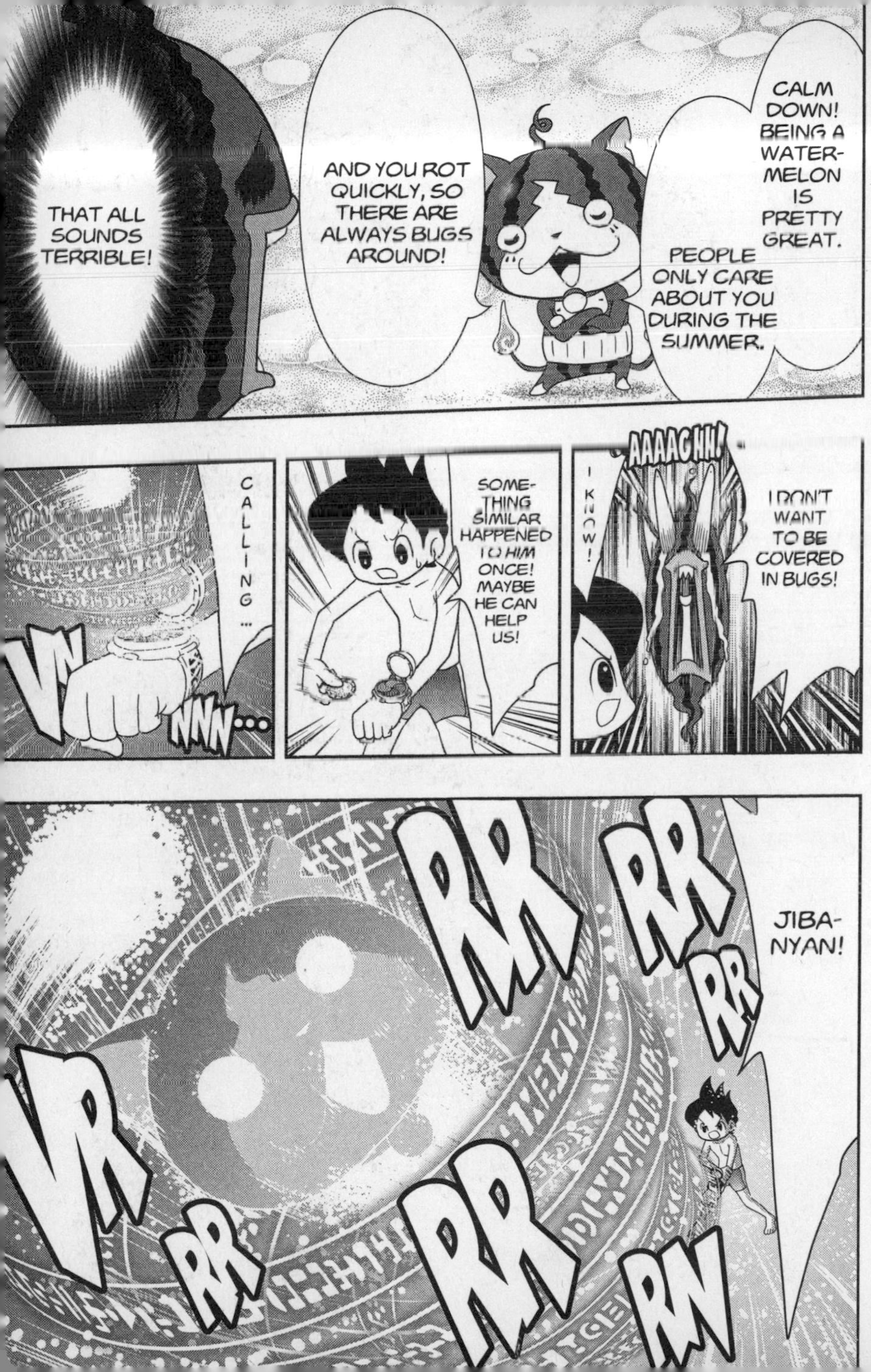
CALM DOWN! BEING A WATER-MELON IS PRETTY GREAT.
PEOPLE ONLY CARE ABOUT YOU DURING THE SUMMER.
AND YOU ROT QUICKLY, SO THERE ARE ALWAYS BUGS AROUND!
THAT ALL SOUNDS TERRIBLE!
AAAACHH!
I DON'T WANT TO BE COVERED IN BUGS!
I KNOW!
SOME-THING SIMILAR HAPPENED TO HIM ONCE! MAYBE HE CAN HELP US!
CALLING...
VNNNN...
JIBA-NYAN!
RR RR RR
VR RR RR RN

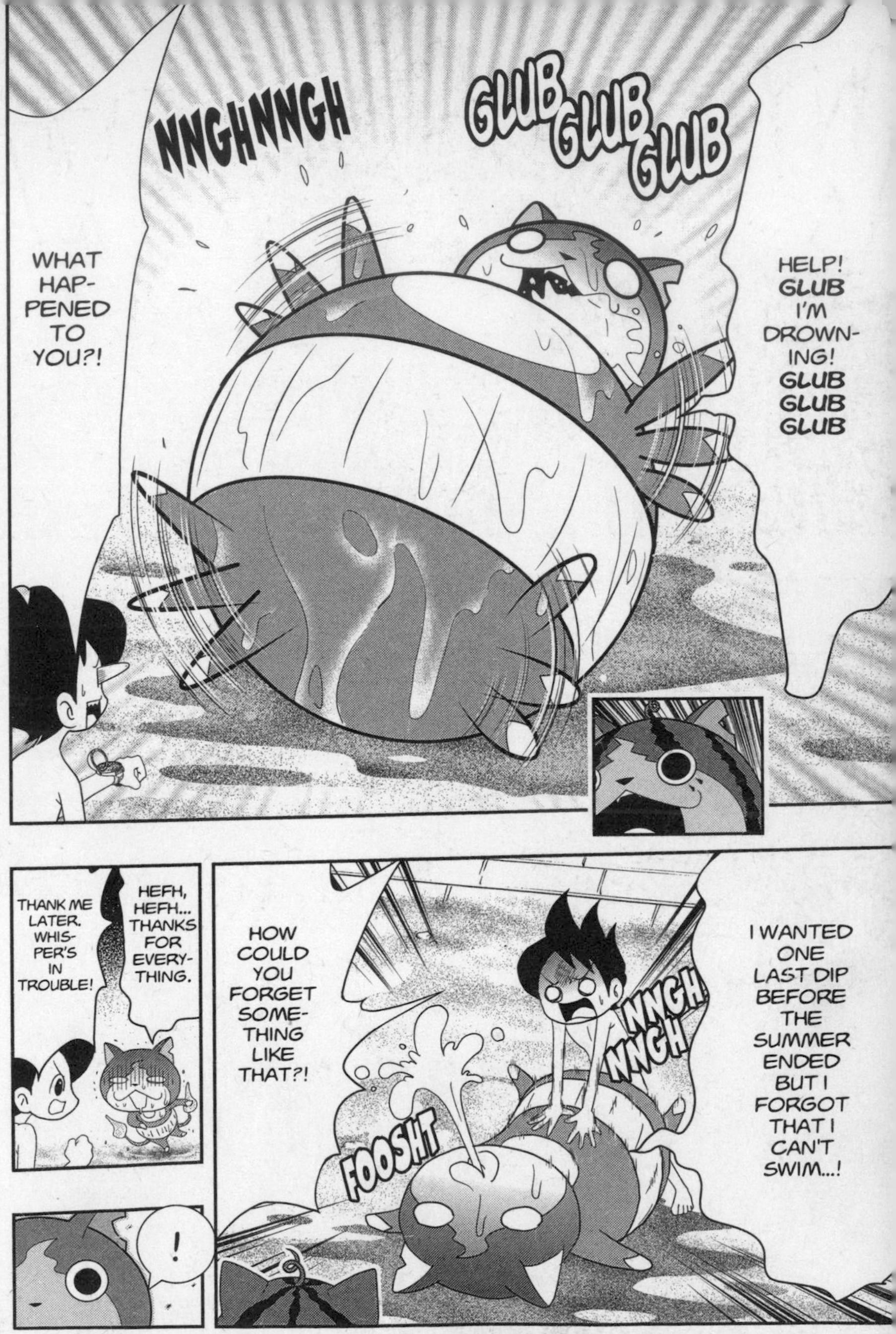
HELP! GLUB I'M DROWNING! GLUB GLUB GLUB
GLUB GLUB GLUB
NNGHNNGH
WHAT HAP-PENED TO YOU?!
I WANTED ONE LAST DIP BEFORE THE SUMMER ENDED BUT I FORGOT THAT I CAN'T SWIM...!
HOW COULD YOU FORGET SOME-THING LIKE THAT?!
NNGH NNGH
FOOSHT
HEFH, HEFH... THANKS FOR EVERY-THING.
THANK ME LATER. WHIS-PER'S IN TROUBLE!
!

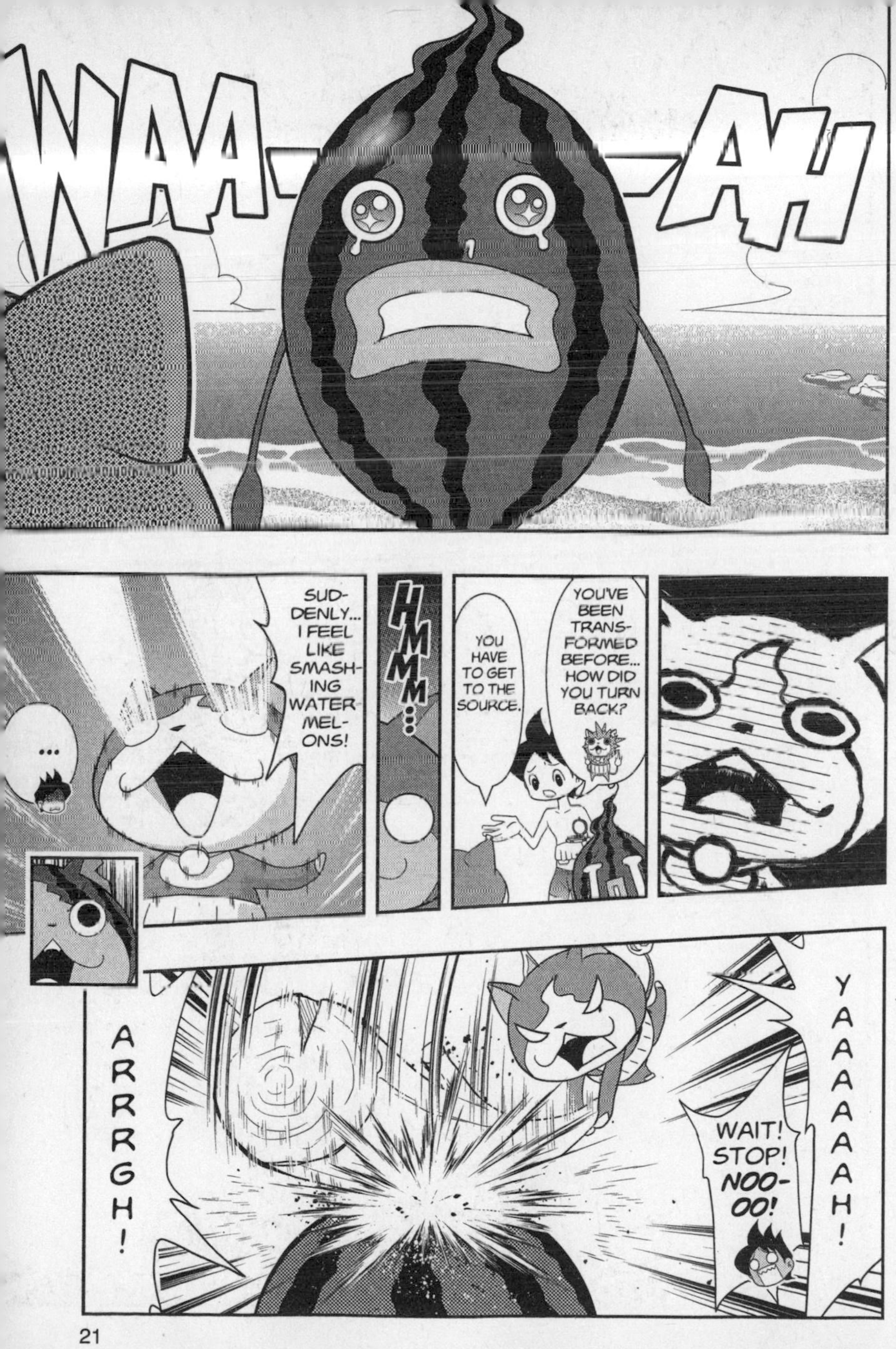
WAA——AH
YOU'VE BEEN TRANS-FORMED BEFORE... HOW DID YOU TURN BACK?
YOU HAVE TO GET TO THE SOURCE.
HMMM...
SUD-DENLY... I FEEL LIKE SMASH-ING WATER-MEL-ONS!
...
YAAAAAAAH!
WAIT! STOP! NOO-OO!
ARRRGH!

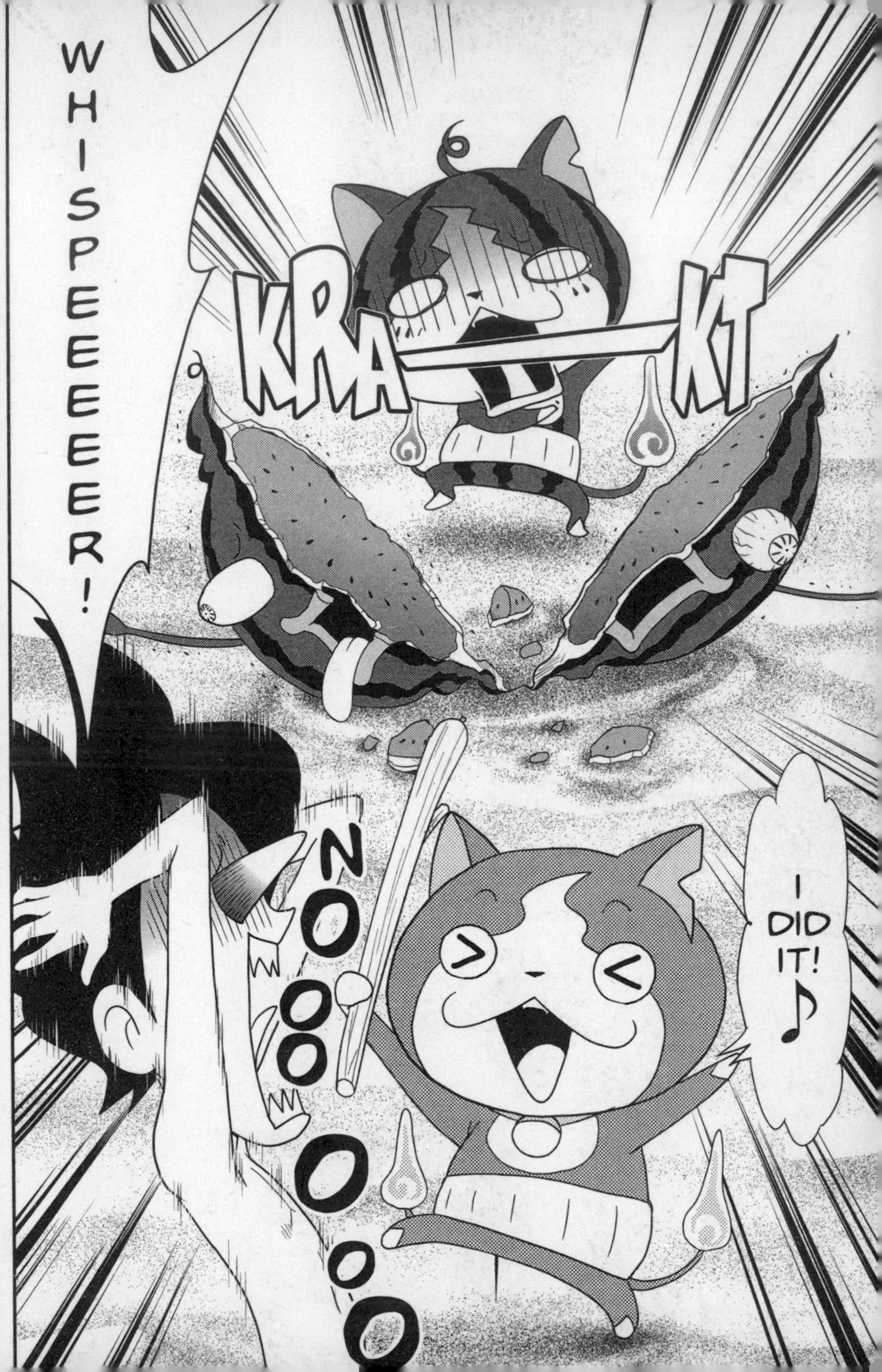
WHISPEEEEER!
KRA KT
I DID IT! ♪
NOOOOOOOO

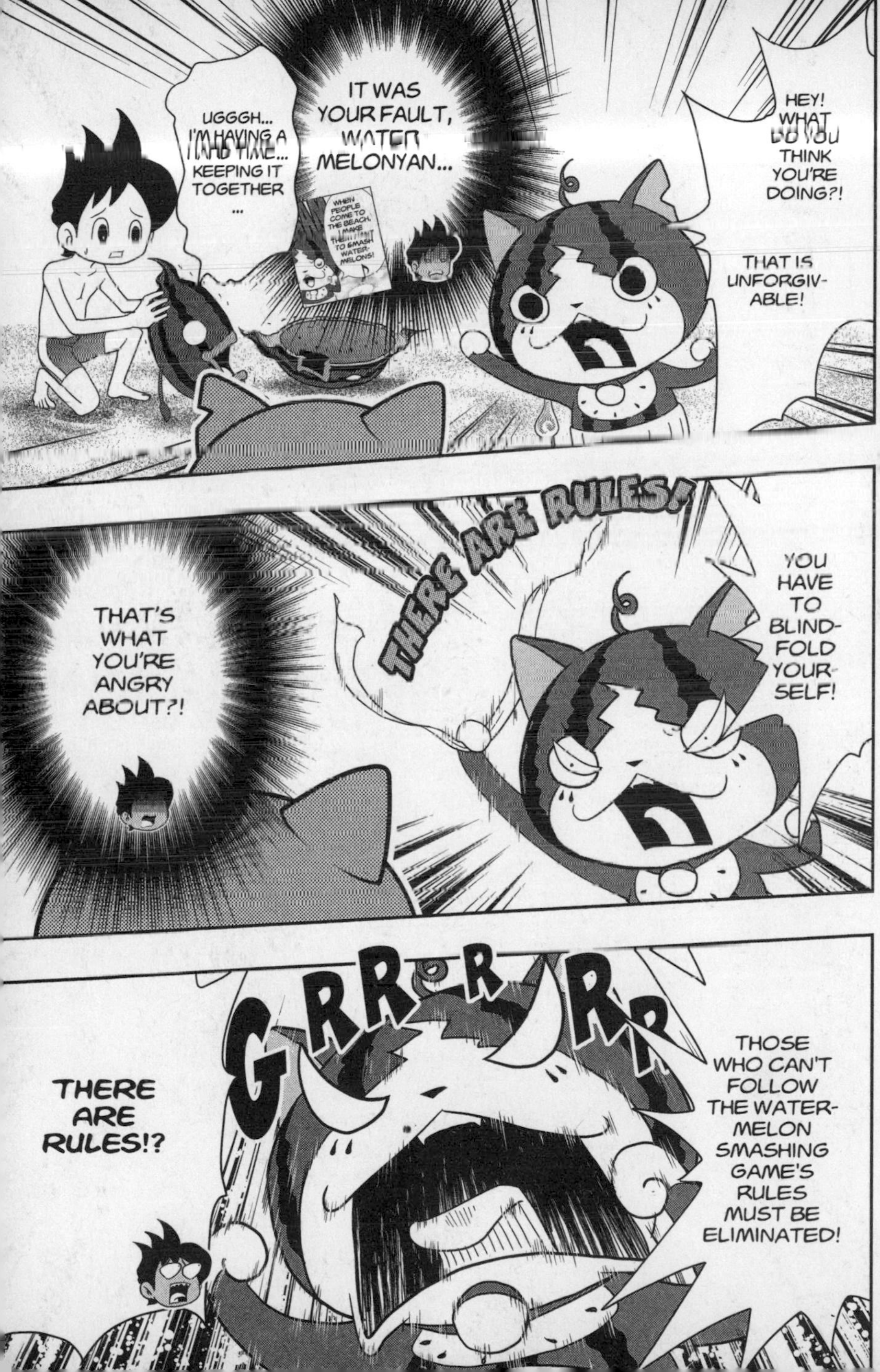
HEY! WHAT DO YOU THINK YOU'RE DOING?!
THAT IS UNFORGIV-ABLE!
IT WAS YOUR FAULT, WATER MELONYAN...
UGGGH... I'M HAVING A HARD TIME... KEEPING IT TOGETHER ...
THERE ARE RULES!
YOU HAVE TO BLIND-FOLD YOUR-SELF!
THAT'S WHAT YOU'RE ANGRY ABOUT?!
GRR-R-R-RR
THOSE WHO CAN'T FOLLOW THE WATER-MELON SMASHING GAME'S RULES MUST BE ELIMINATED!
THERE ARE RULES!?

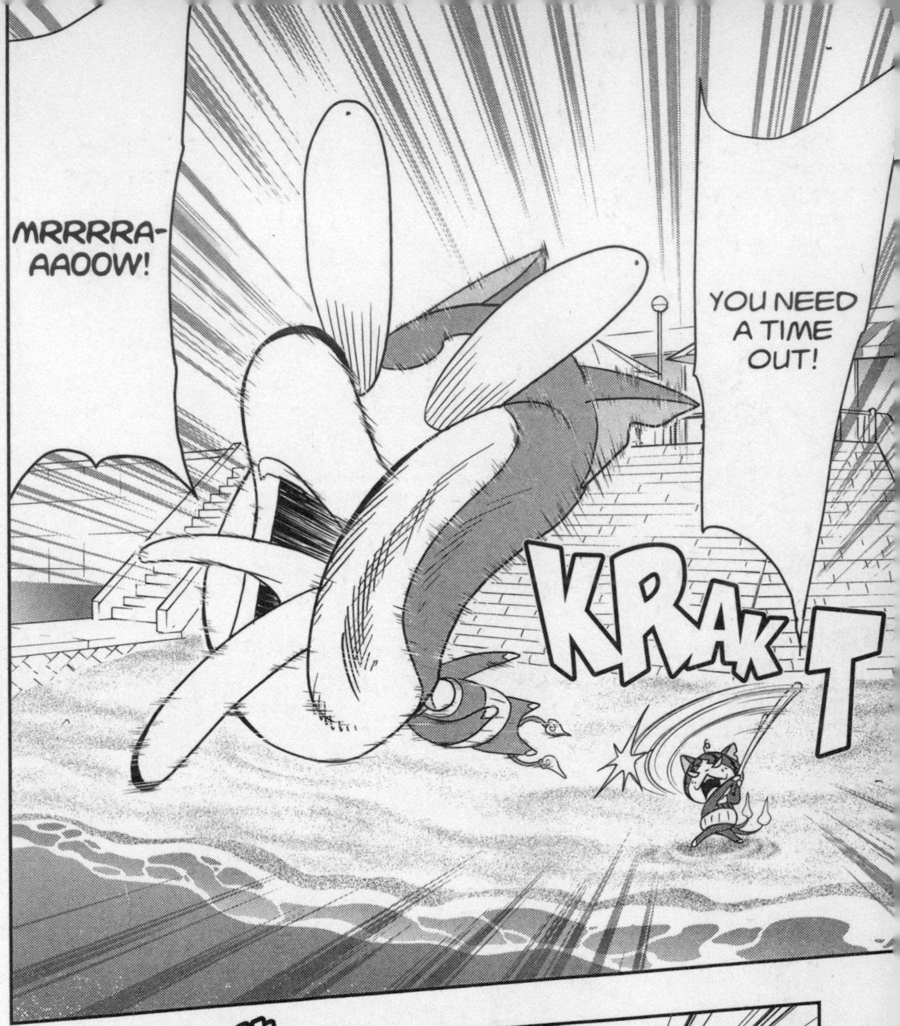
YOU NEED A TIME OUT!
MRRRRA-AAOOW!
KRAKT
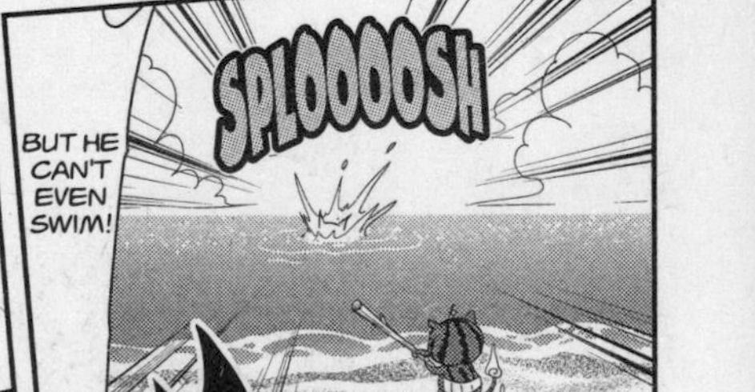
SPLOOOOSH
BUT HE CAN'T EVEN SWIM!
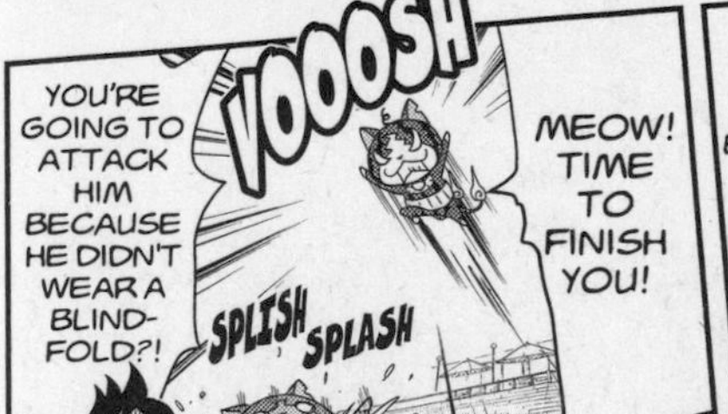
VOOOSH
MEOW! TIME TO FINISH YOU!
YOU'RE GOING TO ATTACK HIM BECAUSE HE DIDN'T WEAR A BLIND-FOLD?!
SPLISH SPLASH

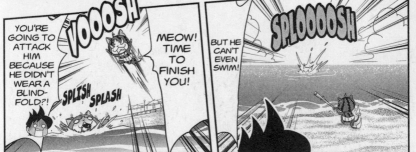

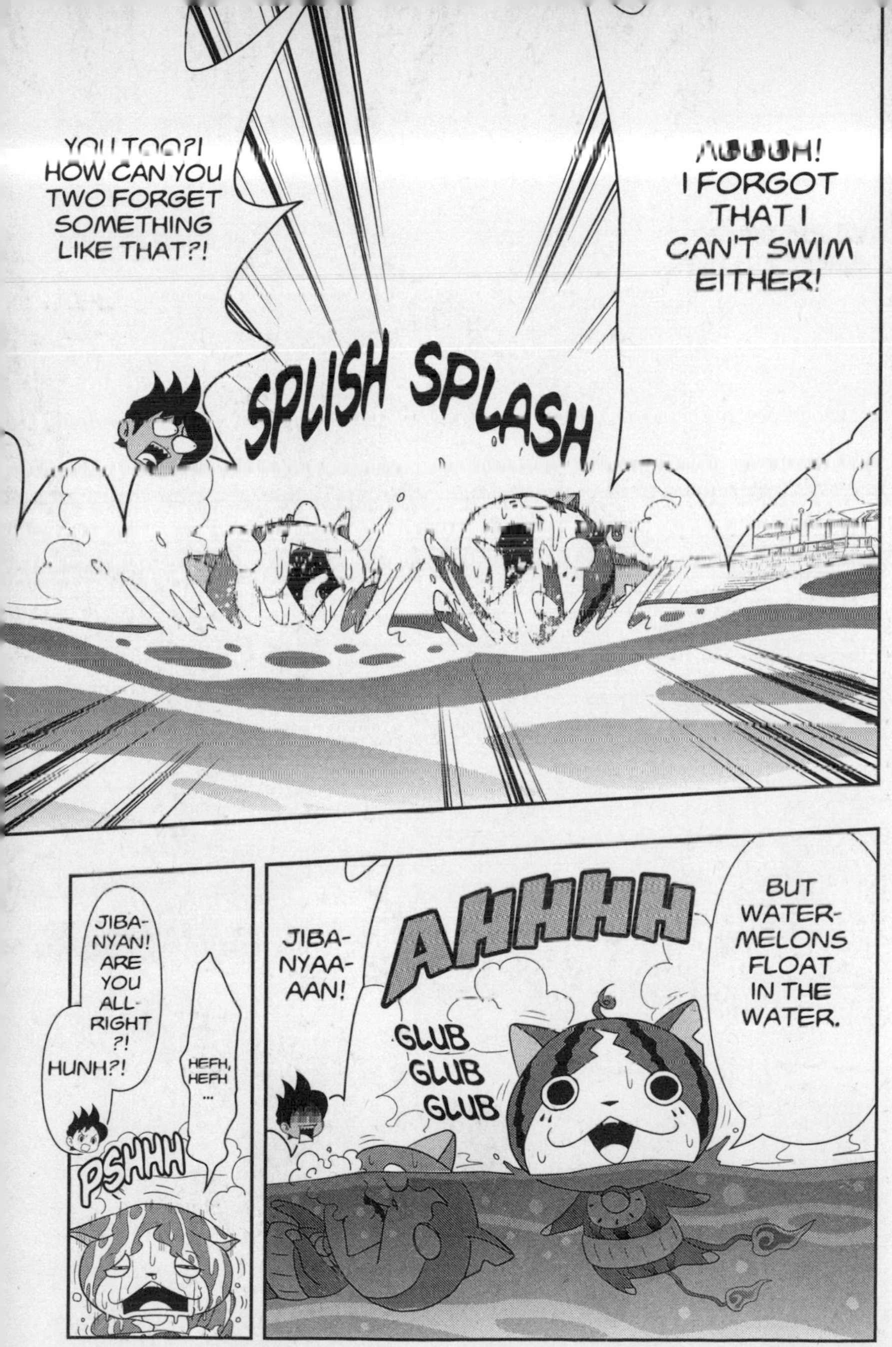
AUUUH! I FORGOT THAT I CAN'T SWIM EITHER!
YOU TOO?! HOW CAN YOU TWO FORGET SOMETHING LIKE THAT?!
SPLISH SPLASH
BUT WATER-MELONS FLOAT IN THE WATER.
AHHHH
JIBA-NYAA-AAN!
GLUB GLUB GLUB
HEFH, HEFH ...
JIBA-NYAN! ARE YOU ALL-RIGHT?!
HUNH?!
PSHHH

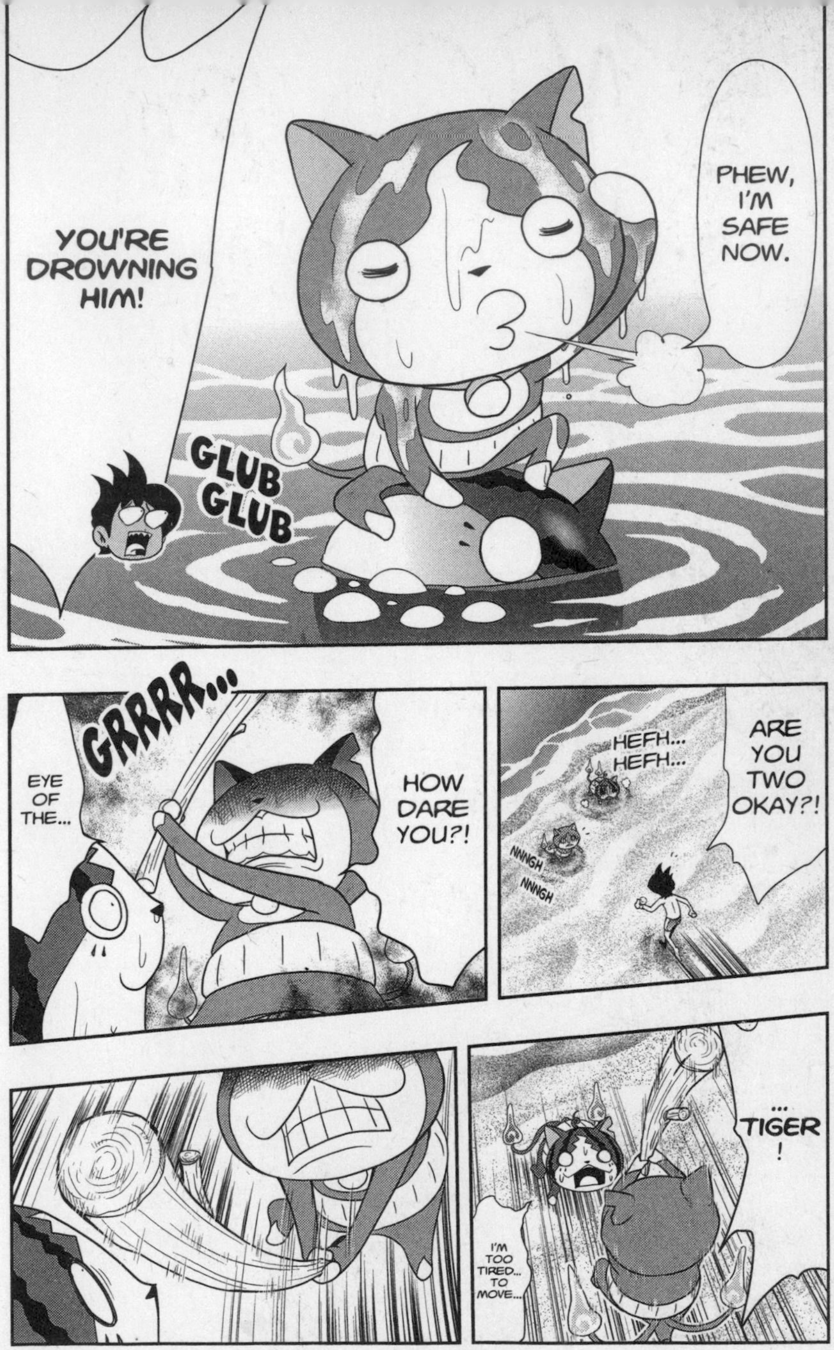
PHEW, I'M SAFE NOW.
YOU'RE DROWNING HIM!
GLUB GLUB
ARE YOU TWO OKAY?!
HEFH... HEFH...
NNNGH NNNGH
GRRRR...
HOW DARE YOU?!
EYE OF THE...
...TIGER!
I'M TOO TIRED... TO MOVE...

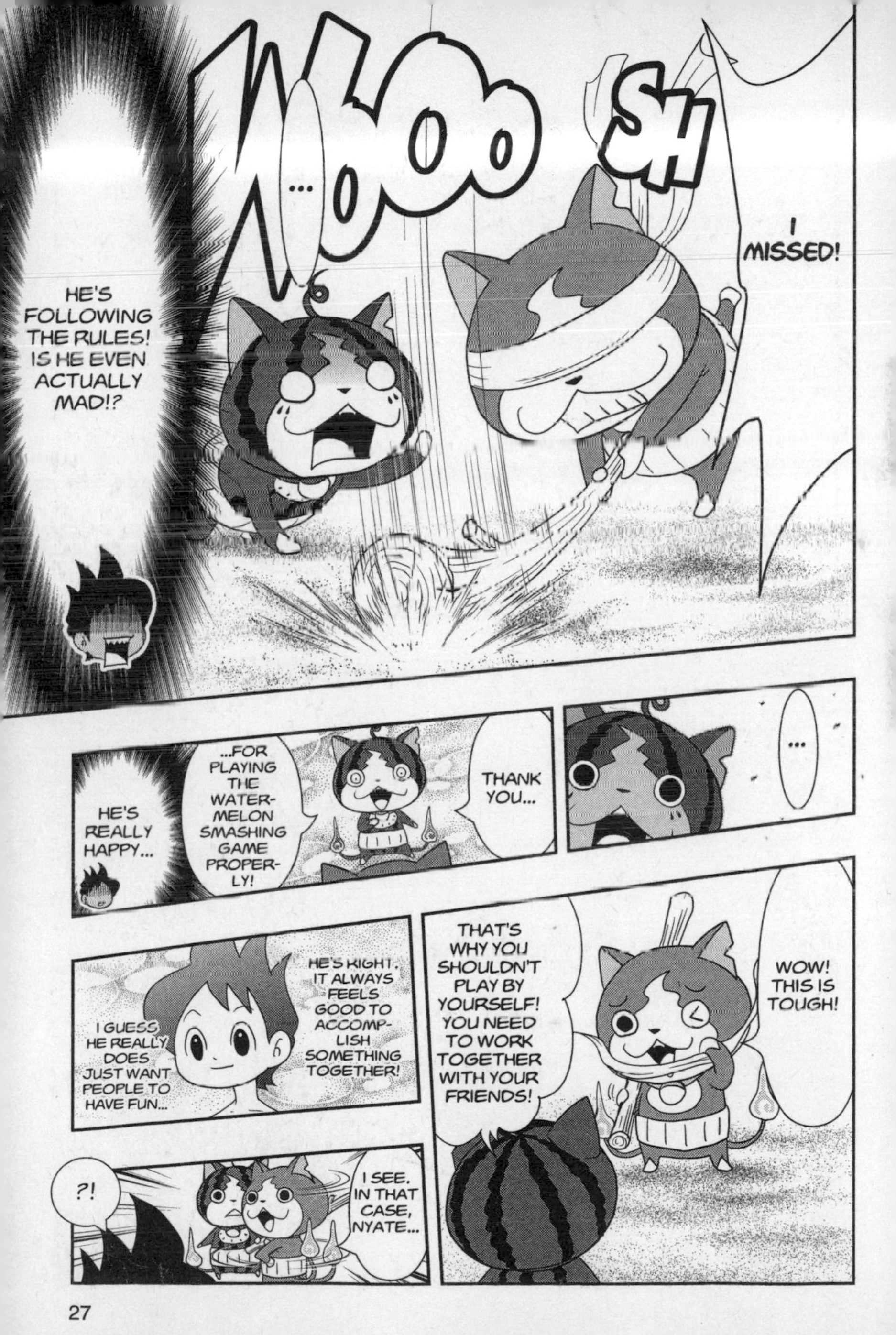
I MISSED!
WHOOSH
...
HE'S FOLLOWING THE RULES! IS HE EVEN ACTUALLY MAD!?
...
THANK YOU...
...FOR PLAYING THE WATER-MELON SMASHING GAME PROPER-LY!
HE'S REALLY HAPPY...
WOW! THIS IS TOUGH!
THAT'S WHY YOU SHOULDN'T PLAY BY YOURSELF! YOU NEED TO WORK TOGETHER WITH YOUR FRIENDS!
HE'S RIGHT. IT ALWAYS FEELS GOOD TO ACCOMP-LISH SOMETHING TOGETHER!
I GUESS HE REALLY DOES JUST WANT PEOPLE TO HAVE FUN...
I SEE. IN THAT CASE, NYATE...
?!

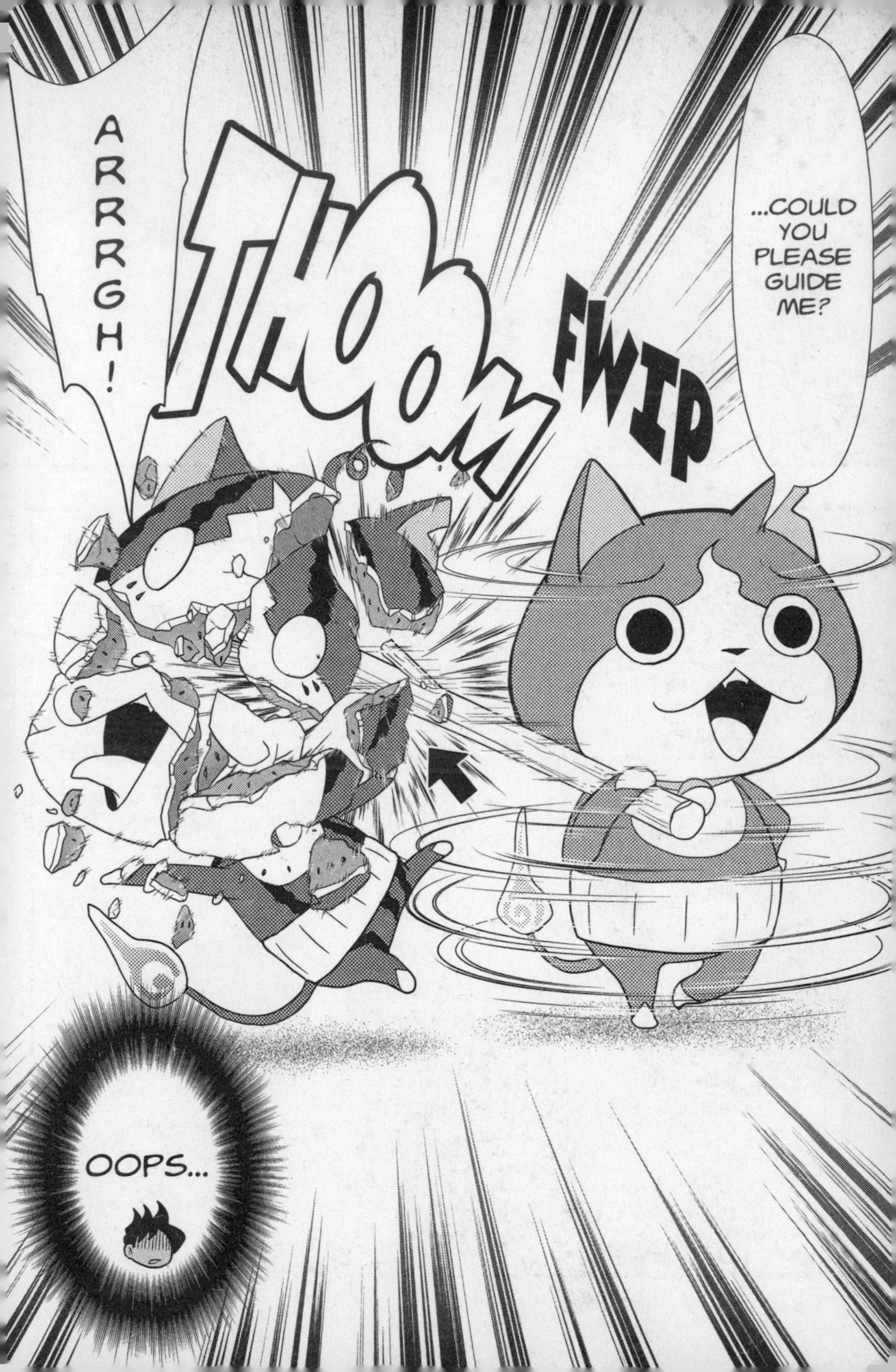
...COULD YOU PLEASE GUIDE ME?
FWIP
THOOM
ARRRGH!
OOPS...

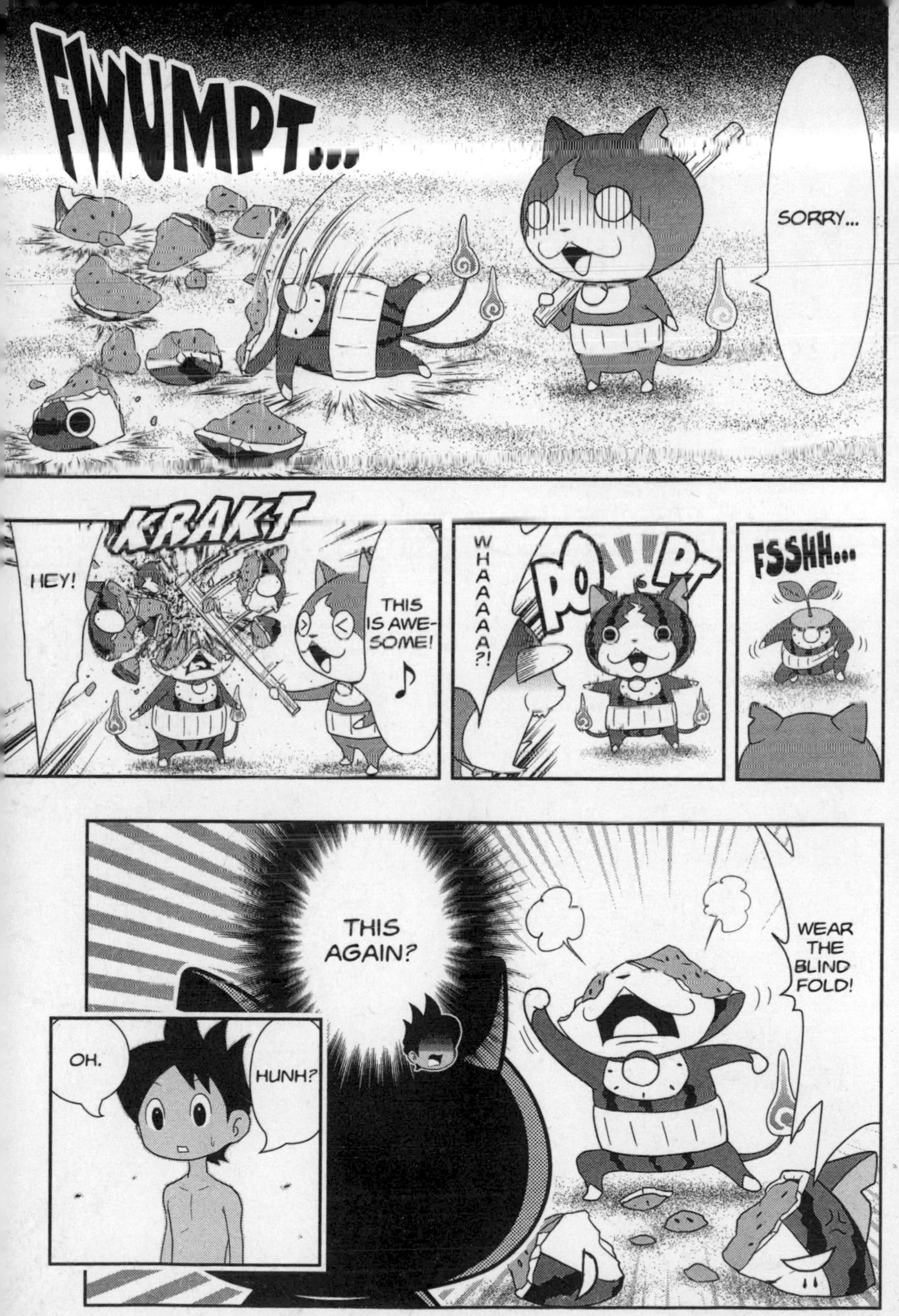
FWUMPT...
SORRY...
FSSHH...
POPT
WHAAAAAA?!
THIS IS AWE-SOME! ♪
KRAKT
HEY!
WEAR THE BLIND FOLD!
THIS AGAIN?
HUNH?
OH.

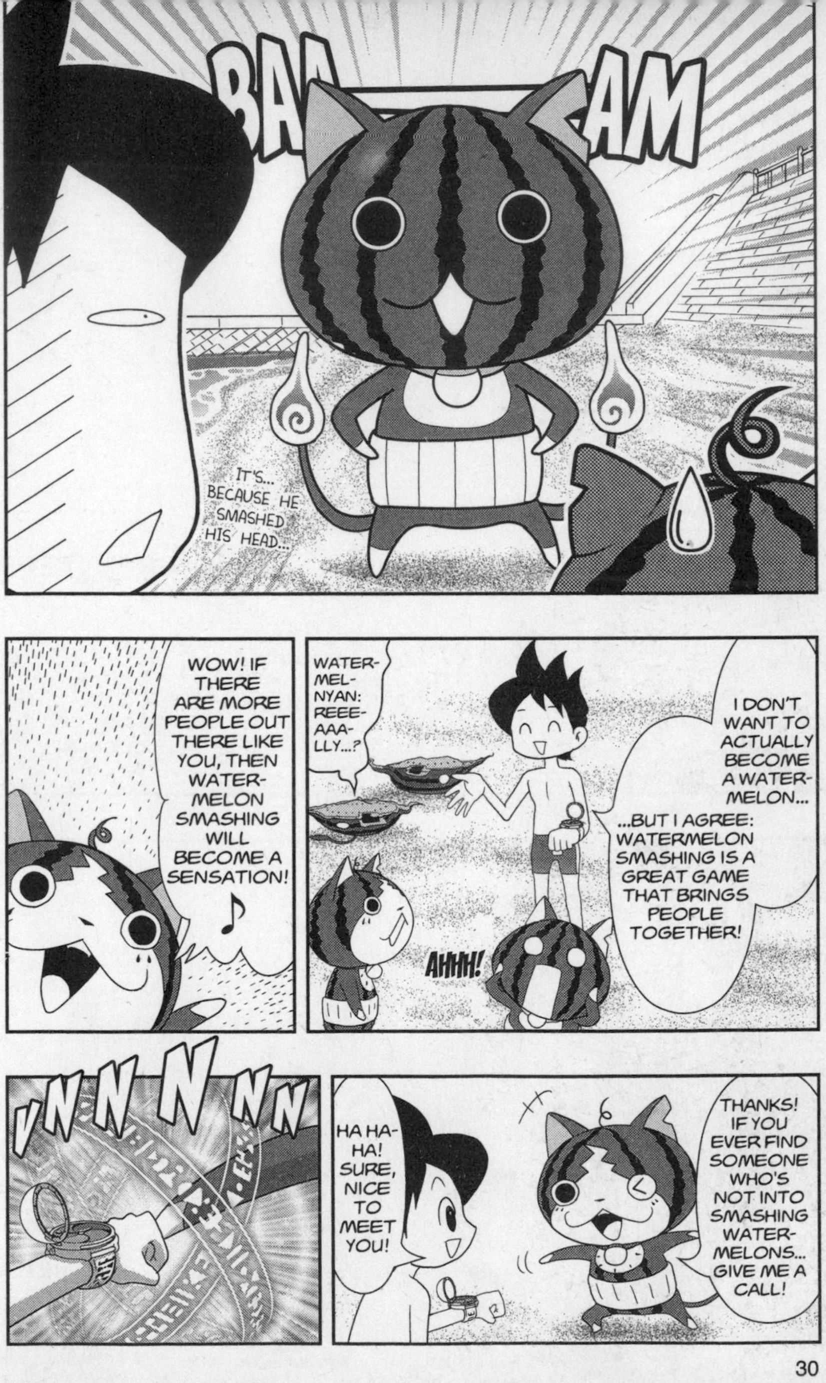
BA
AM
IT'S... BECAUSE HE SMASHED HIS HEAD...
I DON'T WANT TO ACTUALLY BECOME A WATER-MELON...
...BUT I AGREE: WATERMELON SMASHING IS A GREAT GAME THAT BRINGS PEOPLE TOGETHER!
WATER-MEL-NYAN: REEE-AAA-LLY...?
AHHH!
WOW! IF THERE ARE MORE PEOPLE OUT THERE LIKE YOU, THEN WATER-MELON SMASHING WILL BECOME A SENSATION! ♪
THANKS! IF YOU EVER FIND SOMEONE WHO'S NOT INTO SMASHING WATER-MELONS... GIVE ME A CALL!
HA HA-HA! SURE, NICE TO MEET YOU!
VNNNNNN

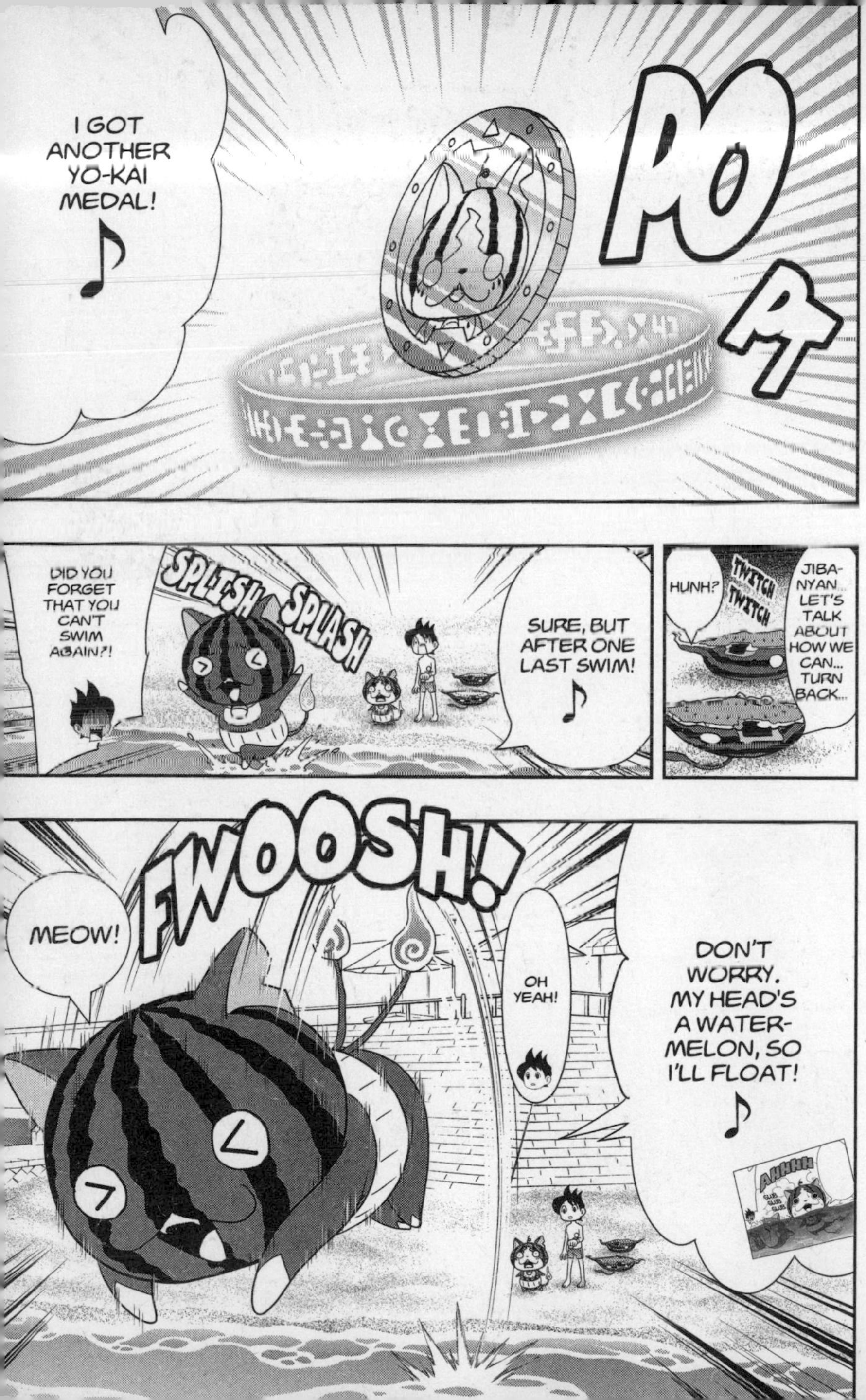
POP
I GOT ANOTHER YO-KAI MEDAL! ♪
JIBA-NYAN... LET'S TALK ABOUT HOW WE CAN... TURN BACK...
TWITCH TWITCH
HUNH?
SURE, BUT AFTER ONE LAST SWIM! ♪
SPLISH SPLASH
DID YOU FORGET THAT YOU CAN'T SWIM AGAIN?!
DON'T WORRY. MY HEAD'S A WATER-MELON, SO I'LL FLOAT! ♪
AHHHH
OH YEAH!
FWOOSH!
MEOW!

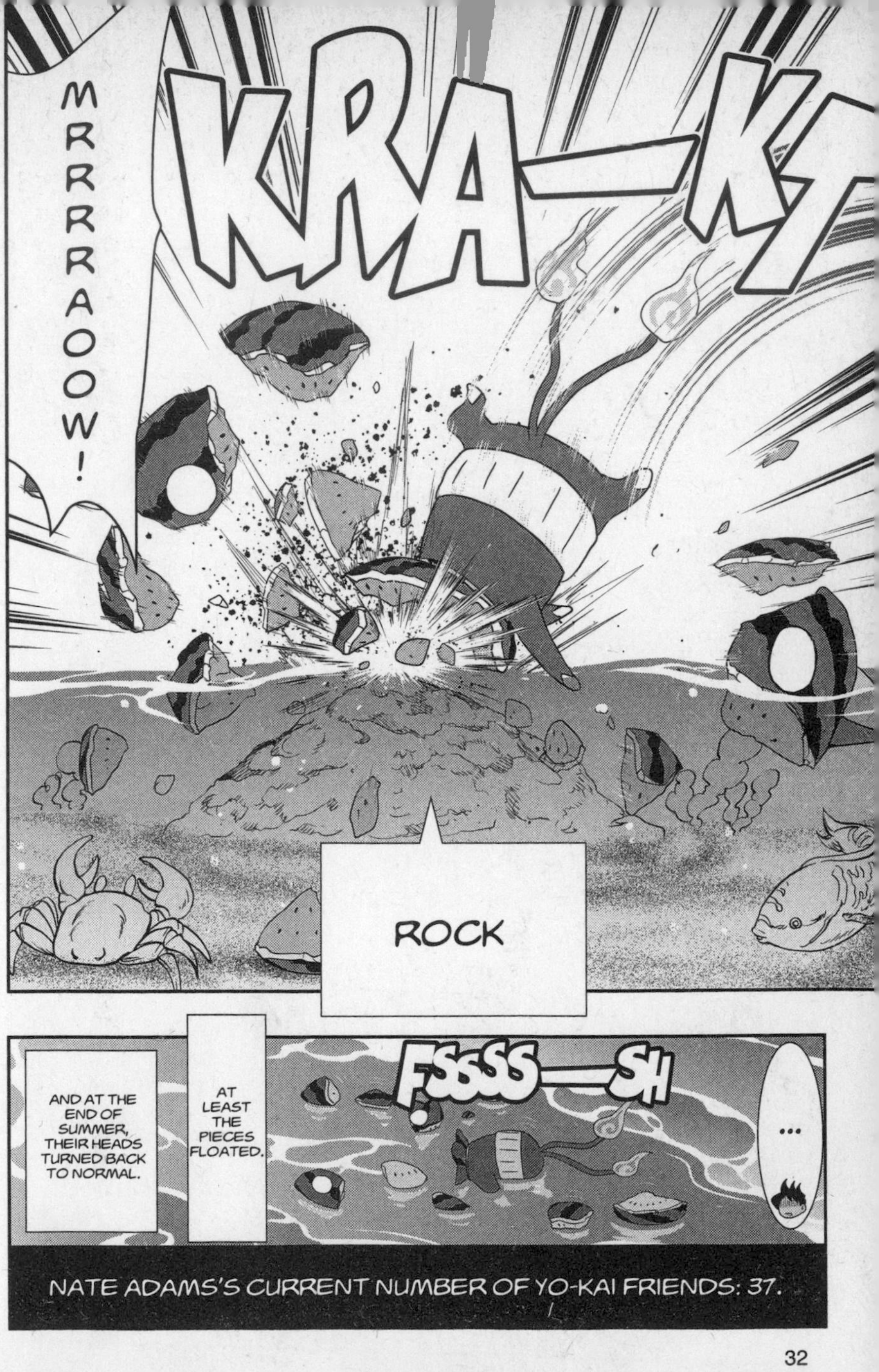
KRA-KT
MRRRRAOOOW!
ROCK
...
FSSSS—SH
AT LEAST THE PIECES FLOATED.
AND AT THE END OF SUMMER, THEIR HEADS TURNED BACK TO NORMAL.
NATE ADAMS'S CURRENT NUMBER OF YO-KAI FRIENDS: 37.

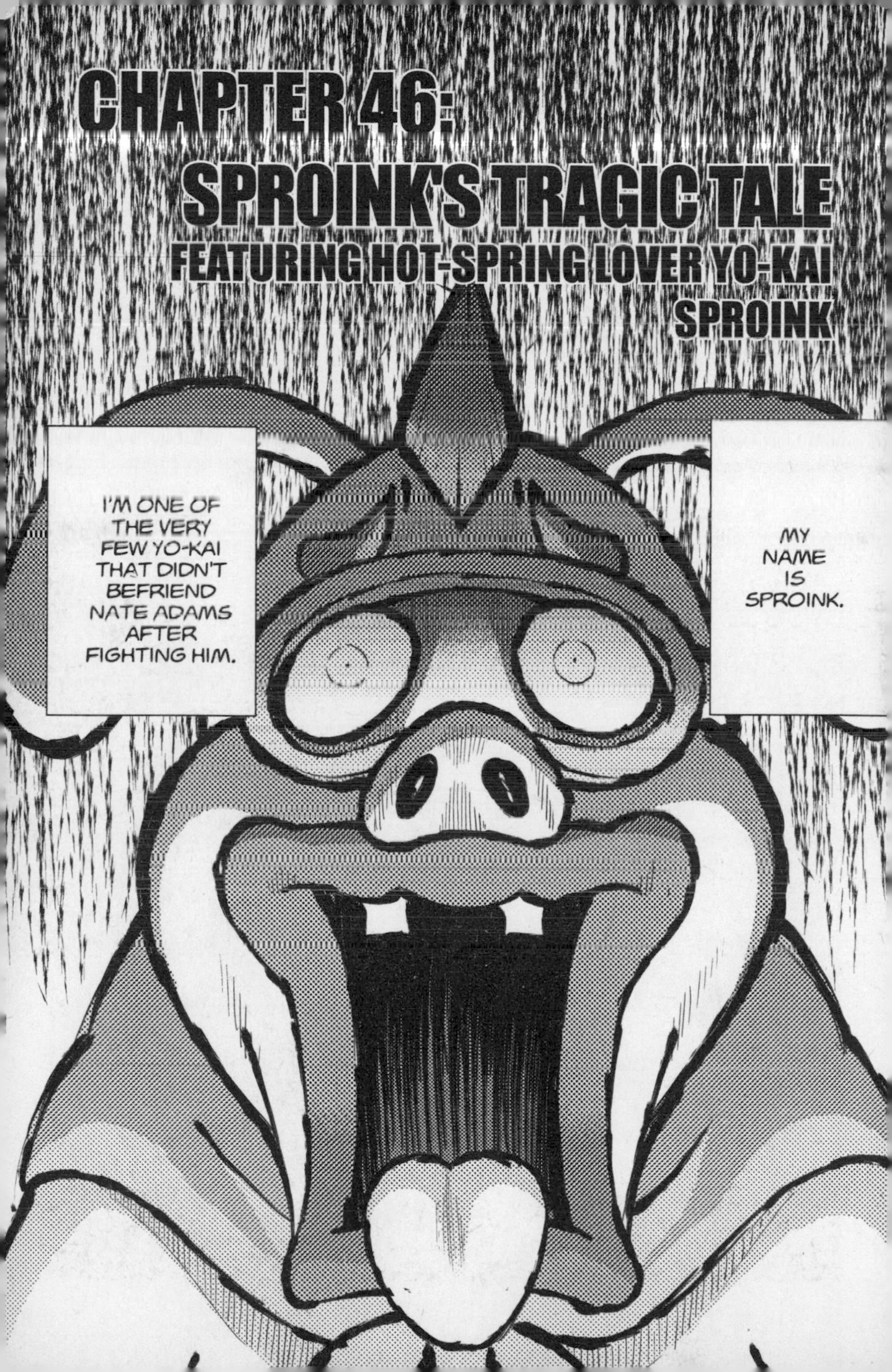
CHAPTER 46:
SPROINK'S TRAGIC TALE
FEATURING HOT-SPRING LOVER YO-KAI SPROINK
MY NAME IS SPROINK.
I'M ONE OF THE VERY FEW YO-KAI THAT DIDN'T BEFRIEND NATE ADAMS AFTER FIGHTING HIM.

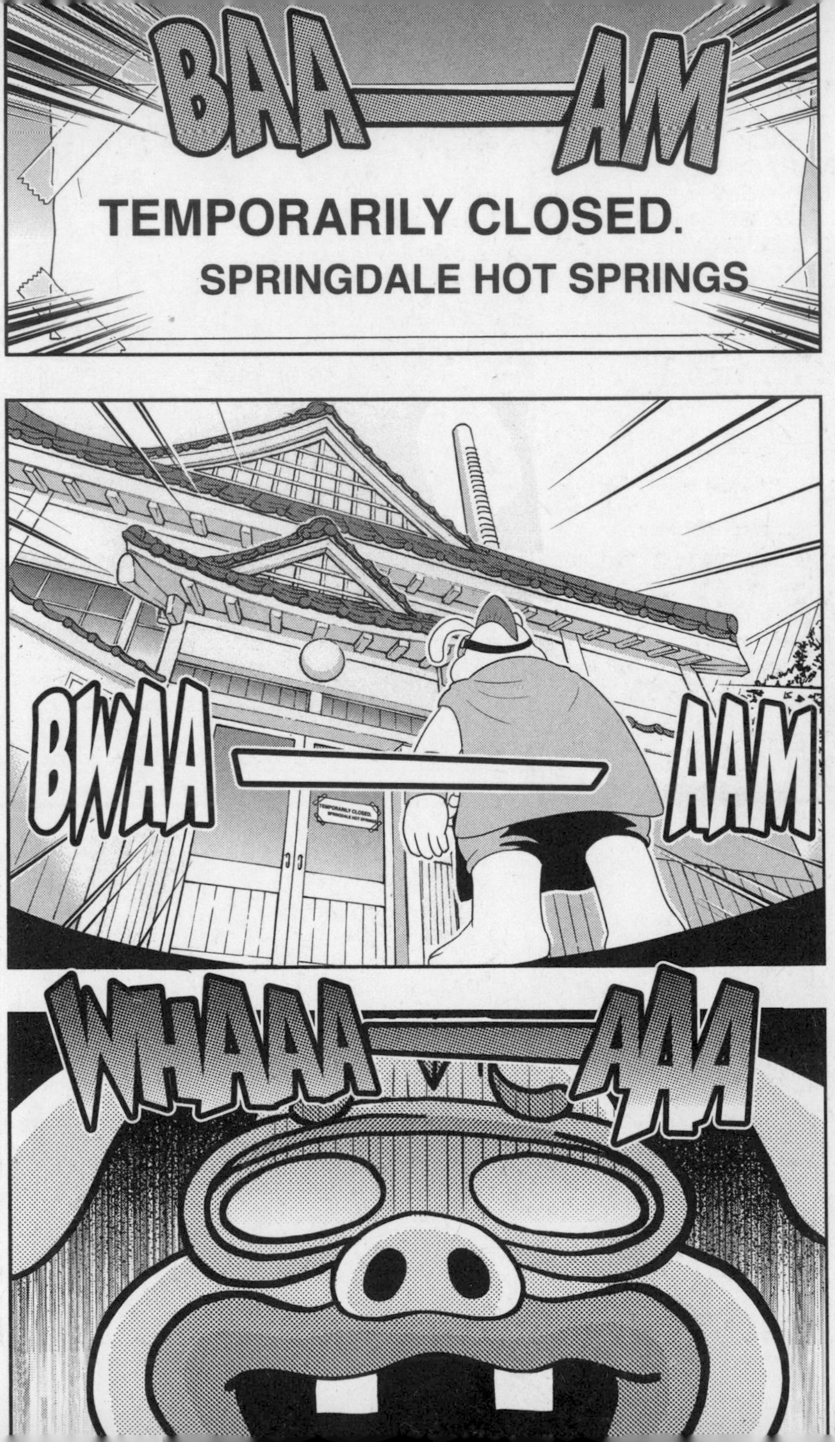
BAA—AM
TEMPORARILY CLOSED.
SPRINGDALE HOT SPRINGS
BWAA—AAM
WHAAA—AAA

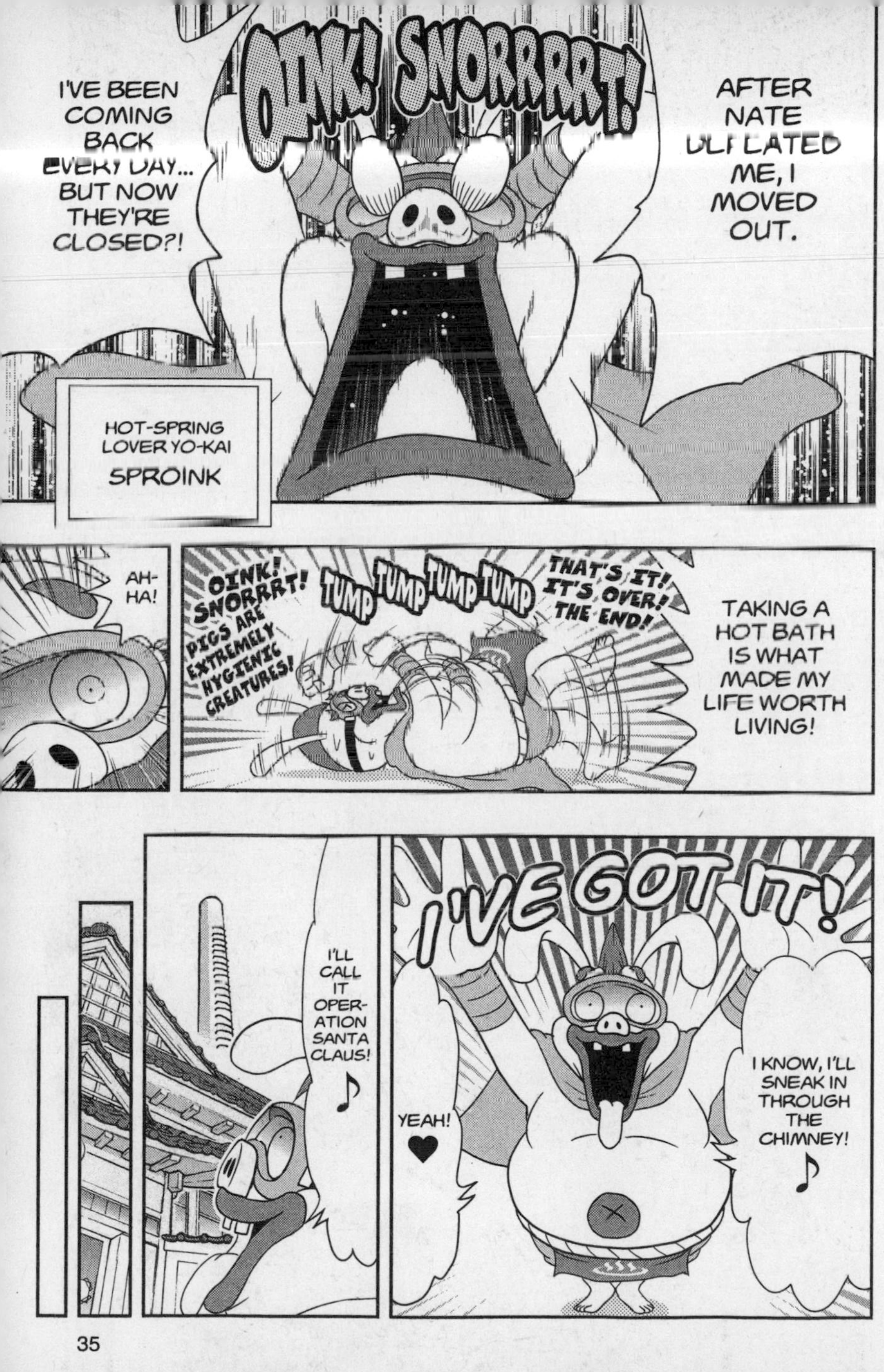
AFTER NATE DEFLATED ME, I MOVED OUT.
OINK! SNORRRRT!
I'VE BEEN COMING BACK EVERY DAY... BUT NOW THEY'RE CLOSED?!
HOT-SPRING LOVER YO-KAI SPROINK
TAKING A HOT BATH IS WHAT MADE MY LIFE WORTH LIVING!
THAT'S IT! IT'S OVER! THE END!
TUMP TUMP TUMP TUMP
OINK! SNORRRT! PIGS ARE EXTREMELY HYGIENIC CREATURES!
AH-HA!
I'VE GOT IT!
I KNOW, I'LL SNEAK IN THROUGH THE CHIMNEY! ♪
YEAH! ♥
I'LL CALL IT OPERATION SANTA CLAUS! ♪

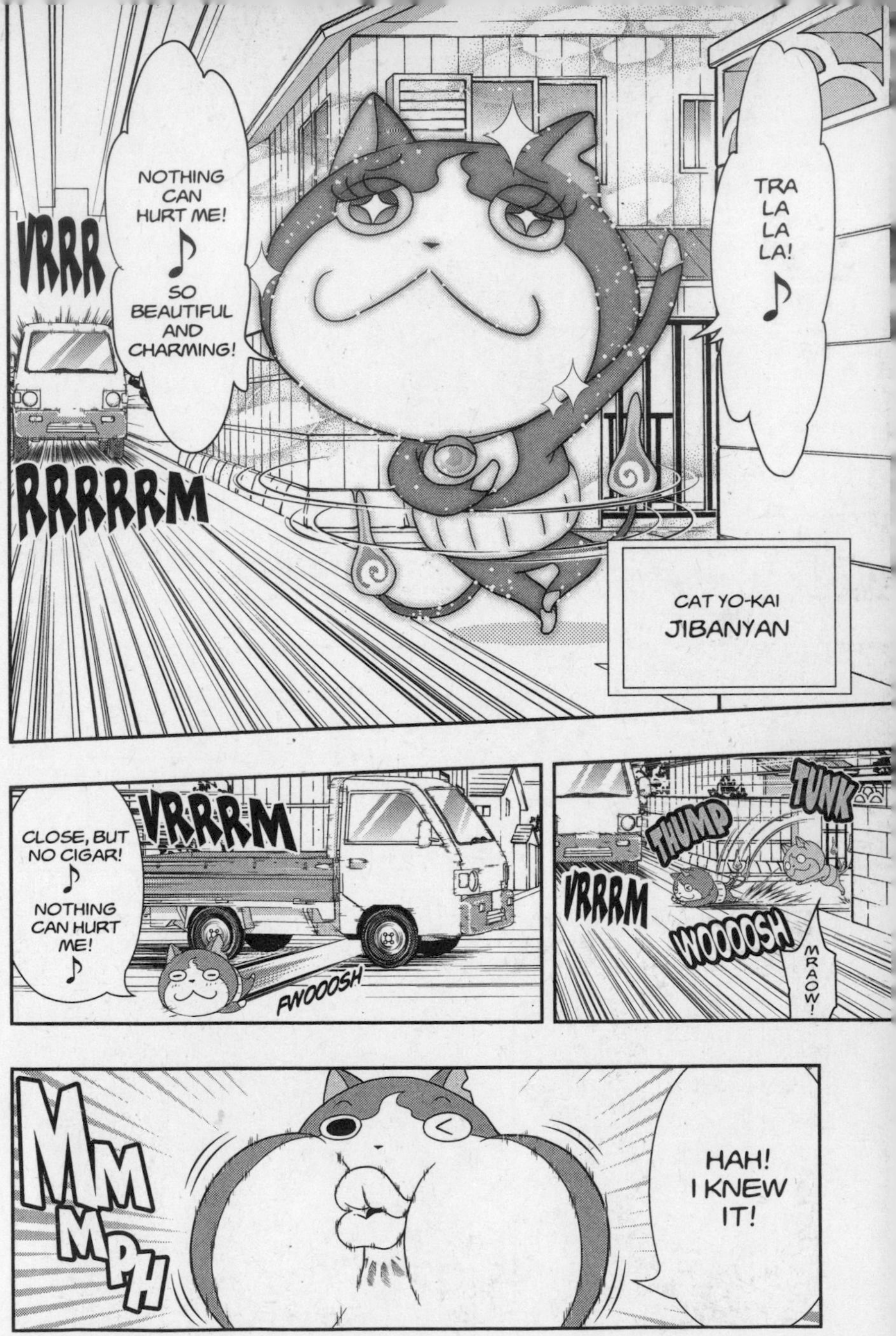
TRA LA LA LA! ♪
NOTHING CAN HURT ME! ♪ SO BEAUTIFUL AND CHARMING!
VRRR
RRRRRM
CAT YO-KAI JIBANYAN
TUNK
THUMP
VRRRM
WOOOOSH
MRAOW!
VRRRM
CLOSE, BUT NO CIGAR! ♪ NOTHING CAN HURT ME! ♪
FWOOOSH
HAH! I KNEW IT!
MMMPH

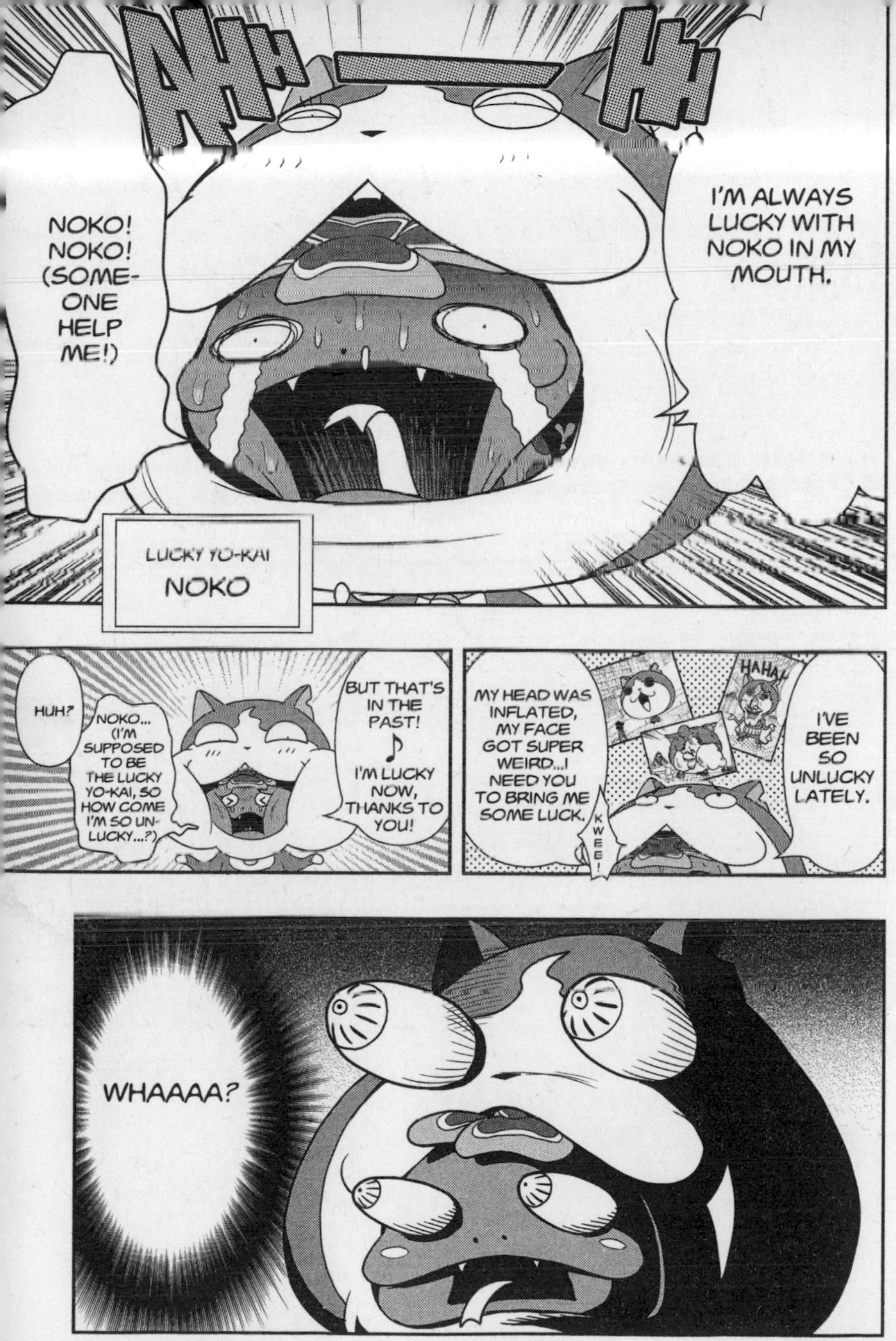
AHH——HH
I'M ALWAYS LUCKY WITH NOKO IN MY MOUTH.
NOKO! NOKO! (SOME-ONE HELP ME!)
LUCKY YO-KAI NOKO
I'VE BEEN SO UNLUCKY LATELY.
HAHA!
MY HEAD WAS INFLATED, MY FACE GOT SUPER WEIRD...I NEED YOU TO BRING ME SOME LUCK.
KWEE!
BUT THAT'S IN THE PAST! ♪ I'M LUCKY NOW, THANKS TO YOU!
NOKO... (I'M SUPPOSED TO BE THE LUCKY YO-KAI, SO HOW COME I'M SO UN-LUCKY...?)
HUH?
WHAAAA?

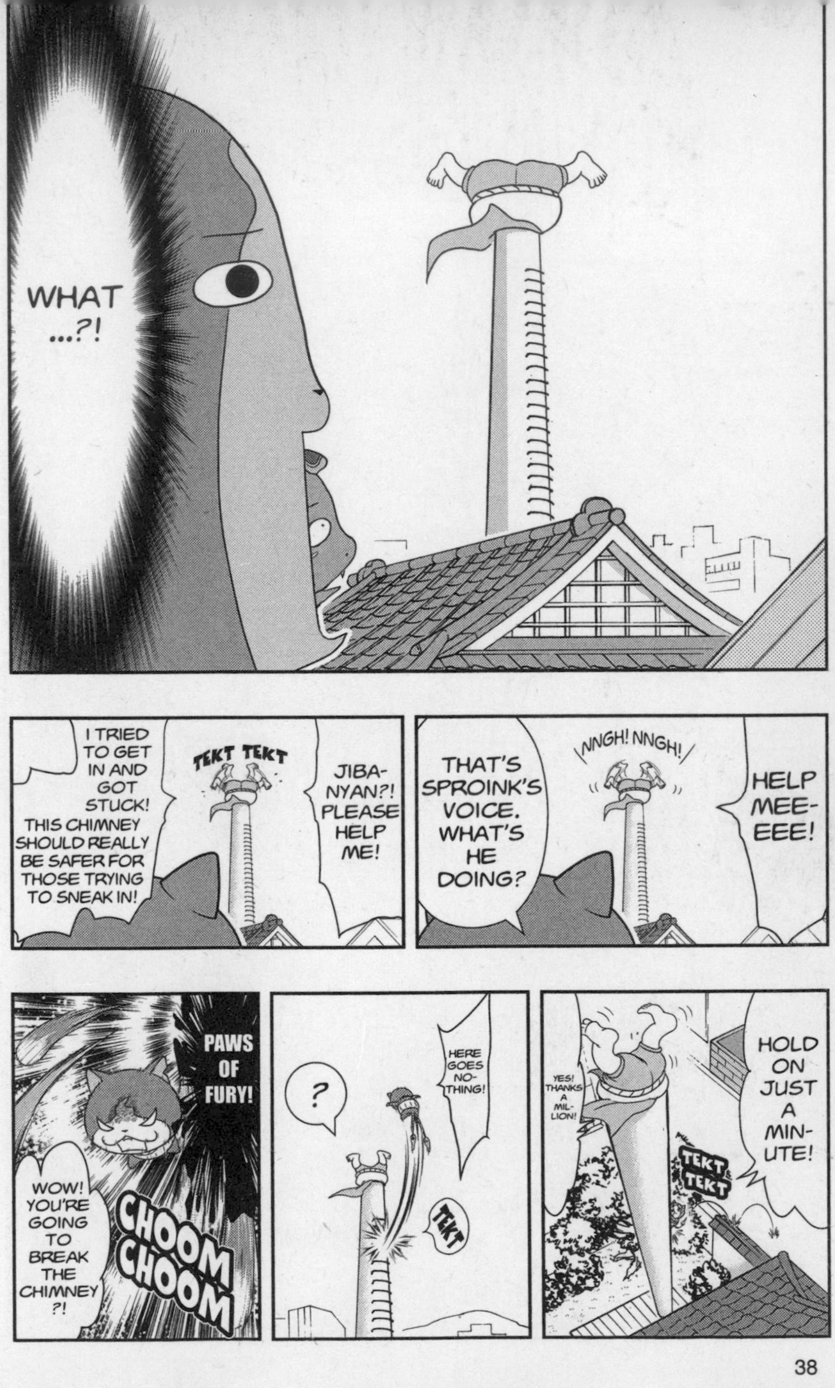
WHAT ...?!
HELP MEEE-EEE!
NNGH! NNGH!
THAT'S SPROINK'S VOICE. WHAT'S HE DOING?
JIBA-NYAN?! PLEASE HELP ME!
TEKT TEKT
I TRIED TO GET IN AND GOT STUCK! THIS CHIMNEY SHOULD REALLY BE SAFER FOR THOSE TRYING TO SNEAK IN!
HOLD ON JUST A MIN-UTE!
YES! THANKS A MIL-LION!
TEKT TEKT
HERE GOES NO-THING!
?
TEKT
PAWS OF FURY!
WOW! YOU'RE GOING TO BREAK THE CHIMNEY?!
CHOOM CHOOM

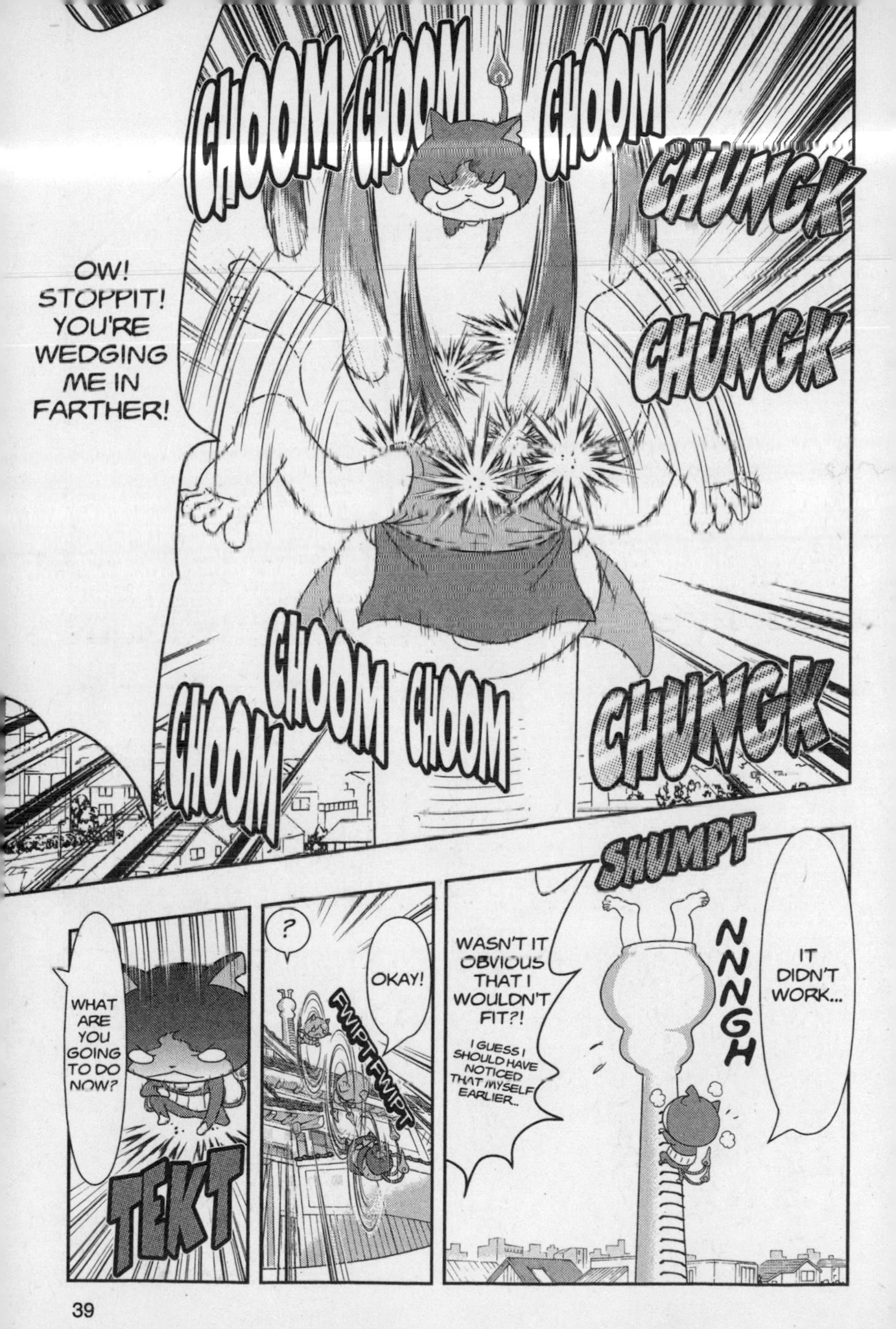
CHOOM CHOOM CHOOM
CHUNCK
CHUNGK
OW! STOPPIT! YOU'RE WEDGING ME IN FARTHER!
CHUNGK
CHOOM CHOOM CHOOM
SHUMPT
IT DIDN'T WORK...
NNNGH
WASN'T IT OBVIOUS THAT I WOULDN'T FIT?!
I GUESS I SHOULD HAVE NOTICED THAT MYSELF EARLIER..
OKAY!
?
FWIPT FWIPT
WHAT ARE YOU GOING TO DO NOW?
TEKT

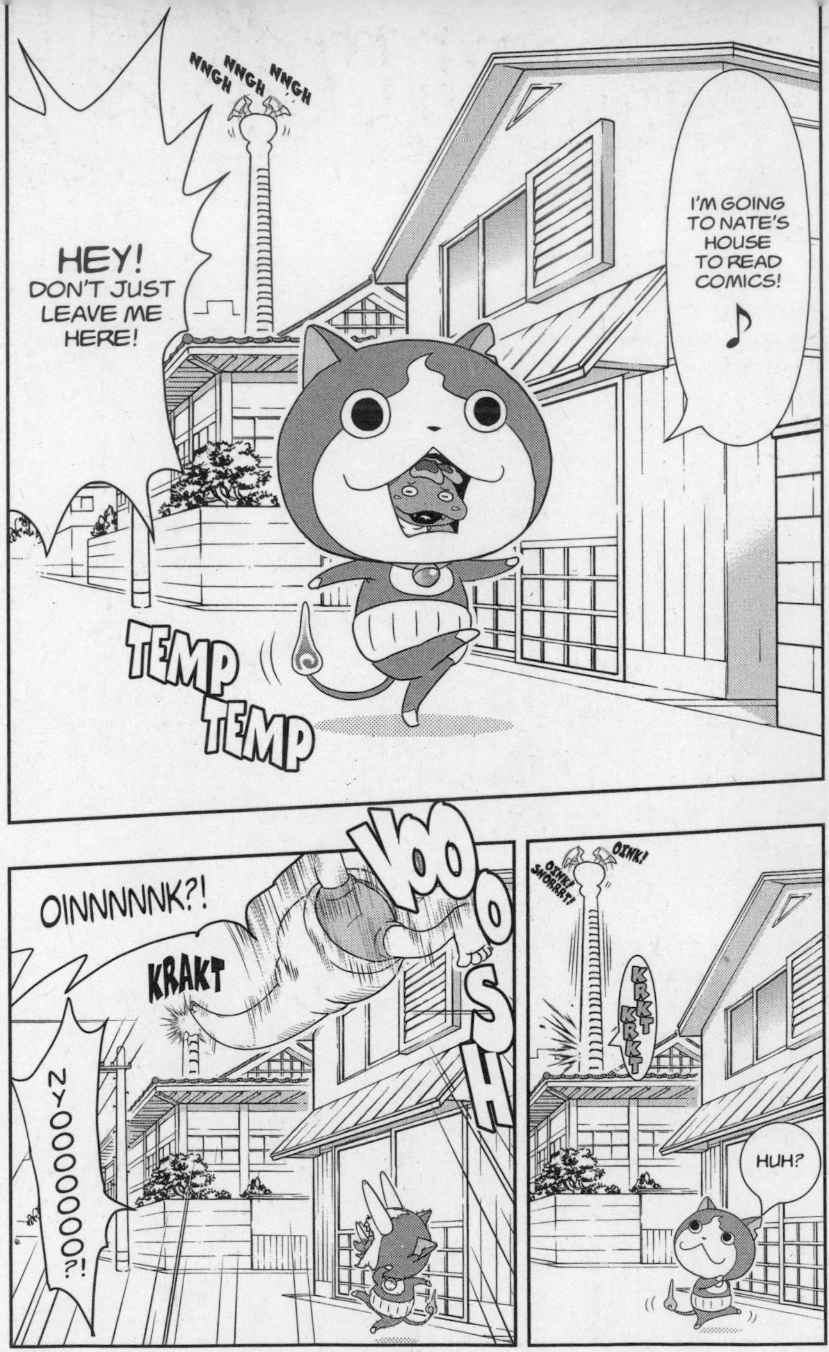
I'M GOING TO NATE'S HOUSE TO READ COMICS! ♪
NNGH NNGH NNGH
HEY! DON'T JUST LEAVE ME HERE!
TEMP TEMP
OINK!
OINK! SNORRRT!
KRKT KRKT KRKT
HUH?
VOOOOSH
OINNNNNK?!
KRAKT
NYOOOOOOOO?!

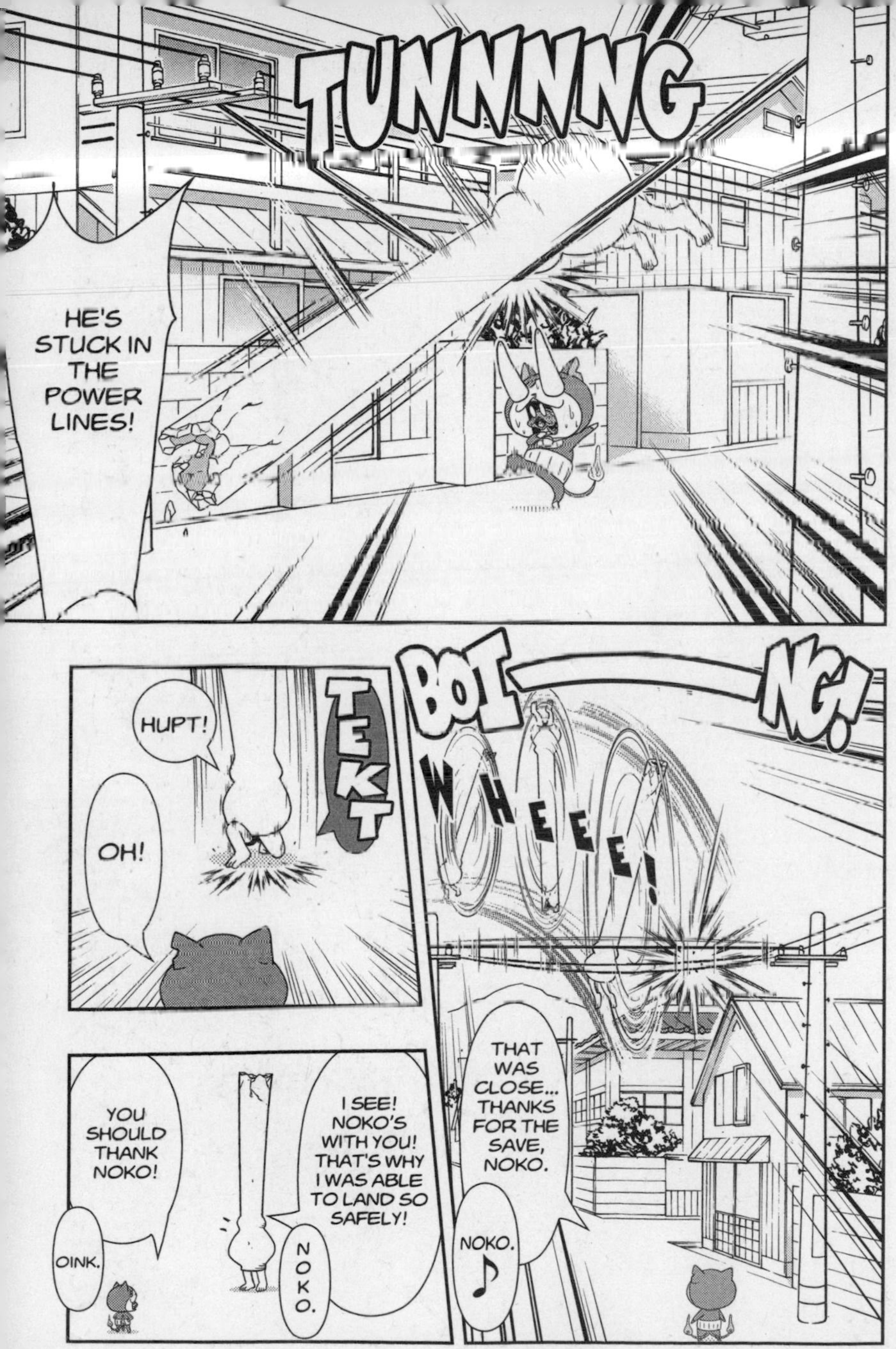
TUNNNNG
HE'S STUCK IN THE POWER LINES!
BOI—NG!
WHEEEE!
TEKT
HUPT!
OH!
THAT WAS CLOSE... THANKS FOR THE SAVE, NOKO.
NOKO. ♪
I SEE! NOKO'S WITH YOU! THAT'S WHY I WAS ABLE TO LAND SO SAFELY!
NOKO.
YOU SHOULD THANK NOKO!
OINK.

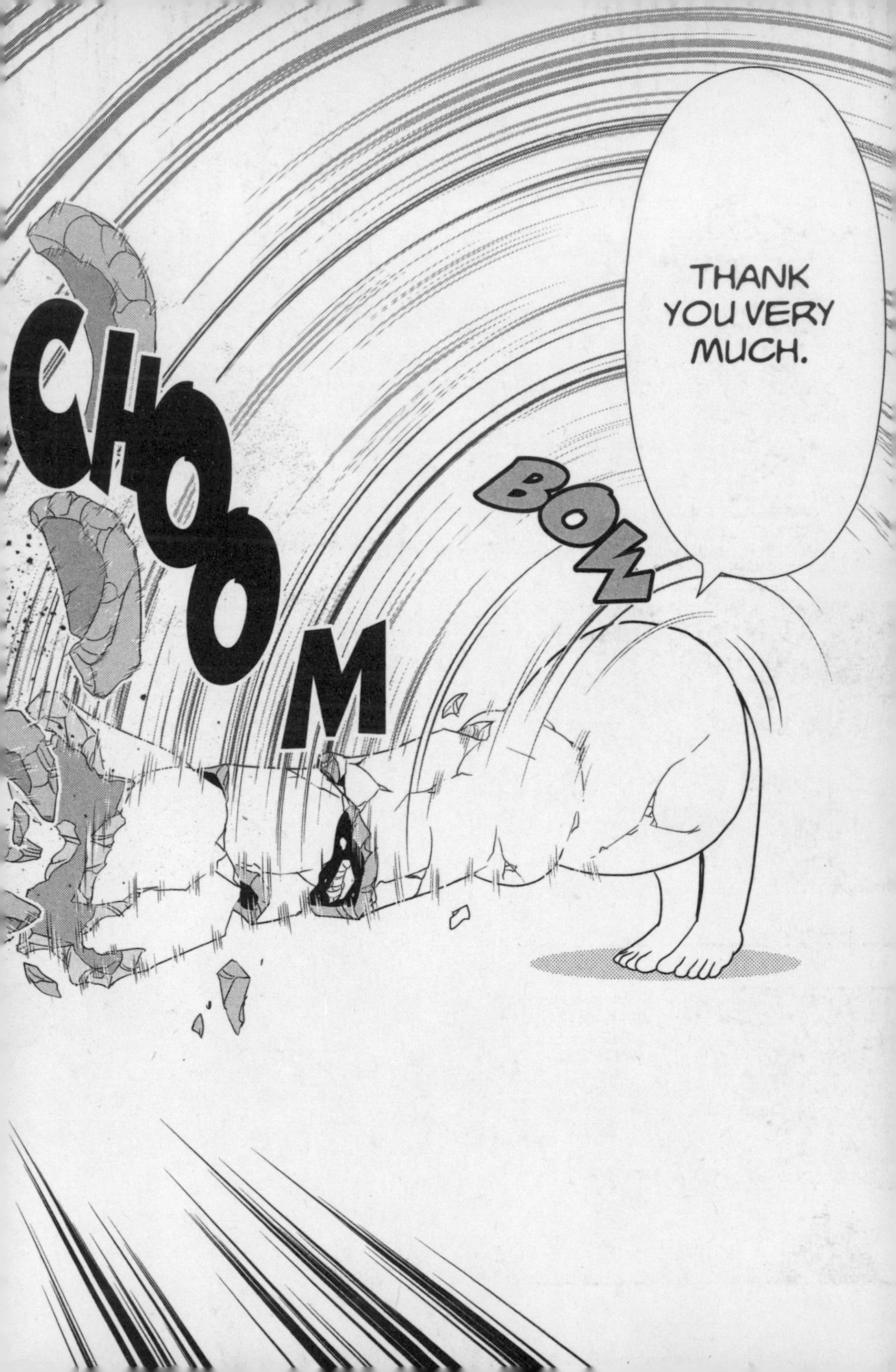
THANK YOU VERY MUCH.
BOW
CHOOOM

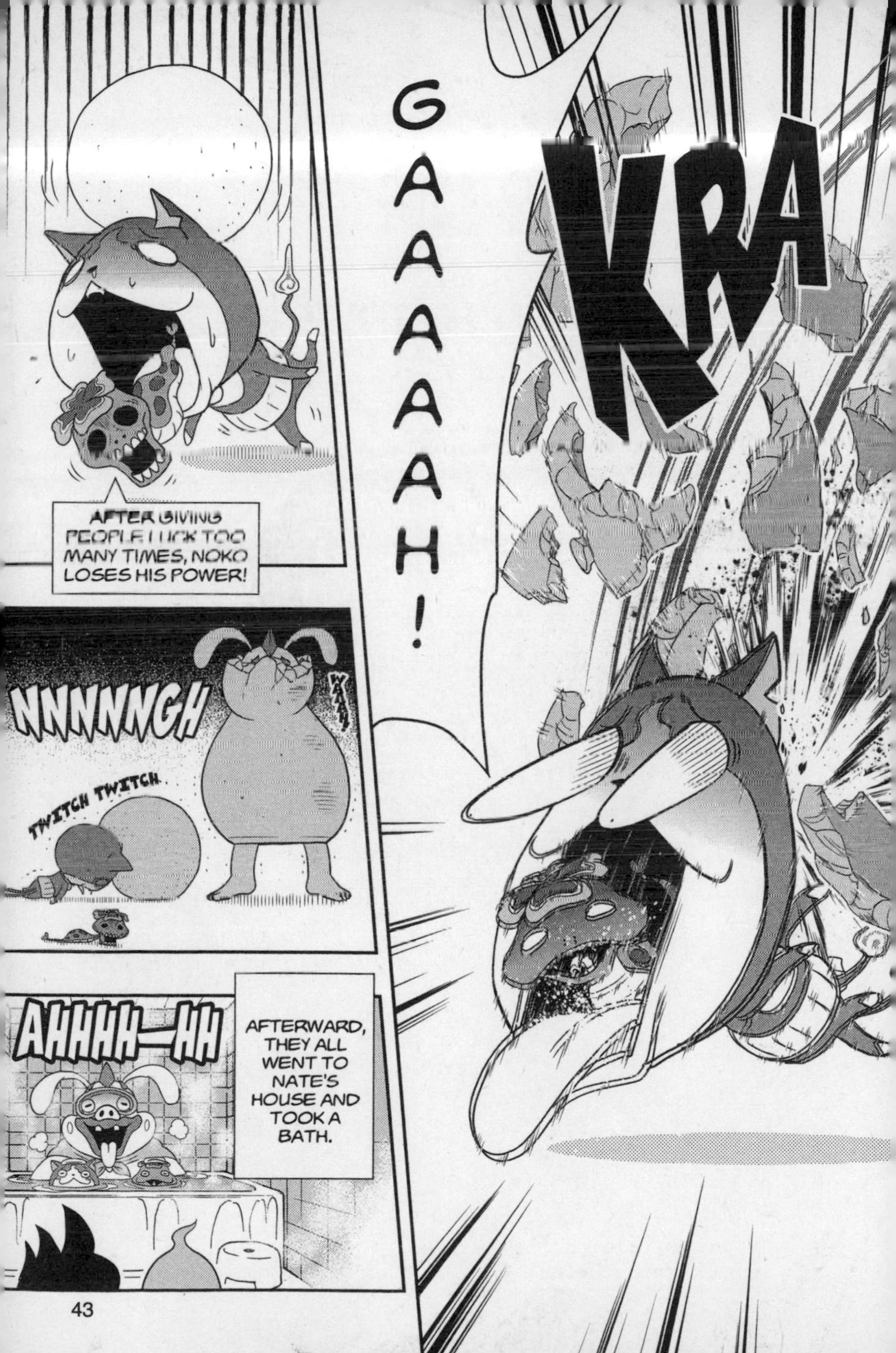
GAAAAAH!
KRA
AFTER GIVING PEOPLE LUCK TOO MANY TIMES, NOKO LOSES HIS POWER!
NNNNNGH
TWITCH TWITCH
AFTERWARD, THEY ALL WENT TO NATE'S HOUSE AND TOOK A BATH.
AHHHH—HH

CHAPTER 47: HONESTY IS THE BEST POLICY?!

FEATURING PUREHEARTED YO-KAI SANDMEH

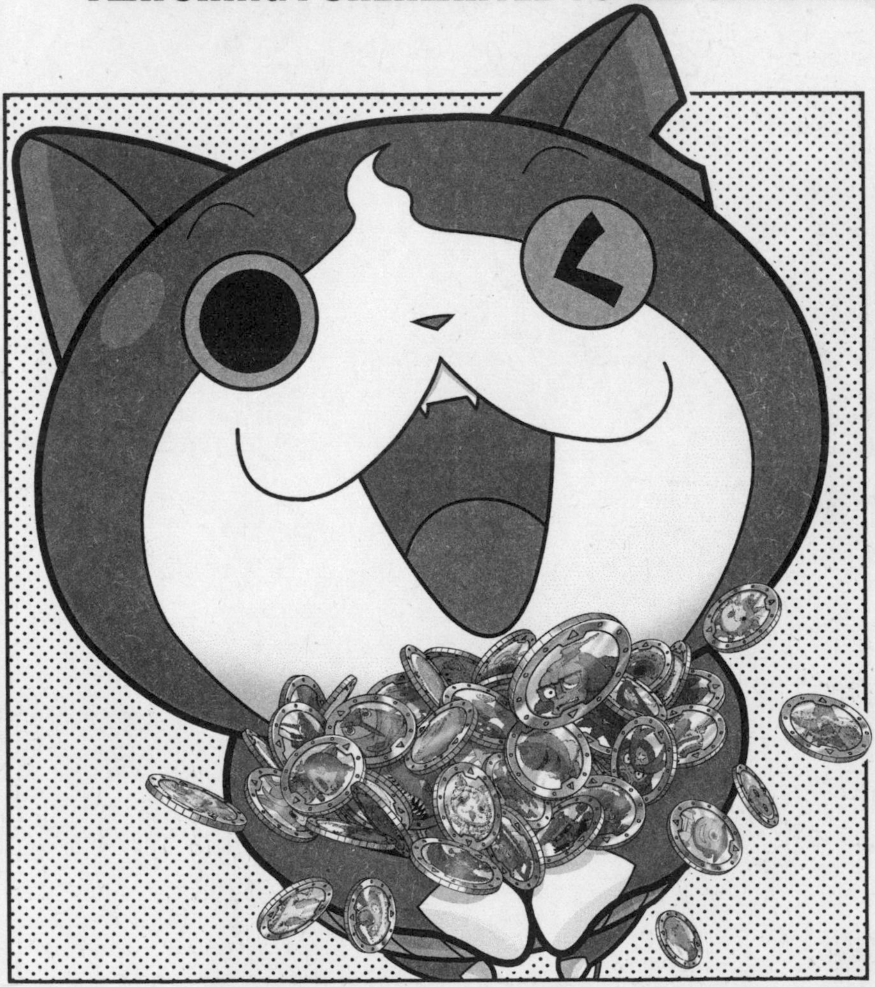

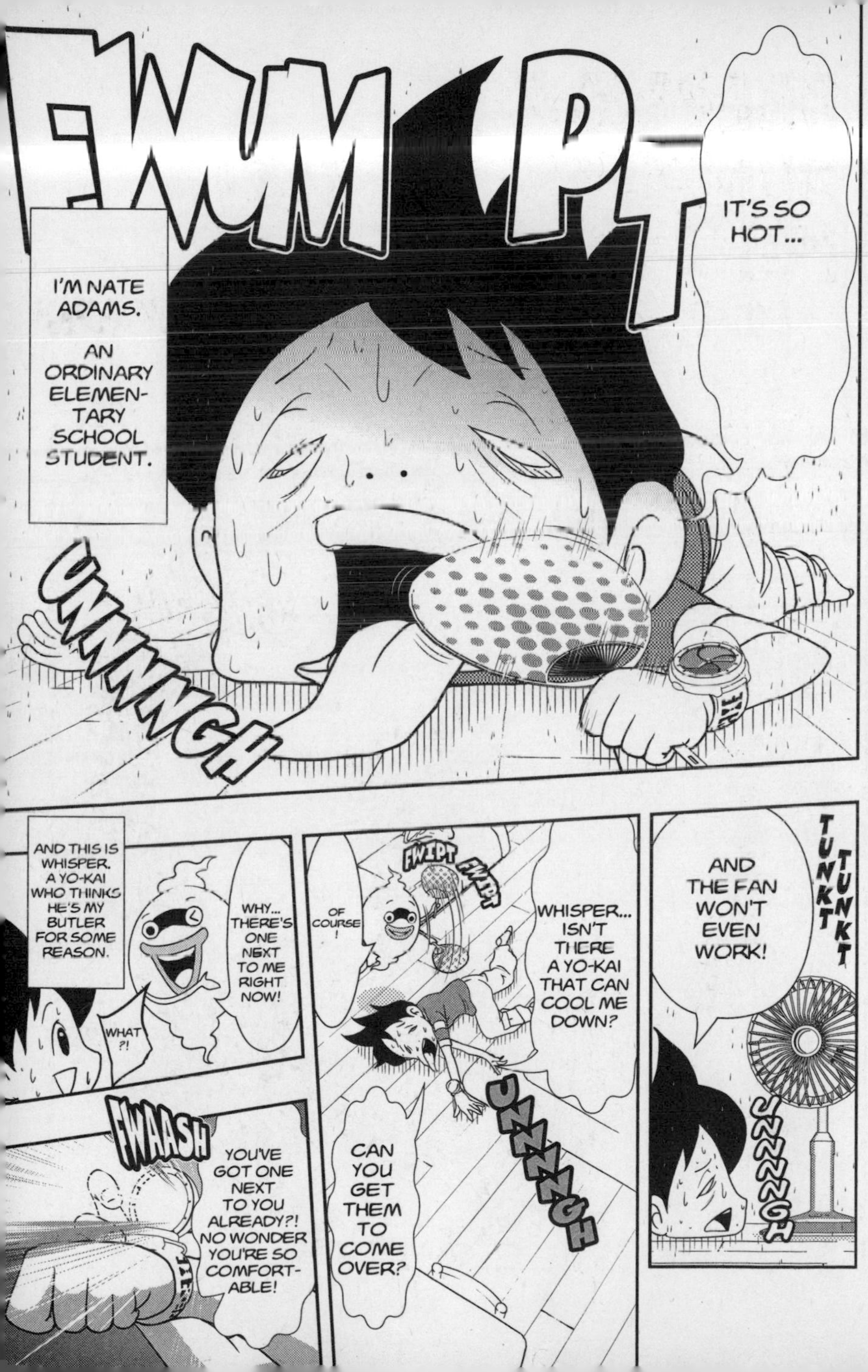
FWUMPT
IT'S SO HOT...
I'M NATE ADAMS.
AN ORDINARY ELEMENTARY SCHOOL STUDENT.
UNNNNGH
AND THE FAN WON'T EVEN WORK!
TUNKT
TUNKT
UNNNNGH
WHISPER... ISN'T THERE A YO-KAI THAT CAN COOL ME DOWN?
FWIPT
FWIPT
OF COURSE!
UNNNGH
CAN YOU GET THEM TO COME OVER?
AND THIS IS WHISPER. A YO-KAI WHO THINKS HE'S MY BUTLER FOR SOME REASON.
WHY... THERE'S ONE NEXT TO ME RIGHT NOW!
WHAT?!
FWAASH
YOU'VE GOT ONE NEXT TO YOU ALREADY?! NO WONDER YOU'RE SO COMFORTABLE!

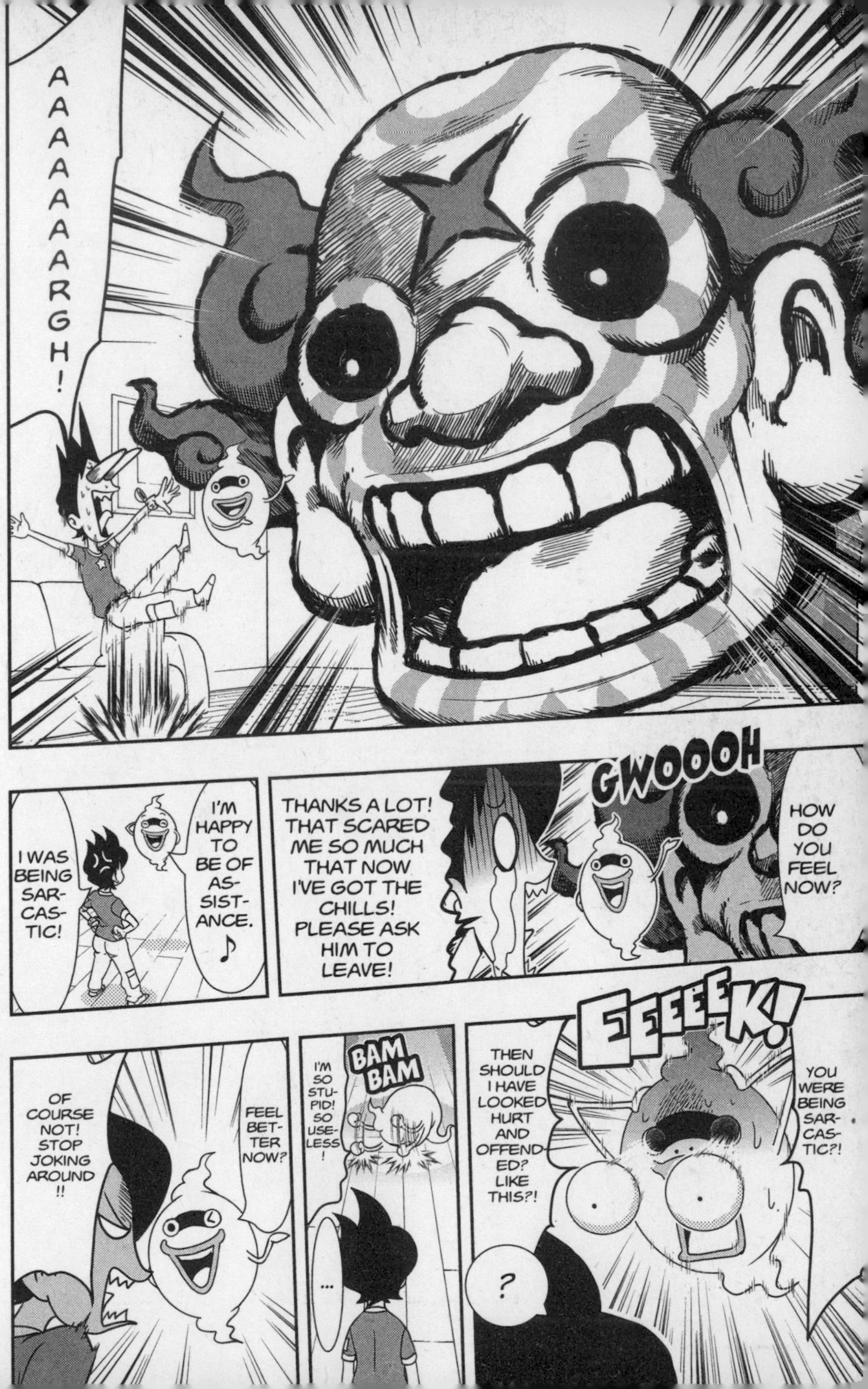
AAAAAAARGH!
GWOOOH
HOW DO YOU FEEL NOW?
THANKS A LOT! THAT SCARED ME SO MUCH THAT NOW I'VE GOT THE CHILLS! PLEASE ASK HIM TO LEAVE!
I'M HAPPY TO BE OF ASSISTANCE. ♪
I WAS BEING SARCASTIC!
EEEEK!
YOU WERE BEING SARCASTIC?!
THEN SHOULD I HAVE LOOKED HURT AND OFFENDED? LIKE THIS?!
?
BAM BAM
I'M SO STUPID! SO USELESS!
...
FEEL BETTER NOW?
OF COURSE NOT! STOP JOKING AROUND!!

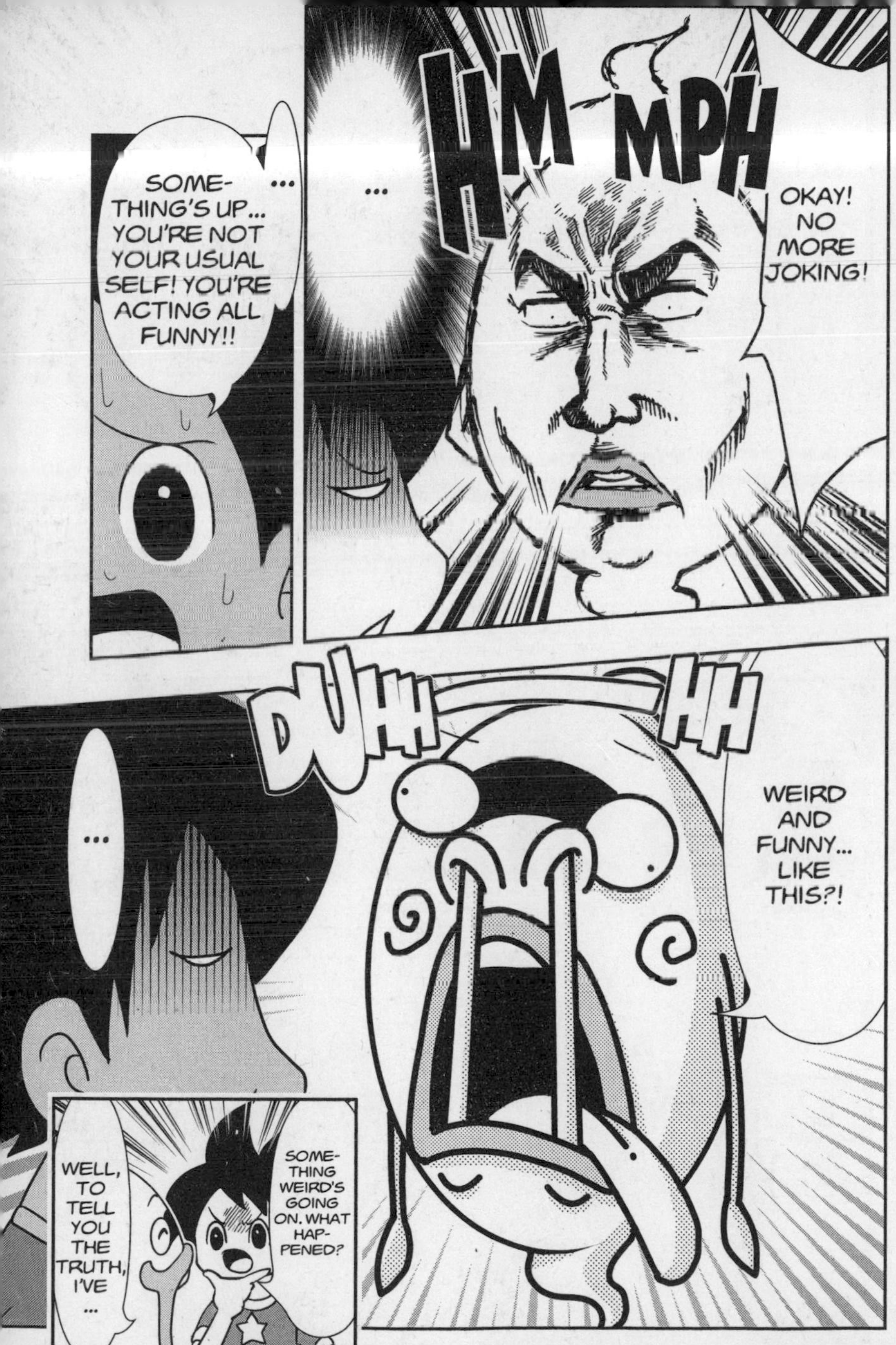
HM-MPH
OKAY! NO MORE JOKING!
...
...
SOME-THING'S UP... YOU'RE NOT YOUR USUAL SELF! YOU'RE ACTING ALL FUNNY!!
DUHHHH
WEIRD AND FUNNY... LIKE THIS?!
...
SOME-THING WEIRD'S GOING ON. WHAT HAP-PENED?
WELL, TO TELL YOU THE TRUTH, I'VE ...

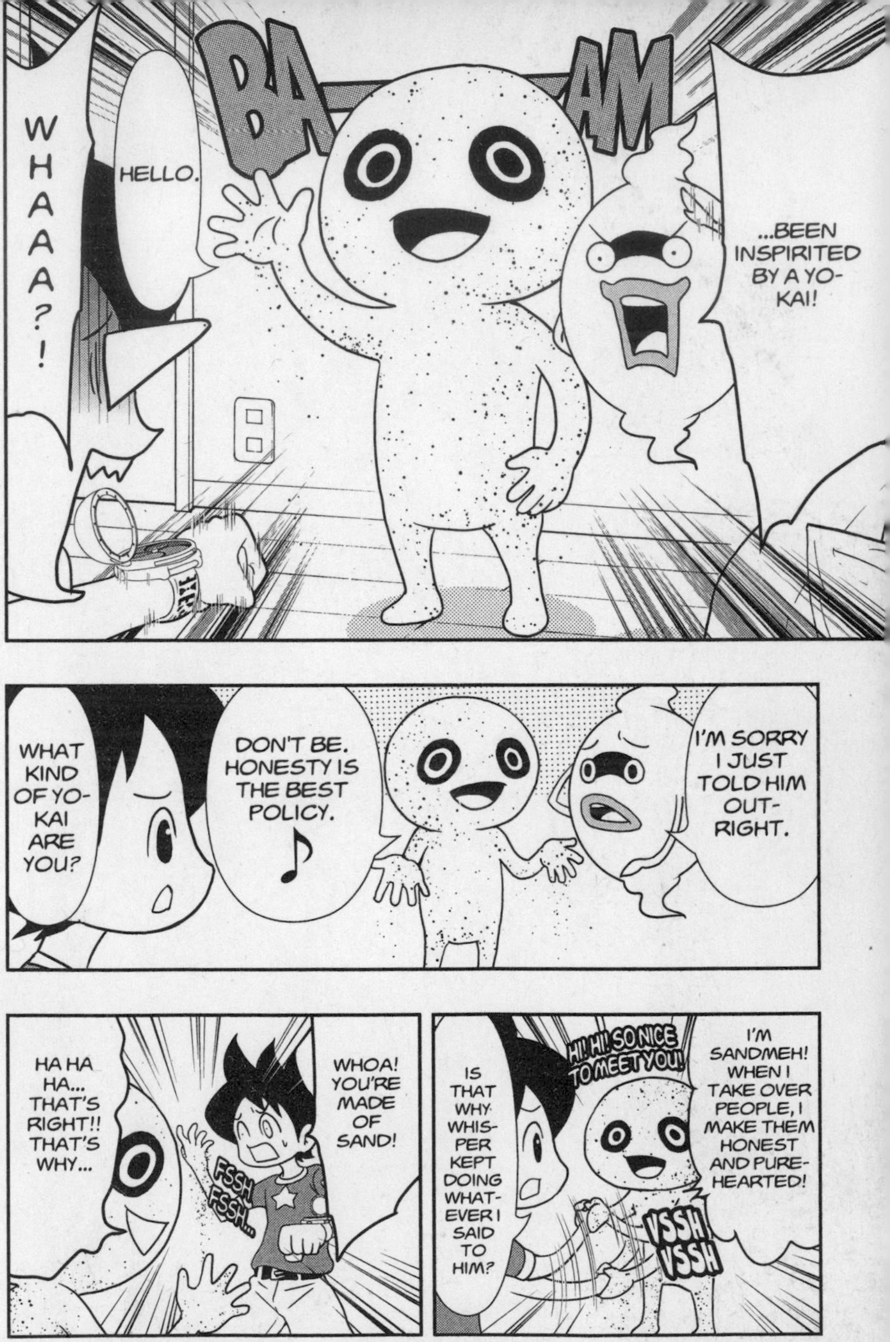
...BEEN INSPIRITED BY A YO-KAI!
BA
AM
HELLO.
WHAAAA?!
I'M SORRY I JUST TOLD HIM OUT-RIGHT.
DON'T BE. HONESTY IS THE BEST POLICY. ♪
WHAT KIND OF YO-KAI ARE YOU?
I'M SANDMEH! WHEN I TAKE OVER PEOPLE, I MAKE THEM HONEST AND PURE-HEARTED!
HI! HI! SO NICE TO MEET YOU!
IS THAT WHY WHISPER KEPT DOING WHATEVER I SAID TO HIM?
VSSH VSSH
WHOA! YOU'RE MADE OF SAND!
FSSH FSSH...
HA HA HA... THAT'S RIGHT!! THAT'S WHY...

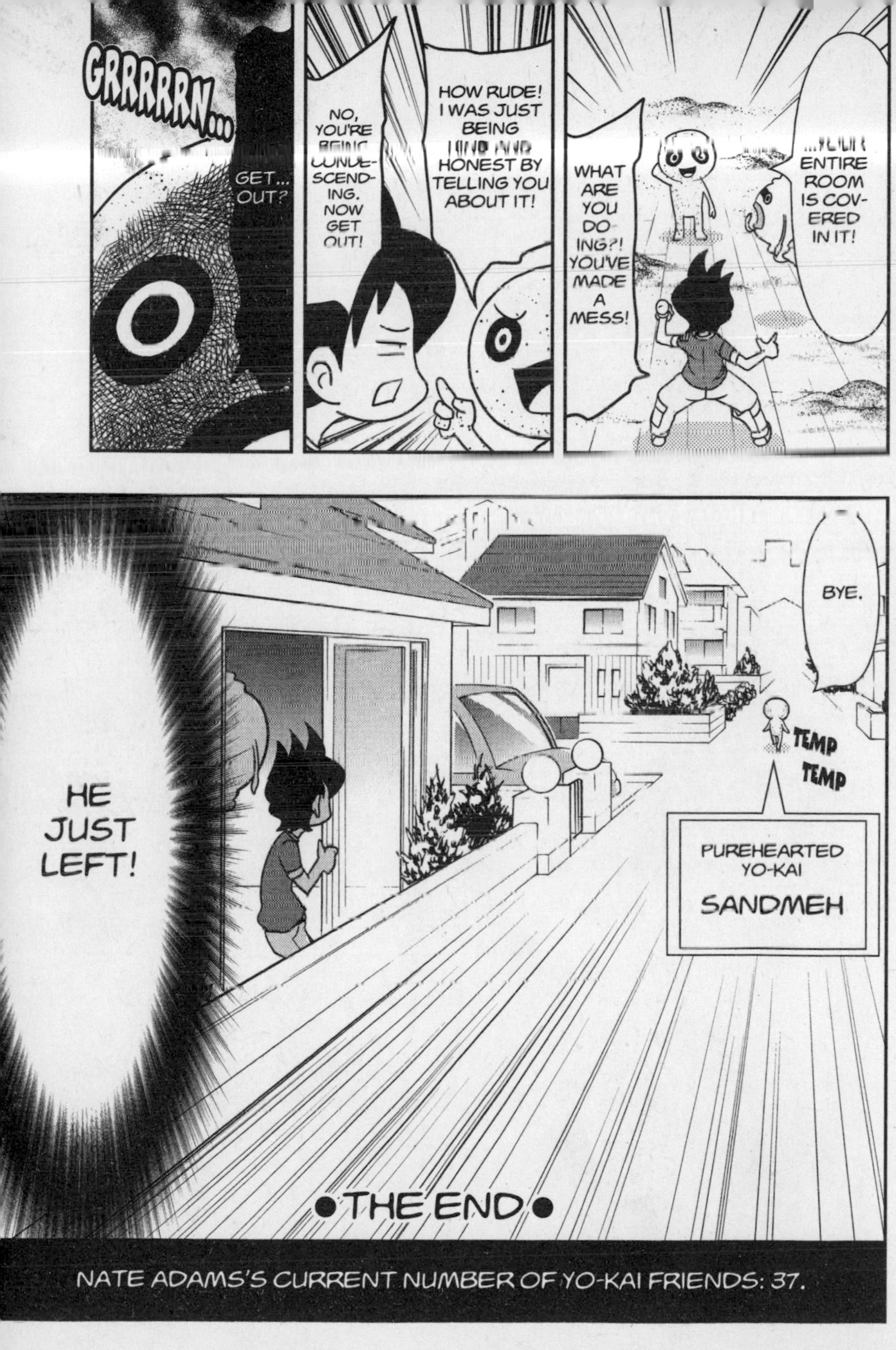
...YOUR ENTIRE ROOM IS COVERED IN IT!
WHAT ARE YOU DOING?! YOU'VE MADE A MESS!
HOW RUDE! I WAS JUST BEING KIND AND HONEST BY TELLING YOU ABOUT IT!
NO, YOU'RE BEING CONDE-SCEND-ING. NOW GET OUT!
GET... OUT?
GRRRRRN...
BYE.
TEMP TEMP
PUREHEARTED YO-KAI
SANDMEH
HE JUST LEFT!
•THE END•
NATE ADAMS'S CURRENT NUMBER OF YO-KAI FRIENDS: 37.

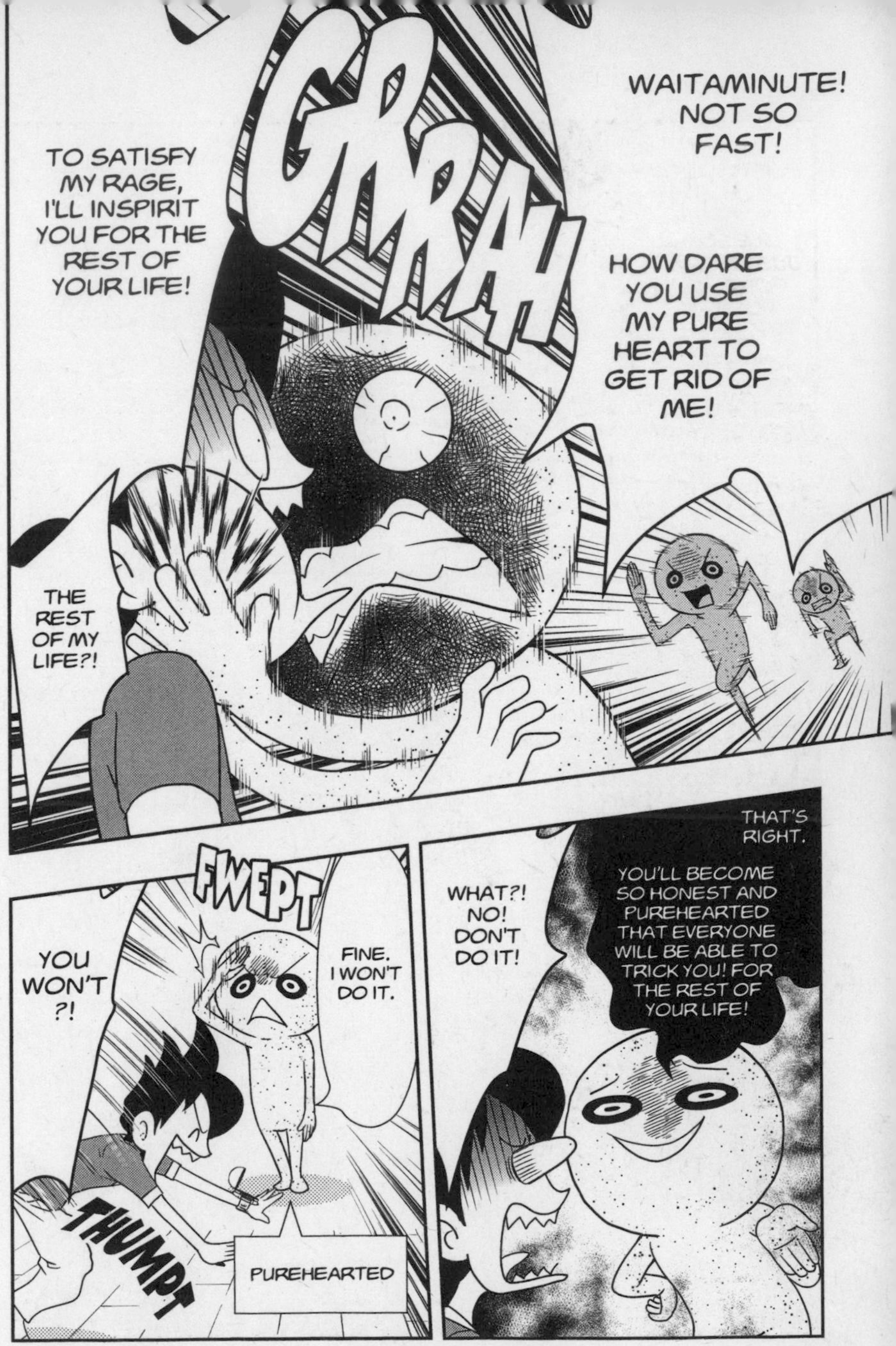
WAITAMINUTE! NOT SO FAST!
HOW DARE YOU USE MY PURE HEART TO GET RID OF ME!
GRRAH
TO SATISFY MY RAGE, I'LL INSPIRIT YOU FOR THE REST OF YOUR LIFE!
THE REST OF MY LIFE?!
THAT'S RIGHT.
YOU'LL BECOME SO HONEST AND PUREHEARTED THAT EVERYONE WILL BE ABLE TO TRICK YOU! FOR THE REST OF YOUR LIFE!
WHAT?! NO! DON'T DO IT!
FWEPT
FINE. I WON'T DO IT.
YOU WON'T ?!
THUMPT
PUREHEARTED

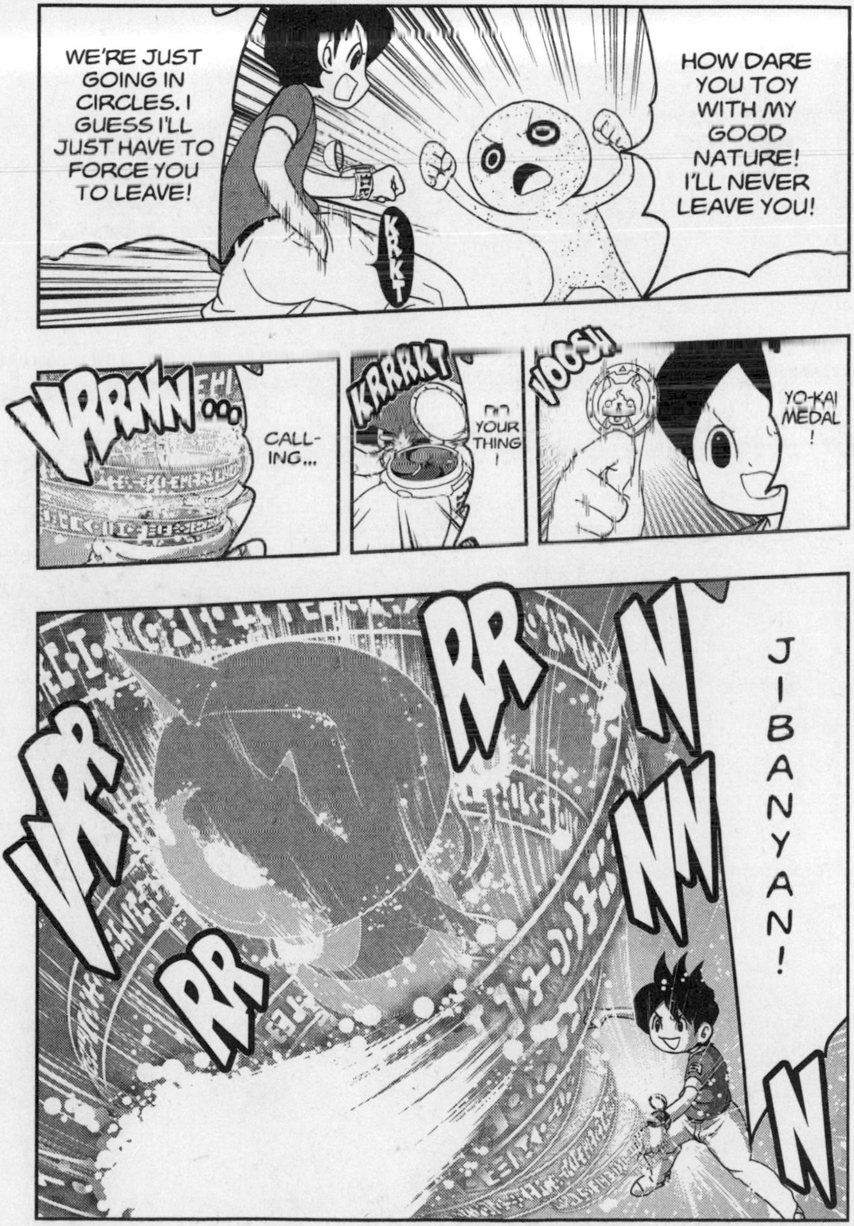
WE'RE JUST GOING IN CIRCLES. I GUESS I'LL JUST HAVE TO FORCE YOU TO LEAVE!
HOW DARE YOU TOY WITH MY GOOD NATURE! I'LL NEVER LEAVE YOU!
KRKT
VRRNN...
CALLING...
KRRRKT
YOUR THING!
VOOSH
YO-KAI MEDAL!
VRRRRNNNNN
JIBANYAN!

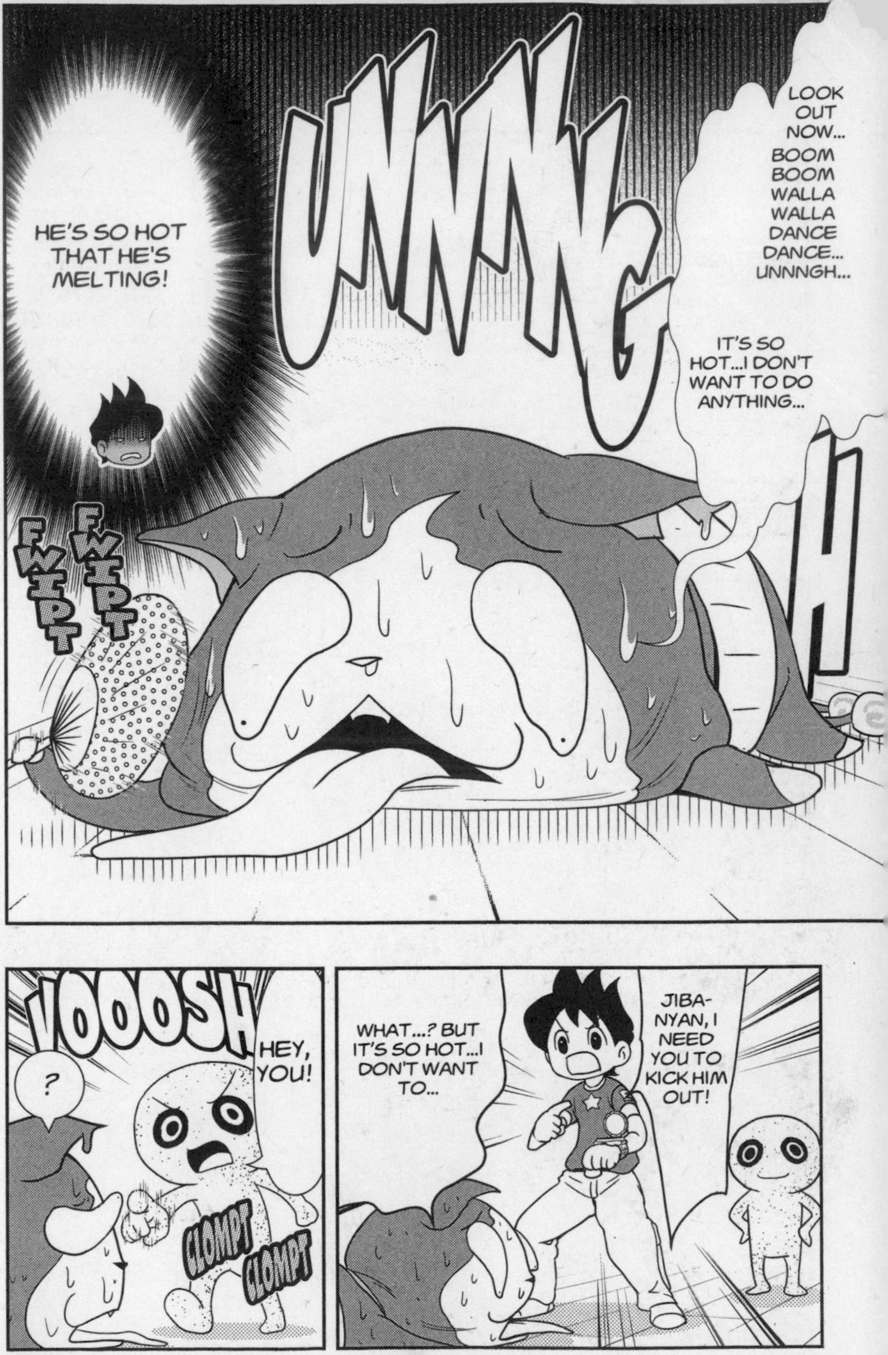
LOOK OUT NOW... BOOM BOOM WALLA WALLA DANCE DANCE... UNNNGH...
UNNNNGH
IT'S SO HOT...I DON'T WANT TO DO ANYTHING...
HE'S SO HOT THAT HE'S MELTING!
FWIPT
FWIPT
JIBA-NYAN, I NEED YOU TO KICK HIM OUT!
WHAT...? BUT IT'S SO HOT...I DON'T WANT TO...
VOOOSH
HEY, YOU!
?
CLOMPT
CLOMPT

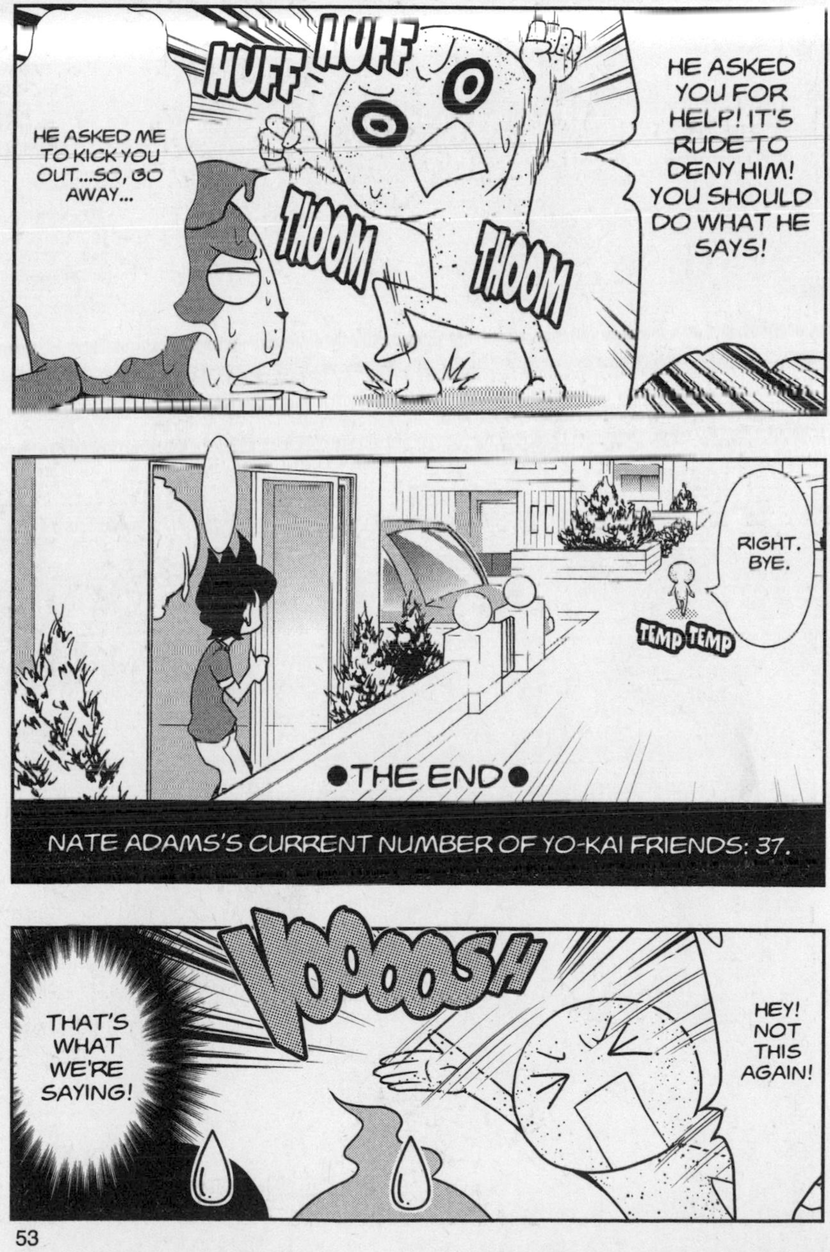
HE ASKED YOU FOR HELP! IT'S RUDE TO DENY HIM! YOU SHOULD DO WHAT HE SAYS!
HUFF HUFF
HE ASKED ME TO KICK YOU OUT...SO, GO AWAY...
THOOM THOOM
RIGHT. BYE.
TEMP TEMP
●THE END●
NATE ADAMS'S CURRENT NUMBER OF YO-KAI FRIENDS: 37.
VOOOOSH
HEY! NOT THIS AGAIN!
THAT'S WHAT WE'RE SAYING!

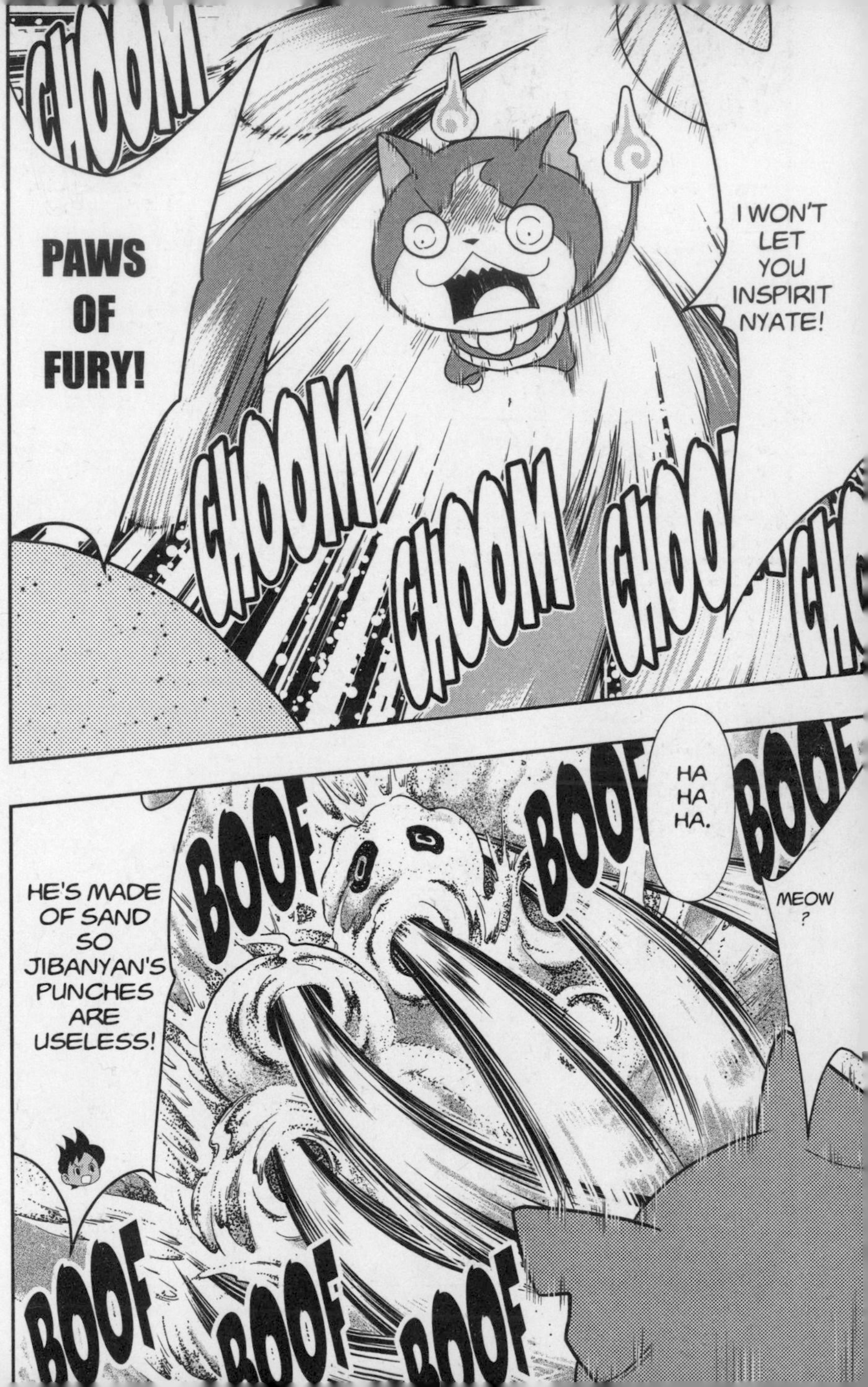
CHOOM
I WON'T LET YOU INSPIRIT NYATE!
PAWS OF FURY!
CHOOM
CHOOM
CHOOM
CHOO
CHO
BOOF
BOOF
HA HA HA.
MEOW?
BOOF
BOOF
HE'S MADE OF SAND SO JIBANYAN'S PUNCHES ARE USELESS!
BOOF
BOOF
BOOF

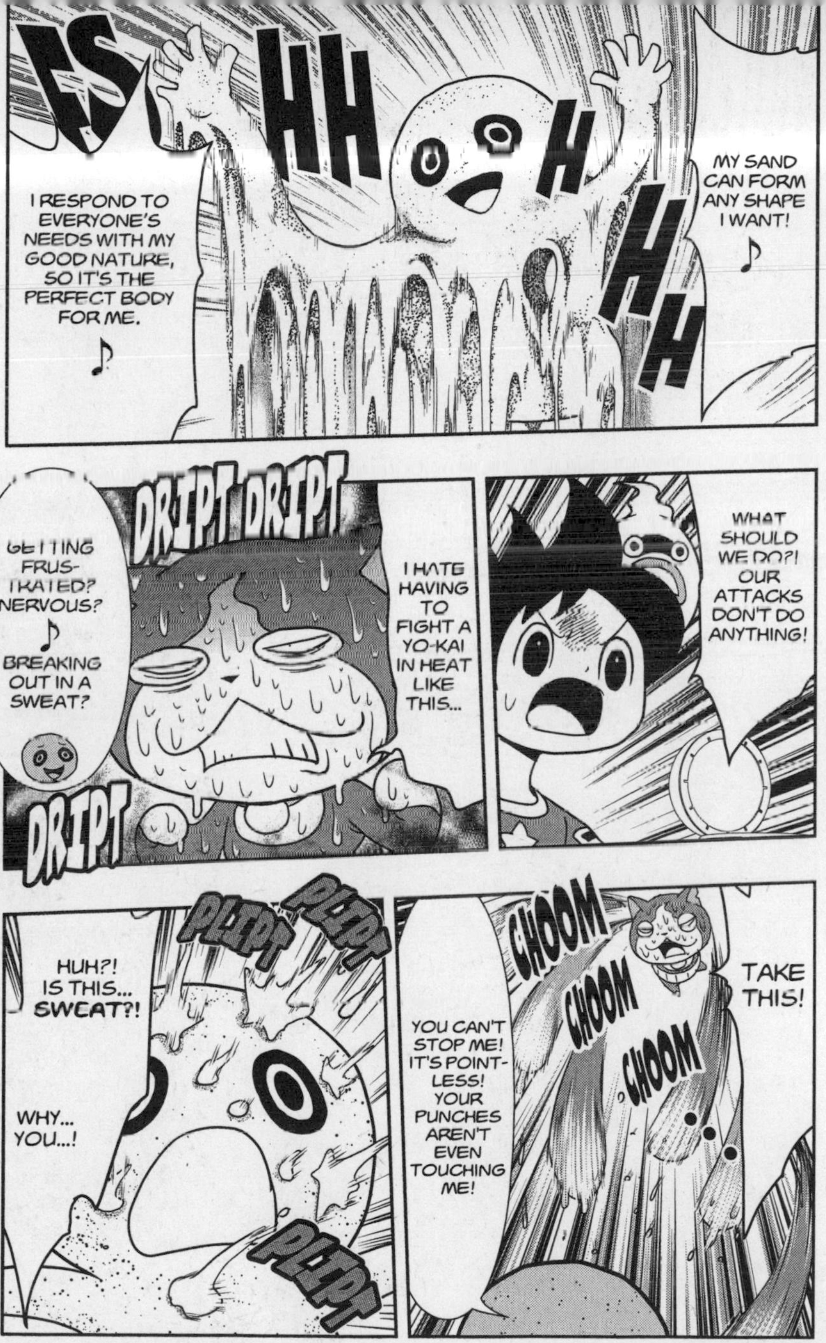
MY SAND CAN FORM ANY SHAPE I WANT! ♪
I RESPOND TO EVERYONE'S NEEDS WITH MY GOOD NATURE, SO IT'S THE PERFECT BODY FOR ME. ♪
WHAT SHOULD WE DO?! OUR ATTACKS DON'T DO ANYTHING!
I HATE HAVING TO FIGHT A YO-KAI IN HEAT LIKE THIS...
DRIPT DRIPT
GETTING FRUS-TRATED? NERVOUS? ♪
BREAKING OUT IN A SWEAT?
DRIPT
TAKE THIS!
CHOOM
CHOOM
CHOOM
YOU CAN'T STOP ME! IT'S POINTLESS! YOUR PUNCHES AREN'T EVEN TOUCHING ME!
PLIPT
PLIPT
HUH?! IS THIS... SWEAT?!
WHY... YOU...!
PLIPT

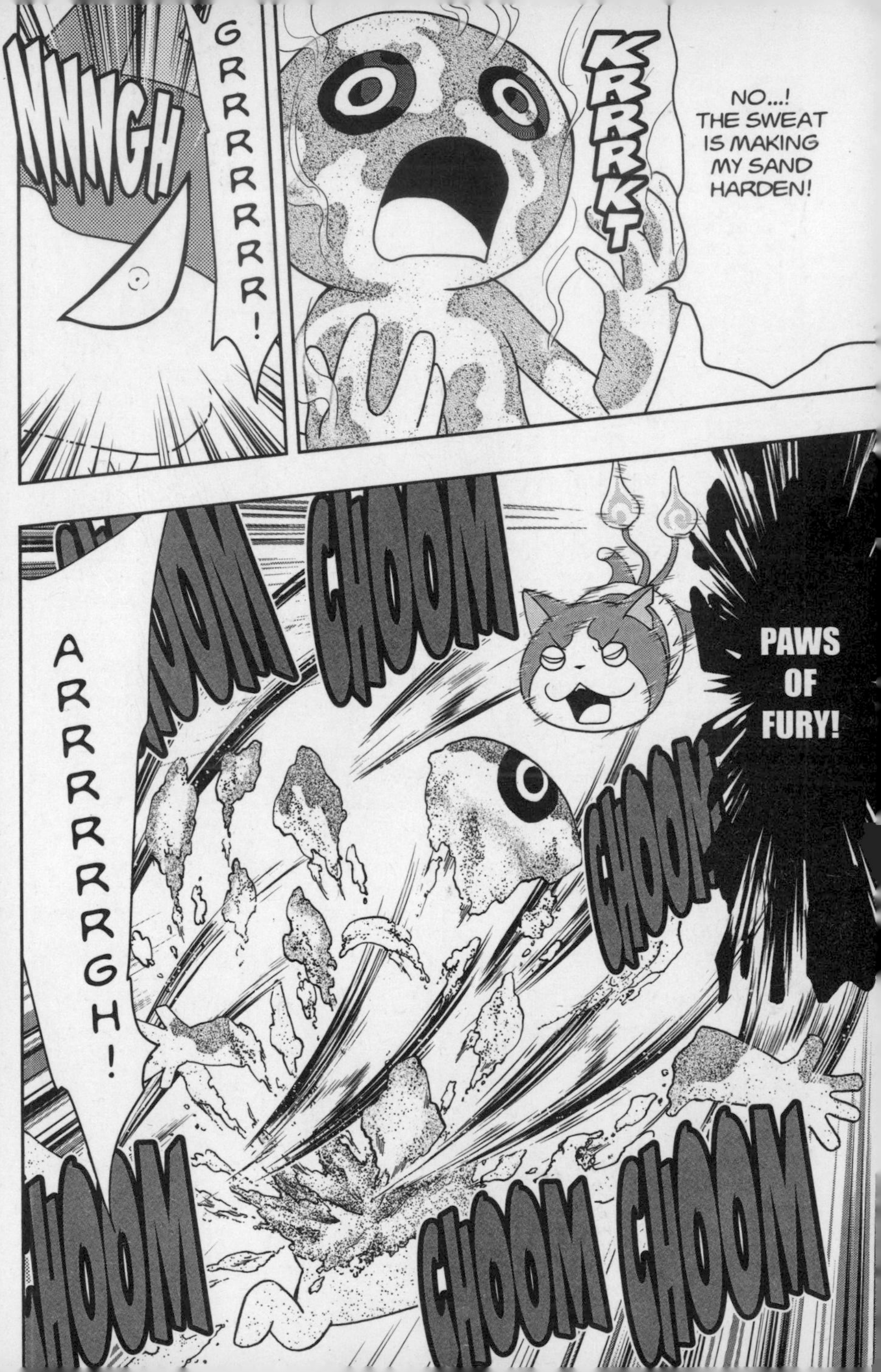
NO...! THE SWEAT IS MAKING MY SAND HARDEN!
KRRRRKT
GRRRRRRRR!
NNNGH
PAWS OF FURY!
CHOOM
CHOOM
CHOOM
CHOOM
ARRRRRRRGH!
CHOOM CHOOM
CHOOM

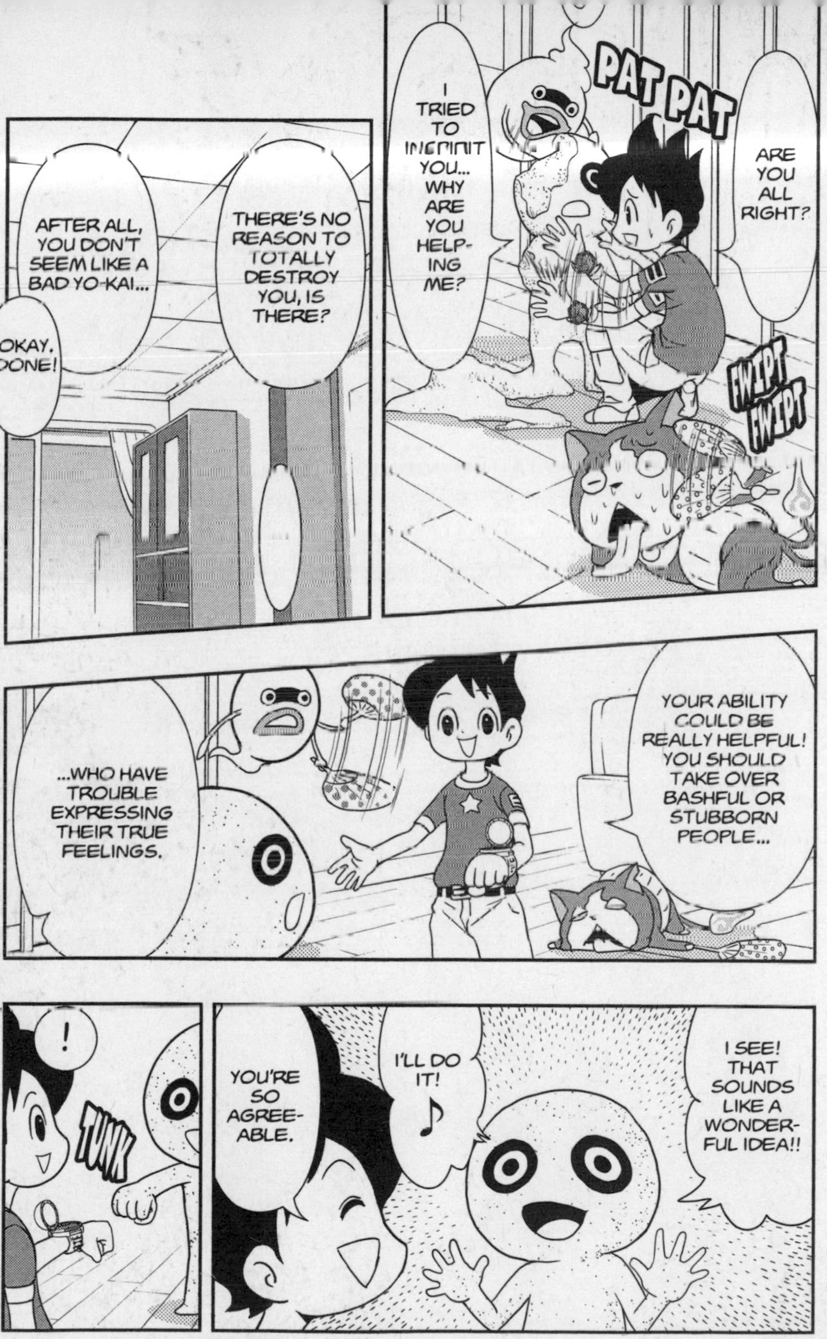
ARE YOU ALL RIGHT?
PAT PAT
I TRIED TO INSPIRIT YOU... WHY ARE YOU HELPING ME?
FWIPT FWIPT
THERE'S NO REASON TO TOTALLY DESTROY YOU, IS THERE?
AFTER ALL, YOU DON'T SEEM LIKE A BAD YO-KAI...
OKAY. DONE!
YOUR ABILITY COULD BE REALLY HELPFUL! YOU SHOULD TAKE OVER BASHFUL OR STUBBORN PEOPLE...
...WHO HAVE TROUBLE EXPRESSING THEIR TRUE FEELINGS.
I SEE! THAT SOUNDS LIKE A WONDERFUL IDEA!!
I'LL DO IT! ♪
YOU'RE SO AGREEABLE.
!
TUNK

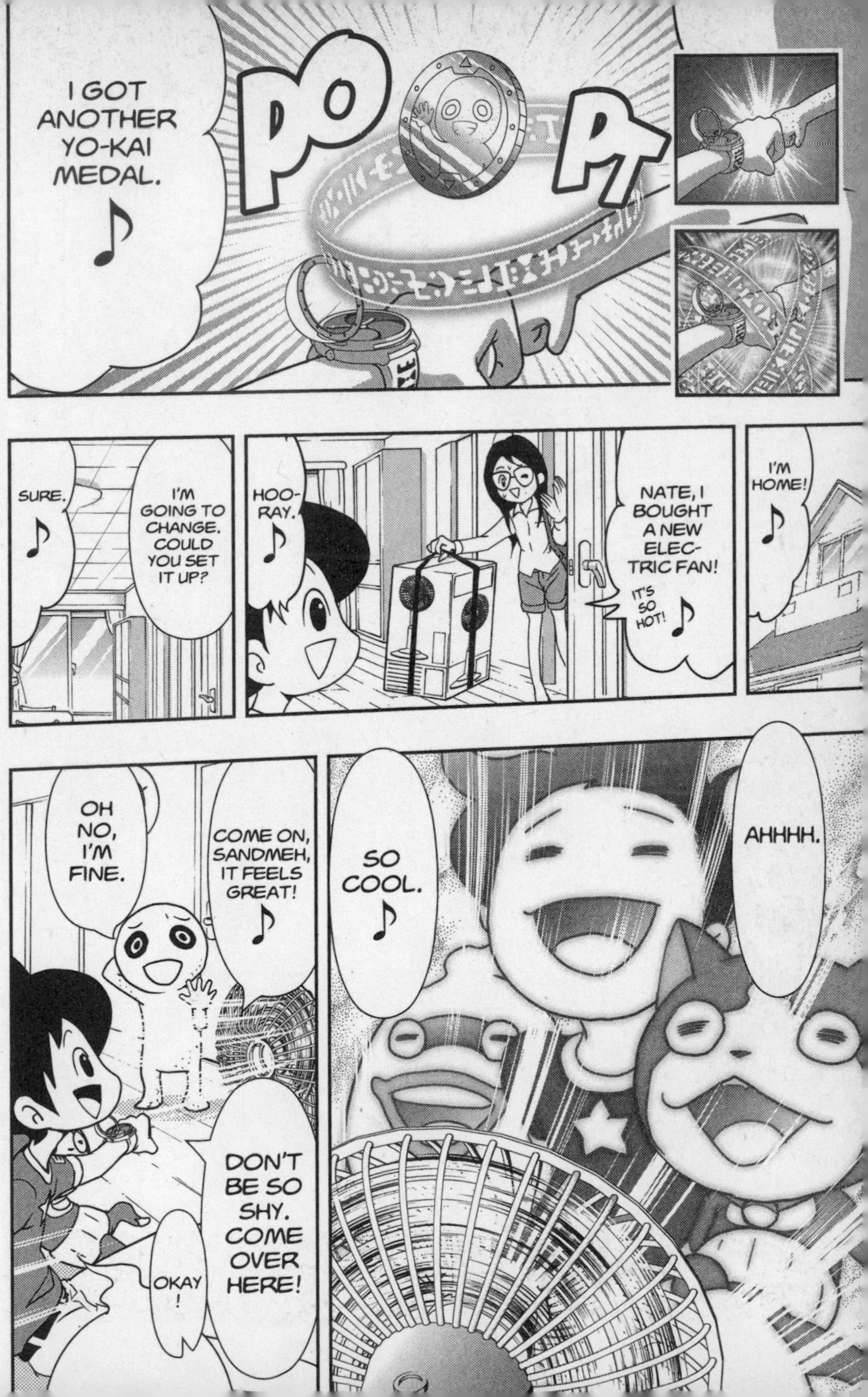
POOPT
I GOT ANOTHER YO-KAI MEDAL. ♪
I'M HOME! ♪
NATE, I BOUGHT A NEW ELECTRIC FAN!
IT'S SO HOT! ♪
HOORAY. ♪
I'M GOING TO CHANGE. COULD YOU SET IT UP?
SURE. ♪
AHHHH.
SO COOL. ♪
COME ON, SANDMEH, IT FEELS GREAT! ♪
OH NO, I'M FINE.
DON'T BE SO SHY. COME OVER HERE!
OKAY!

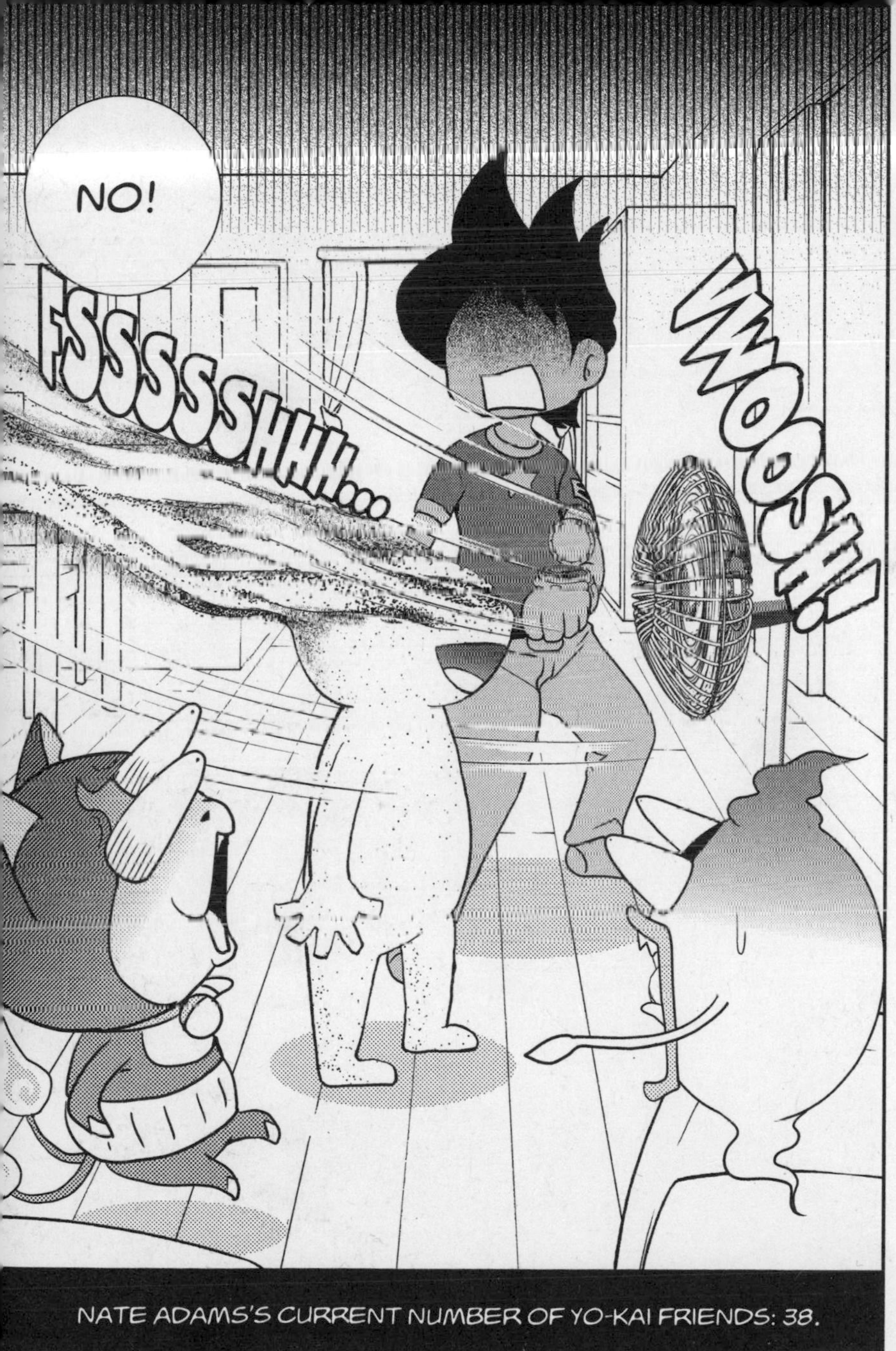

NO!
WOOSH!!
FSSSSHHH...
NATE ADAMS'S CURRENT NUMBER OF YO-KAI FRIENDS: 38.

CLAP CLAP

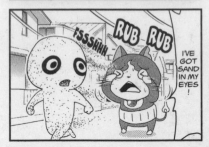

RUB RUB
I'VE GOT SAND IN MY EYES!
FSSSHHH
KEEP BLINKING! FAST! CLAP YOUR EYELIDS TO-GETHER!
SHWOOO
?
POPT
...
KLAP KLAP KLAP KLAP
HE'S ACTUALLY CLAPPING! I MADE HIM TOO PURE-HEARTED!

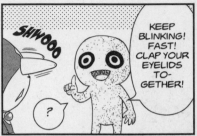

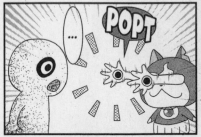

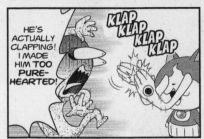

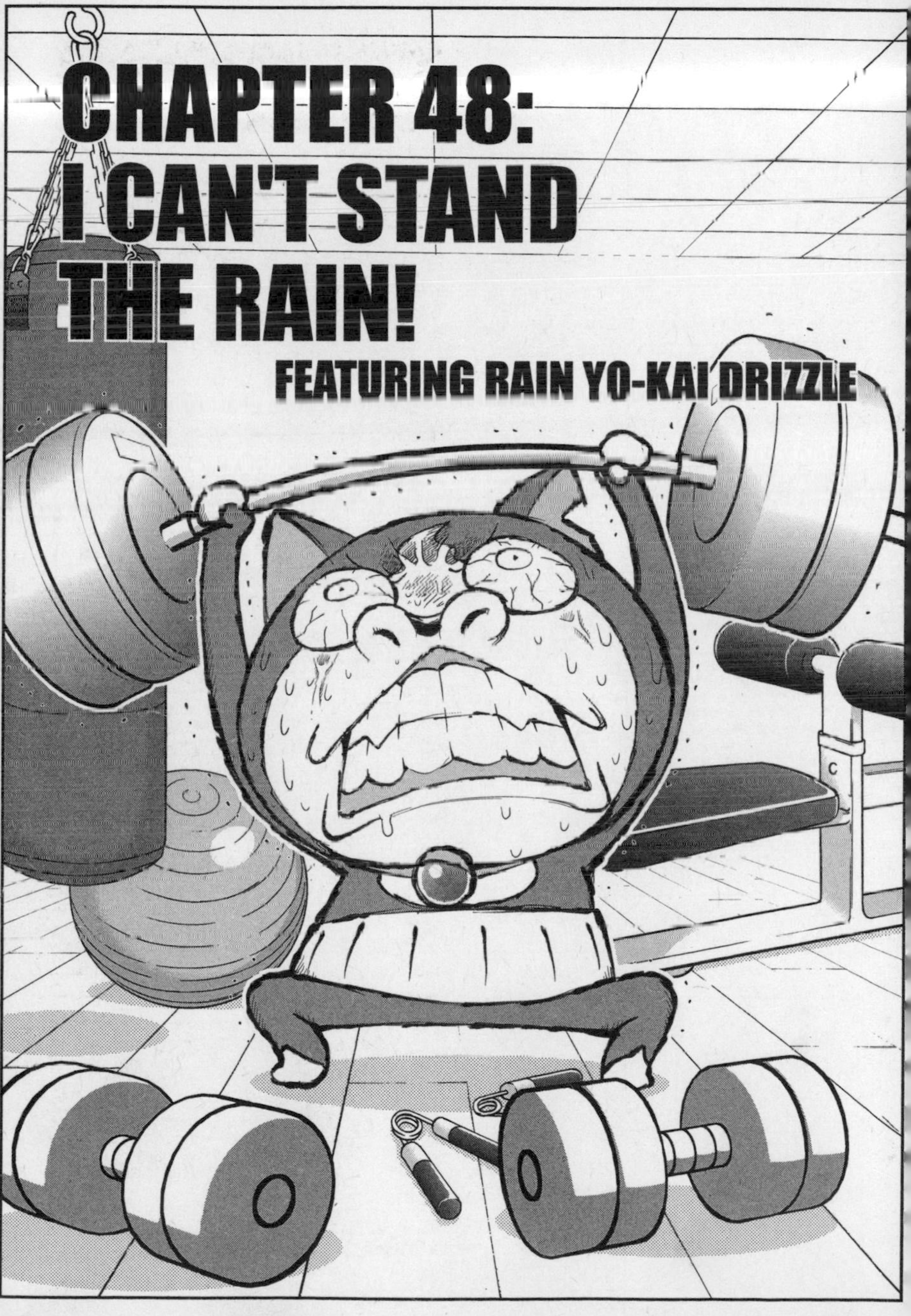
CHAPTER 48:
I CAN'T STAND THE RAIN!
FEATURING RAIN YO-KAI DRIZZLE

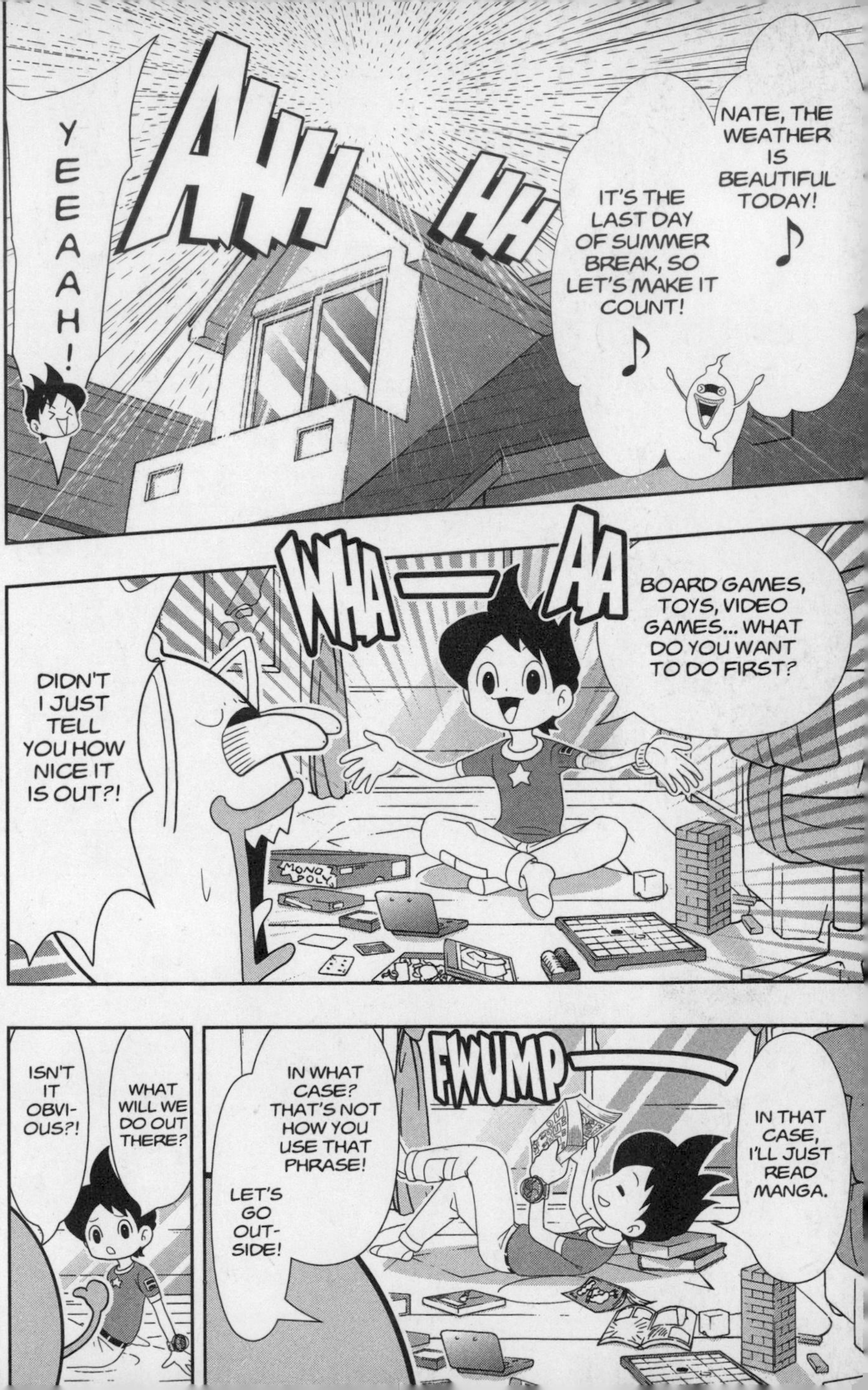
NATE, THE WEATHER IS BEAUTIFUL TODAY! ♪
IT'S THE LAST DAY OF SUMMER BREAK, SO LET'S MAKE IT COUNT! ♪
AHHHH
YEEAAAH!
BOARD GAMES, TOYS, VIDEO GAMES... WHAT DO YOU WANT TO DO FIRST?
WHA—AA
DIDN'T I JUST TELL YOU HOW NICE IT IS OUT?!
MONOPOLY
IN THAT CASE, I'LL JUST READ MANGA.
FWUMP—
IN WHAT CASE? THAT'S NOT HOW YOU USE THAT PHRASE!
LET'S GO OUT-SIDE!
WHAT WILL WE DO OUT THERE?
ISN'T IT OBVIOUS?!

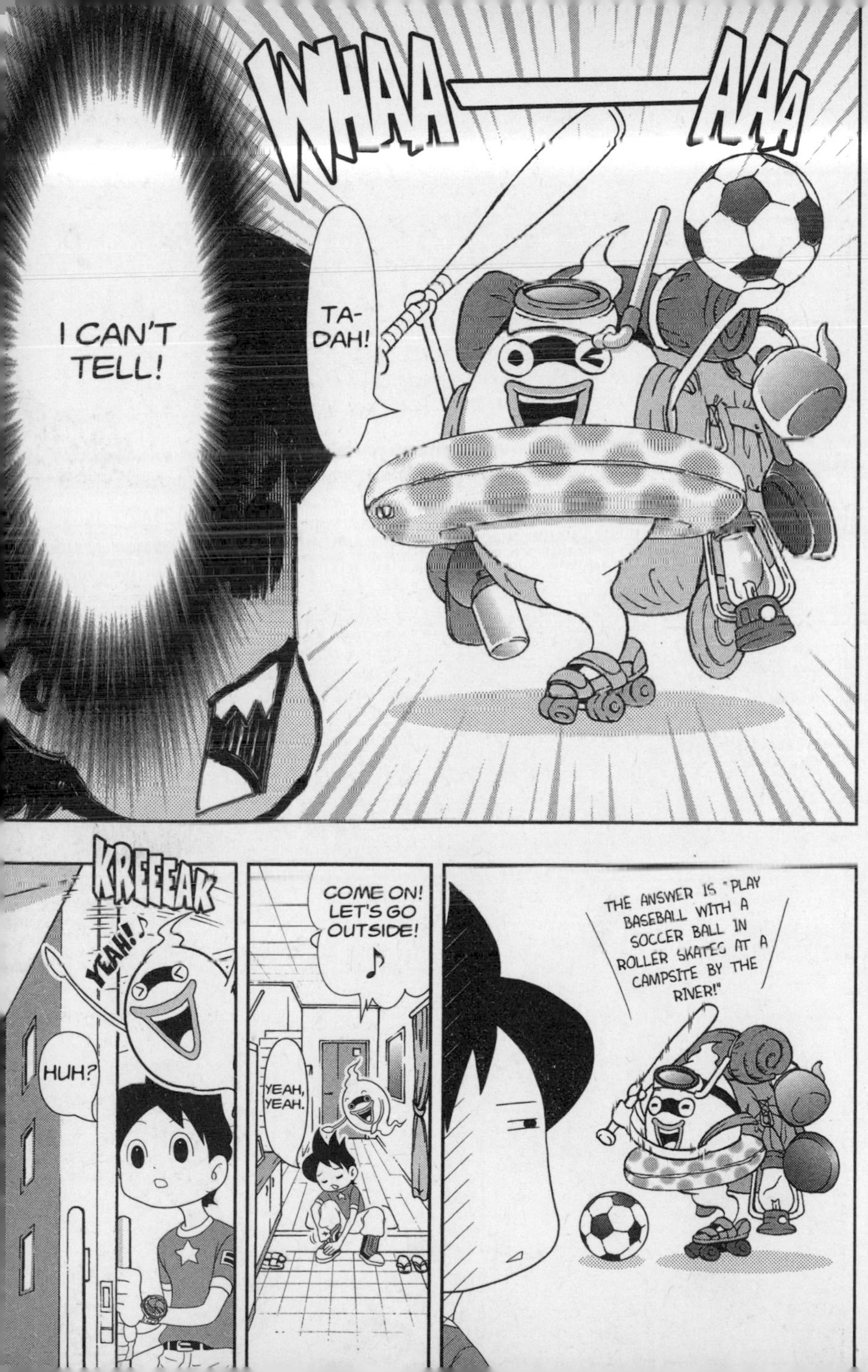
WHAA——AAA
TA-DAH!
I CAN'T TELL!
THE ANSWER IS "PLAY BASEBALL WITH A SOCCER BALL IN ROLLER SKATES AT A CAMPSITE BY THE RIVER!"
COME ON! LET'S GO OUTSIDE! ♪
YEAH, YEAH.
KREEEAK
YEAH! ♪
HUH?

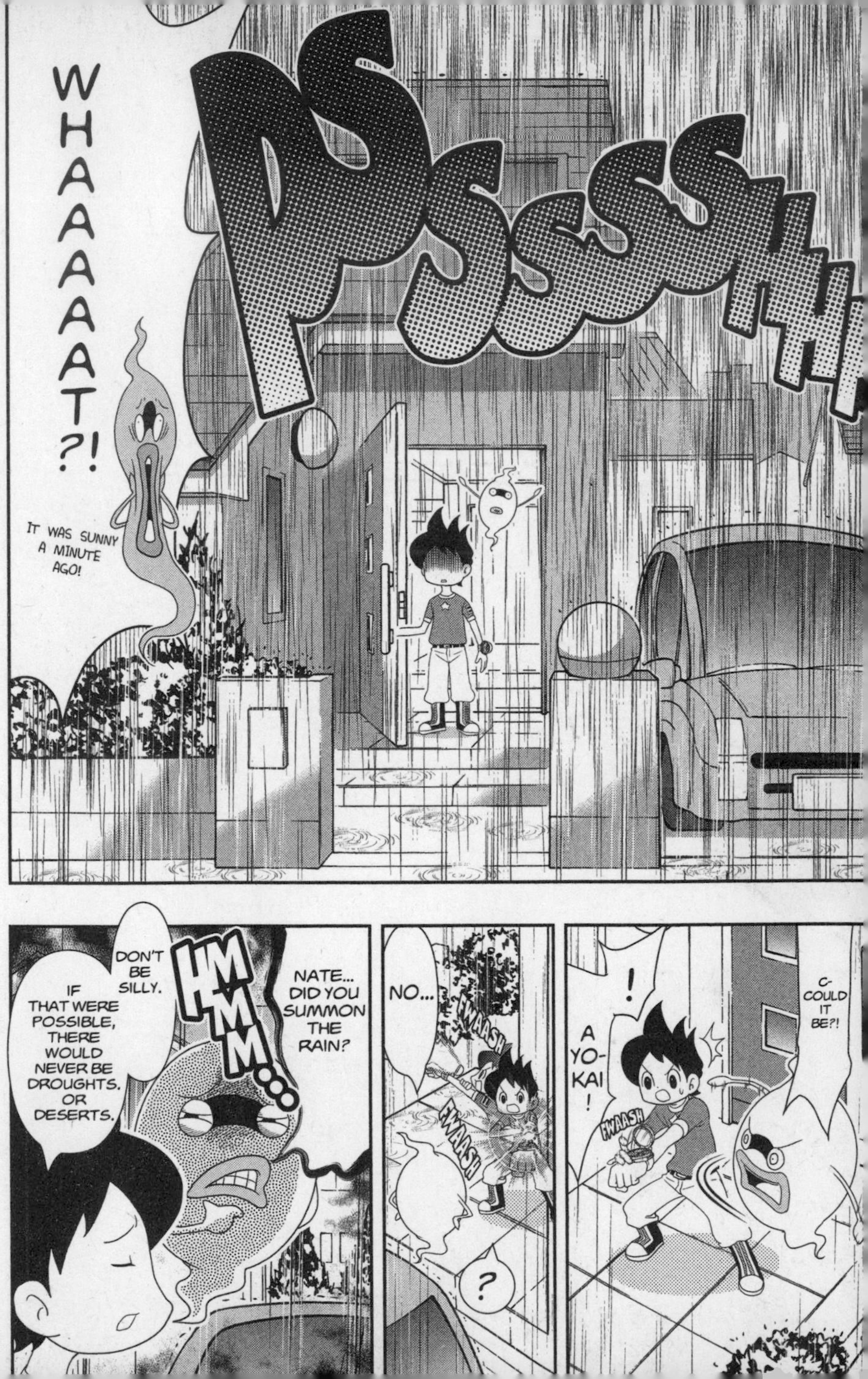
DSSSSSHH
WHAAAAAT?!
IT WAS SUNNY A MINUTE AGO!
C-COULD IT BE?!
!
A YO-KAI!
FWAASH
NO...
FWAASH
FWAASH
?
NATE... DID YOU SUMMON THE RAIN?
HMMM...
DON'T BE SILLY.
IF THAT WERE POSSIBLE, THERE WOULD NEVER BE DROUGHTS. OR DESERTS.

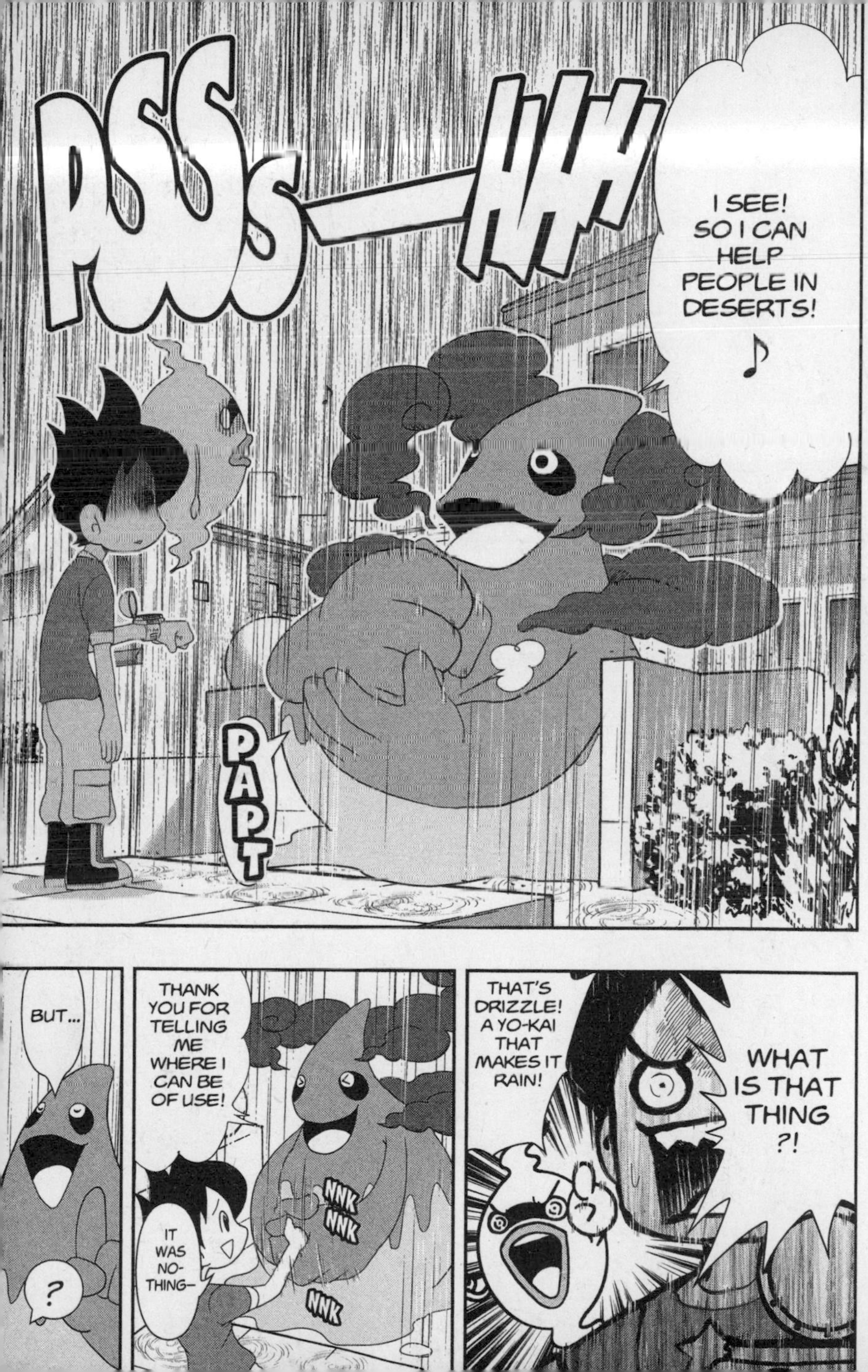
PSSSS—HHH
I SEE! SO I CAN HELP PEOPLE IN DESERTS! ♪
PAPT
WHAT IS THAT THING?!
THAT'S DRIZZLE! A YO-KAI THAT MAKES IT RAIN!
THANK YOU FOR TELLING ME WHERE I CAN BE OF USE!
IT WAS NO-THING—
NNK NNK
NNK
BUT...
?

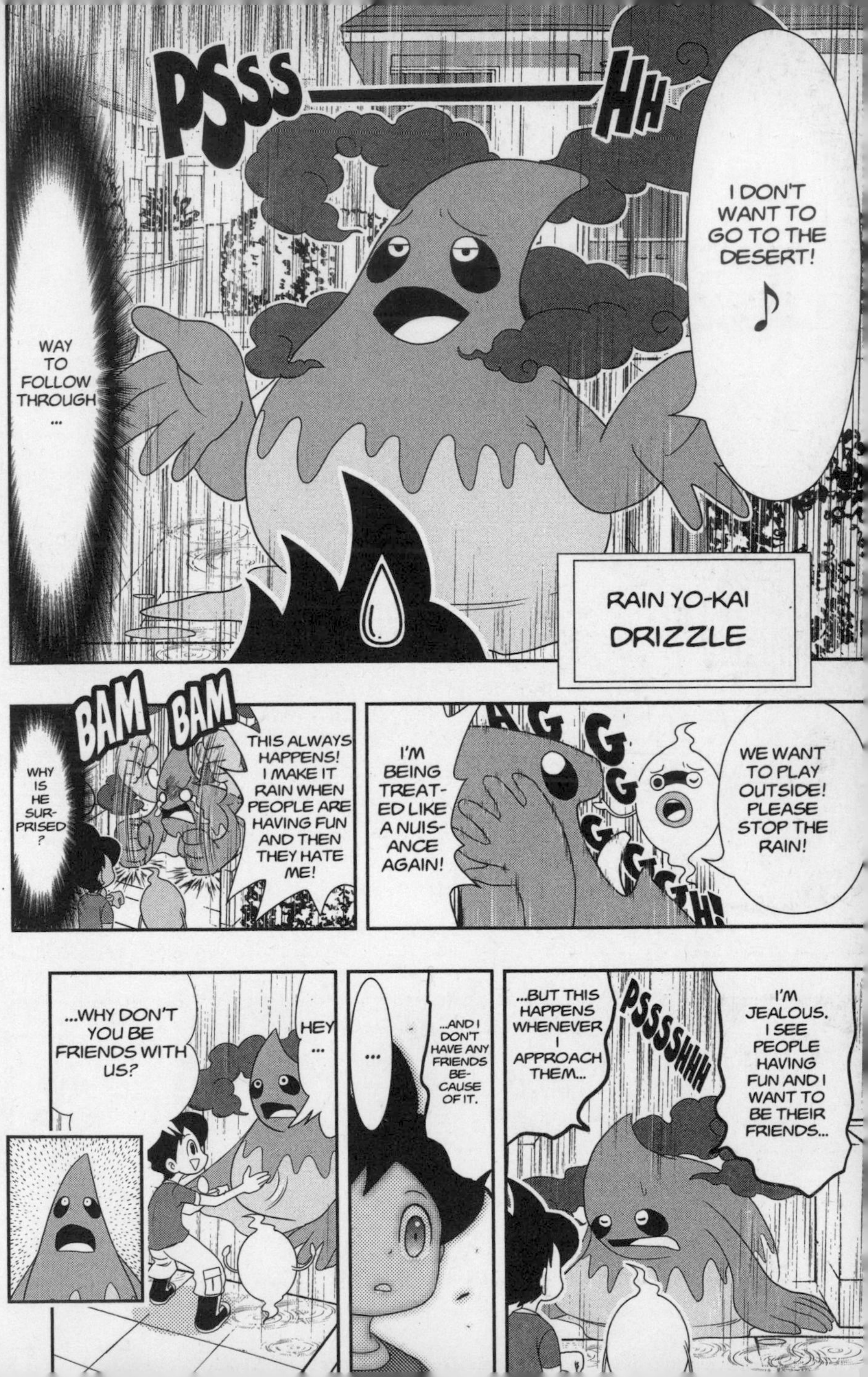
PSSS—HH
I DON'T WANT TO GO TO THE DESERT! ♪
RAIN YO-KAI DRIZZLE
WAY TO FOLLOW THROUGH ...
WE WANT TO PLAY OUTSIDE! PLEASE STOP THE RAIN!
I'M BEING TREATED LIKE A NUISANCE AGAIN!
BAM BAM
THIS ALWAYS HAPPENS! I MAKE IT RAIN WHEN PEOPLE ARE HAVING FUN AND THEN THEY HATE ME!
WHY IS HE SURPRISED?
I'M JEALOUS. I SEE PEOPLE HAVING FUN AND I WANT TO BE THEIR FRIENDS...
PSSSSHHH
...BUT THIS HAPPENS WHENEVER I APPROACH THEM...
...AND I DON'T HAVE ANY FRIENDS BECAUSE OF IT.
...
HEY ...
...WHY DON'T YOU BE FRIENDS WITH US?

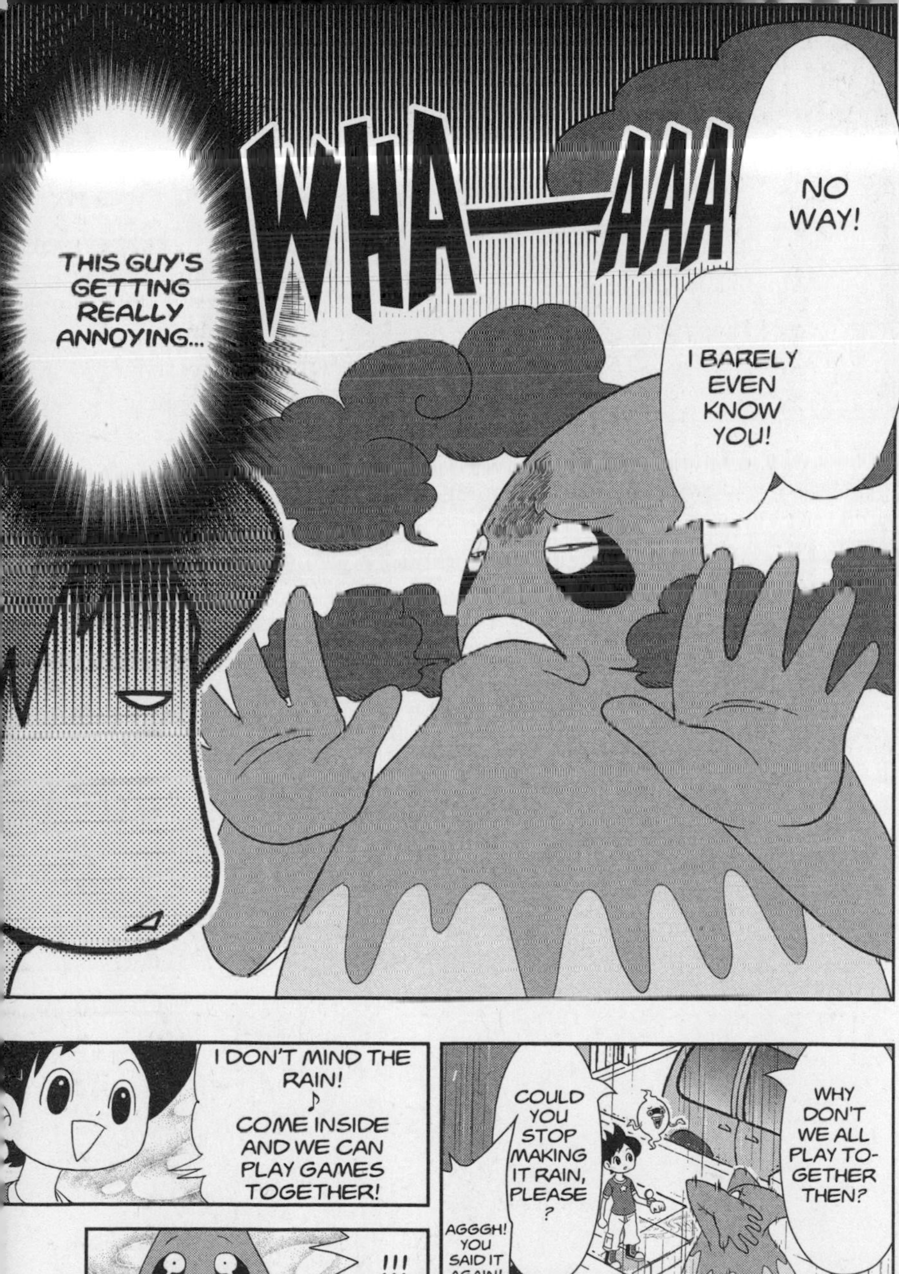
NO WAY!
I BARELY EVEN KNOW YOU!
WHA—AAA
THIS GUY'S GETTING REALLY ANNOYING...
WHY DON'T WE ALL PLAY TO-GETHER THEN?
COULD YOU STOP MAKING IT RAIN, PLEASE?
AGGGH! YOU SAID IT AGAIN!
I DON'T MIND THE RAIN! ♪ COME INSIDE AND WE CAN PLAY GAMES TOGETHER!
!!!

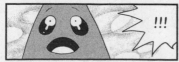

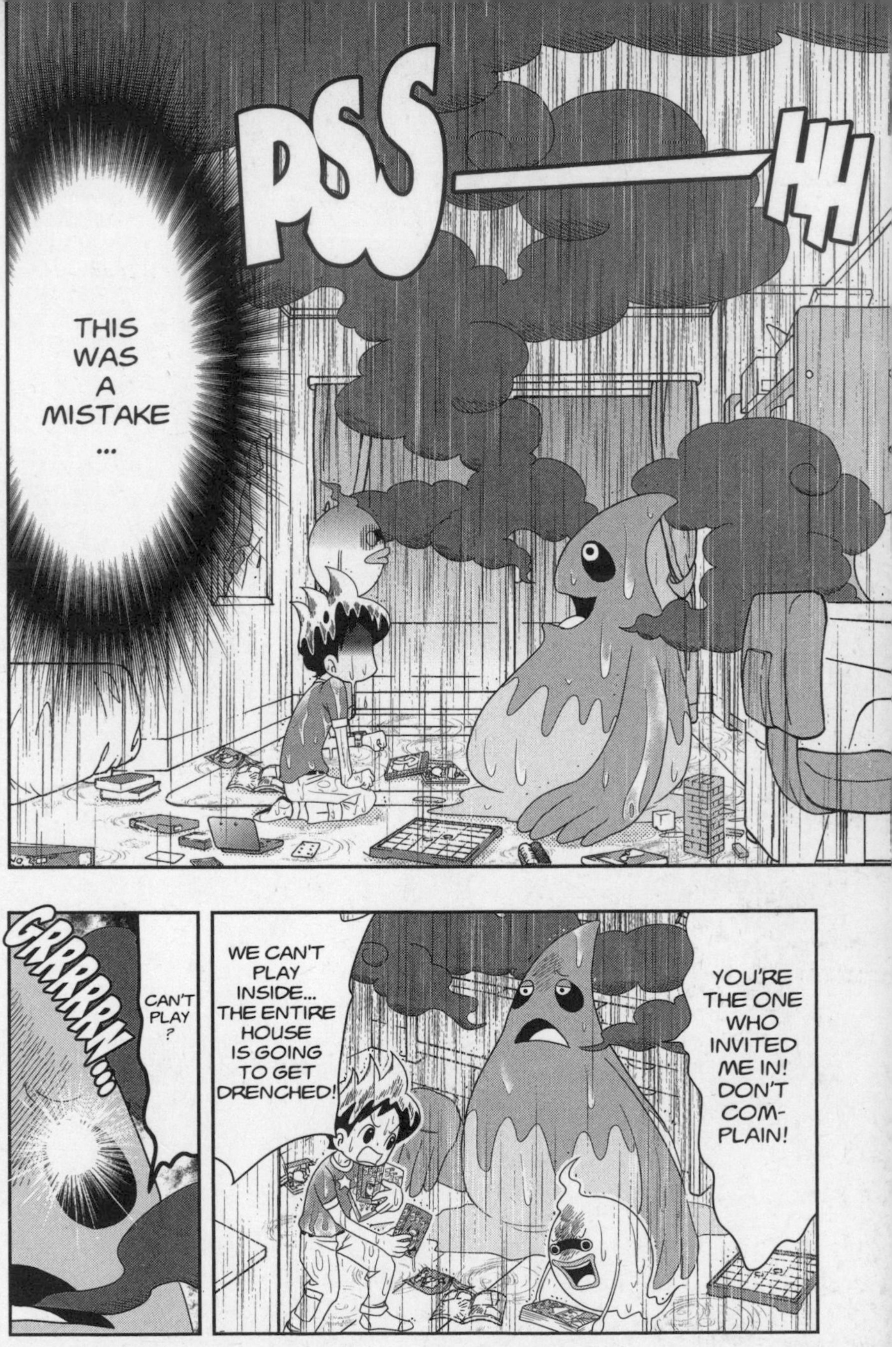
PSS—HH
THIS WAS A MISTAKE ...
YOU'RE THE ONE WHO INVITED ME IN! DON'T COM-PLAIN!
WE CAN'T PLAY INSIDE... THE ENTIRE HOUSE IS GOING TO GET DRENCHED!
CAN'T PLAY ?
GRRRRRN...

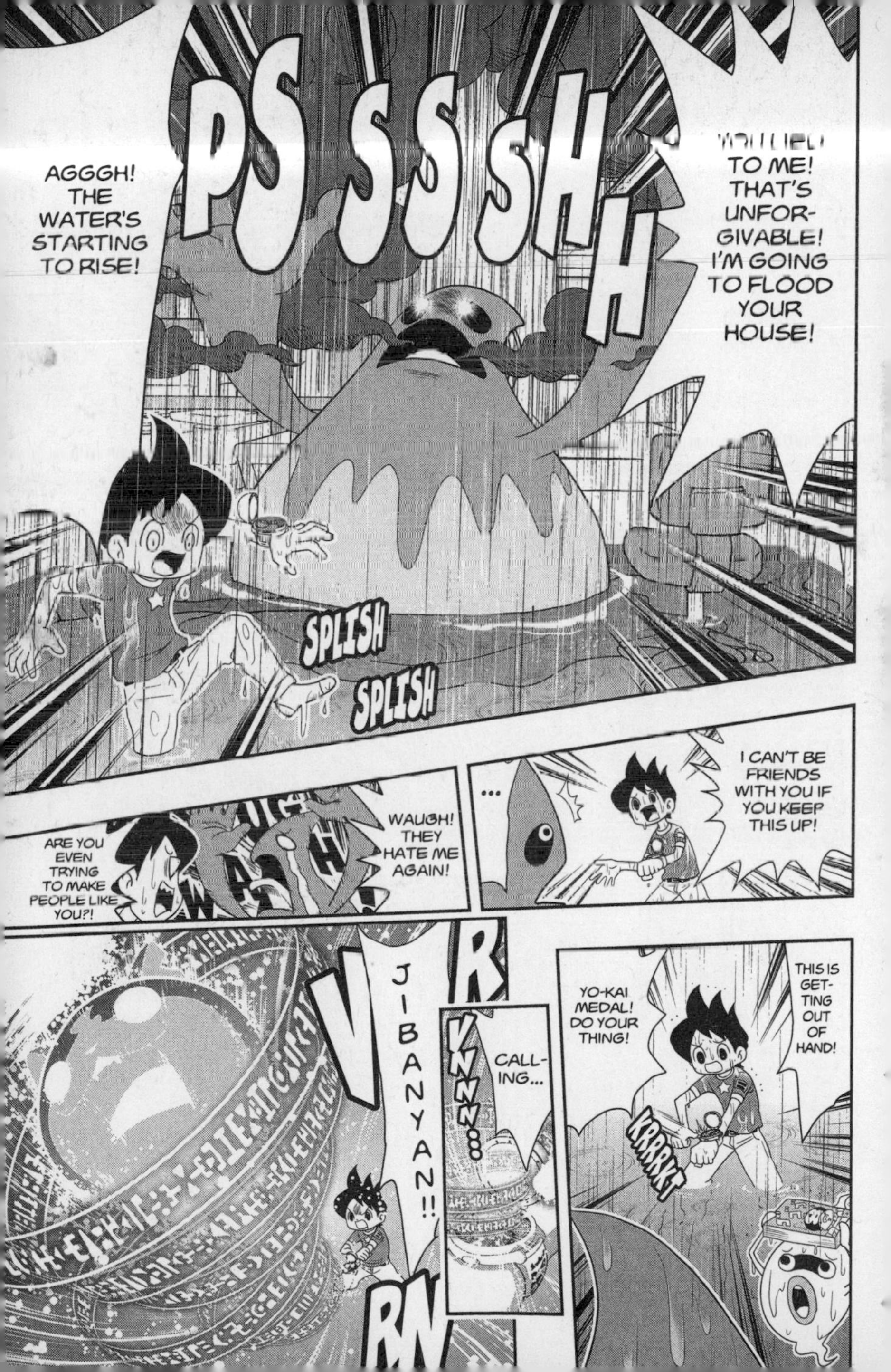

TO ME! THAT'S UNFORGIVABLE! I'M GOING TO FLOOD YOUR HOUSE!
PSSSSHH
AGGGH! THE WATER'S STARTING TO RISE!
SPLISH
SPLISH
I CAN'T BE FRIENDS WITH YOU IF YOU KEEP THIS UP!
...
WAUGH! THEY HATE ME AGAIN!
ARE YOU EVEN TRYING TO MAKE PEOPLE LIKE YOU?!
THIS IS GETTING OUT OF HAND!
YO-KAI MEDAL! DO YOUR THING!
KRRRKT
VNNN...
CALLING...
JIBANYAN!!
VRRN

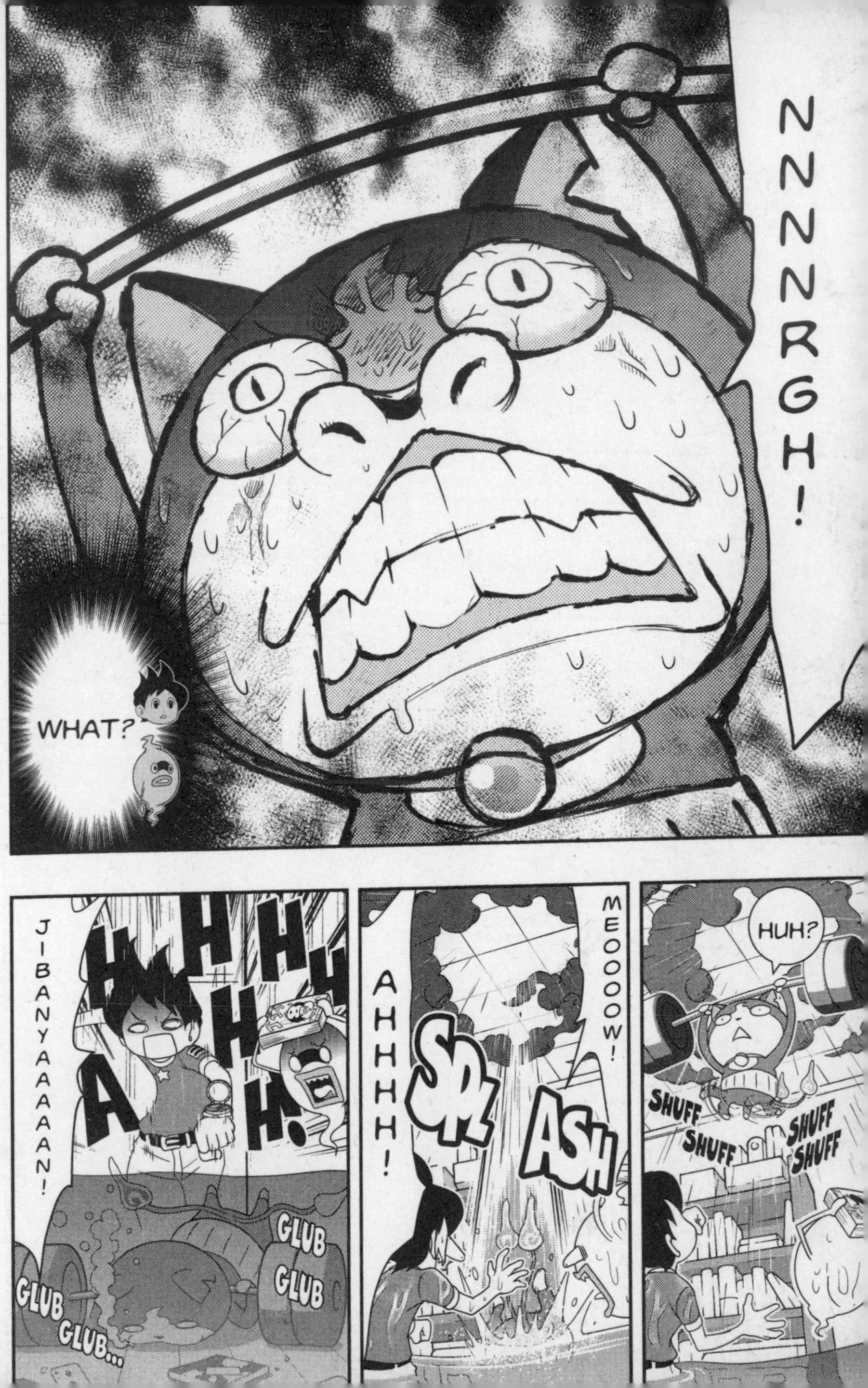
NNNNRGH!
WHAT?
HUH?
SHUFF SHUFF
SHUFF SHUFF
MEOOOOOW!
AHHHHH!
SPLASH
JIBANYAAAAAAN!
AHHHHHH!
GLUB GLUB
GLUB GLUB...

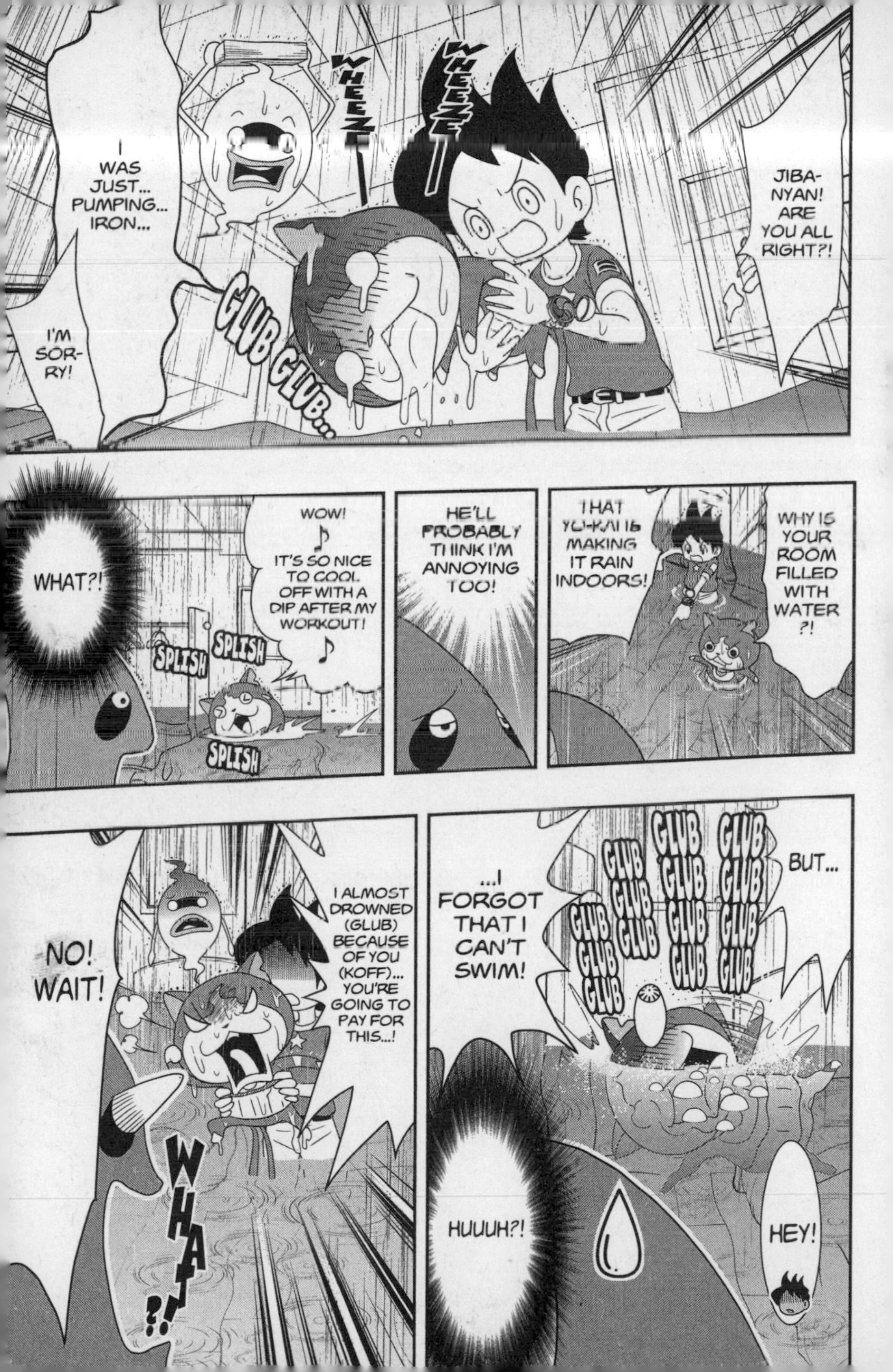
JIBA-NYAN! ARE YOU ALL RIGHT?!
WHEEZE
WHEEZE
I WAS JUST... PUMPING... IRON...
GLUB GLUB...
I'M SOR-RY!
WHY IS YOUR ROOM FILLED WITH WATER?!
THAT YO-KAI IS MAKING IT RAIN INDOORS!
HE'LL PROBABLY THINK I'M ANNOYING TOO!
WOW! ♪ IT'S SO NICE TO COOL OFF WITH A DIP AFTER MY WORKOUT! ♪
SPLISH
SPLISH
SPLISH
WHAT?!
BUT...
GLUB GLUB GLUB GLUB
GLUB GLUB GLUB GLUB
GLUB GLUB GLUB
GLUB GLUB GLUB
...I FORGOT THAT I CAN'T SWIM!
HEY!
HUUUH?!
I ALMOST DROWNED (GLUB) BECAUSE OF YOU (KOFF)... YOU'RE GOING TO PAY FOR THIS...!
NO! WAIT!
WHAT?!

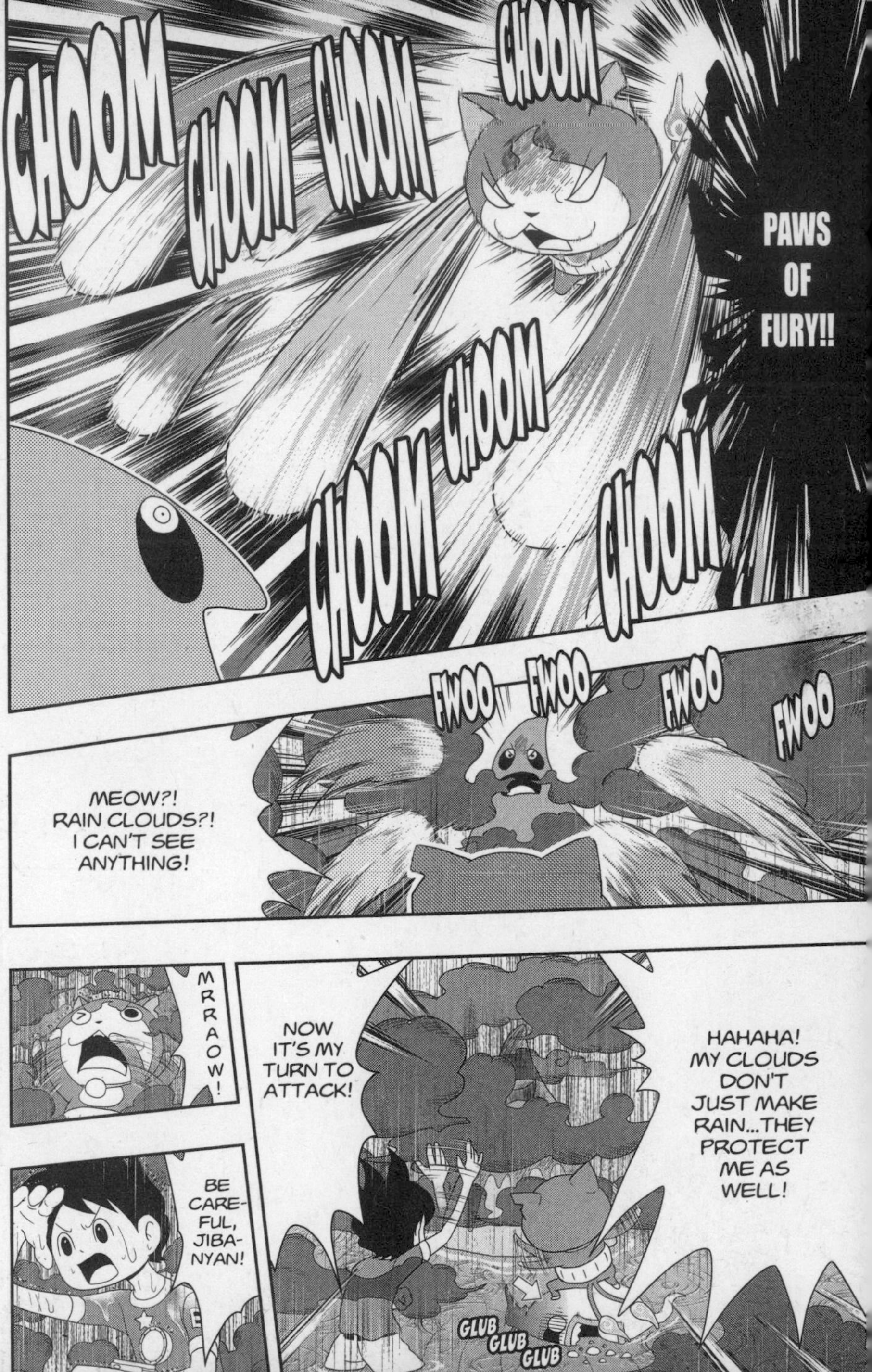
PAWS OF FURY!!
CHOOM
CHOOM
CHOOM
CHOOM
CHOOM
CHOOM
CHOOM
FWOO
FWOO
FWOO
FWOO
MEOW?! RAIN CLOUDS?! I CAN'T SEE ANYTHING!
HAHAHA! MY CLOUDS DON'T JUST MAKE RAIN...THEY PROTECT ME AS WELL!
NOW IT'S MY TURN TO ATTACK!
GLUB GLUB GLUB
MRRAOW!
BE CARE-FUL, JIBA-NYAN!

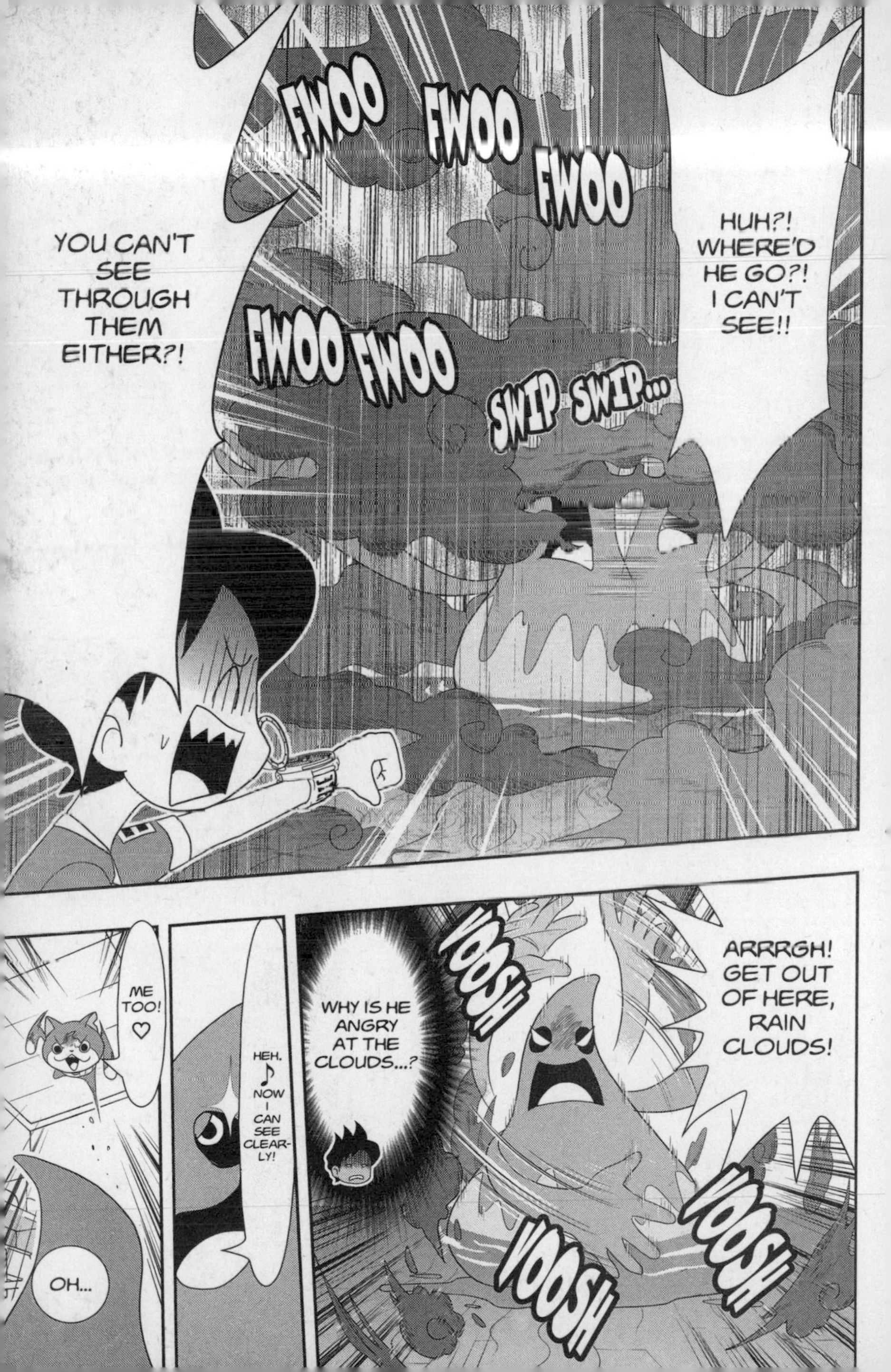
FWOO FWOO FWOO
HUH?! WHERE'D HE GO?! I CAN'T SEE!!
FWOO FWOO
SWIP SWIP...
YOU CAN'T SEE THROUGH THEM EITHER?!
VOOSH
ARRRGH! GET OUT OF HERE, RAIN CLOUDS!
VOOSH VOOSH
WHY IS HE ANGRY AT THE CLOUDS...?
HEH. ♪ NOW I CAN SEE CLEAR-LY!
ME TOO! ♡
OH...

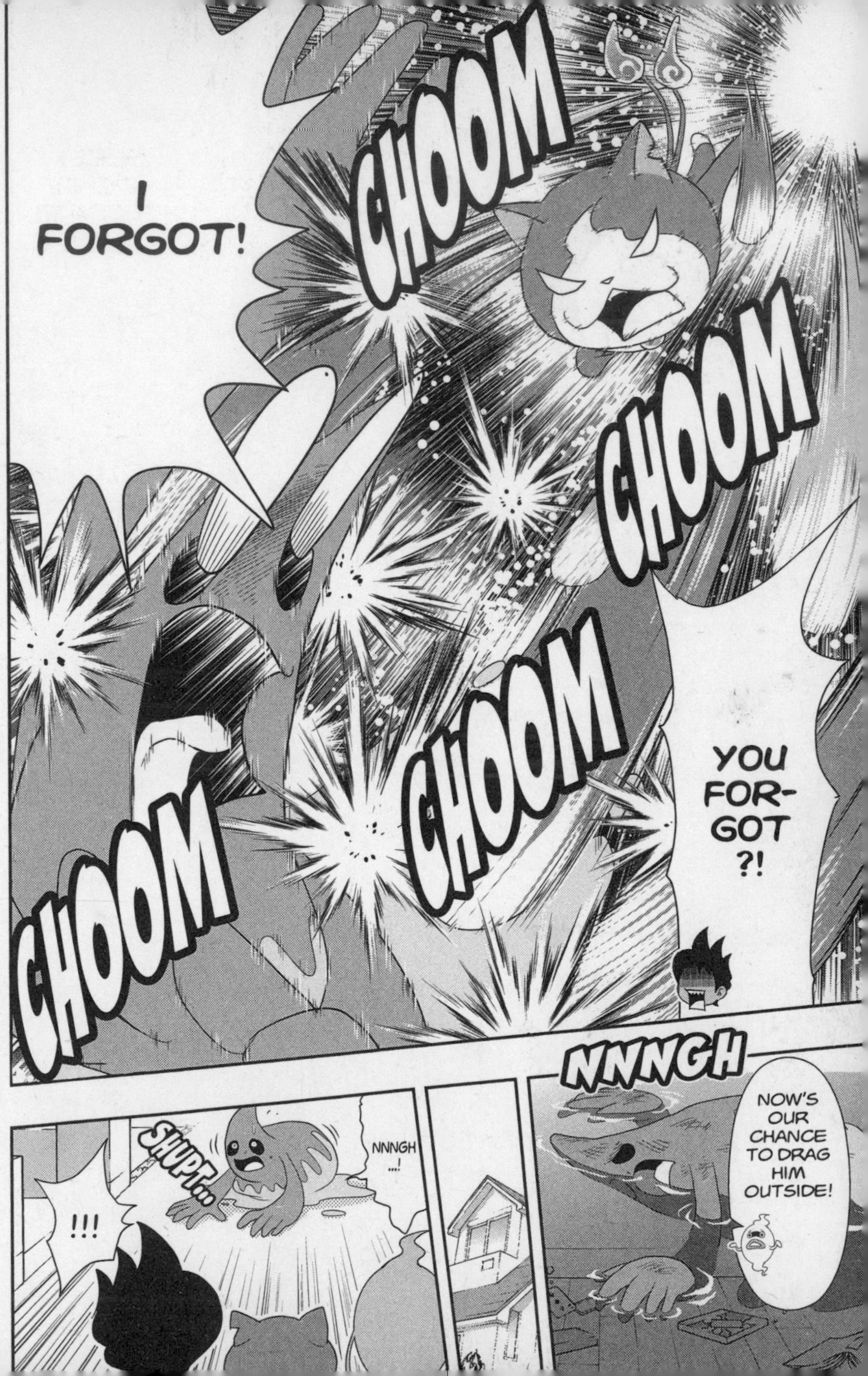
CHOOM
I FORGOT!
CHOOM
CHOOM
YOU FOR-GOT?!
CHOOM
NNNGH
NOW'S OUR CHANCE TO DRAG HIM OUTSIDE!
NNNGH...!
SHUPT...
!!!

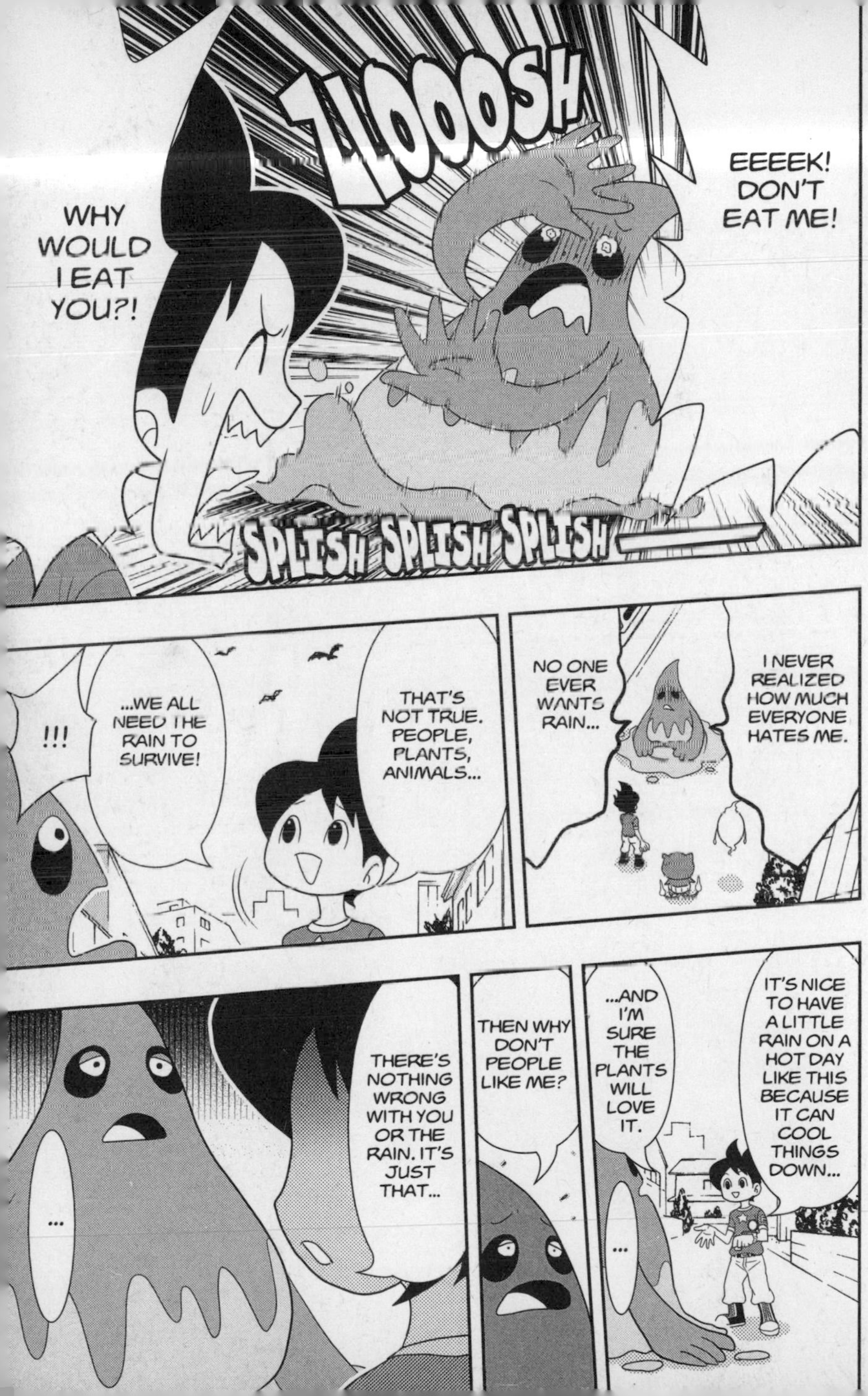
WHOOOSH
EEEEK! DON'T EAT ME!
WHY WOULD I EAT YOU?!
SPLISH SPLISH SPLISH
I NEVER REALIZED HOW MUCH EVERYONE HATES ME.
NO ONE EVER WANTS RAIN...
THAT'S NOT TRUE. PEOPLE, PLANTS, ANIMALS...
...WE ALL NEED THE RAIN TO SURVIVE!
!!!
IT'S NICE TO HAVE A LITTLE RAIN ON A HOT DAY LIKE THIS BECAUSE IT CAN COOL THINGS DOWN...
...AND I'M SURE THE PLANTS WILL LOVE IT.
...
THEN WHY DON'T PEOPLE LIKE ME?
THERE'S NOTHING WRONG WITH YOU OR THE RAIN. IT'S JUST THAT...
...

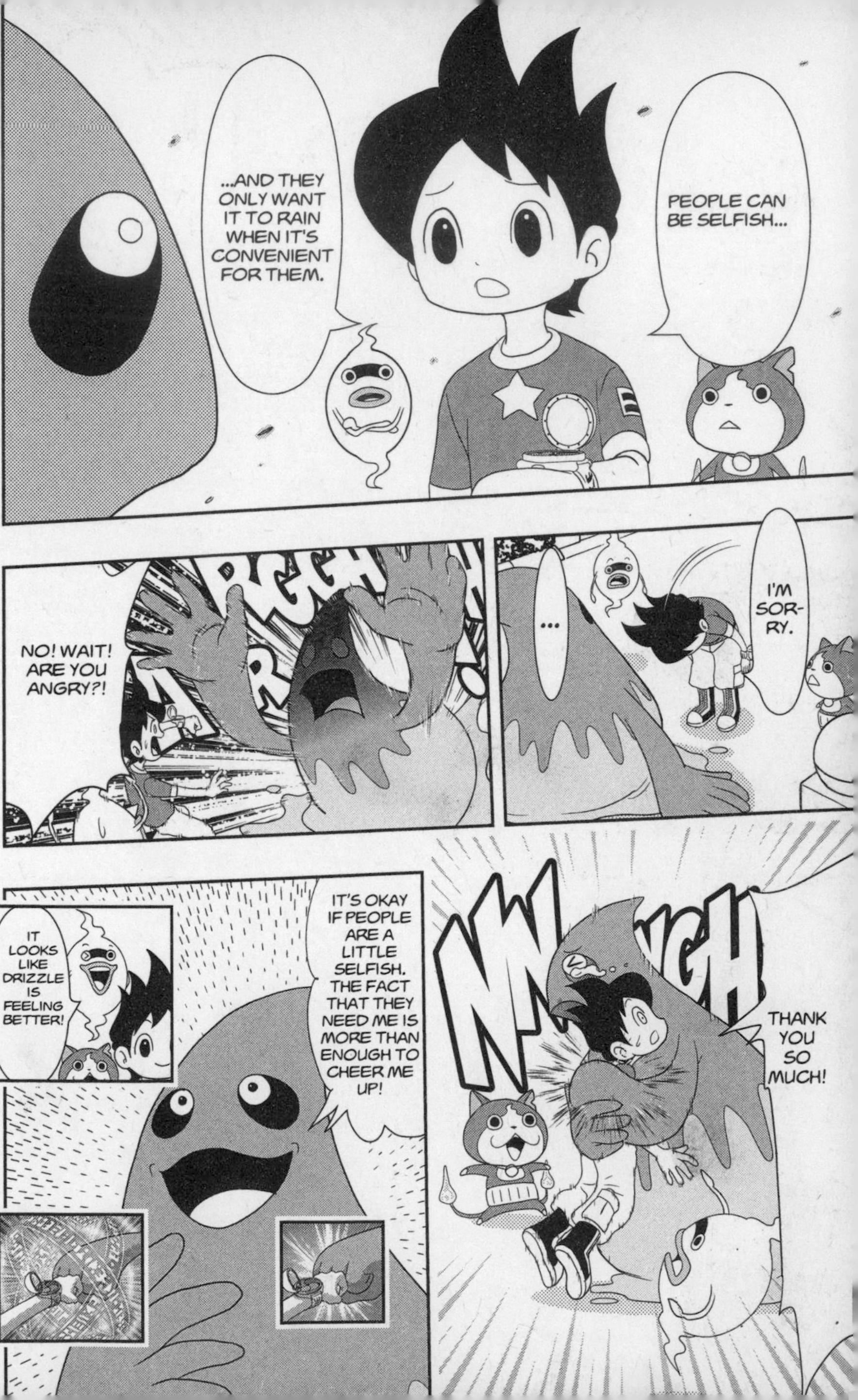
PEOPLE CAN BE SELFISH...
...AND THEY ONLY WANT IT TO RAIN WHEN IT'S CONVENIENT FOR THEM.
I'M SORRY.
...
NO! WAIT! ARE YOU ANGRY?!
THANK YOU SO MUCH!
IT'S OKAY IF PEOPLE ARE A LITTLE SELFISH. THE FACT THAT THEY NEED ME IS MORE THAN ENOUGH TO CHEER ME UP!
IT LOOKS LIKE DRIZZLE IS FEELING BETTER!

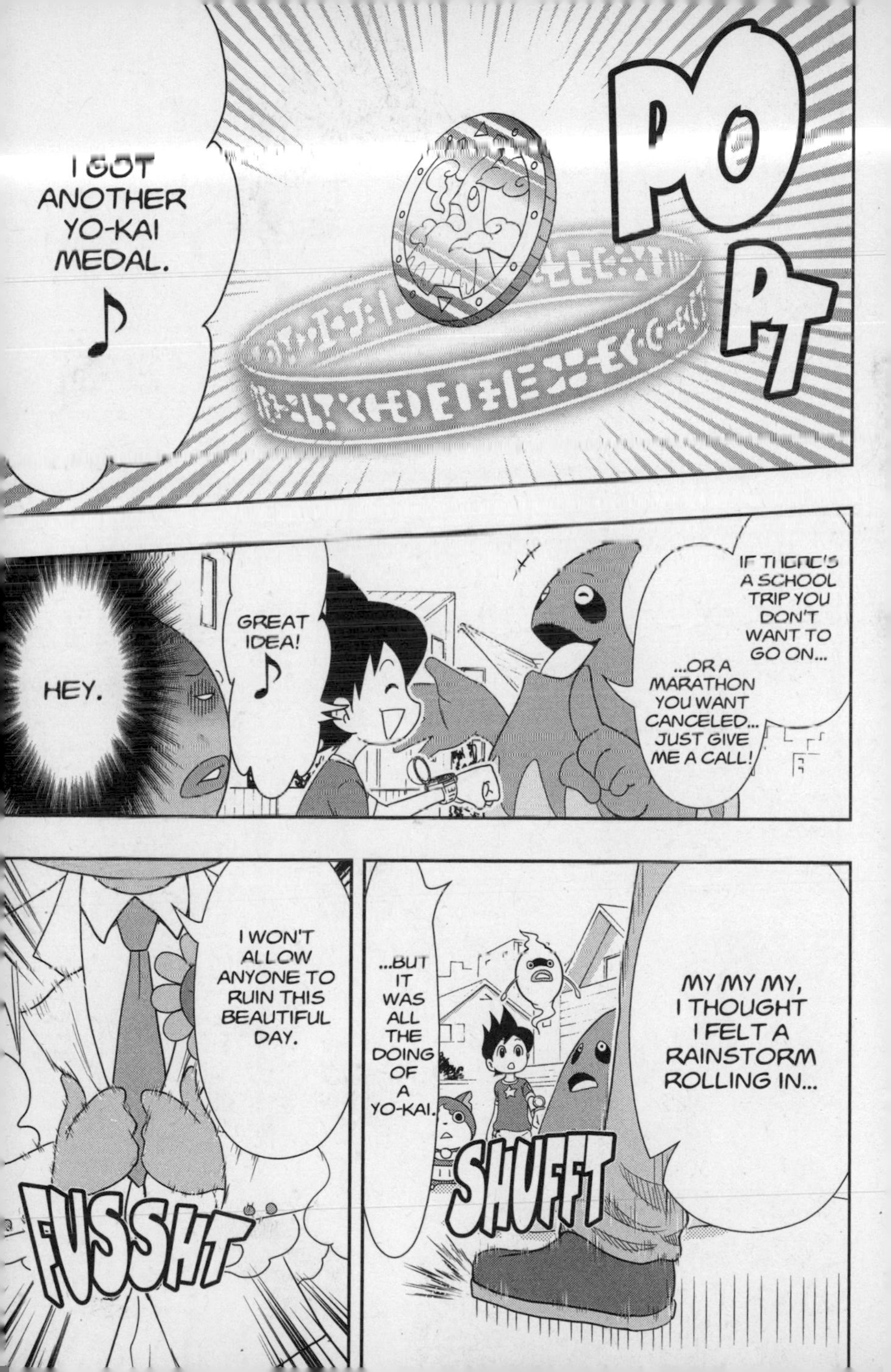
POPT
I GOT ANOTHER YO-KAI MEDAL. ♪
IF THERE'S A SCHOOL TRIP YOU DON'T WANT TO GO ON...
...OR A MARATHON YOU WANT CANCELED... JUST GIVE ME A CALL!
GREAT IDEA! ♪
HEY.
MY MY MY, I THOUGHT I FELT A RAINSTORM ROLLING IN...
SHUFFT
...BUT IT WAS ALL THE DOING OF A YO-KAI.
I WON'T ALLOW ANYONE TO RUIN THIS BEAUTIFUL DAY.
FUSSHT

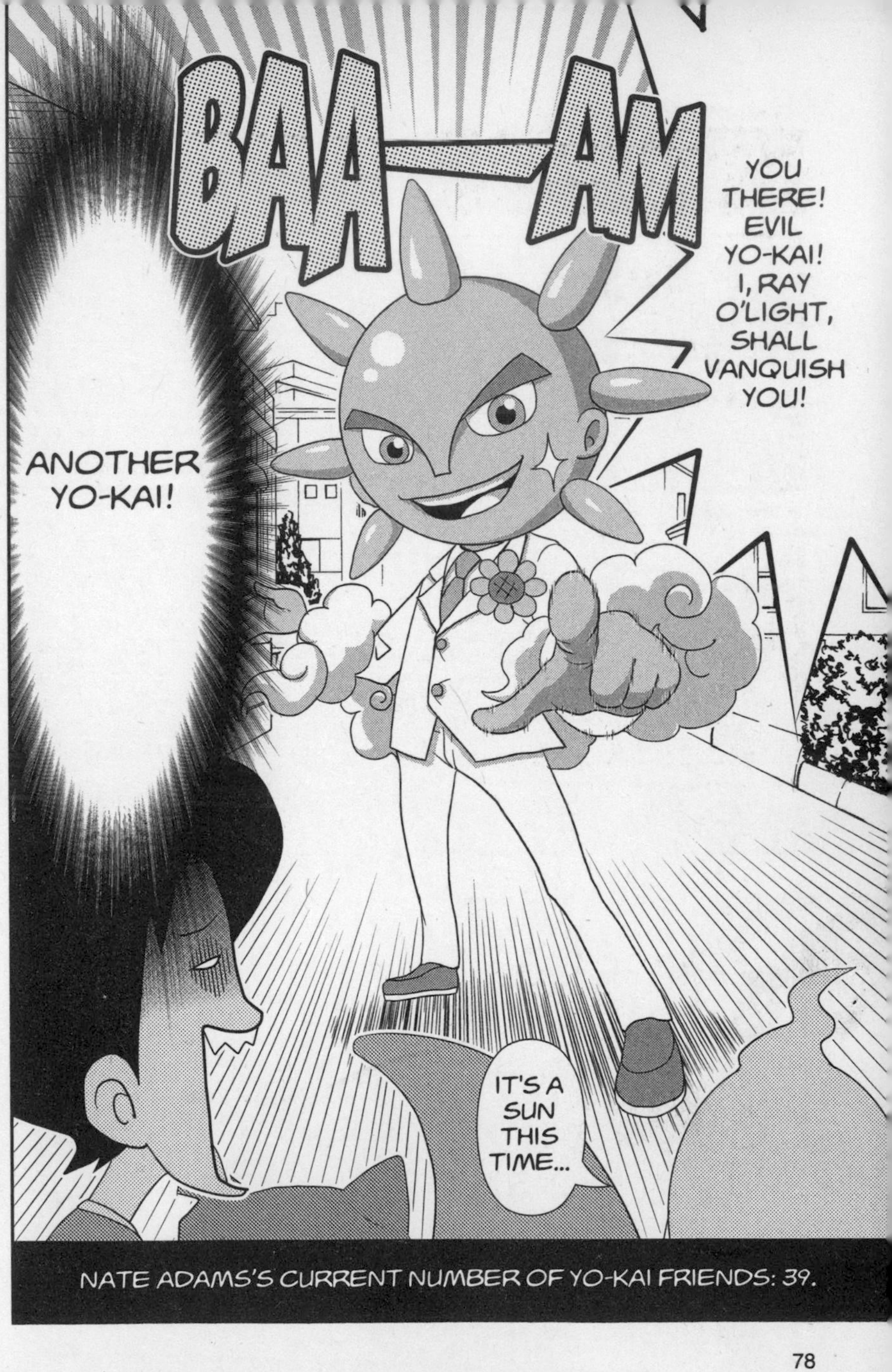
BAA—AM
YOU THERE! EVIL YO-KAI! I, RAY O'LIGHT, SHALL VANQUISH YOU!
ANOTHER YO-KAI!
IT'S A SUN THIS TIME...
NATE ADAMS'S CURRENT NUMBER OF YO-KAI FRIENDS: 39.

YO-KAI WATCH ⑥

DRIZZELDA'S YO-KAI

IT ALWAYS RAINS WHEREVER I GO.
PSSSSHHH
DRIZ-ZELDA.
PEOPLE DON'T LIKE ME...
...BUT THERE'S A YO-KAI WHO I'M JUST RIGHT FOR.
OOH. ♪
HE'S A LITTLE CLINGY THOUGH...
BLUSH
YOU DON'T SEEM TO MIND IT!
WHAT KIND OF YO-KAI IS IT?
RAIN, RAIN, COME AND STAY! ♪
HE'S THE REASON IT'S ALWAYS RAINING!
YOU!

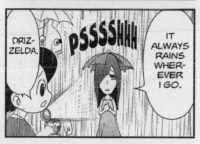

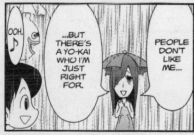

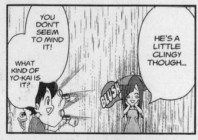

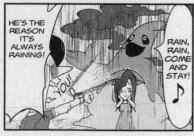

CHAPTER 49:
SUNSHINE VS. RAIN: THE INCREDIBLE WEATHER BATTLE!

FEATURING SUNSHINE YO-KAI RAY O'LIGHT

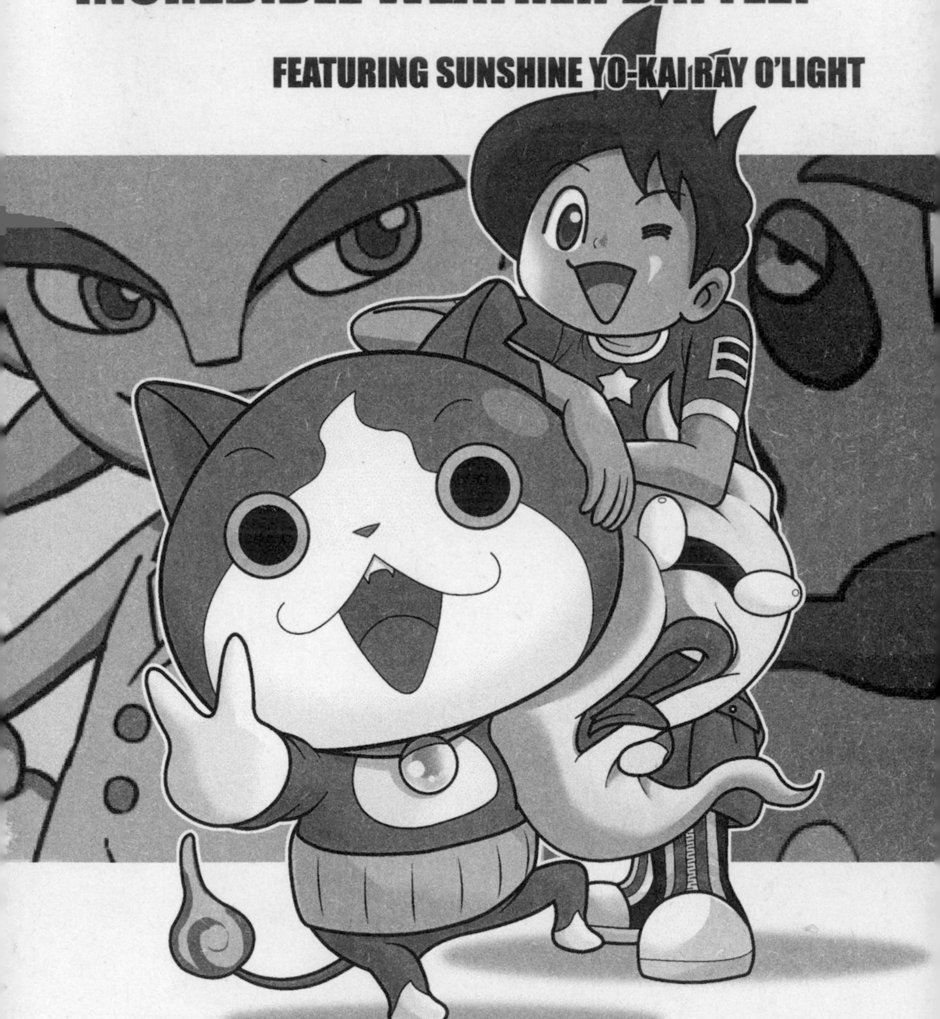

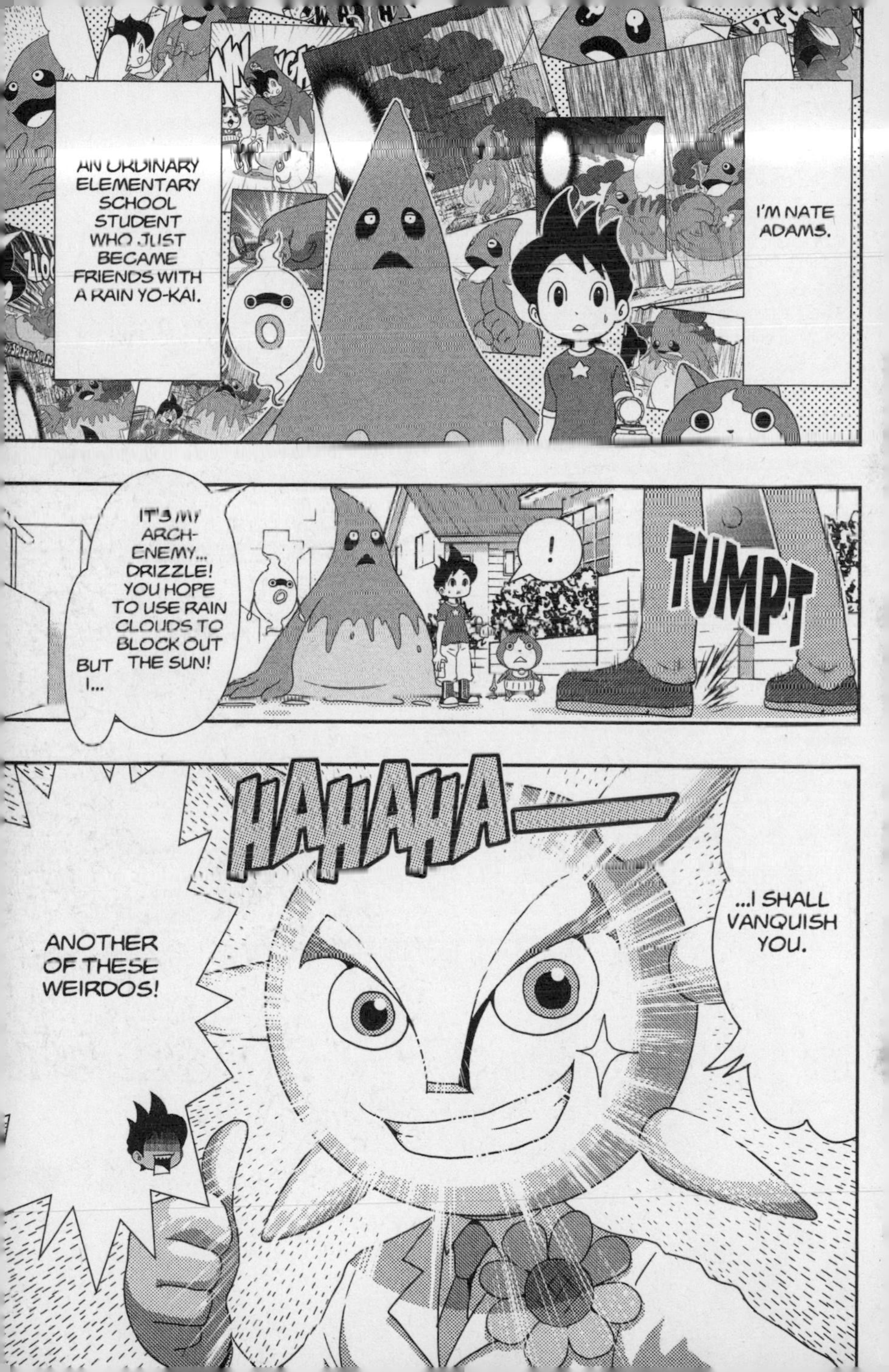

I'M NATE ADAMS.
AN ORDINARY ELEMENTARY SCHOOL STUDENT WHO JUST BECAME FRIENDS WITH A RAIN YO-KAI.
TUMPT
!
IT'S MY ARCH-ENEMY... DRIZZLE! YOU HOPE TO USE RAIN CLOUDS TO BLOCK OUT THE SUN! BUT I...
HAHAHA—
...I SHALL VANQUISH YOU.
ANOTHER OF THESE WEIRDOS!

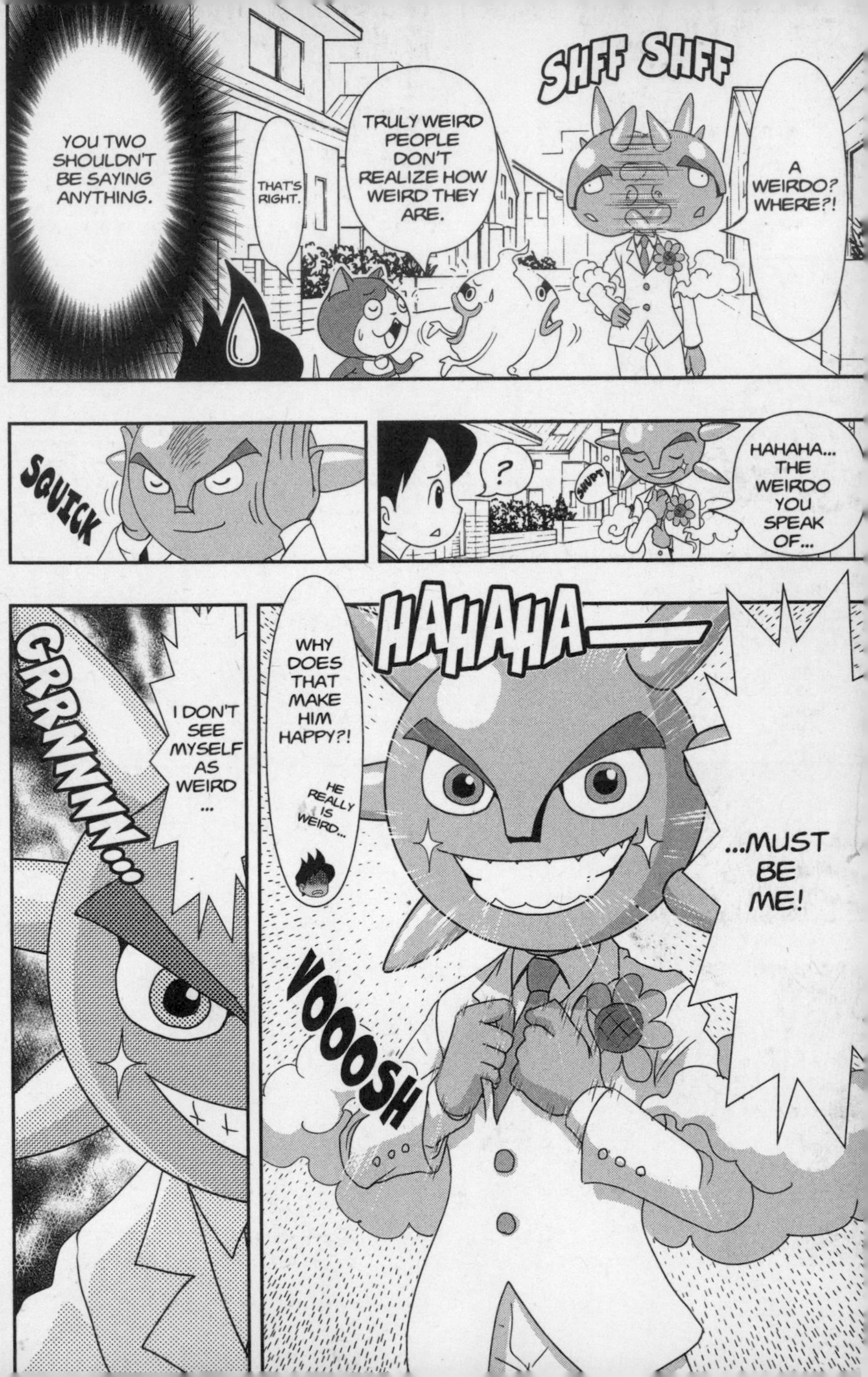
SHFF SHFF
A WEIRDO? WHERE?!
TRULY WEIRD PEOPLE DON'T REALIZE HOW WEIRD THEY ARE.
THAT'S RIGHT.
YOU TWO SHOULDN'T BE SAYING ANYTHING.
HAHAHA... THE WEIRDO YOU SPEAK OF...
SHUPT
?
SQUICK
HAHAHA—
...MUST BE ME!
WHY DOES THAT MAKE HIM HAPPY?!
HE REALLY IS WEIRD...
VOOOSH
I DON'T SEE MYSELF AS WEIRD ...
GRRNNNN...

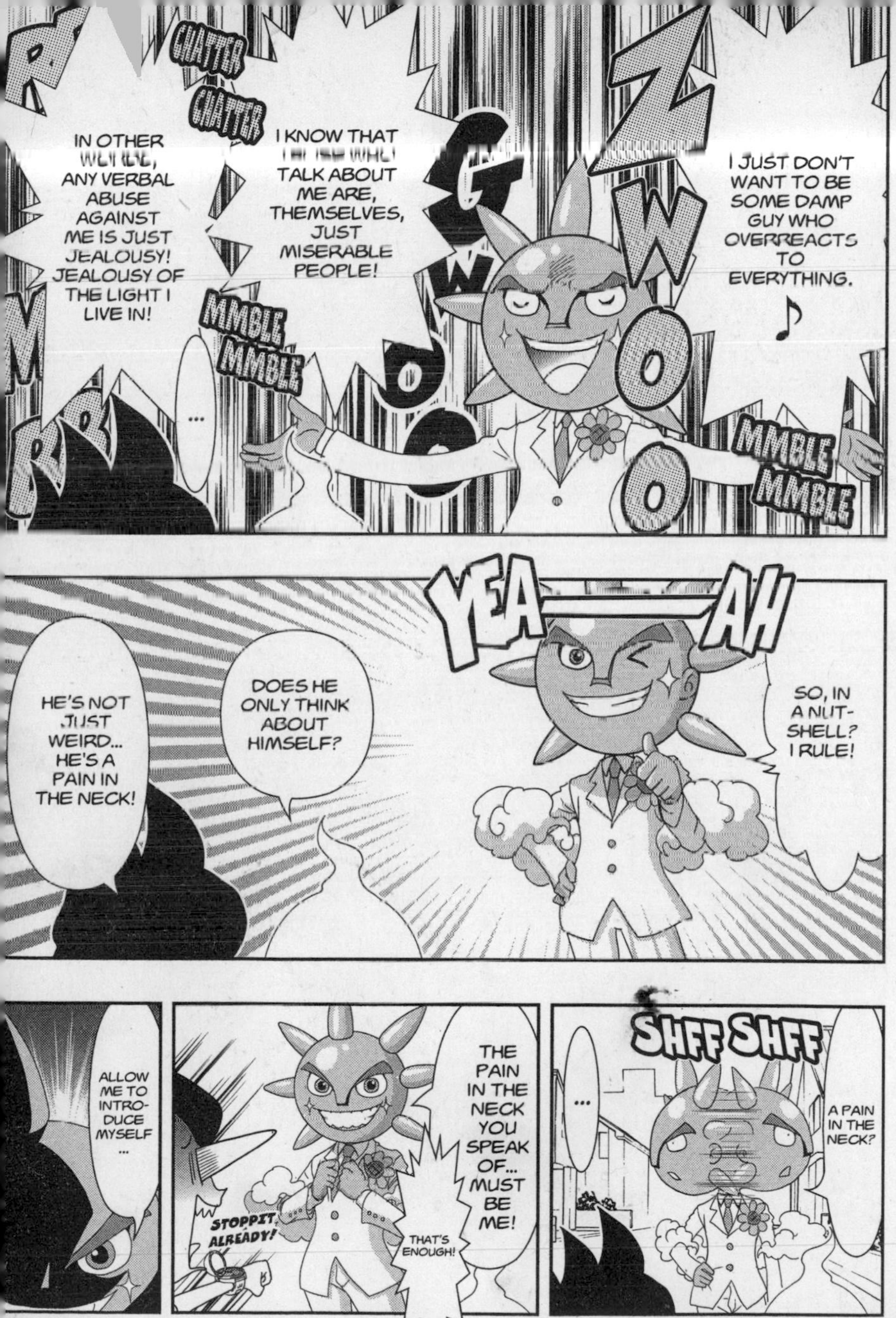
I JUST DON'T WANT TO BE SOME DAMP GUY WHO OVERREACTS TO EVERYTHING. ♪
ZWOOO
MMBLE MMBLE
I KNOW THAT TALK ABOUT ME ARE, THEMSELVES, JUST MISERABLE PEOPLE!
GWJO
CHATTER CHATTER
IN OTHER ANY VERBAL ABUSE AGAINST ME IS JUST JEALOUSY! JEALOUSY OF THE LIGHT I LIVE IN!
MMBLE MMBLE
...
SO, IN A NUT-SHELL? I RULE!
YEA—AH
DOES HE ONLY THINK ABOUT HIMSELF?
HE'S NOT JUST WEIRD... HE'S A PAIN IN THE NECK!
SHFF SHFF
A PAIN IN THE NECK?
...
THE PAIN IN THE NECK YOU SPEAK OF... MUST BE ME!
THAT'S ENOUGH!
STOPPIT, ALREADY!
ALLOW ME TO INTRO-DUCE MYSELF ...

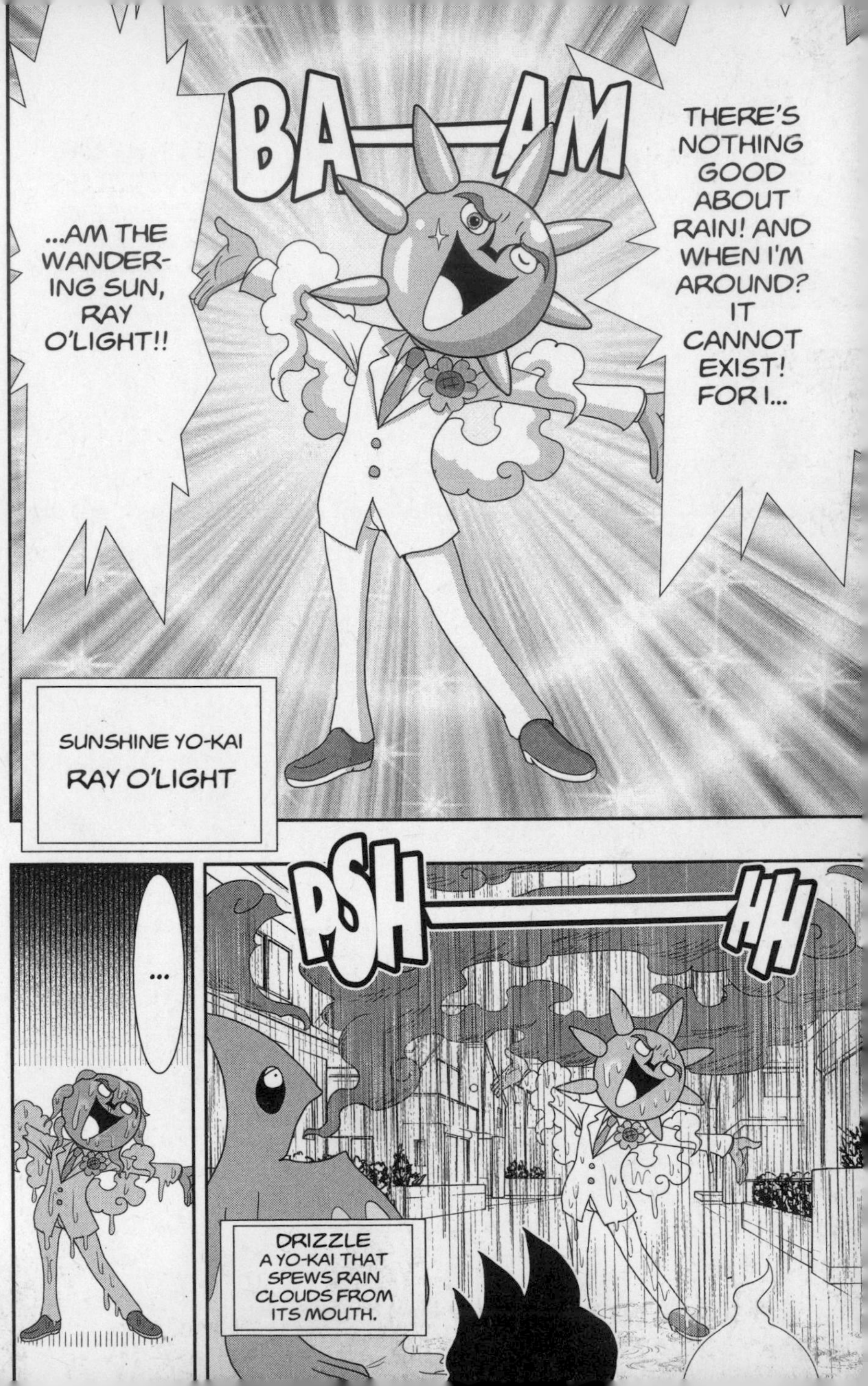
THERE'S NOTHING GOOD ABOUT RAIN! AND WHEN I'M AROUND? IT CANNOT EXIST! FOR I...
BA—AM
...AM THE WANDER-ING SUN, RAY O'LIGHT!!
SUNSHINE YO-KAI
RAY O'LIGHT
PSH—HH
DRIZZLE
A YO-KAI THAT SPEWS RAIN CLOUDS FROM ITS MOUTH.
...

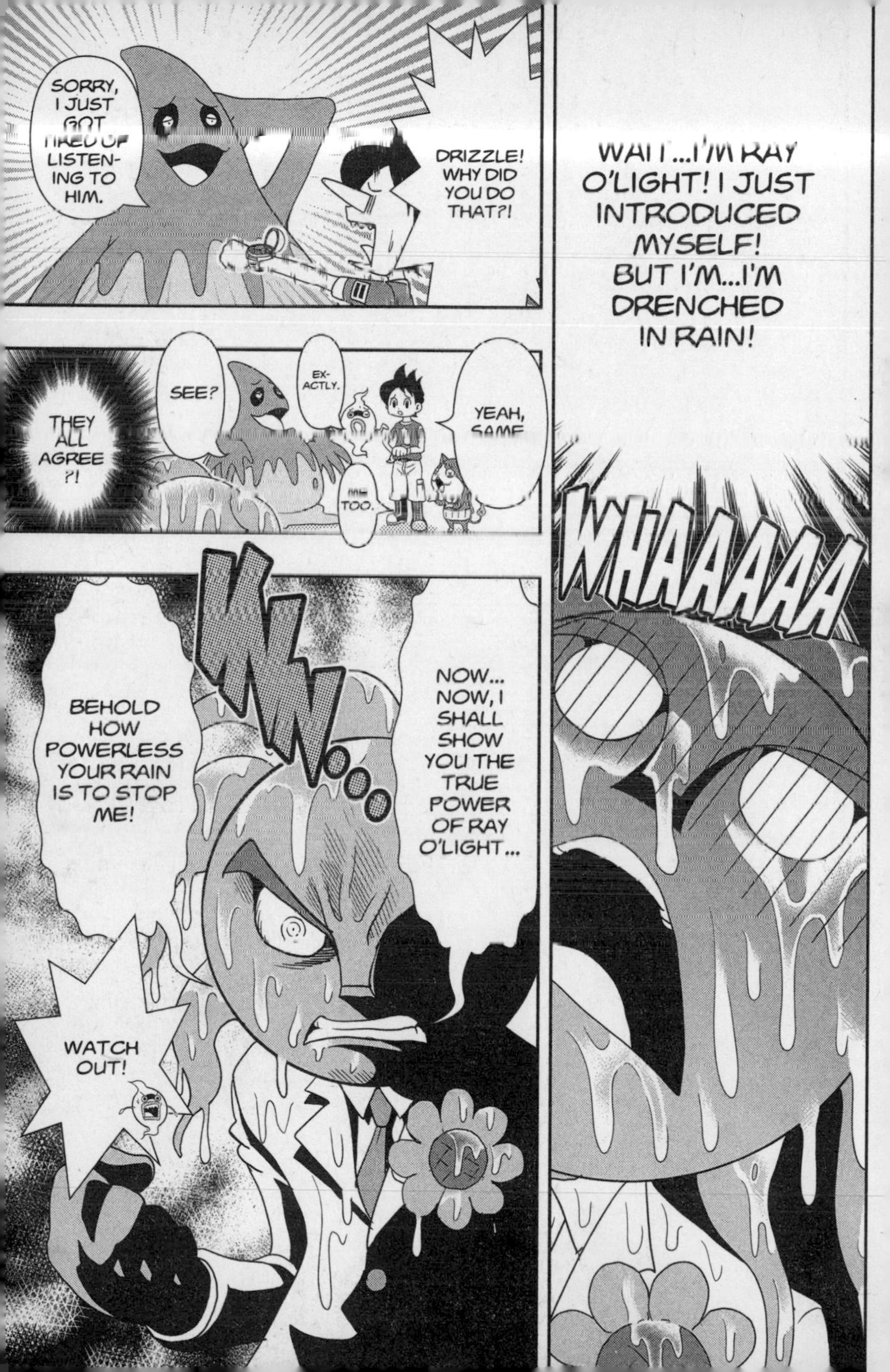
WAIT...I'M RAY O'LIGHT! I JUST INTRODUCED MYSELF! BUT I'M...I'M DRENCHED IN RAIN!
WHAAAAAA
DRIZZLE! WHY DID YOU DO THAT?!
SORRY, I JUST GOT TIRED OF LISTENING TO HIM.
YEAH, SAME
EX-ACTLY.
SEE?
ME TOO.
THEY ALL AGREE ?!
NOW... NOW, I SHALL SHOW YOU THE TRUE POWER OF RAY O'LIGHT...
WWN...
BEHOLD HOW POWERLESS YOUR RAIN IS TO STOP ME!
WATCH OUT!

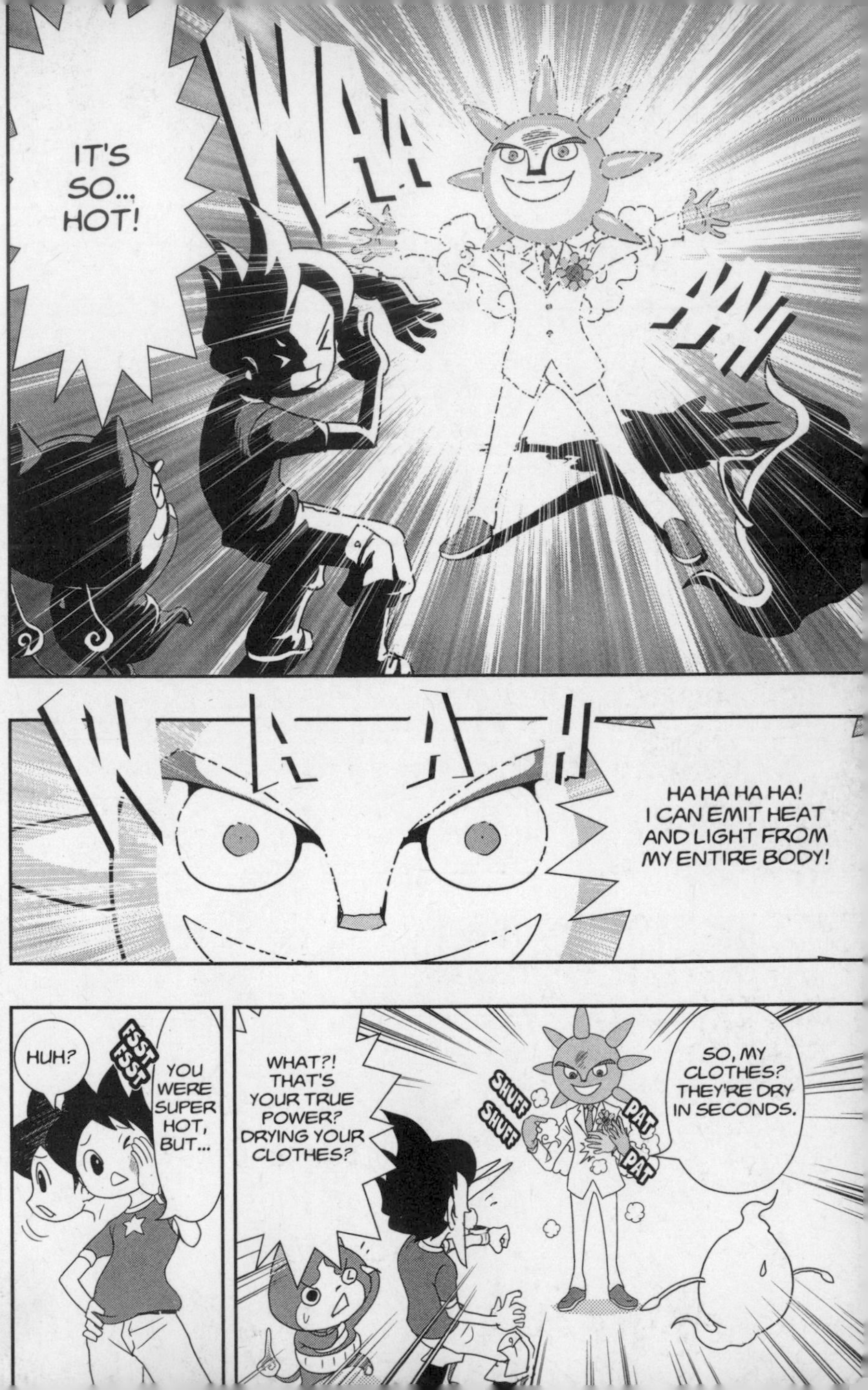
WAA
AH
IT'S SO... HOT!
WAAH
HA HA HA HA! I CAN EMIT HEAT AND LIGHT FROM MY ENTIRE BODY!
SO, MY CLOTHES? THEY'RE DRY IN SECONDS.
PAT PAT
SHUFF SHUFF
WHAT?! THAT'S YOUR TRUE POWER? DRYING YOUR CLOTHES?
YOU WERE SUPER HOT, BUT...
FSST FSST
HUH?

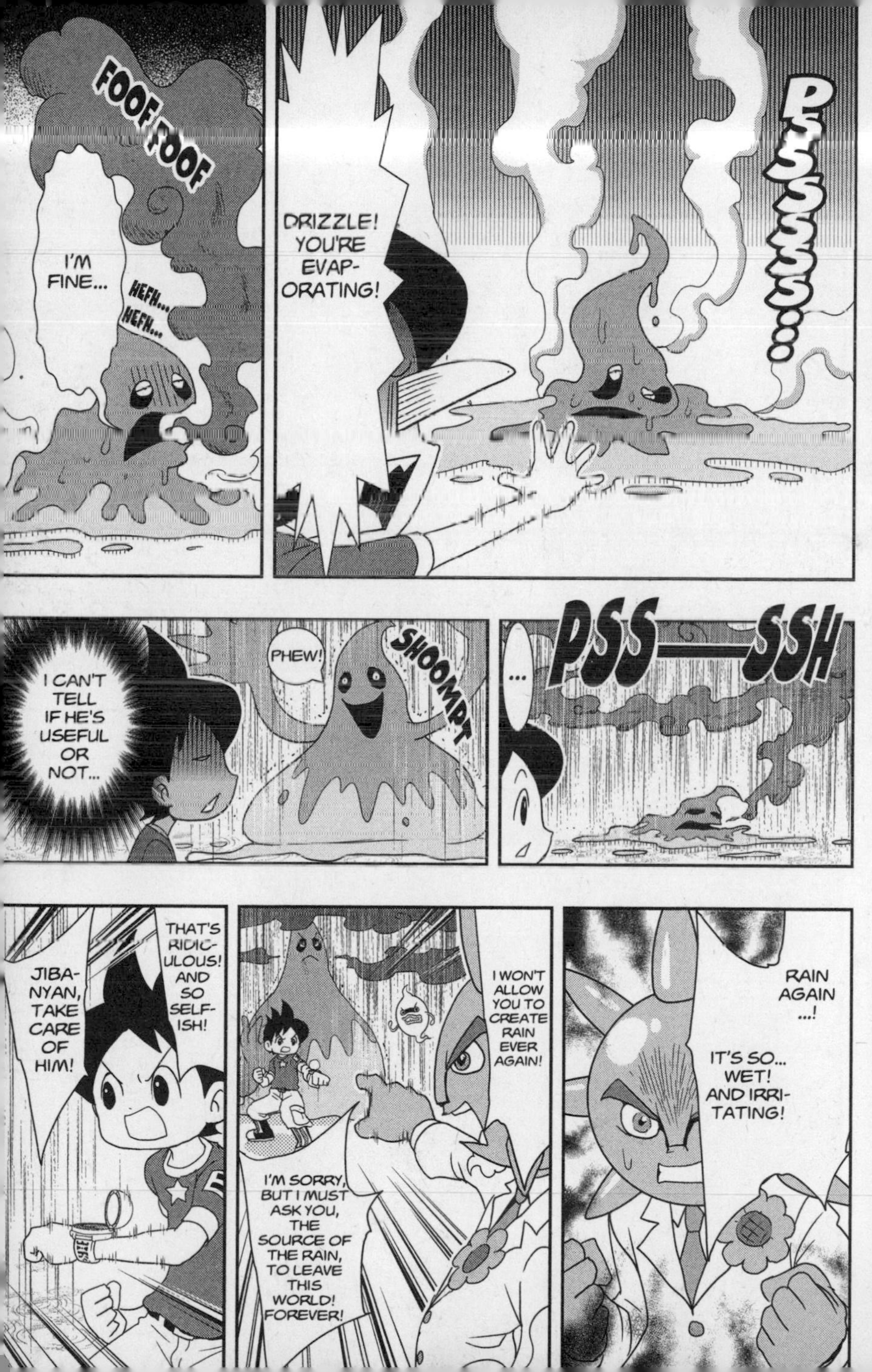
PSSSSSS...
DRIZZLE! YOU'RE EVAPORATING!
FOOF FOOF
I'M FINE...
HEFH... HEFH...
PSS—SSH
...
SHOOMPT
PHEW!
I CAN'T TELL IF HE'S USEFUL OR NOT...
RAIN AGAIN...!
IT'S SO... WET! AND IRRITATING!
I WON'T ALLOW YOU TO CREATE RAIN EVER AGAIN!
I'M SORRY, BUT I MUST ASK YOU, THE SOURCE OF THE RAIN, TO LEAVE THIS WORLD! FOREVER!
THAT'S RIDICULOUS! AND SO SELFISH!
JIBANYAN, TAKE CARE OF HIM!

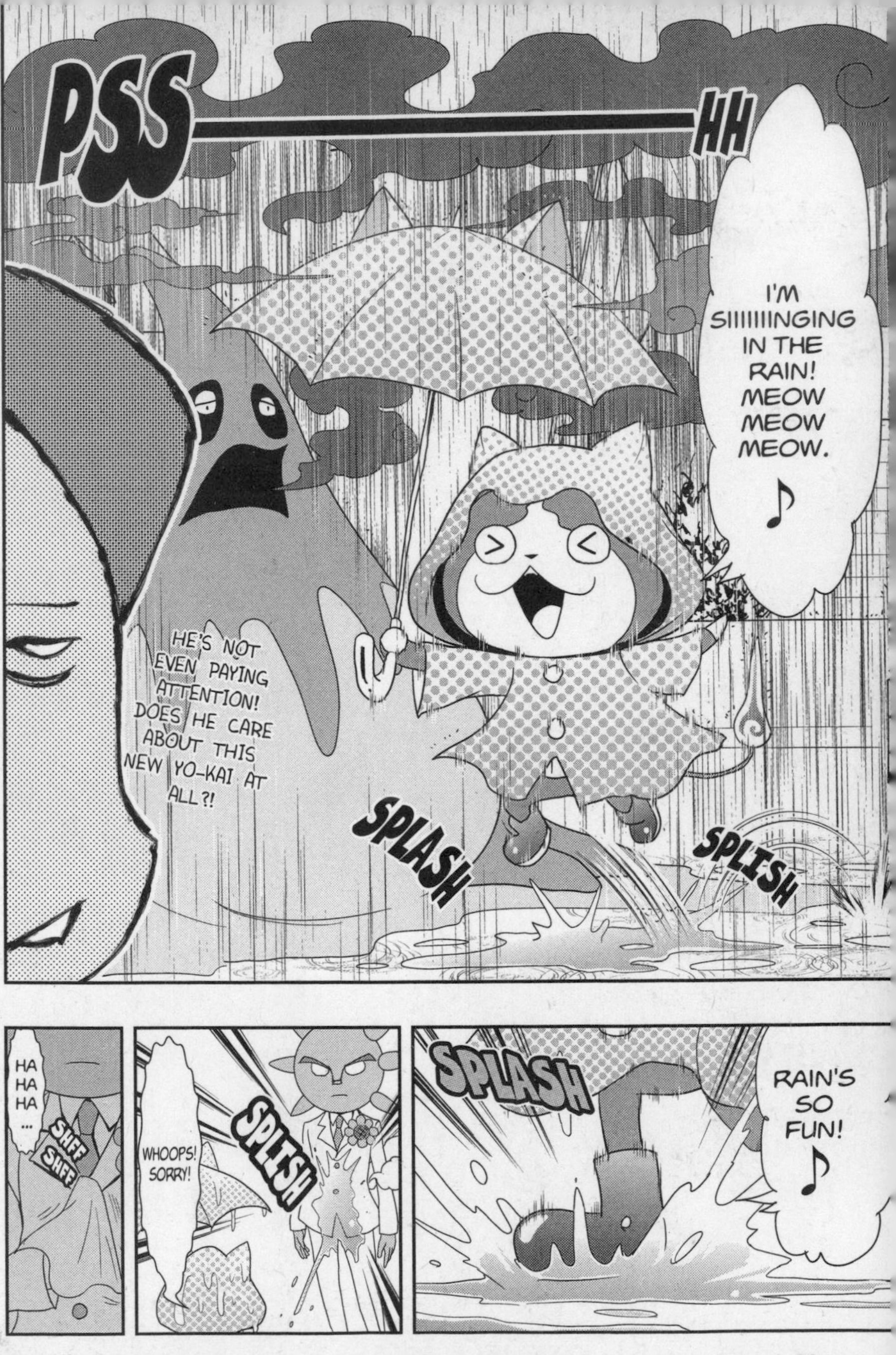
PSS———HH
I'M SIIIIIIIINGING IN THE RAIN! MEOW MEOW MEOW. ♪
SPLISH
SPLASH
HE'S NOT EVEN PAYING ATTENTION! DOES HE CARE ABOUT THIS NEW YO-KAI AT ALL?!
SPLASH
RAIN'S SO FUN! ♪
SPLISH
WHOOPS! SORRY!
HA HA HA ...
SHFF SHFF

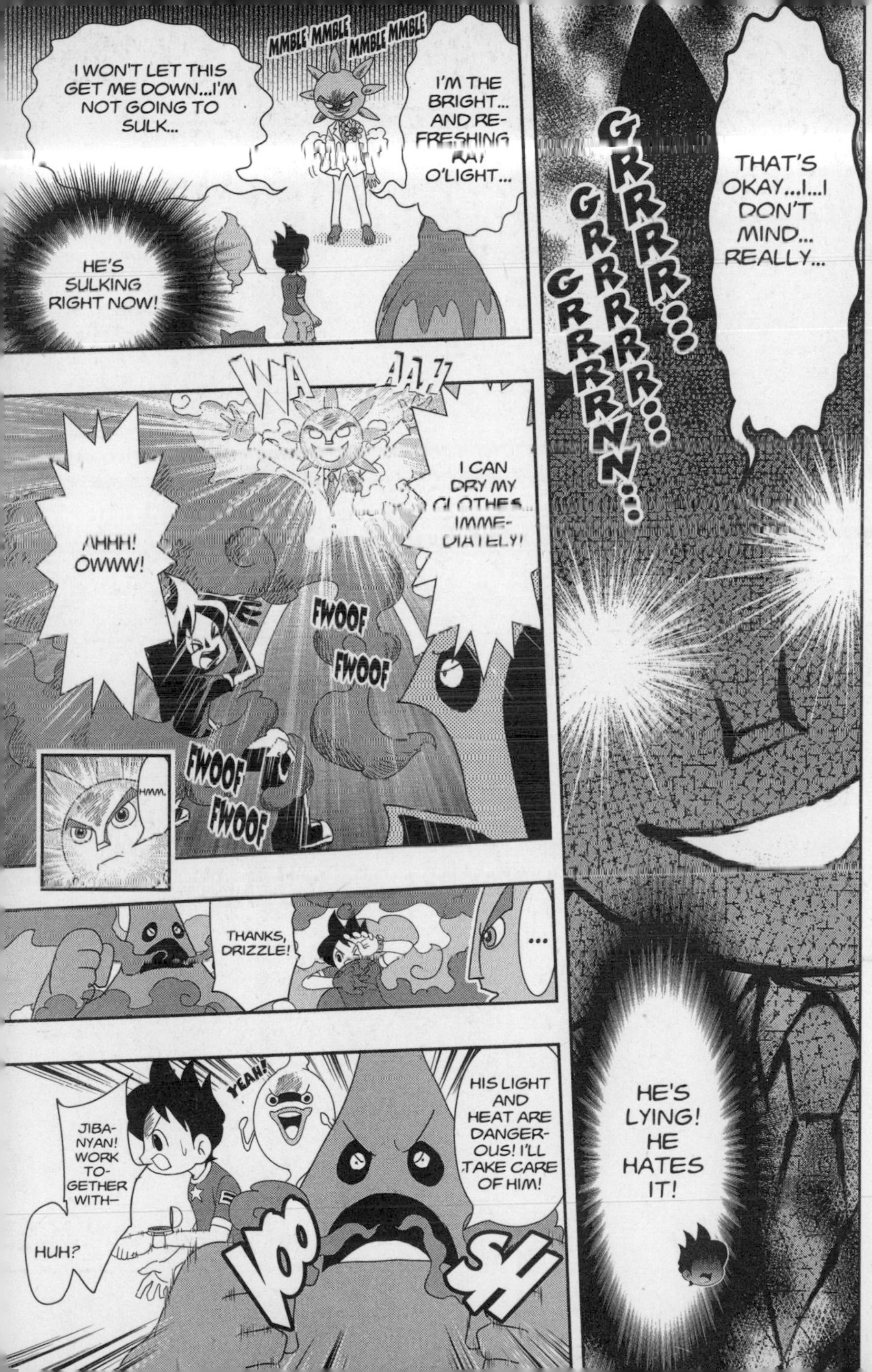
THAT'S OKAY...I...I DON'T MIND... REALLY...
GRRRR...
GRRRRRR...
GRRRRRN...
HE'S LYING! HE HATES IT!
MMBLE MMBLE MMBLE MMBLE
I'M THE BRIGHT... AND RE-FRESHING RAY O'LIGHT...
I WON'T LET THIS GET ME DOWN...I'M NOT GOING TO SULK...
HE'S SULKING RIGHT NOW!
WAAAH
I CAN DRY MY CLOTHES IMME-DIATELY!
FWOOF
FWOOF
AHHH! OWWW!
FWOOF
FWOOF
HMM.
...
THANKS, DRIZZLE!
HIS LIGHT AND HEAT ARE DANGER-OUS! I'LL TAKE CARE OF HIM!
WOOSH
YEAH!
JIBA-NYAN! WORK TO-GETHER WITH—
HUH?

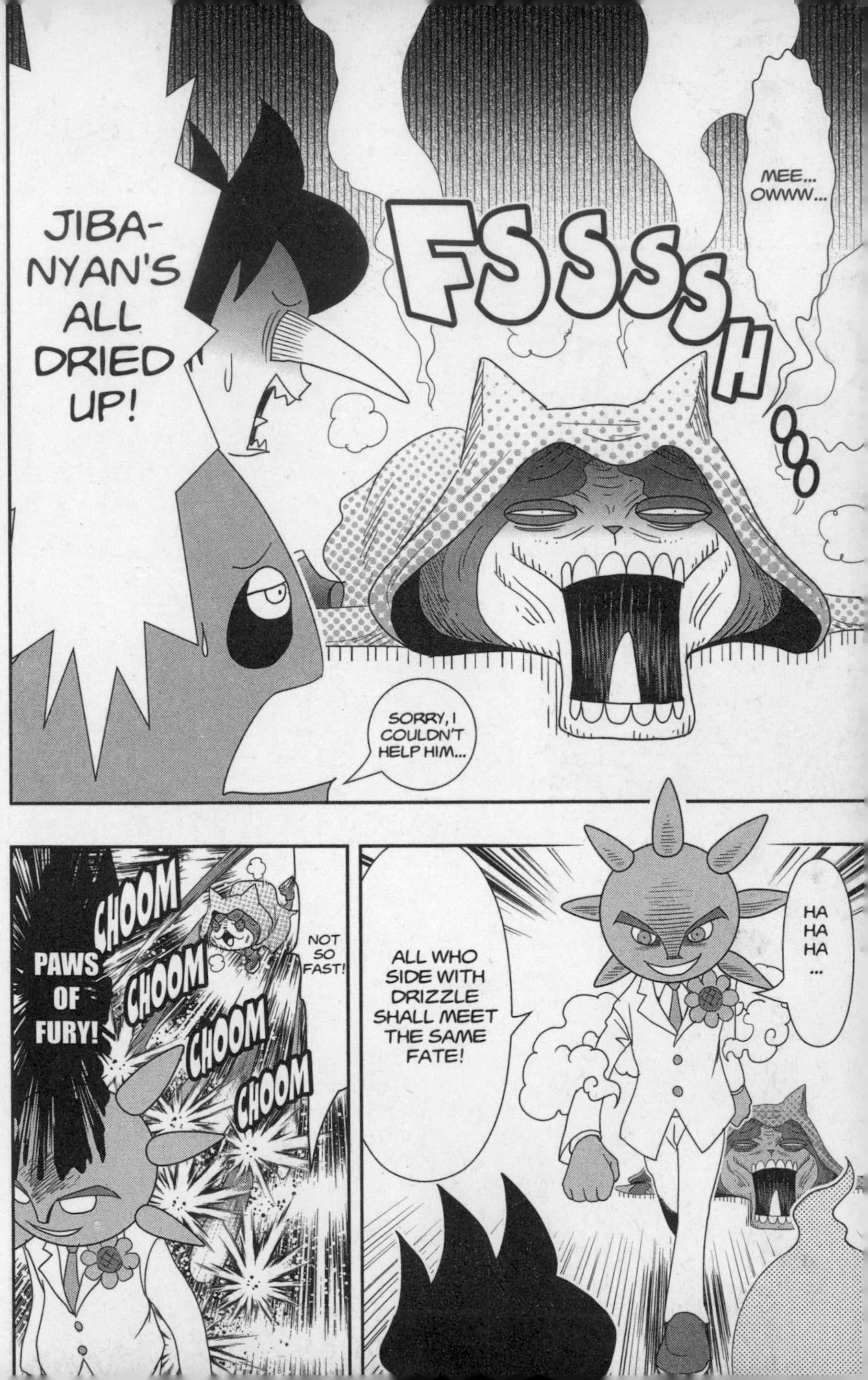
MEE... OWWW...
FSSSSH...
JIBA-NYAN'S ALL DRIED UP!
SORRY, I COULDN'T HELP HIM...
HA HA HA ...
ALL WHO SIDE WITH DRIZZLE SHALL MEET THE SAME FATE!
NOT SO FAST!
CHOOM CHOOM CHOOM CHOOM
PAWS OF FURY!

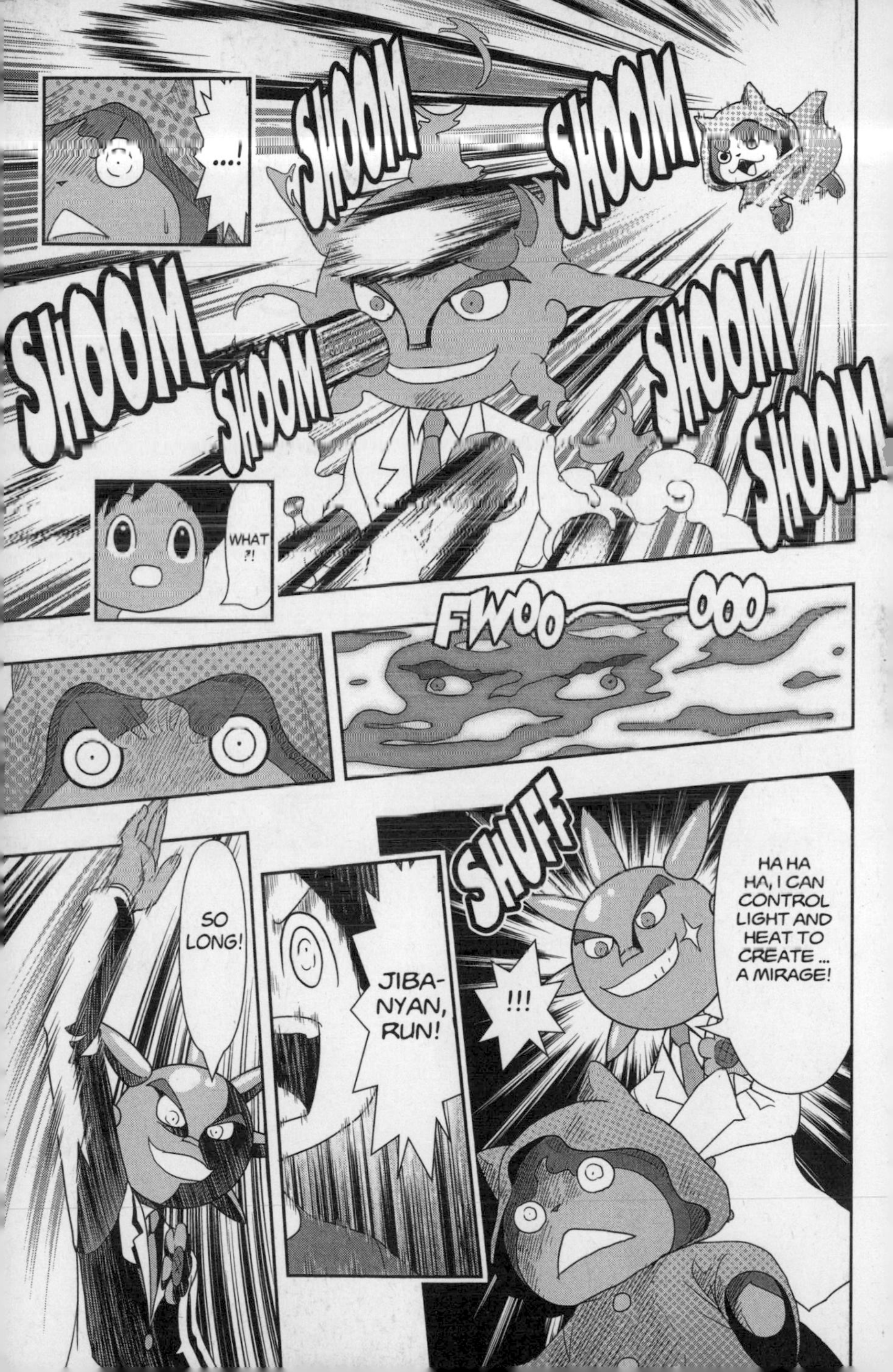
SHOOM
SHOOM
SHOOM
SHOOM
SHOOM
SHOOM
SHOOM
...!
WHAT ?!
FWOO——OOO
SHUFF
HA HA HA, I CAN CONTROL LIGHT AND HEAT TO CREATE ... A MIRAGE!
!!!
JIBA-NYAN, RUN!
SO LONG!

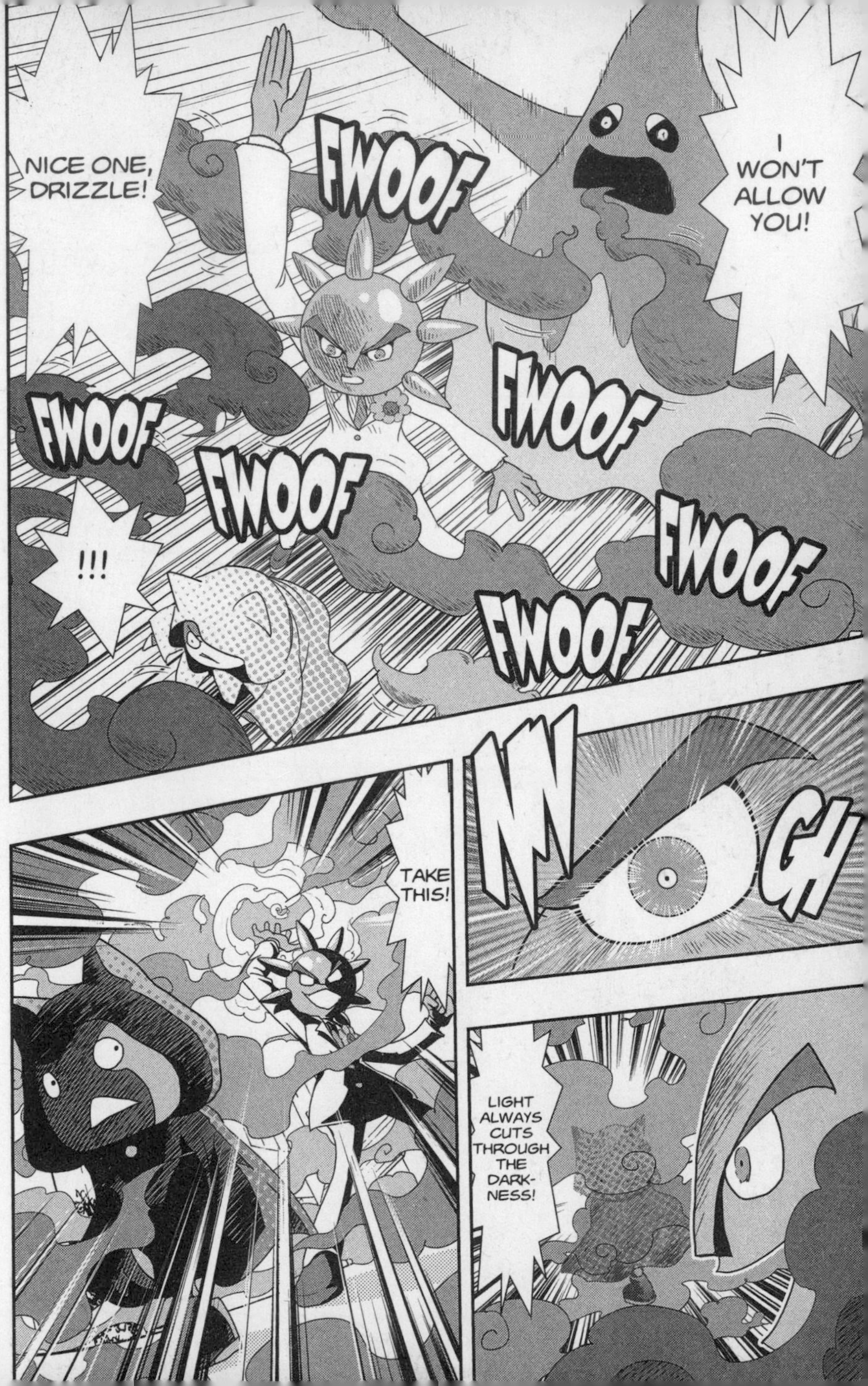
I WON'T ALLOW YOU!
FWOOF
NICE ONE, DRIZZLE!
FWOOF
FWOOF
FWOOF
FWOOF
FWOOF
!!!
MNGH
LIGHT ALWAYS CUTS THROUGH THE DARKNESS!
TAKE THIS!

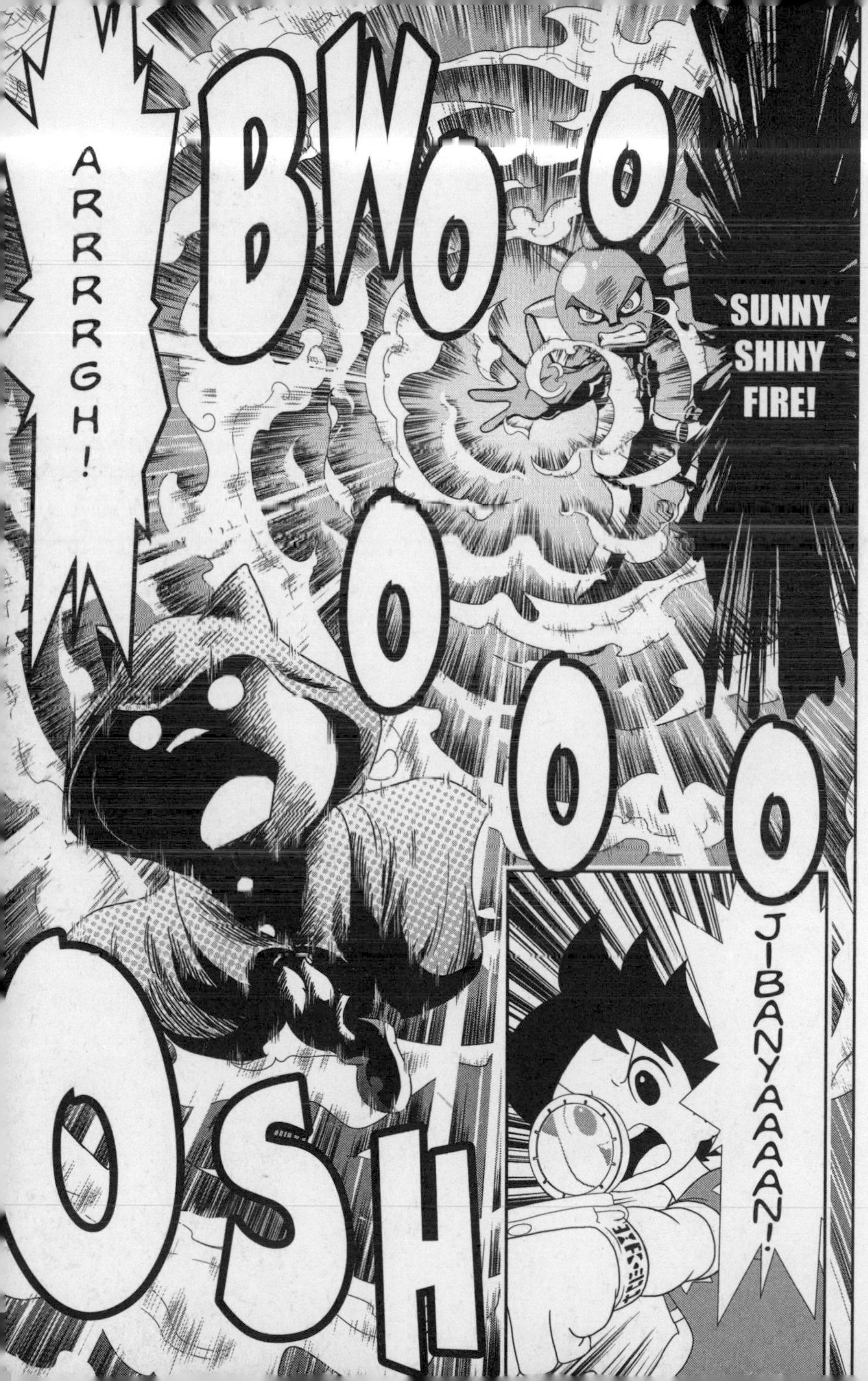
SUNNY SHINY FIRE!
BWOOOOOOOSH
ARRRRGH!
JIBANYAAAAAN!

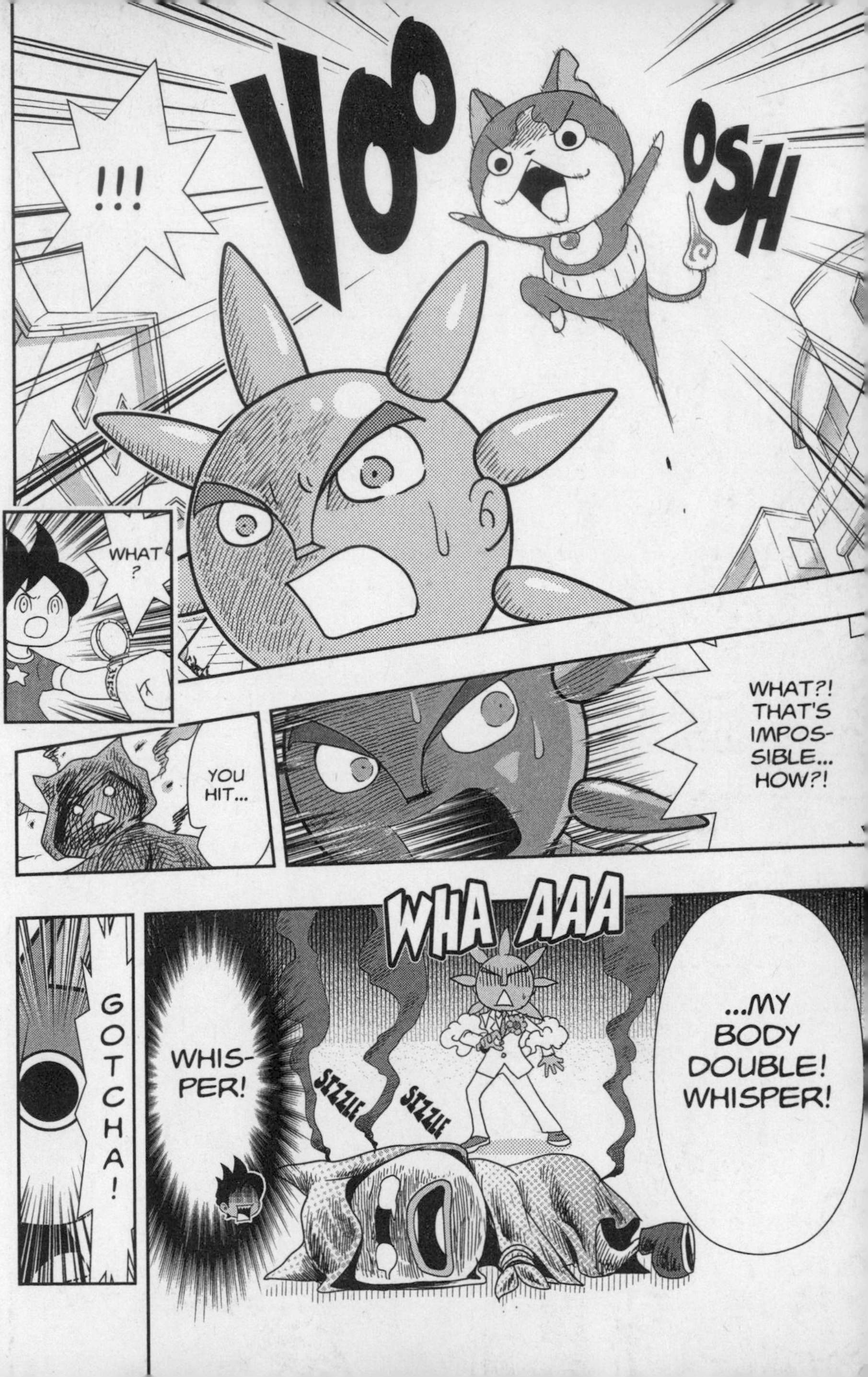
VOO OSH
!!!
WHAT?
WHAT?! THAT'S IMPOSSIBLE... HOW?!
YOU HIT...
...MY BODY DOUBLE! WHISPER!
WHA AAA
SIZZLE
SIZZLE
WHISPER!
GOTCHA!

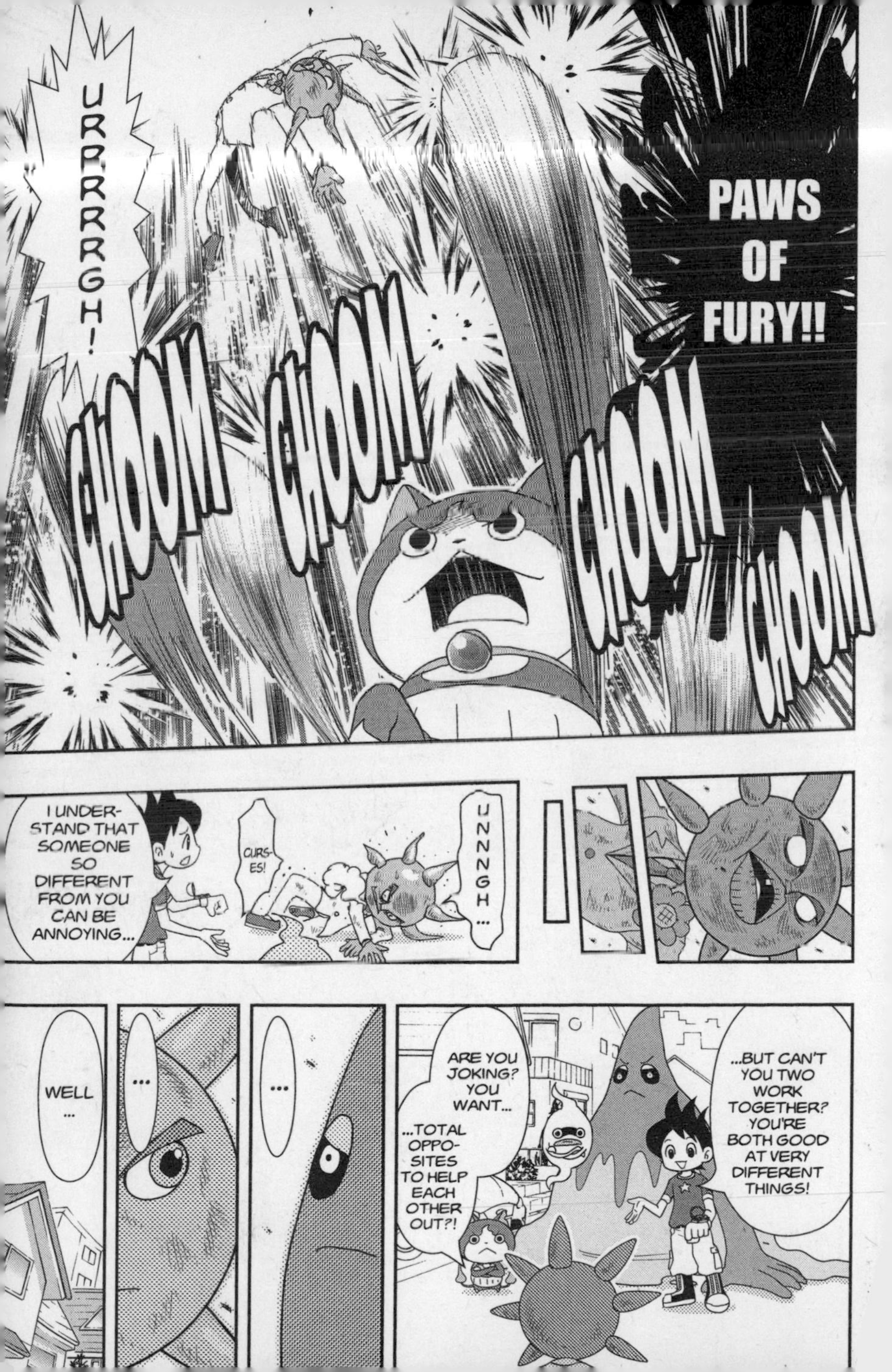
PAWS OF FURY!!
CHOOM
CHOOM
CHOOM
CHOOM
URRRRRGH!
UNNNGH...
CURSES!
I UNDERSTAND THAT SOMEONE SO DIFFERENT FROM YOU CAN BE ANNOYING...
...BUT CAN'T YOU TWO WORK TOGETHER? YOU'RE BOTH GOOD AT VERY DIFFERENT THINGS!
ARE YOU JOKING? YOU WANT...
...TOTAL OPPOSITES TO HELP EACH OTHER OUT?!
...
...
WELL ...

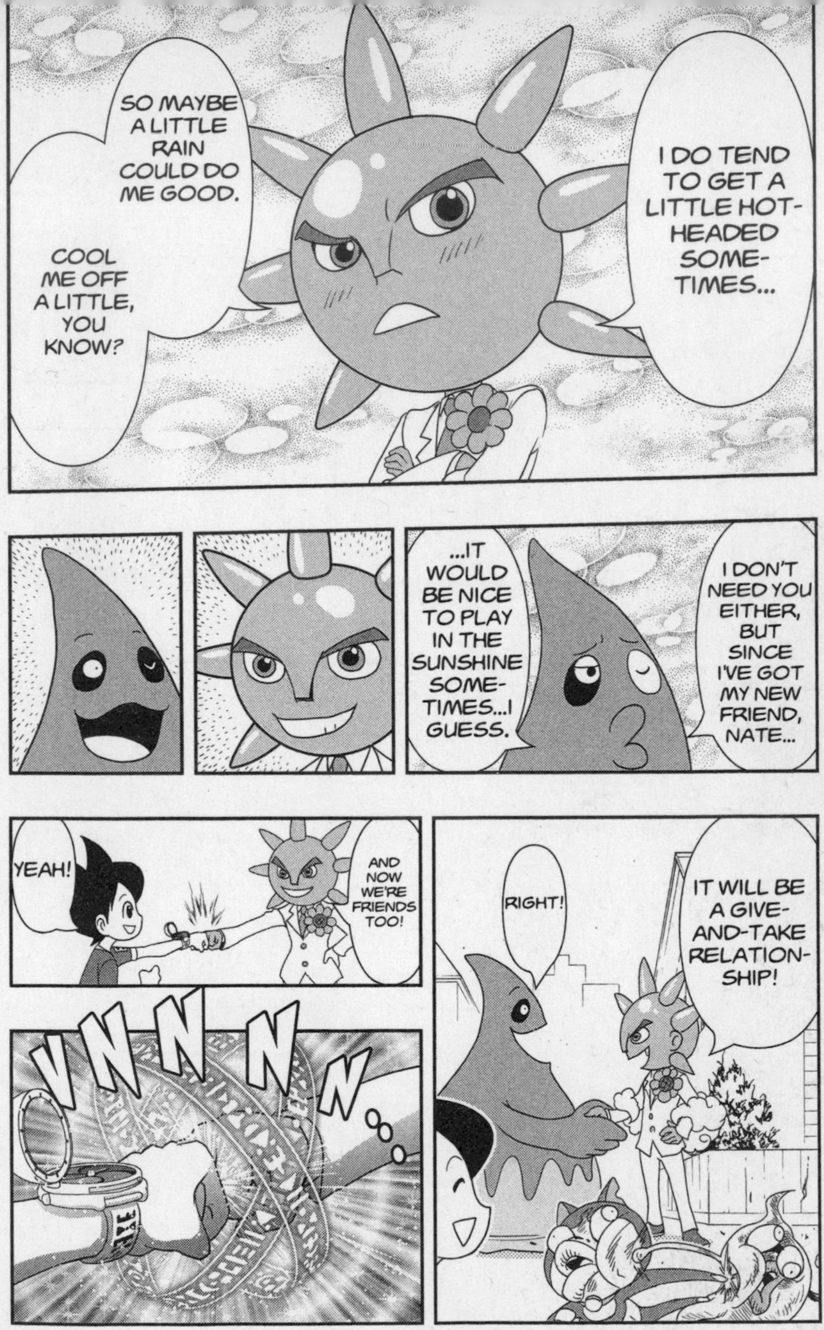
I DO TEND TO GET A LITTLE HOT-HEADED SOME-TIMES...
SO MAYBE A LITTLE RAIN COULD DO ME GOOD.
COOL ME OFF A LITTLE, YOU KNOW?
I DON'T NEED YOU EITHER, BUT SINCE I'VE GOT MY NEW FRIEND, NATE...
...IT WOULD BE NICE TO PLAY IN THE SUNSHINE SOME-TIMES...I GUESS.
IT WILL BE A GIVE-AND-TAKE RELATION-SHIP!
RIGHT!
AND NOW WE'RE FRIENDS TOO!
YEAH!
VNNNNN

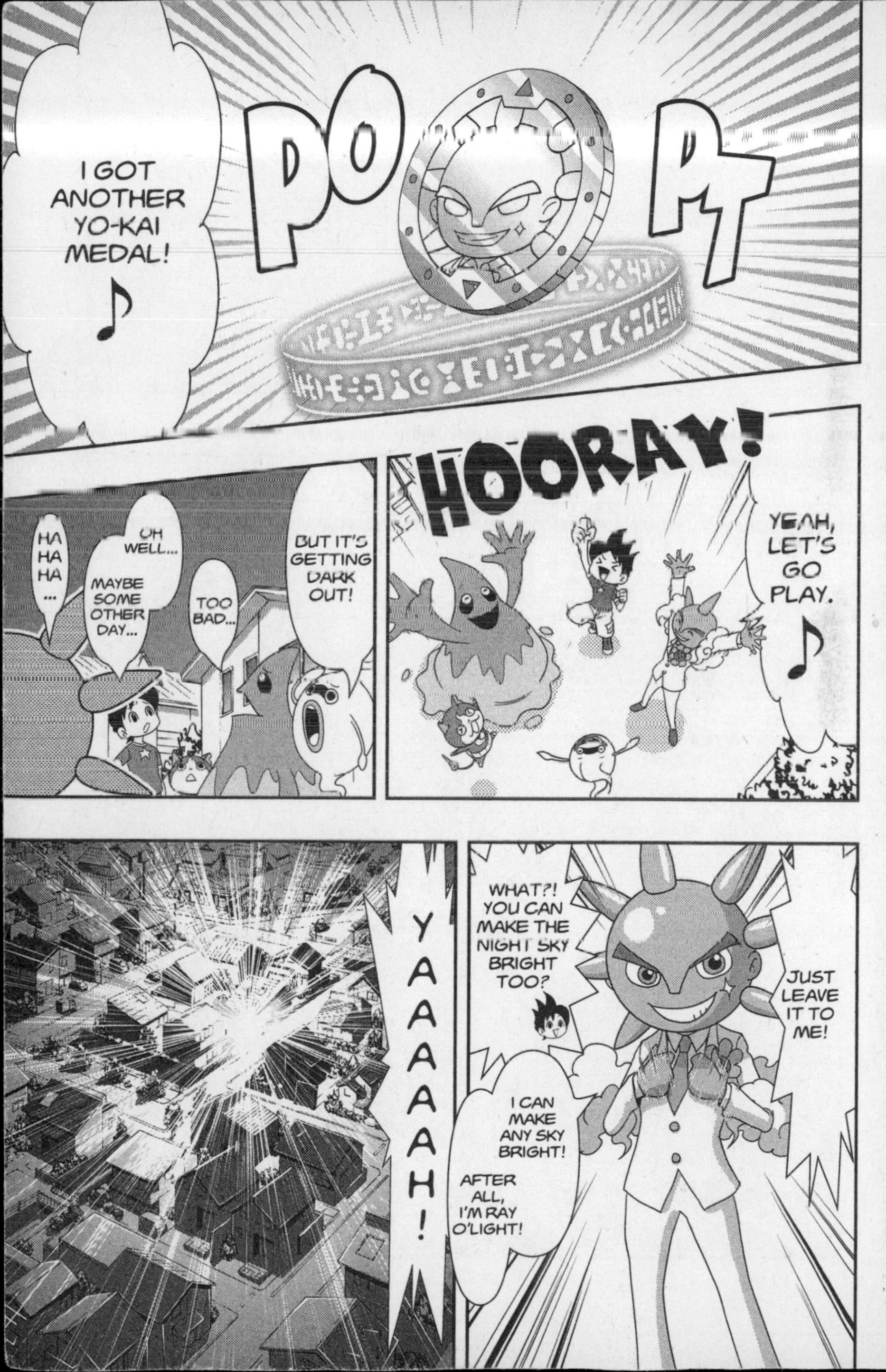
POP
I GOT ANOTHER YO-KAI MEDAL! ♪
HOORAY!
YEAH, LET'S GO PLAY. ♪
BUT IT'S GETTING DARK OUT!
TOO BAD...
OH WELL...
MAYBE SOME OTHER DAY...
HA HA HA...
WHAT?! YOU CAN MAKE THE NIGHT SKY BRIGHT TOO?
JUST LEAVE IT TO ME!
I CAN MAKE ANY SKY BRIGHT!
AFTER ALL, I'M RAY O'LIGHT!
YAAAAAAH!

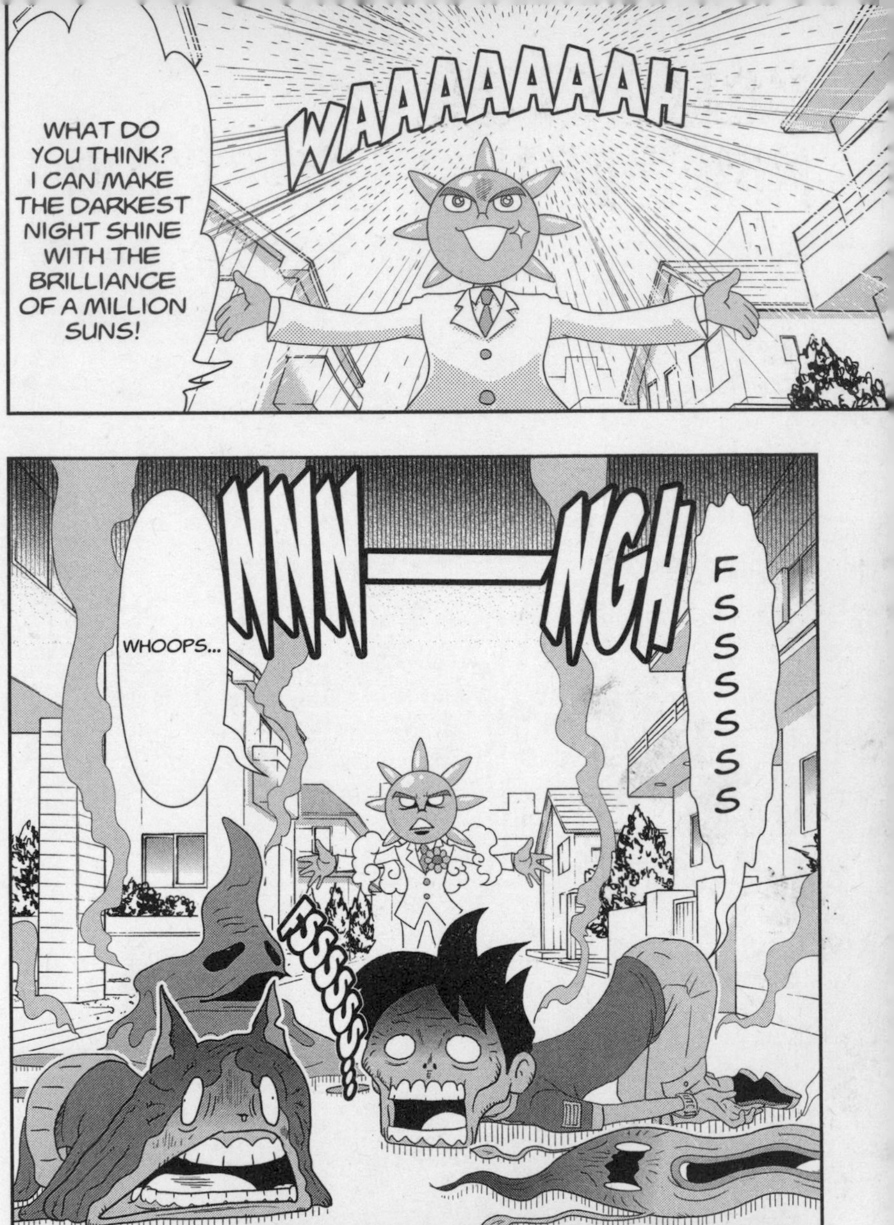
WAAAAAAAH
WHAT DO YOU THINK? I CAN MAKE THE DARKEST NIGHT SHINE WITH THE BRILLIANCE OF A MILLION SUNS!
FSSSSSSS
NNN—NGH
WHOOPS...
FSSSSSS...
NATE ADAMS'S CURRENT NUMBER OF YO-KAI FRIENDS: 40.

CHAPTER 50: NONSTOP FART EXPLOSION!

FEATURING FART YO-KAI CHEEKSQUEEK

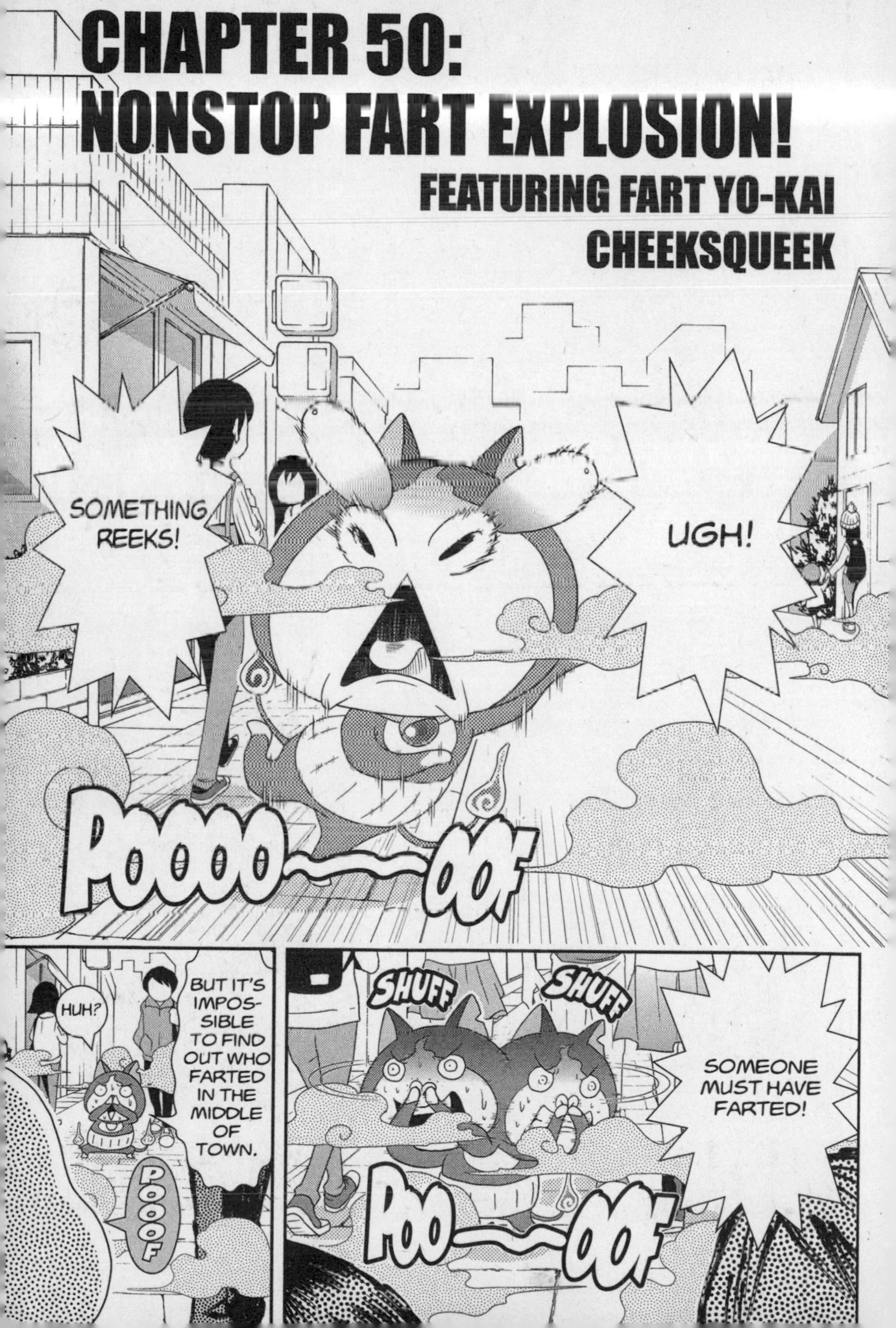
UGH!
SOMETHING REEKS!
POOOO——OOF
SHUFF
SHUFF
SOMEONE MUST HAVE FARTED!
POO——OOF
BUT IT'S IMPOSSIBLE TO FIND OUT WHO FARTED IN THE MIDDLE OF TOWN.
HUH?
POOOF

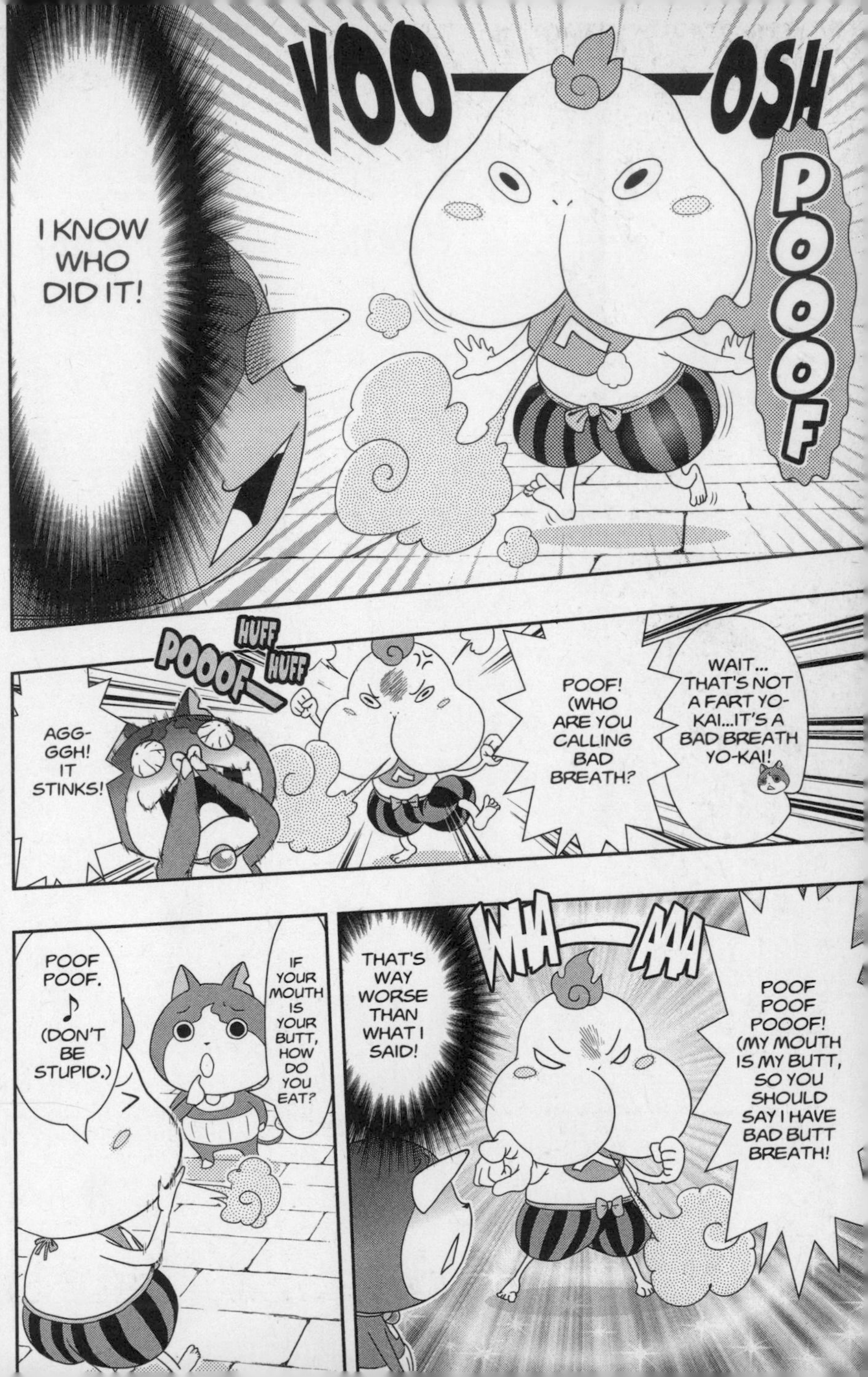
VOO—OSH
POOOOF
I KNOW WHO DID IT!
WAIT... THAT'S NOT A FART YO-KAI...IT'S A BAD BREATH YO-KAI!
POOF! (WHO ARE YOU CALLING BAD BREATH?
HUFF HUFF
POOOF—
AGG-GGH! IT STINKS!
WHA—AAA
POOF POOF POOOF! (MY MOUTH IS MY BUTT, SO YOU SHOULD SAY I HAVE BAD BUTT BREATH!
THAT'S WAY WORSE THAN WHAT I SAID!
IF YOUR MOUTH IS YOUR BUTT, HOW DO YOU EAT?
POOF POOF. ♪ (DON'T BE STUPID.)

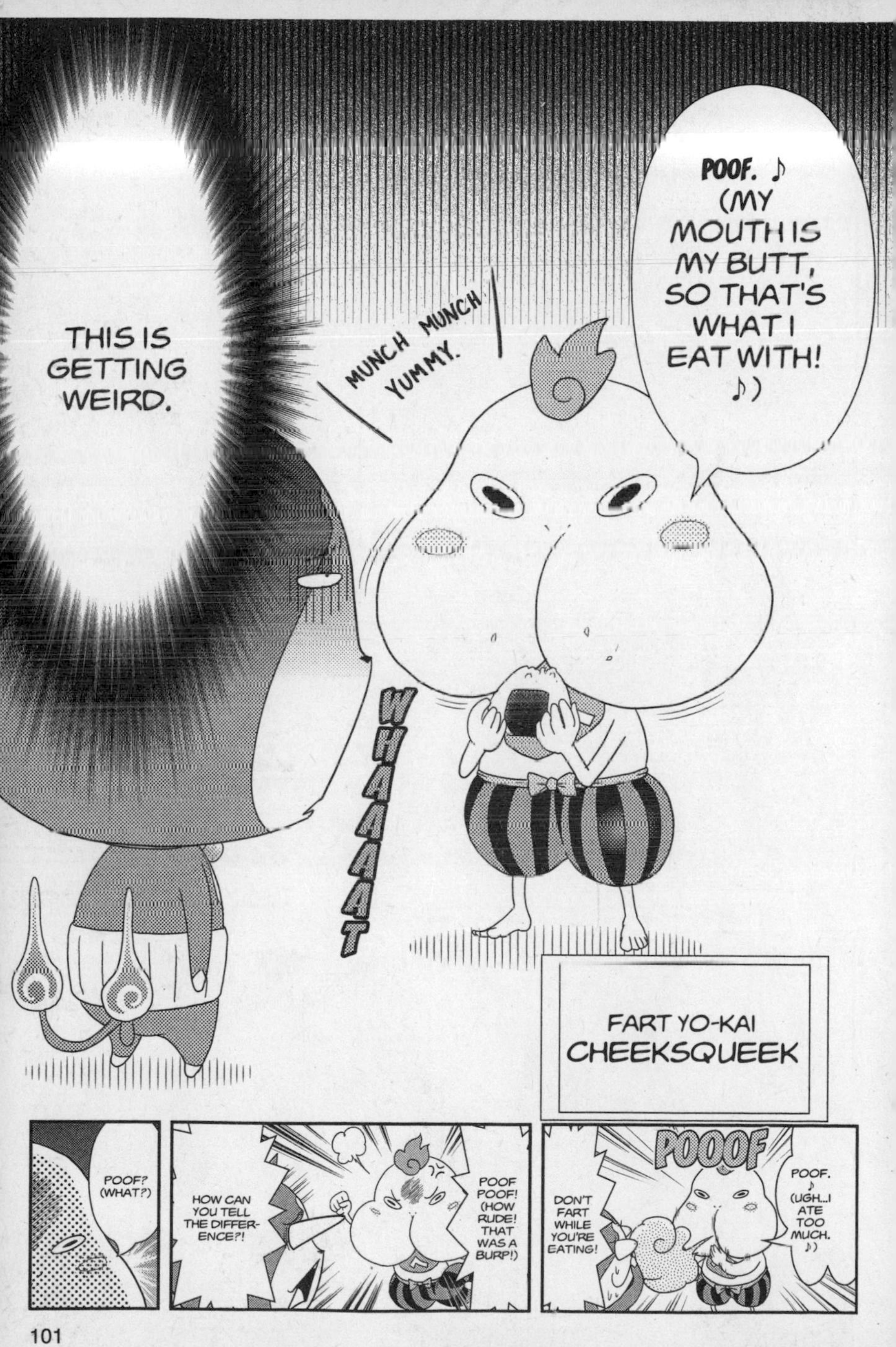
POOF. ♪
(MY MOUTH IS MY BUTT, SO THAT'S WHAT I EAT WITH! ♪)
MUNCH MUNCH
YUMMY.
WHAAAAT
THIS IS GETTING WEIRD.
FART YO-KAI CHEEKSQUEEK
POOF. ♪ (UGH...I ATE TOO MUCH. ♪)
POOOF
DON'T FART WHILE YOU'RE EATING!
POOF POOF! (HOW RUDE! THAT WAS A BURP!)
HOW CAN YOU TELL THE DIFFER-ENCE?!
POOF? (WHAT?)

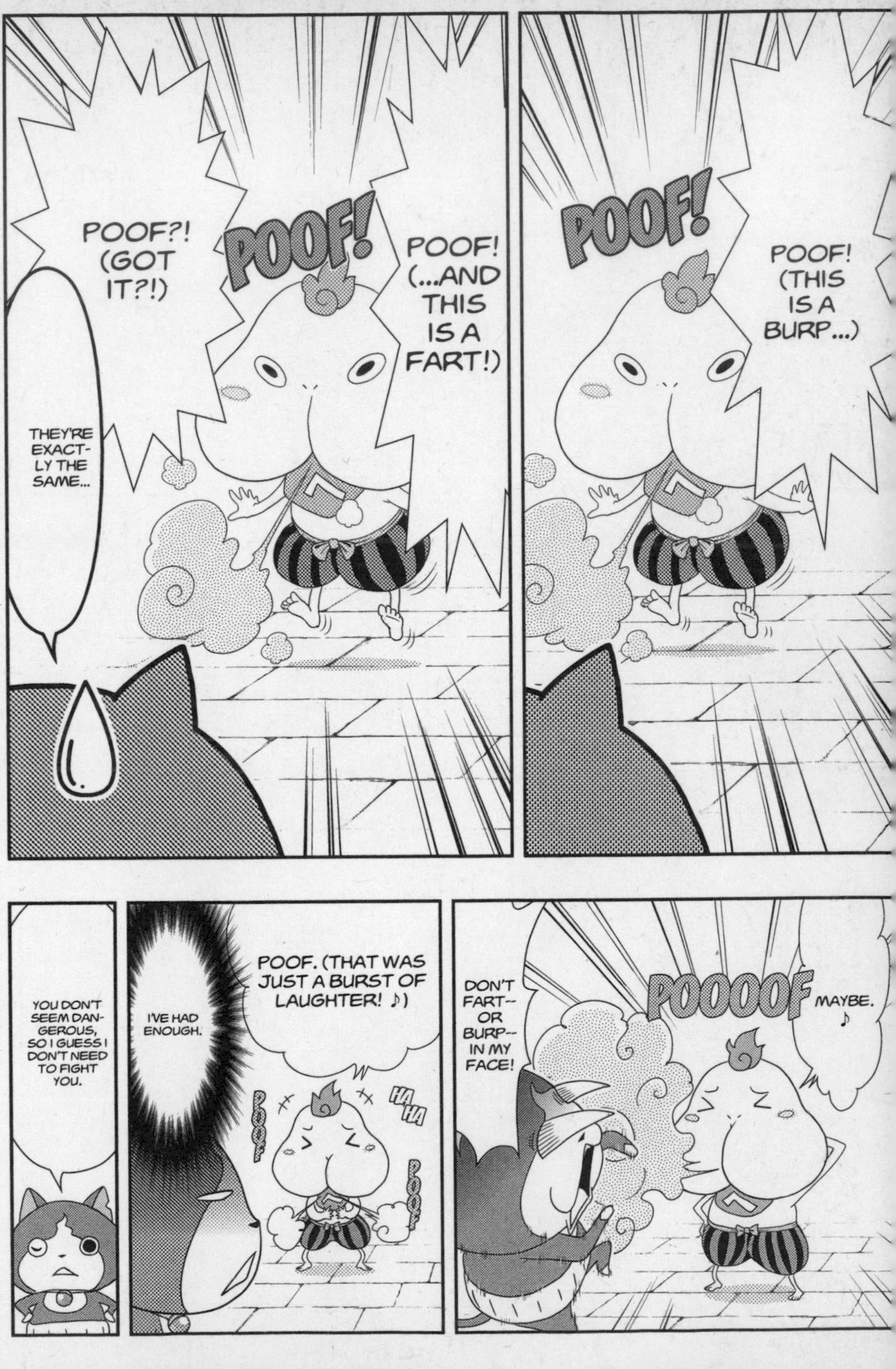
POOF!
POOF! (THIS IS A BURP...)
POOF!
POOF! (...AND THIS IS A FART!)
POOF?! (GOT IT?!)
THEY'RE EXACT-LY THE SAME...
MAYBE. ♪
POOOOF
DON'T FART-- OR BURP-- IN MY FACE!
POOF. (THAT WAS JUST A BURST OF LAUGHTER! ♪)
HA HA
POOF
POOF
I'VE HAD ENOUGH.
YOU DON'T SEEM DAN-GEROUS, SO I GUESS I DON'T NEED TO FIGHT YOU.

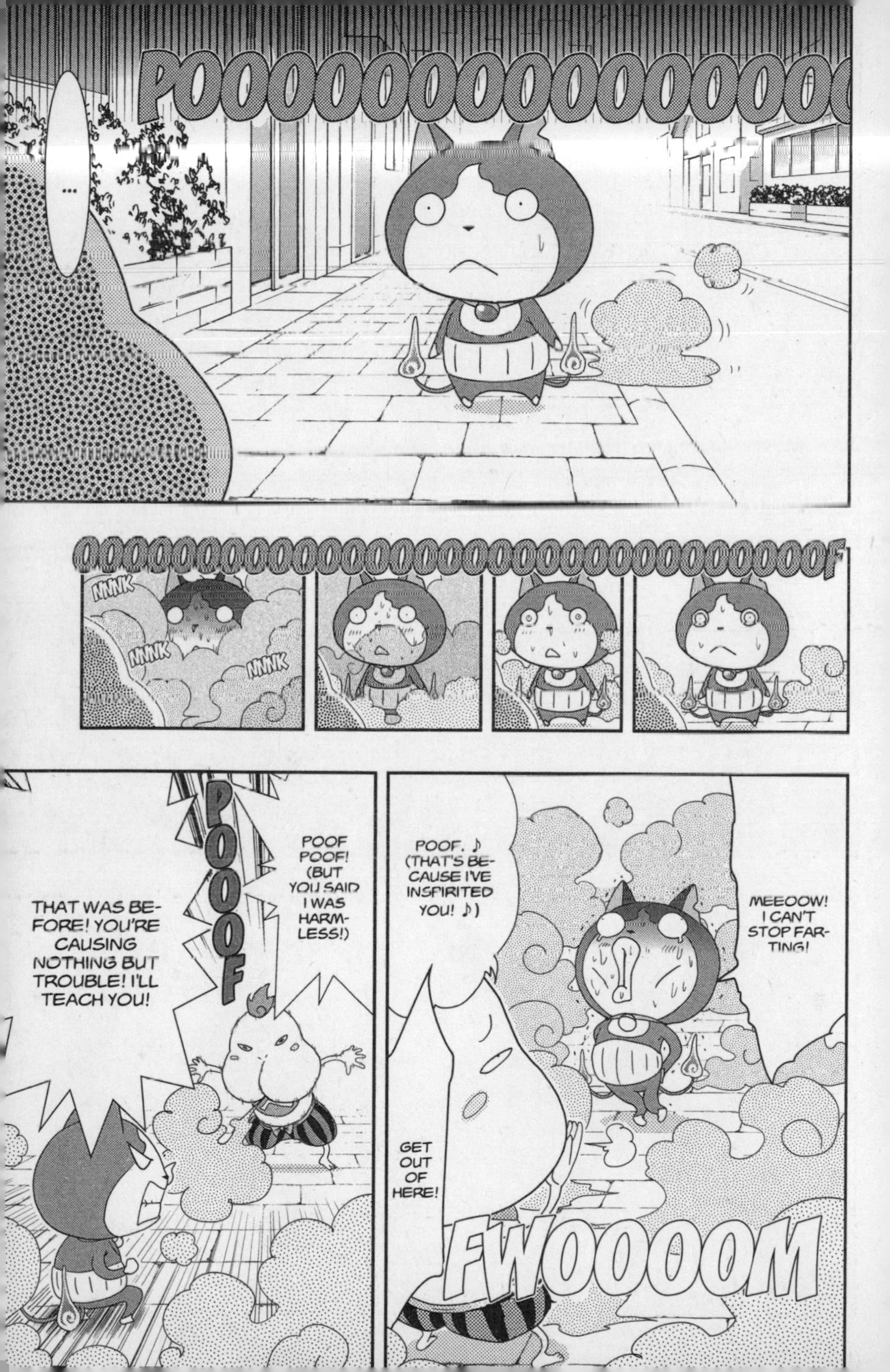
POOOOOOOOOOOOO
...
OOOOOOOOOOOOOOOOOOOOOOOOOOOOOOOF
NNNK
NNNK
NNNK
MEEOOW! I CAN'T STOP FARTING!
POOF. ♪ (THAT'S BECAUSE I'VE INSPIRITED YOU! ♪)
GET OUT OF HERE!
FWOOOOM
POOF POOF! (BUT YOU SAID I WAS HARMLESS!)
POOOF
THAT WAS BEFORE! YOU'RE CAUSING NOTHING BUT TROUBLE! I'LL TEACH YOU!

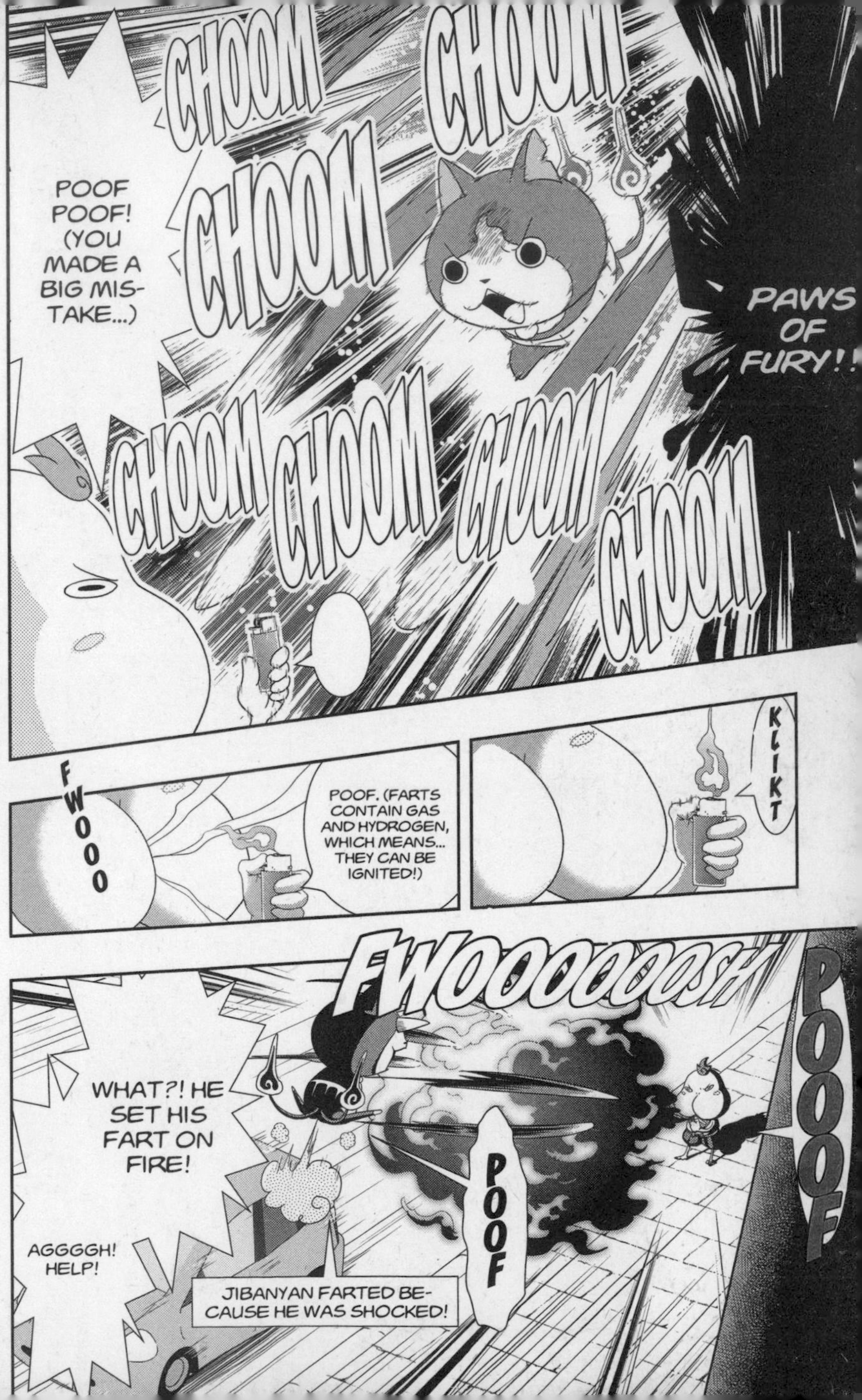
CHOOM
CHOOM
PAWS OF FURY!!
CHOOM
POOF POOF! (YOU MADE A BIG MIS-TAKE...)
CHOOM CHOOM CHOOM CHOOM
KLIKT
POOF. (FARTS CONTAIN GAS AND HYDROGEN, WHICH MEANS... THEY CAN BE IGNITED!)
FWOOO
FWOOOOOOSH
POOOF
POOF
WHAT?! HE SET HIS FART ON FIRE!
JIBANYAN FARTED BE-CAUSE HE WAS SHOCKED!
AGGGGH! HELP!

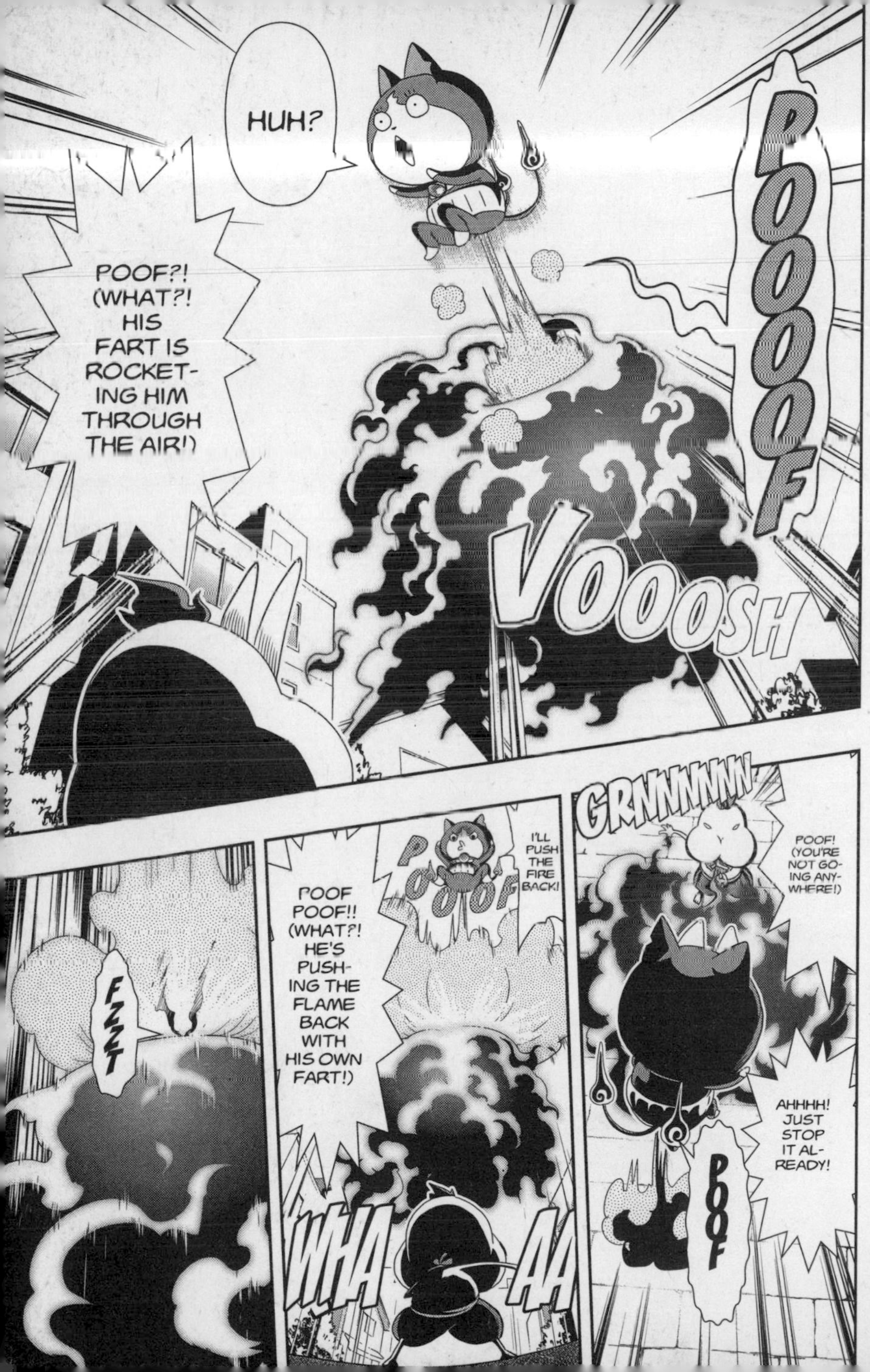
POOOOOF
HUH?
VOOOSH
POOF?! (WHAT?! HIS FART IS ROCKETING HIM THROUGH THE AIR!)
GRNNNNNN
POOF! (YOU'RE NOT GOING ANYWHERE!)
AHHHH! JUST STOP IT ALREADY!
POOF
I'LL PUSH THE FIRE BACK!
POOOF
POOF POOF!! (WHAT?! HE'S PUSHING THE FLAME BACK WITH HIS OWN FART!)
WHA
AA
FZZT

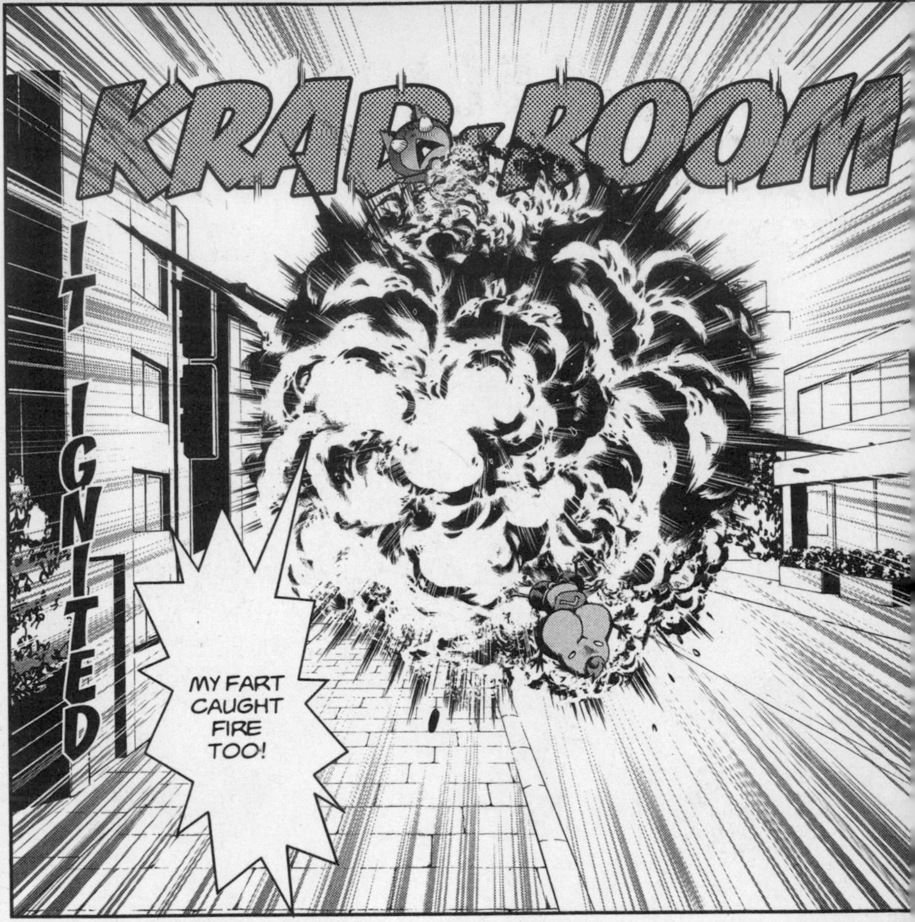
KRAB-BOOM
IT IGNITED
MY FART CAUGHT FIRE TOO!

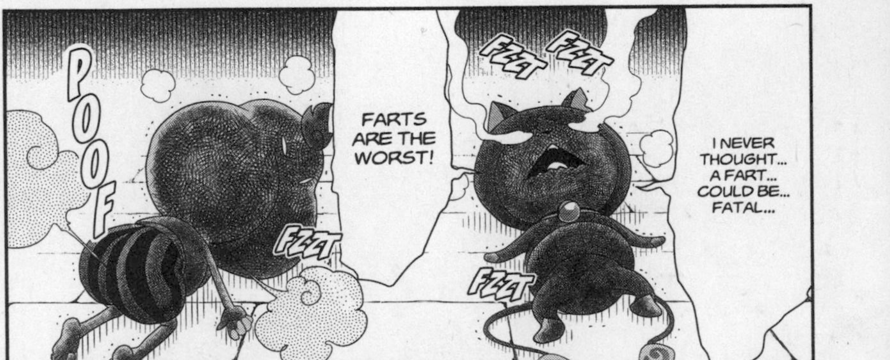
FZZT
FZZT
I NEVER THOUGHT... A FART... COULD BE... FATAL...
FZZT
FARTS ARE THE WORST!
FZZT
POOF

CHAPTER 51: I CAN READ YOU LIKE A BOOK!

FEATURING MIND-READING YO-KAI ESPY

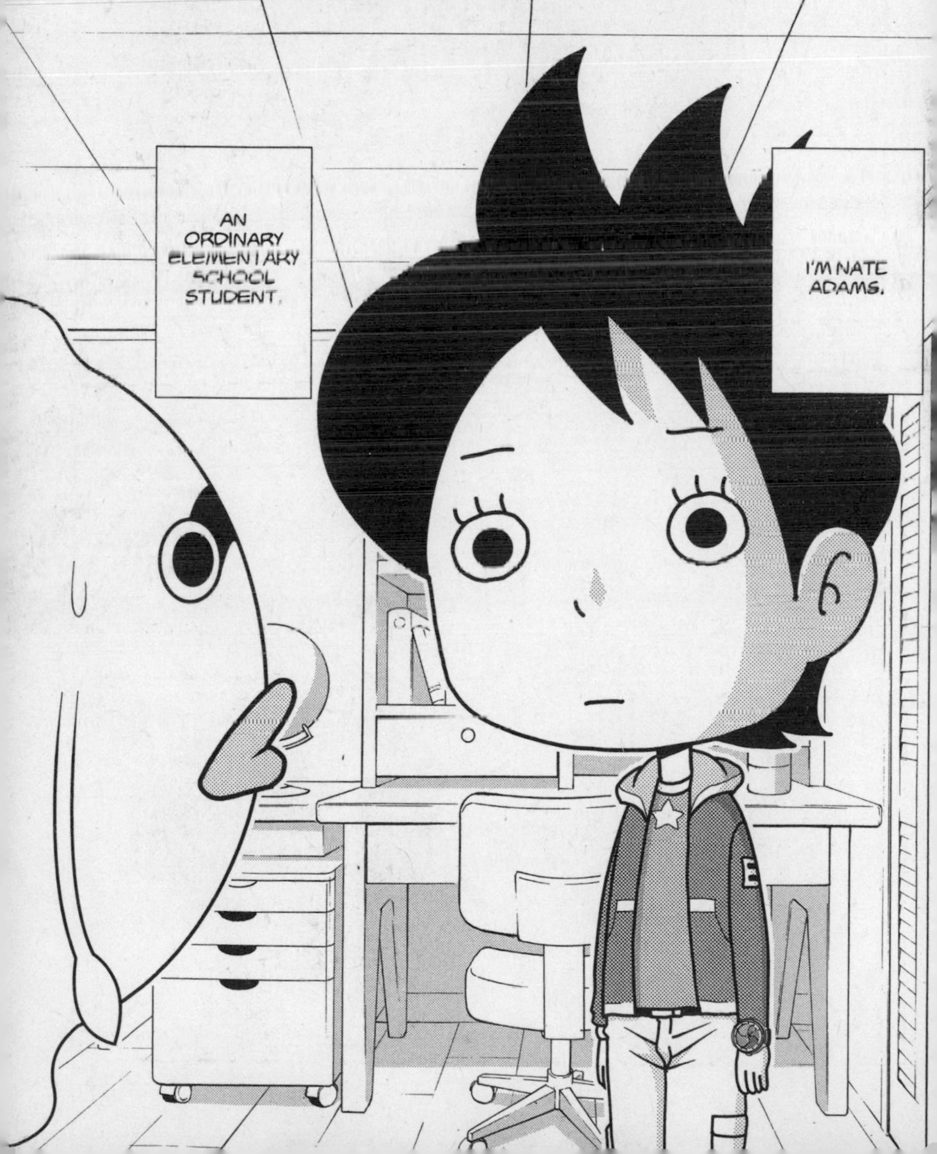
I'M NATE ADAMS.
AN ORDINARY ELEMENTARY SCHOOL STUDENT.

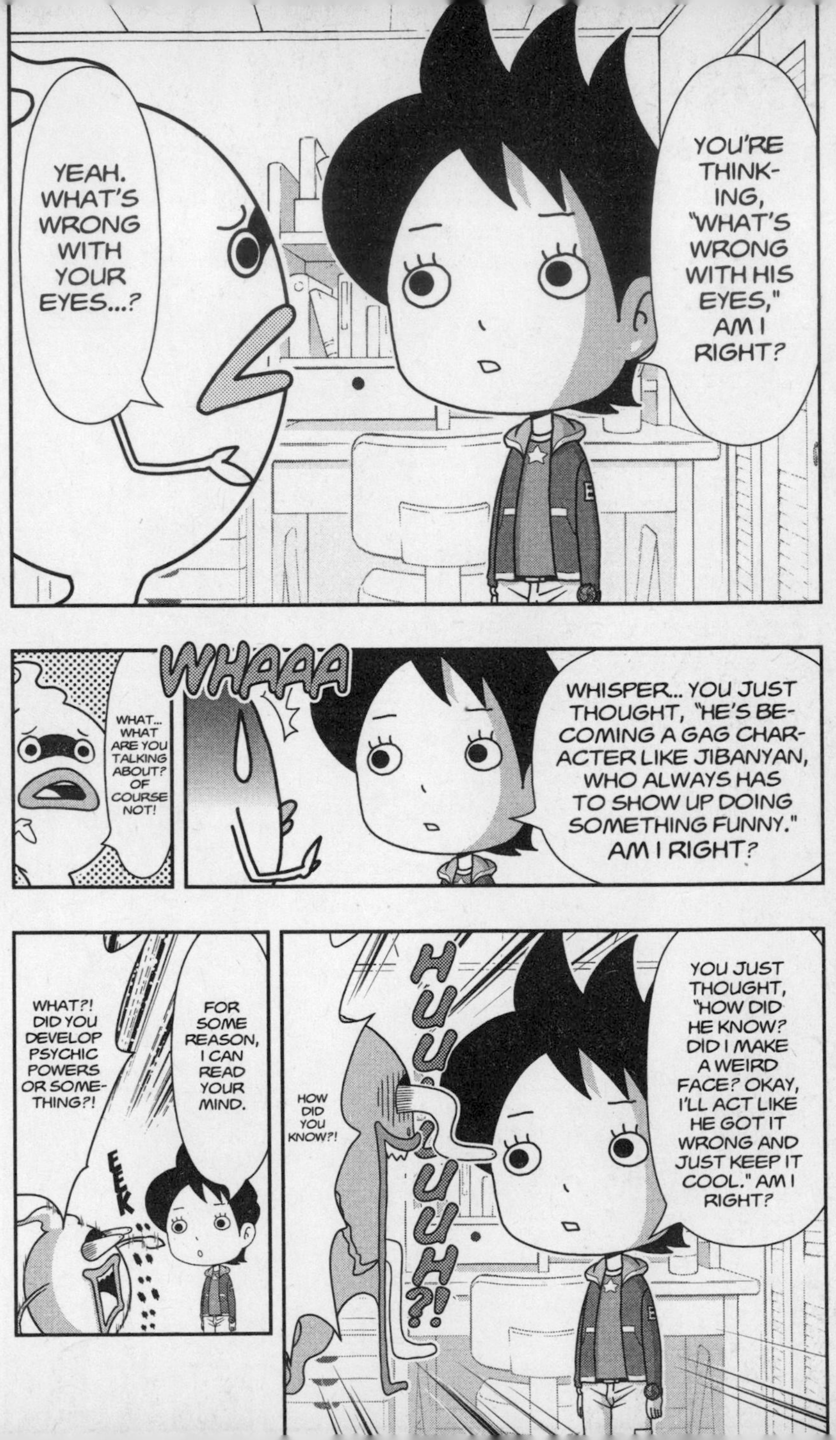
YOU'RE THINKING, "WHAT'S WRONG WITH HIS EYES," AM I RIGHT?
YEAH. WHAT'S WRONG WITH YOUR EYES...?
WHISPER... YOU JUST THOUGHT, "HE'S BECOMING A GAG CHARACTER LIKE JIBANYAN, WHO ALWAYS HAS TO SHOW UP DOING SOMETHING FUNNY." AM I RIGHT?
WHAAA
WHAT... WHAT ARE YOU TALKING ABOUT? OF COURSE NOT!
YOU JUST THOUGHT, "HOW DID HE KNOW? DID I MAKE A WEIRD FACE? OKAY, I'LL ACT LIKE HE GOT IT WRONG AND JUST KEEP IT COOL." AM I RIGHT?
HUUUUUH?!
HOW DID YOU KNOW?!
FOR SOME REASON, I CAN READ YOUR MIND.
WHAT?! DID YOU DEVELOP PSYCHIC POWERS OR SOMETHING?!
EEK

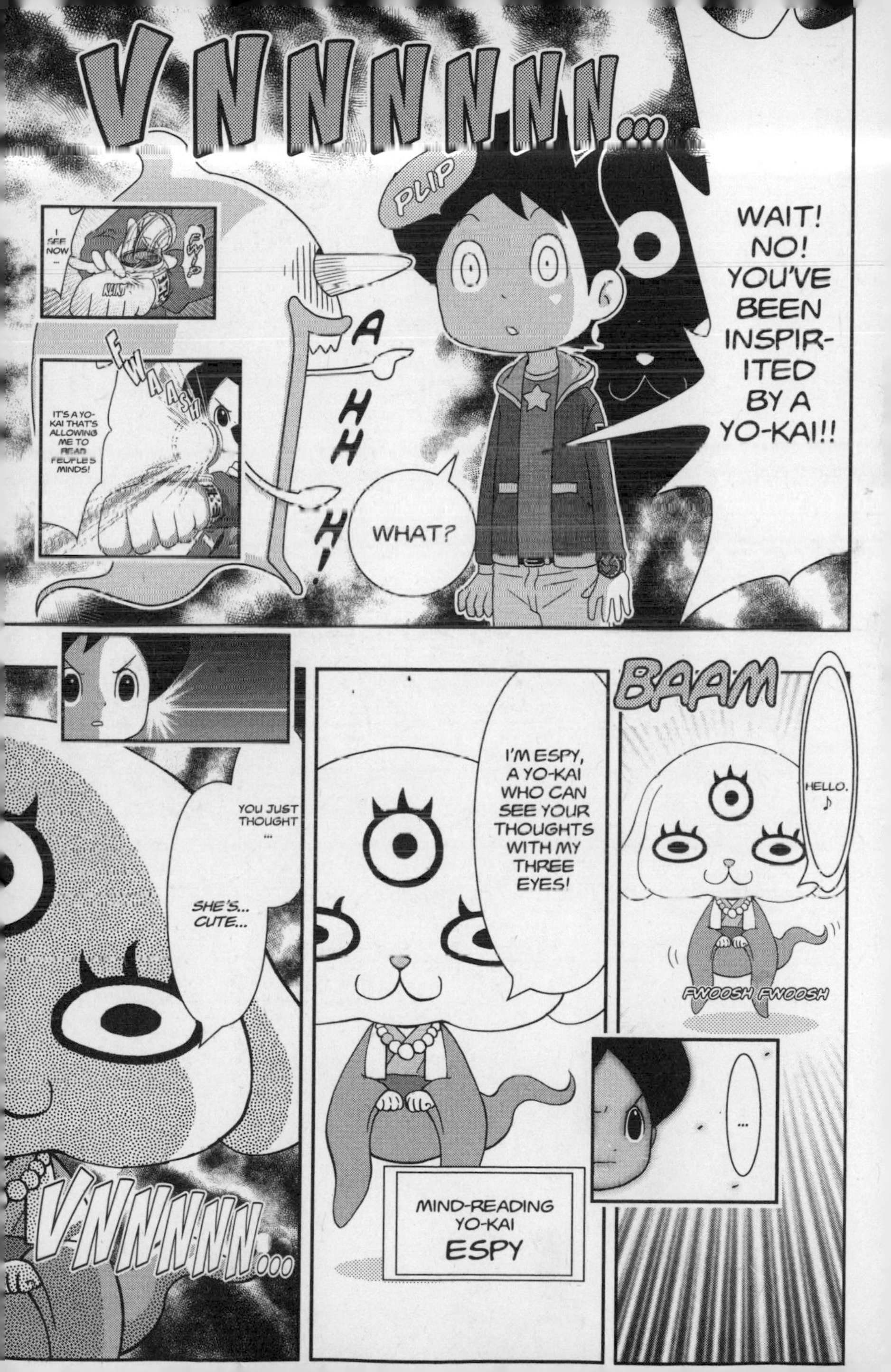

VNNNNNN...
PLIP
WAIT! NO! YOU'VE BEEN INSPIRITED BY A YO-KAI!!
WHAT?
AHHH!
I SEE NOW...
FWAASH
IT'S A YO-KAI THAT'S ALLOWING ME TO READ PEOPLE'S MINDS!
BAAM
HELLO. ♪
FWOOSH FWOOSH
...
I'M ESPY, A YO-KAI WHO CAN SEE YOUR THOUGHTS WITH MY THREE EYES!
MIND-READING YO-KAI ESPY
YOU JUST THOUGHT...
SHE'S... CUTE...
VNNNNNN...

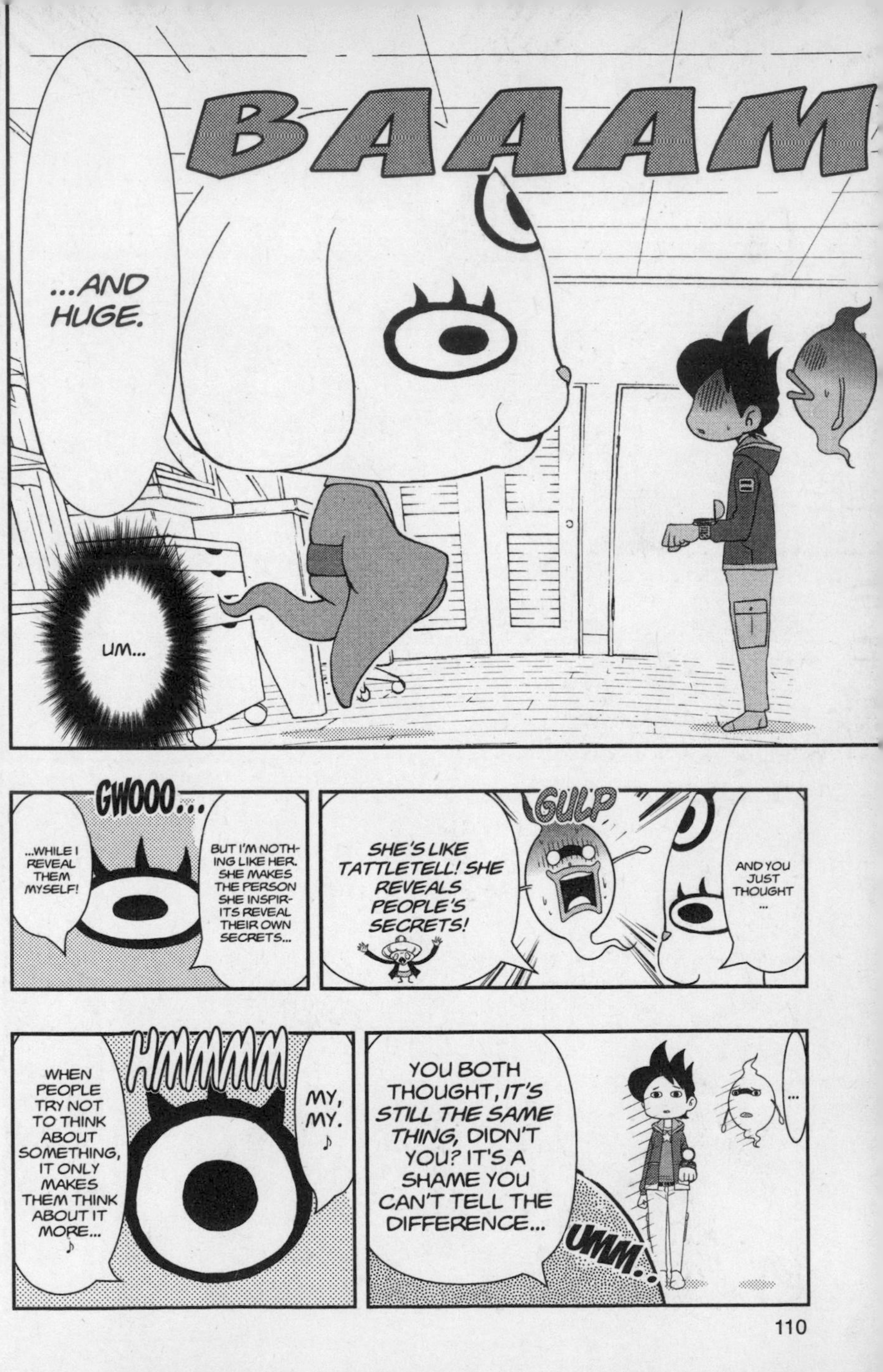
BAAAM
...AND HUGE.
UM...
AND YOU JUST THOUGHT ...
GULP
SHE'S LIKE TATTLETELL! SHE REVEALS PEOPLE'S SECRETS!
GWOOO...
BUT I'M NOTHING LIKE HER. SHE MAKES THE PERSON SHE INSPIRITS REVEAL THEIR OWN SECRETS...
...WHILE I REVEAL THEM MYSELF!
...
YOU BOTH THOUGHT, *IT'S STILL THE SAME THING*, DIDN'T YOU? IT'S A SHAME YOU CAN'T TELL THE DIFFERENCE...
UMM...
HMMMM
MY, MY. ♪
WHEN PEOPLE TRY NOT TO THINK ABOUT SOMETHING, IT ONLY MAKES THEM THINK ABOUT IT MORE... ♪

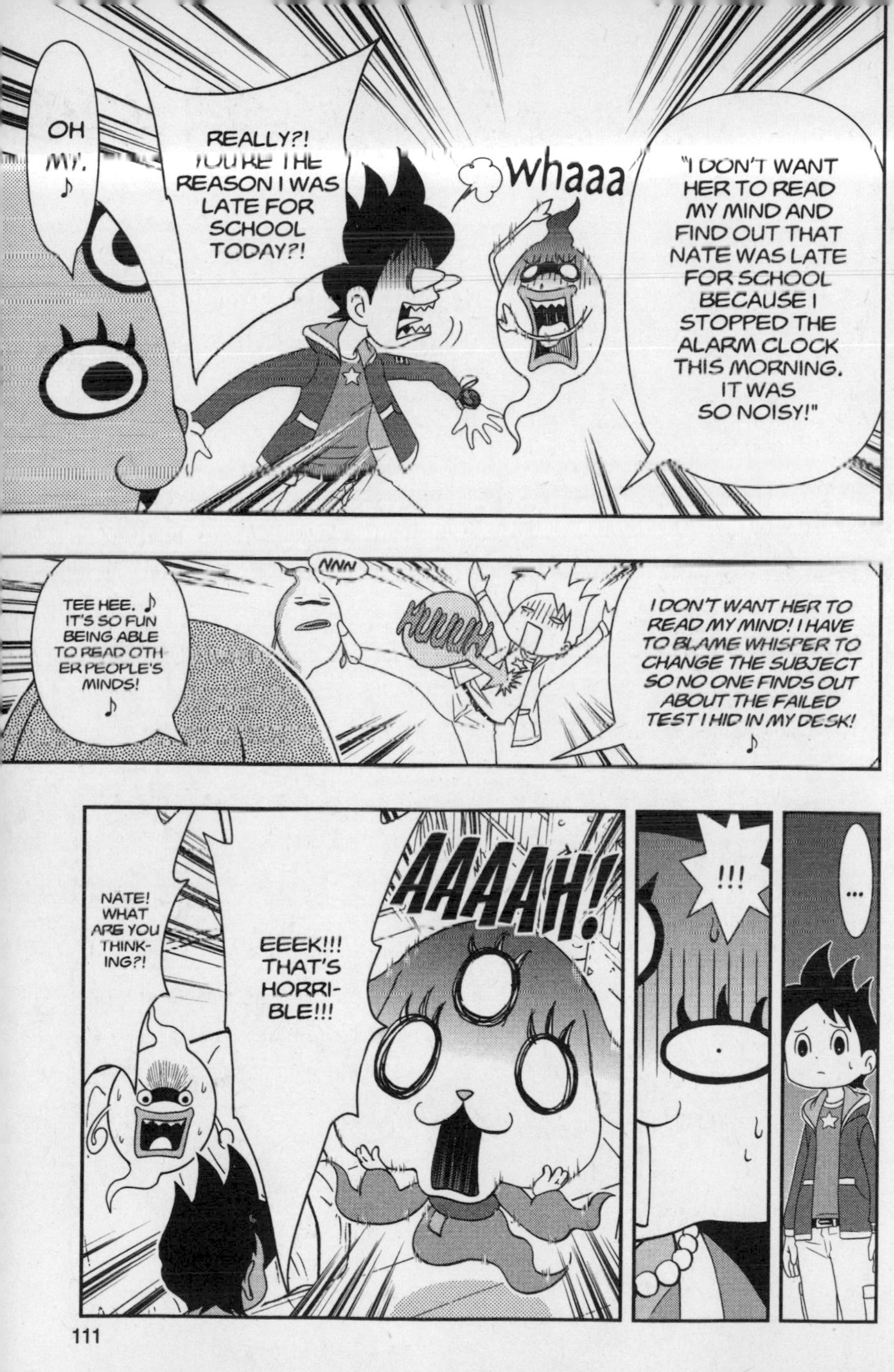

"I DON'T WANT HER TO READ MY MIND AND FIND OUT THAT NATE WAS LATE FOR SCHOOL BECAUSE I STOPPED THE ALARM CLOCK THIS MORNING. IT WAS SO NOISY!"
whaaa
REALLY?! YOU'RE THE REASON I WAS LATE FOR SCHOOL TODAY?!
OH MY. ♪
I DON'T WANT HER TO READ MY MIND! I HAVE TO BLAME WHISPER TO CHANGE THE SUBJECT SO NO ONE FINDS OUT ABOUT THE FAILED TEST I HID IN MY DESK! ♪
NNN
TEE HEE. ♪ IT'S SO FUN BEING ABLE TO READ OTHER PEOPLE'S MINDS! ♪
...
!!!
AAAAH!
EEEK!!! THAT'S HORRIBLE!!!
NATE! WHAT ARE YOU THINKING?!

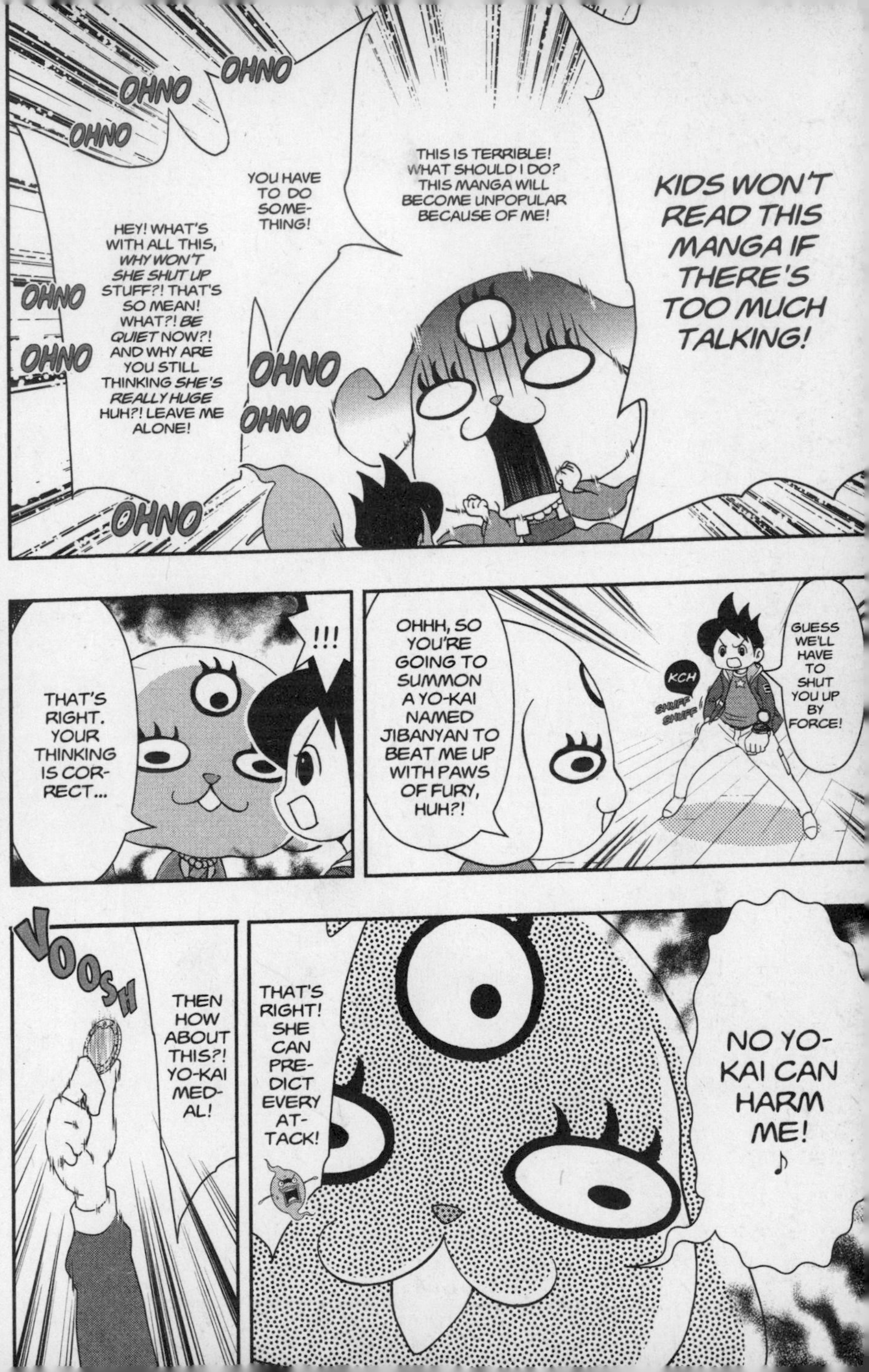
KIDS WON'T READ THIS MANGA IF THERE'S TOO MUCH TALKING!
THIS IS TERRIBLE! WHAT SHOULD I DO? THIS MANGA WILL BECOME UNPOPULAR BECAUSE OF ME!
YOU HAVE TO DO SOMETHING!
HEY! WHAT'S WITH ALL THIS, *WHY WON'T SHE SHUT UP* STUFF?! THAT'S SO MEAN! WHAT?! *BE QUIET* NOW?! AND WHY ARE YOU STILL THINKING *SHE'S REALLY HUGE* HUH?! LEAVE ME ALONE!
OHNO OHNO OHNO OHNO OHNO OHNO OHNO OHNO
GUESS WE'LL HAVE TO SHUT YOU UP BY FORCE!
KCH
SHUFF SHUFF
OHHH, SO YOU'RE GOING TO SUMMON A YO-KAI NAMED JIBANYAN TO BEAT ME UP WITH PAWS OF FURY, HUH?!
!!!
THAT'S RIGHT. YOUR THINKING IS CORRECT...
NO YO-KAI CAN HARM ME! ♪
THAT'S RIGHT! SHE CAN PREDICT EVERY ATTACK!
THEN HOW ABOUT THIS?! YO-KAI MEDAL!
VOOSH

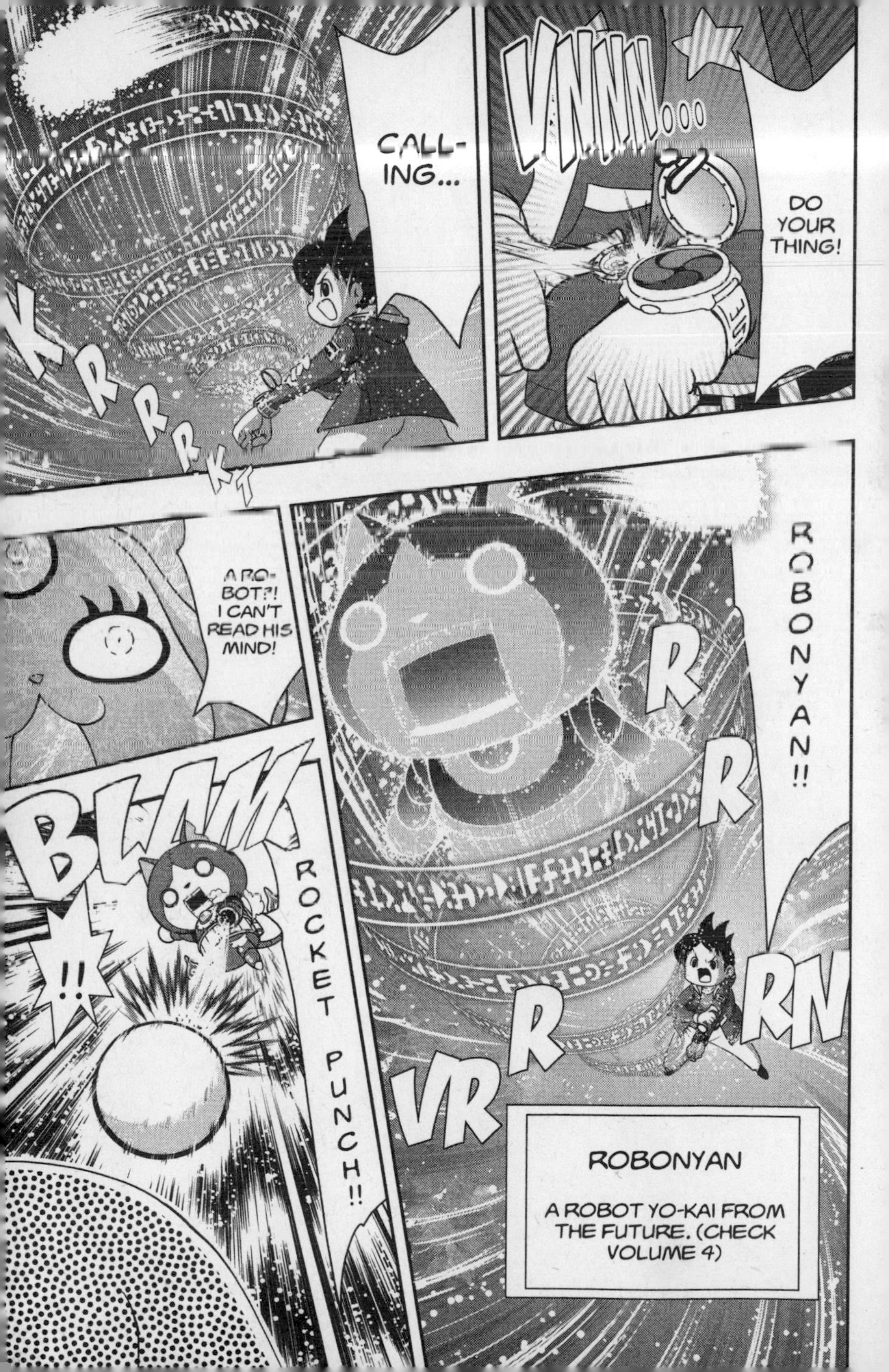
VNNNN...
DO YOUR THING!
CALLING...
KRRRRKT
ROBONYAN!!
RRR
VRRRN
ROBONYAN
A ROBOT YO-KAI FROM THE FUTURE. (CHECK VOLUME 4)
A RO-BOT?! I CAN'T READ HIS MIND!
BLAM
!!
ROCKET PUNCH!!

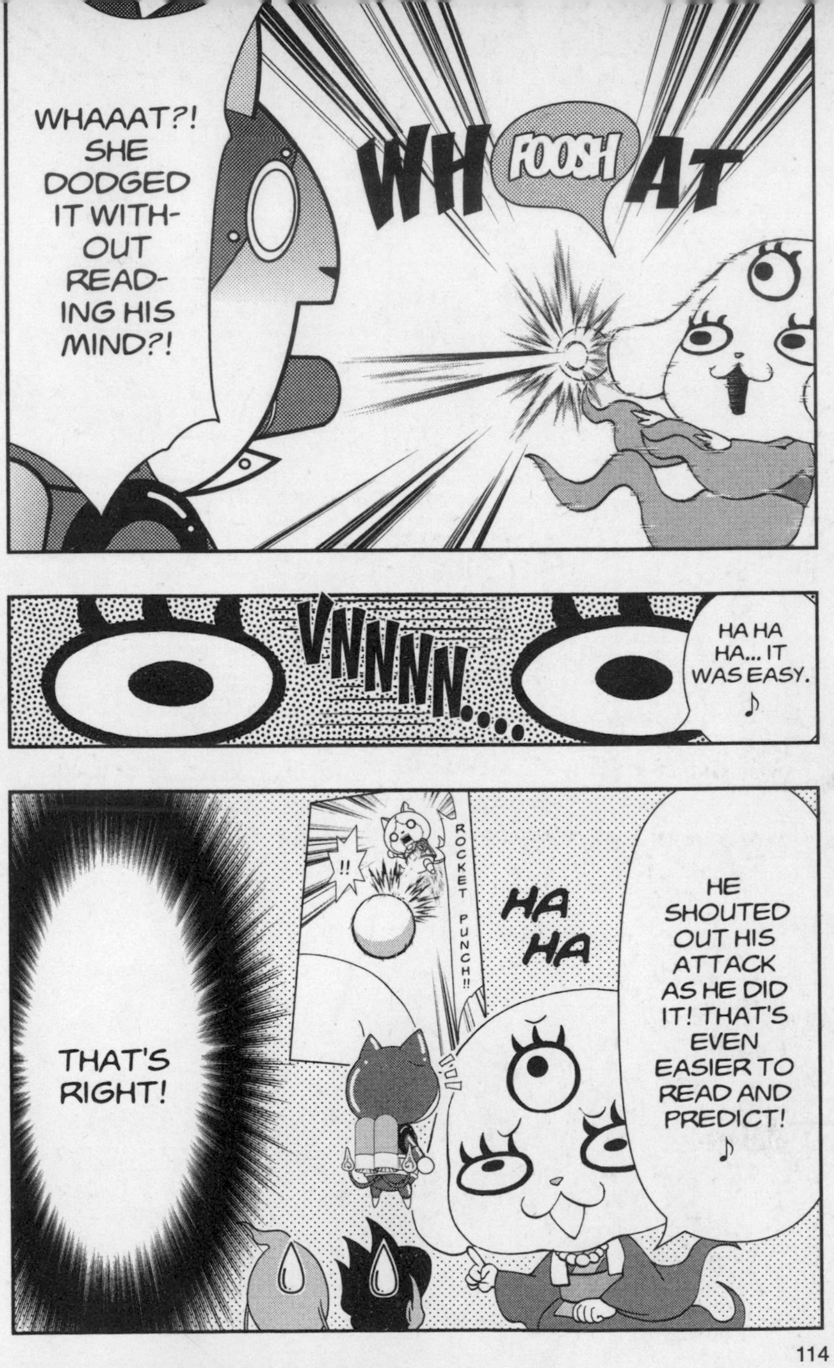
WH AT
FOOSH
WHAAAT?! SHE DODGED IT WITH-OUT READ-ING HIS MIND?!
HA HA HA... IT WAS EASY. ♪
VNNNN....
HE SHOUTED OUT HIS ATTACK AS HE DID IT! THAT'S EVEN EASIER TO READ AND PREDICT! ♪
HA HA
ROCKET PUNCH!!
!!
THAT'S RIGHT!

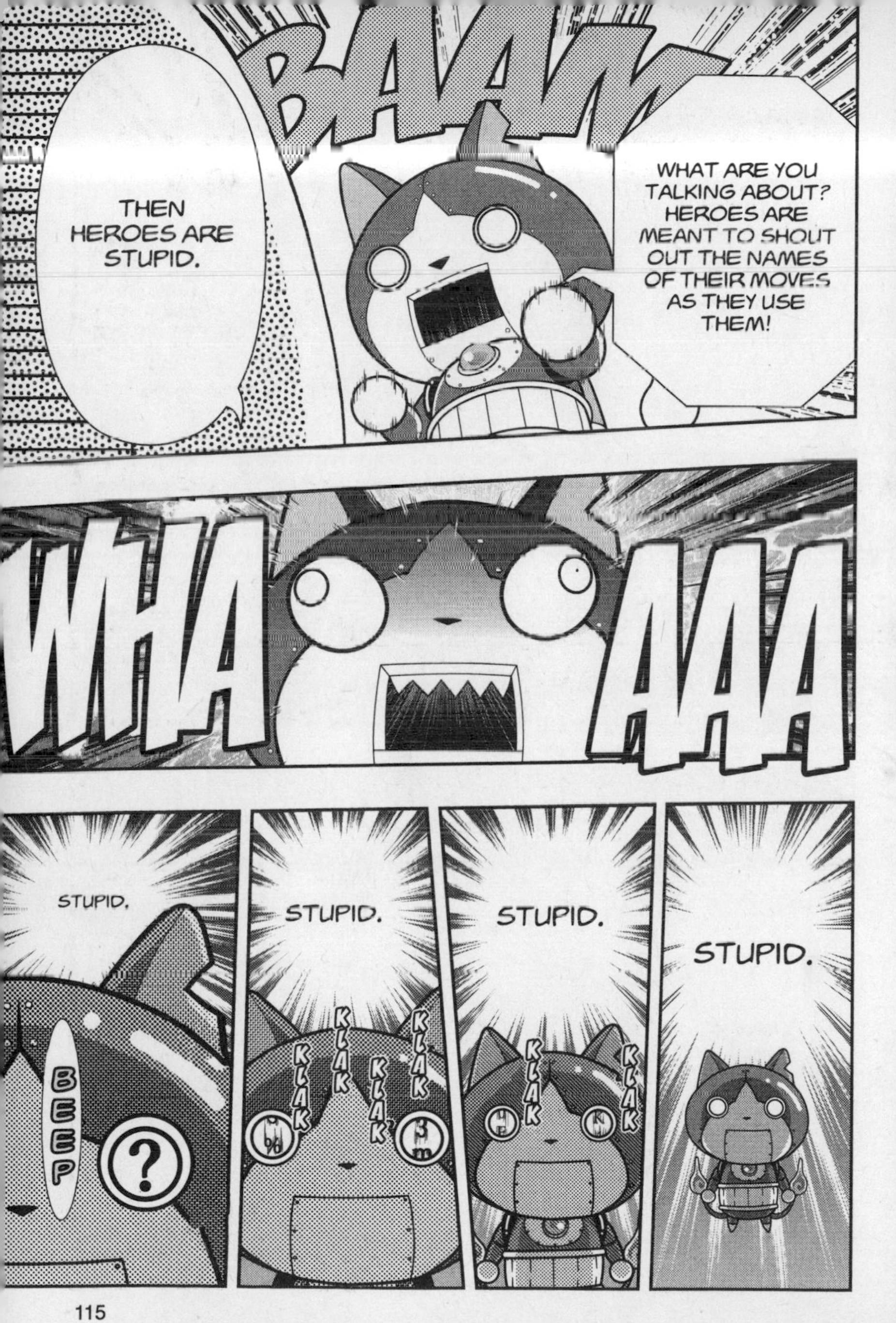
WHAT ARE YOU TALKING ABOUT? HEROES ARE MEANT TO SHOUT OUT THE NAMES OF THEIR MOVES AS THEY USE THEM!
BAAM
THEN HEROES ARE STUPID.
WHA AAA
STUPID.
STUPID.
KLAK
KLAK
STUPID.
KLAK
KLAK
KLAK
STUPID.
BEEP

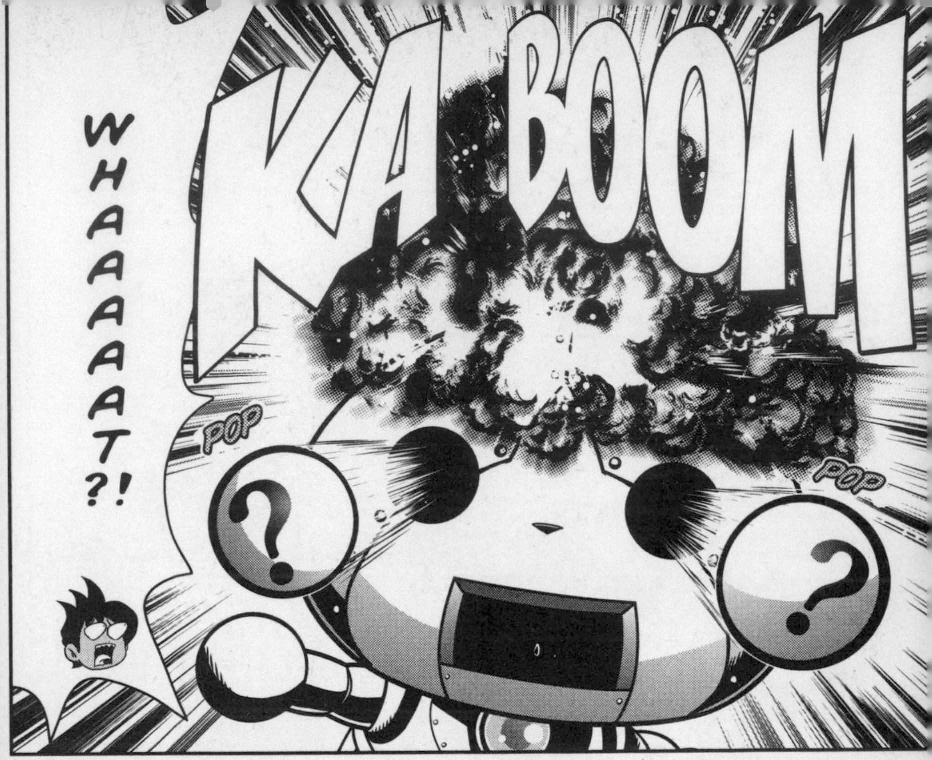
KA-BOOM
POP
POP
WHAAAAAAT?!

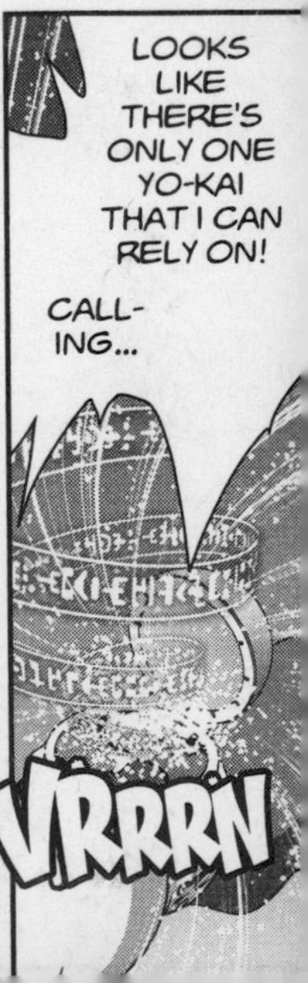
LOOKS LIKE THERE'S ONLY ONE YO-KAI THAT I CAN RELY ON!
CALLING...
VRRRN

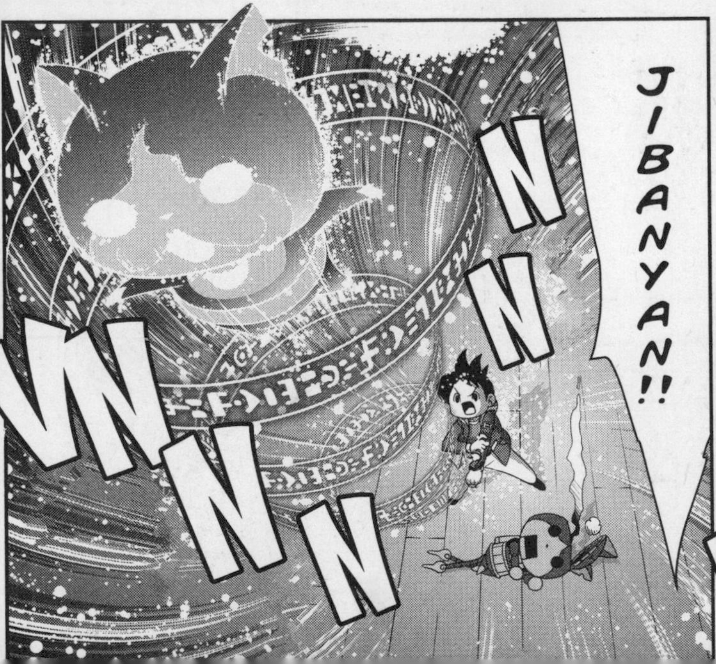
JIBANYAN!!
WNNNNN

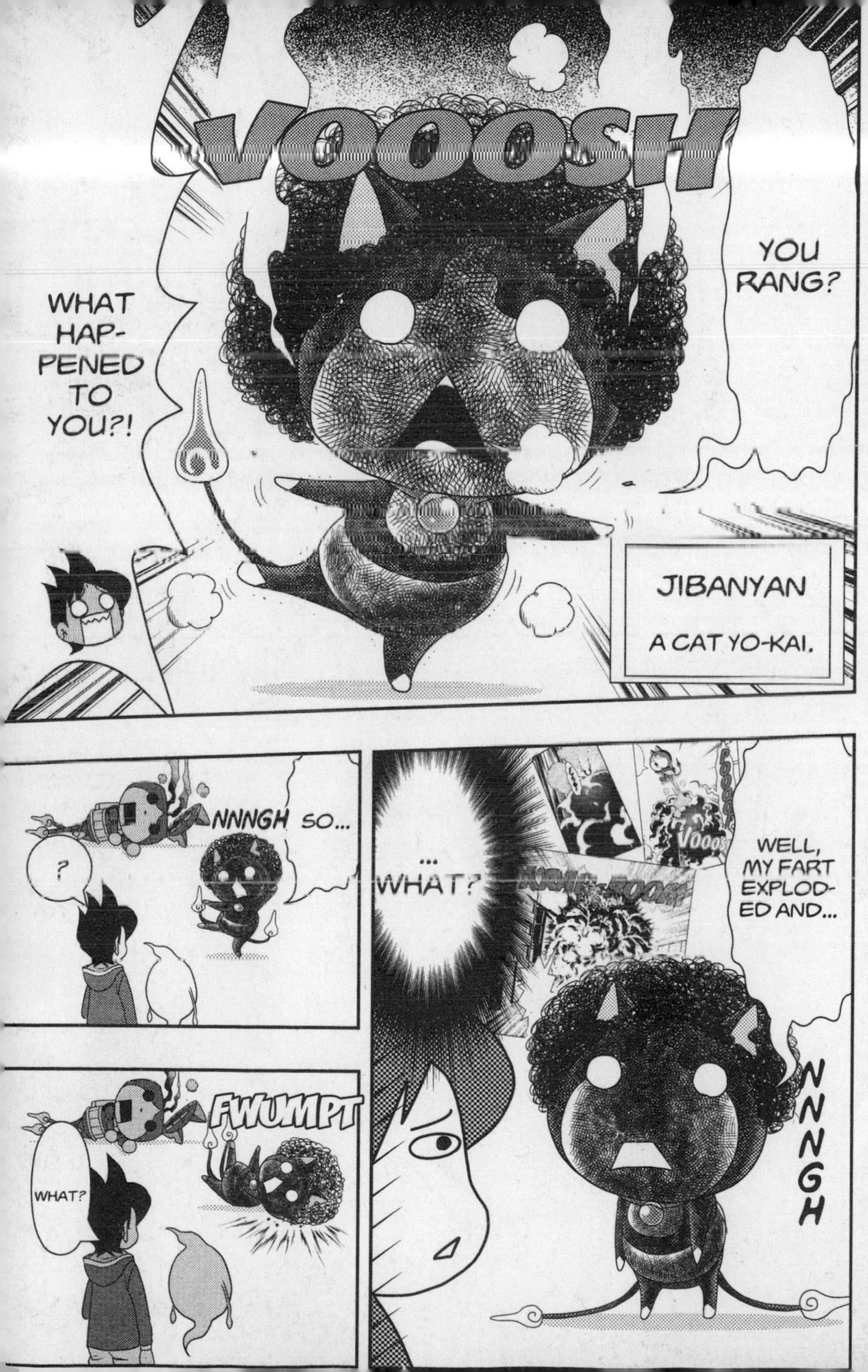
VOOSH
YOU RANG?
JIBANYAN
A CAT YO-KAI.
WHAT HAP-PENED TO YOU?!
WELL, MY FART EXPLOD-ED AND...
... WHAT?
NNNNGH
NNNGH SO...
?
FWUMPT
WHAT?

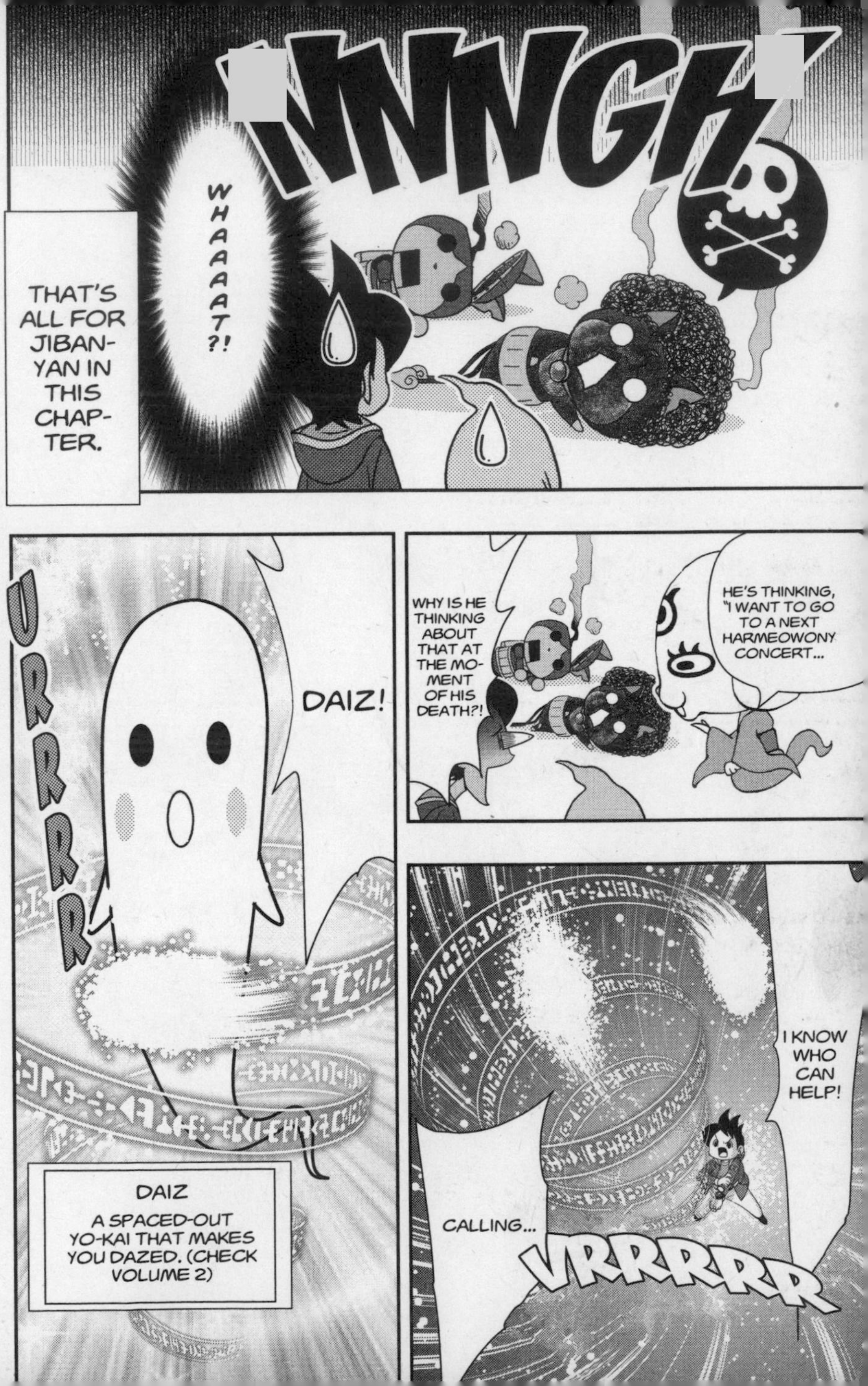
NNNGH!
WHAAAAAT?!
THAT'S ALL FOR JIBAN-YAN IN THIS CHAP-TER.
HE'S THINKING, "I WANT TO GO TO A NEXT HARMEOWONY CONCERT...
WHY IS HE THINKING ABOUT THAT AT THE MO-MENT OF HIS DEATH?!
I KNOW WHO CAN HELP!
CALLING...
VRRRRRR
URRRRR
DAIZ!
DAIZ
A SPACED-OUT YO-KAI THAT MAKES YOU DAZED. (CHECK VOLUME 2)

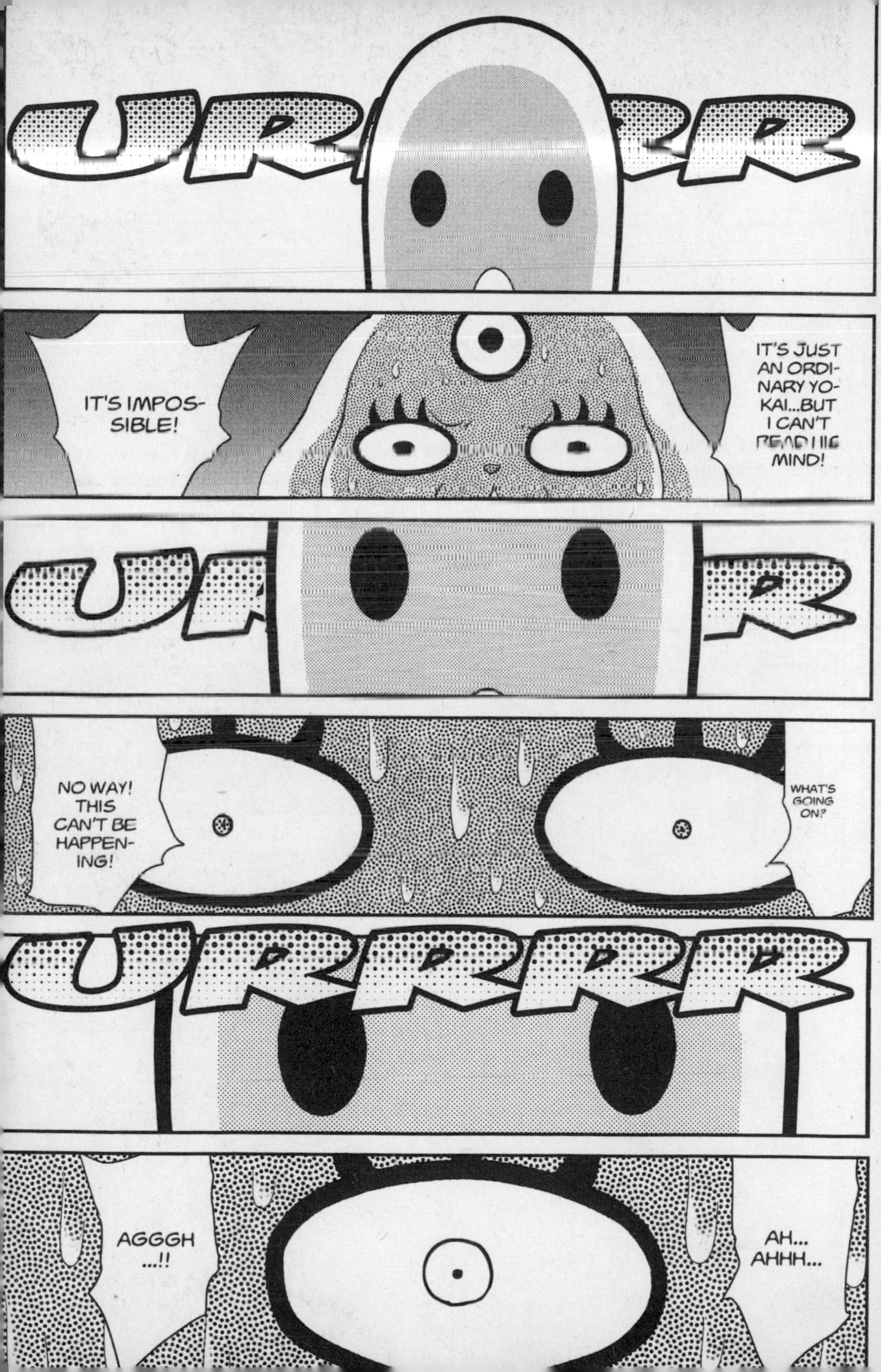
UR RR
IT'S JUST AN ORDINARY YOKAI...BUT I CAN'T READ HIS MIND!
IT'S IMPOSSIBLE!
U R
WHAT'S GOING ON?
NO WAY! THIS CAN'T BE HAPPENING!
URRRR
AH... AHHH...
AGGGH ...!!

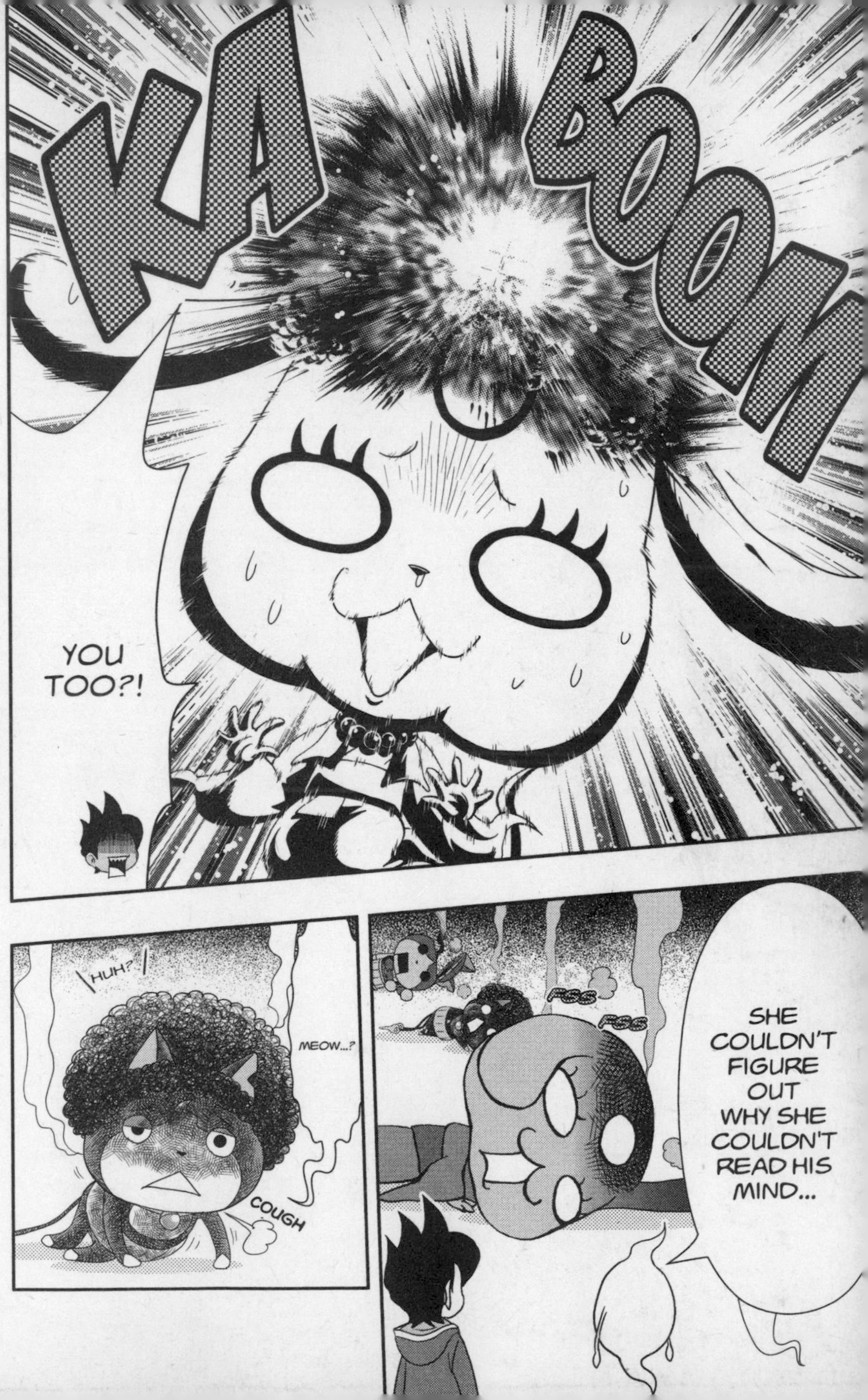
KA
BOOM
YOU TOO?!
FSS
FSS
SHE COULDN'T FIGURE OUT WHY SHE COULDN'T READ HIS MIND...
HUH?
MEOW...?
COUGH

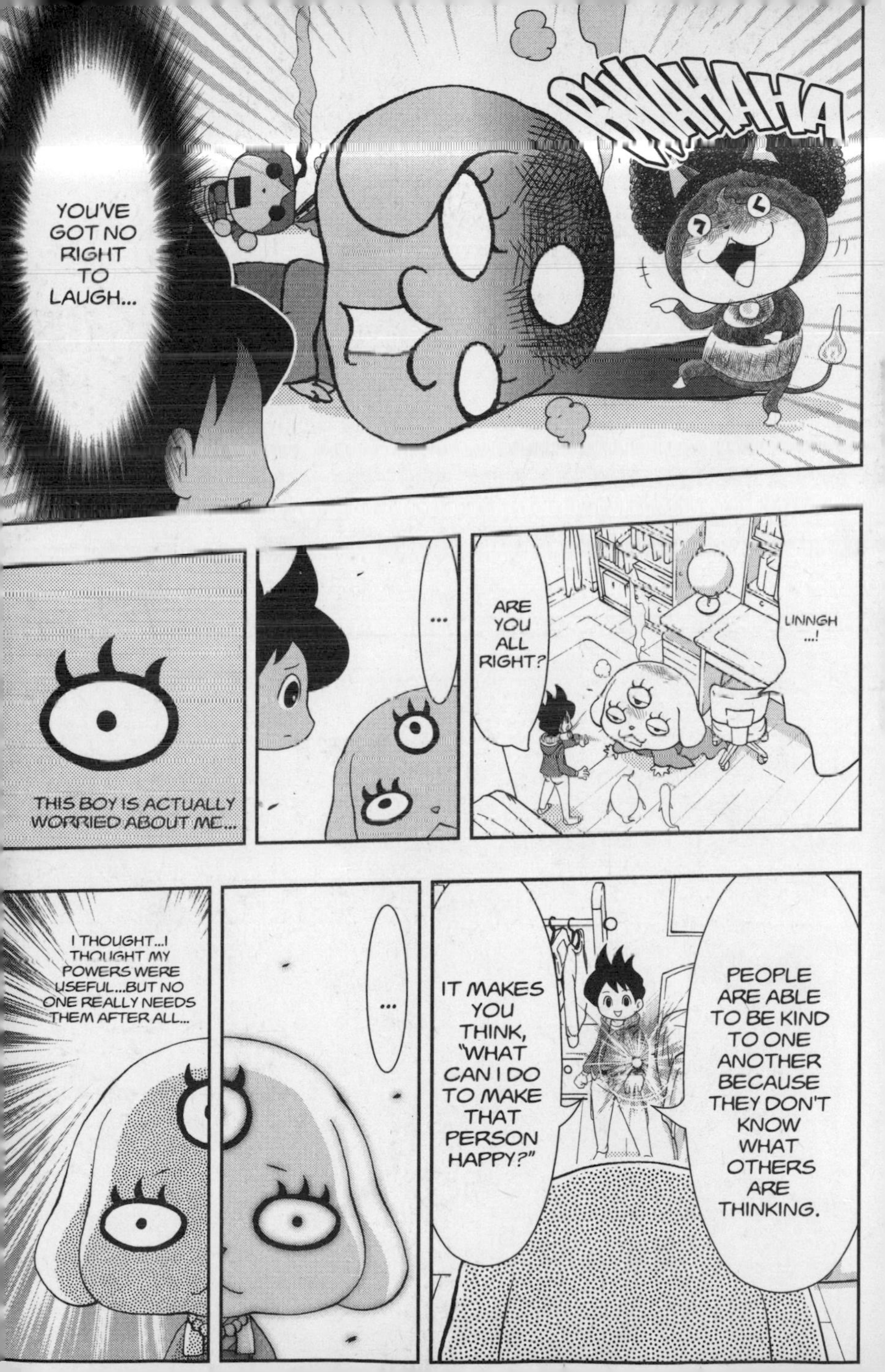
BWAHAHA
YOU'VE GOT NO RIGHT TO LAUGH...
LINNGH ...!
ARE YOU ALL RIGHT?
...
THIS BOY IS ACTUALLY WORRIED ABOUT ME...
PEOPLE ARE ABLE TO BE KIND TO ONE ANOTHER BECAUSE THEY DON'T KNOW WHAT OTHERS ARE THINKING.
IT MAKES YOU THINK, "WHAT CAN I DO TO MAKE THAT PERSON HAPPY?"
...
I THOUGHT...I THOUGHT MY POWERS WERE USEFUL...BUT NO ONE REALLY NEEDS THEM AFTER ALL...

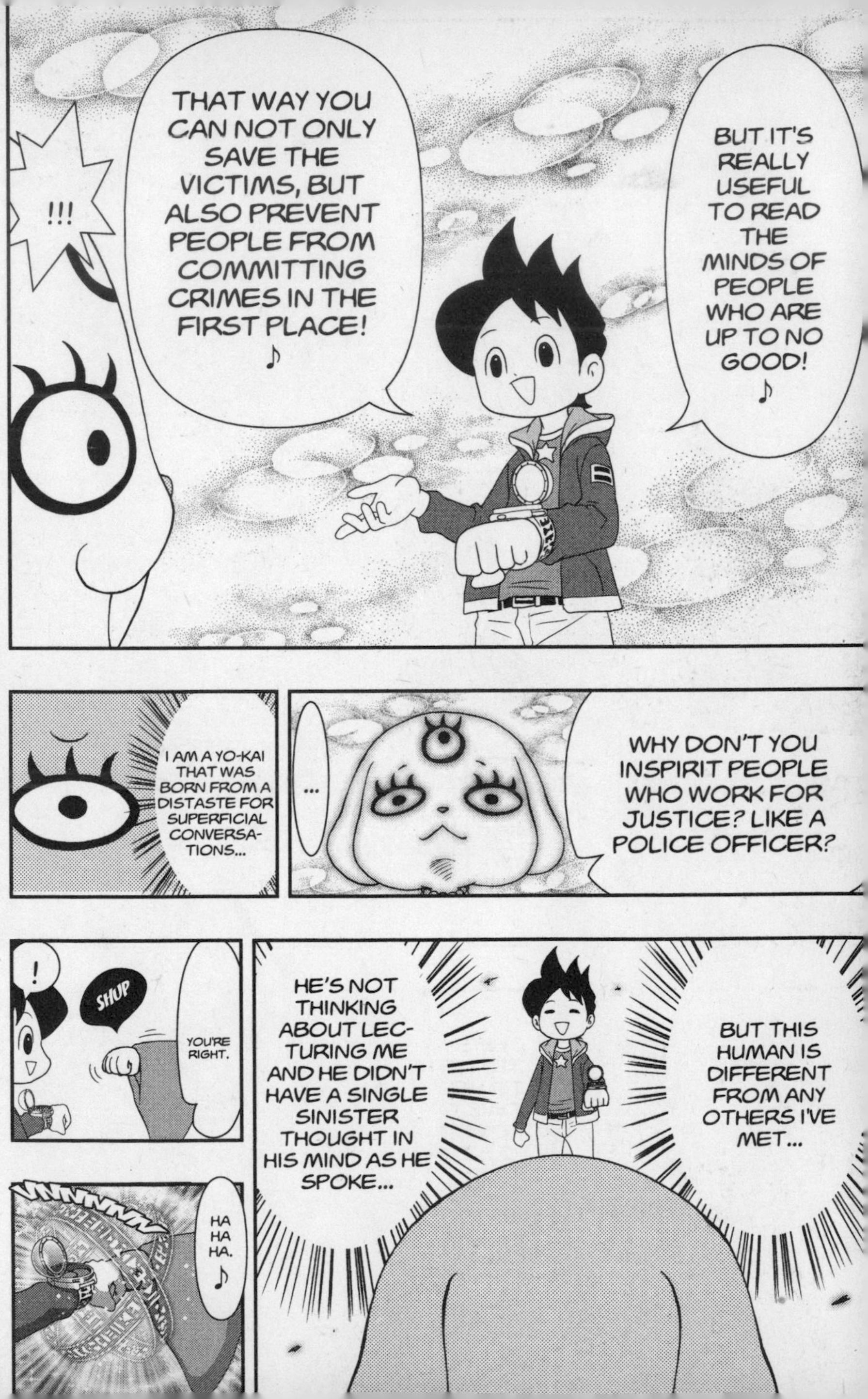
BUT IT'S REALLY USEFUL TO READ THE MINDS OF PEOPLE WHO ARE UP TO NO GOOD! ♪
THAT WAY YOU CAN NOT ONLY SAVE THE VICTIMS, BUT ALSO PREVENT PEOPLE FROM COMMITTING CRIMES IN THE FIRST PLACE! ♪
!!!
WHY DON'T YOU INSPIRIT PEOPLE WHO WORK FOR JUSTICE? LIKE A POLICE OFFICER?
...
I AM A YO-KAI THAT WAS BORN FROM A DISTASTE FOR SUPERFICIAL CONVERSA-TIONS...
BUT THIS HUMAN IS DIFFERENT FROM ANY OTHERS I'VE MET...
HE'S NOT THINKING ABOUT LEC-TURING ME AND HE DIDN'T HAVE A SINGLE SINISTER THOUGHT IN HIS MIND AS HE SPOKE...
YOU'RE RIGHT.
SHUP
!
HA HA HA. ♪

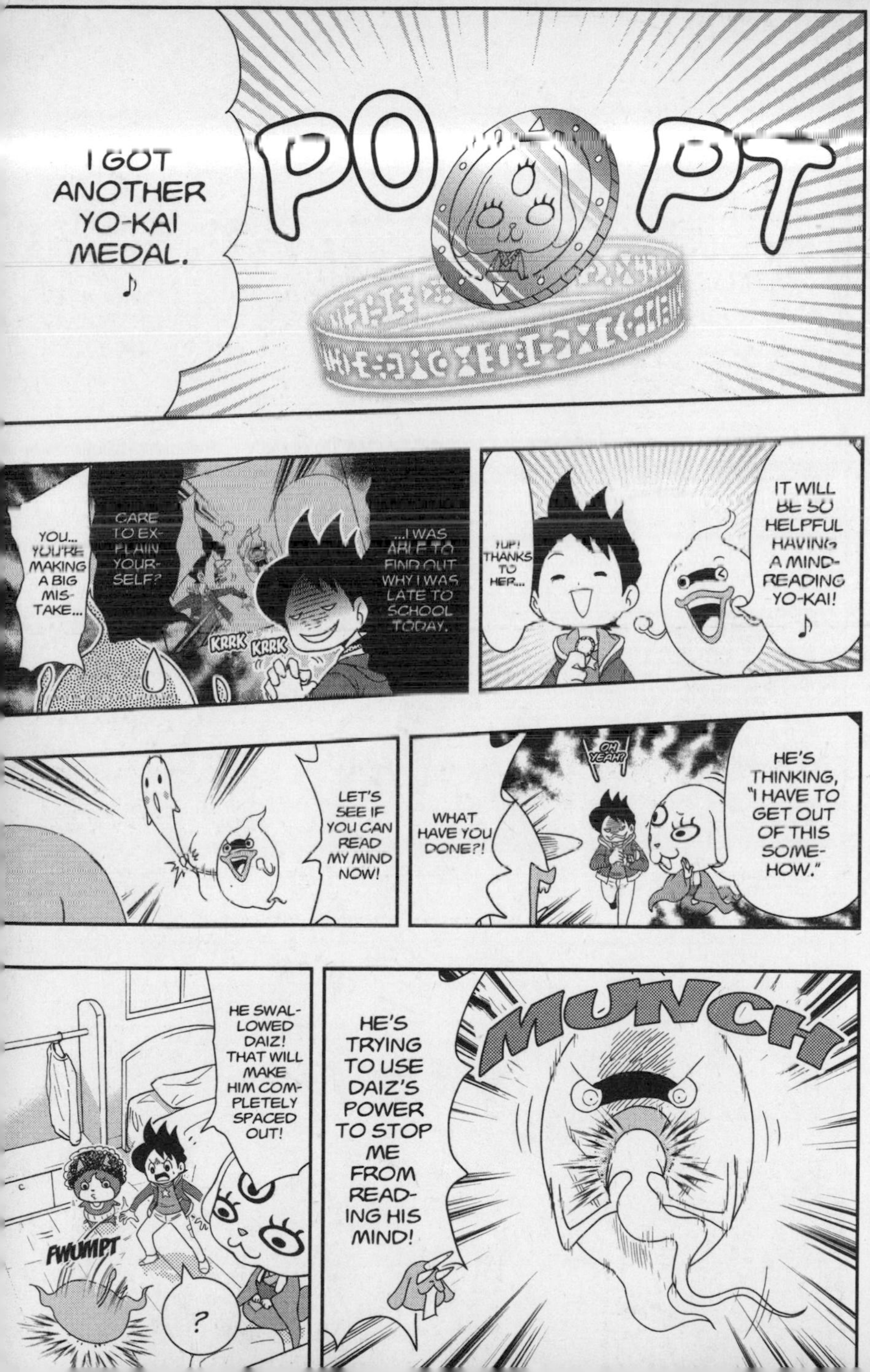
POPT
I GOT ANOTHER YO-KAI MEDAL. ♪
IT WILL BE SO HELPFUL HAVING A MIND-READING YO-KAI! ♪
YUP! THANKS TO HER...
...I WAS ABLE TO FIND OUT WHY I WAS LATE TO SCHOOL TODAY.
CARE TO EXPLAIN YOURSELF?
KRRK KRRK
YOU... YOU'RE MAKING A BIG MISTAKE...
HE'S THINKING, "I HAVE TO GET OUT OF THIS SOMEHOW."
OH YEAH?
WHAT HAVE YOU DONE?!
LET'S SEE IF YOU CAN READ MY MIND NOW!
MUNCH
HE'S TRYING TO USE DAIZ'S POWER TO STOP ME FROM READING HIS MIND!
HE SWALLOWED DAIZ! THAT WILL MAKE HIM COMPLETELY SPACED OUT!
FWUMPT
?

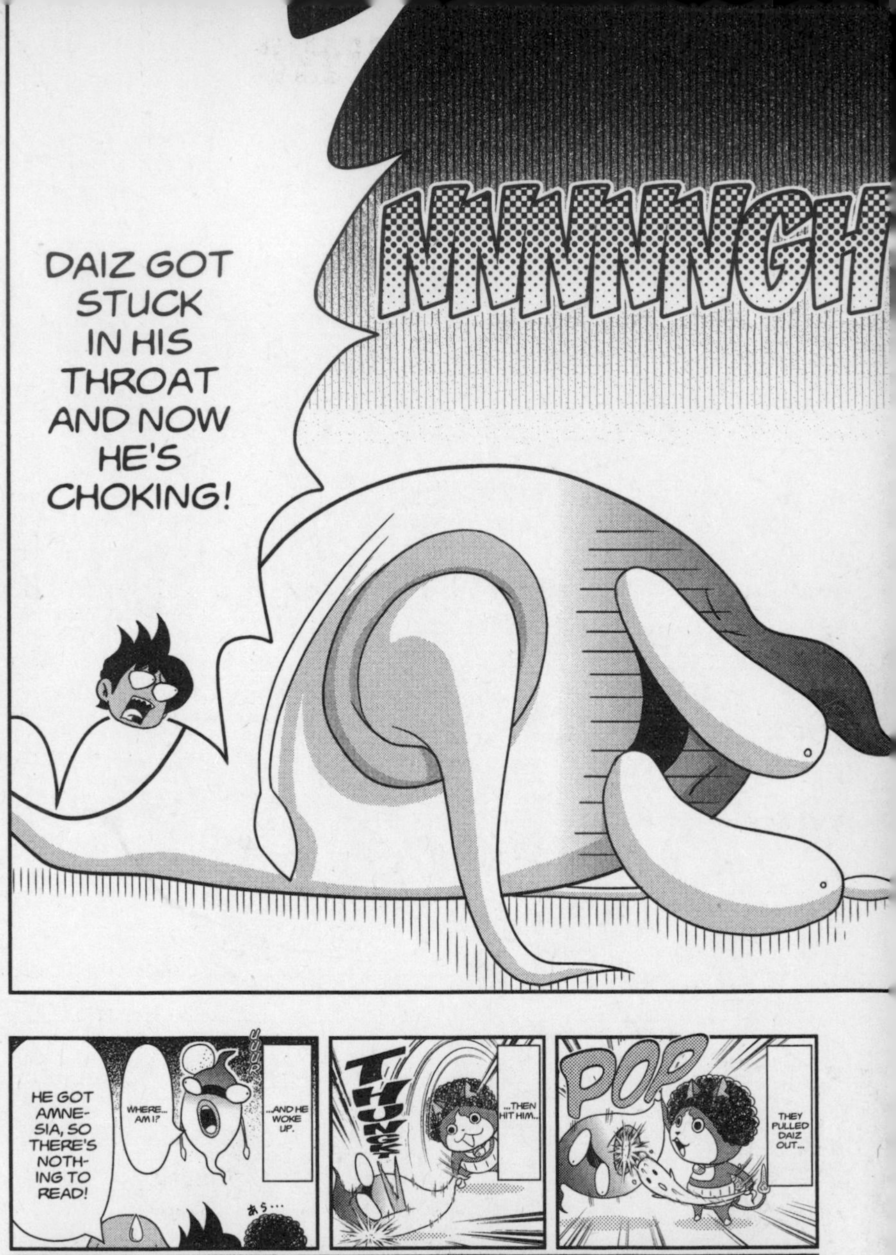
MNNNNNGH
DAIZ GOT STUCK IN HIS THROAT AND NOW HE'S CHOKING!
POP
THEY PULLED DAIZ OUT...
...THEN HIT HIM...
THUNK
...AND HE WOKE UP.
UUUR
WHERE... AM I?
HE GOT AMNE-SIA, SO THERE'S NOTH-ING TO READ!
あら…

NATE ADAMS'S CURRENT NUMBER OF YO-KAI FRIENDS: 41.

CHAPTER 52: A CHILLING TALE!

FEATURING SHIVERING-COLD YO-KAI PUPSICLE

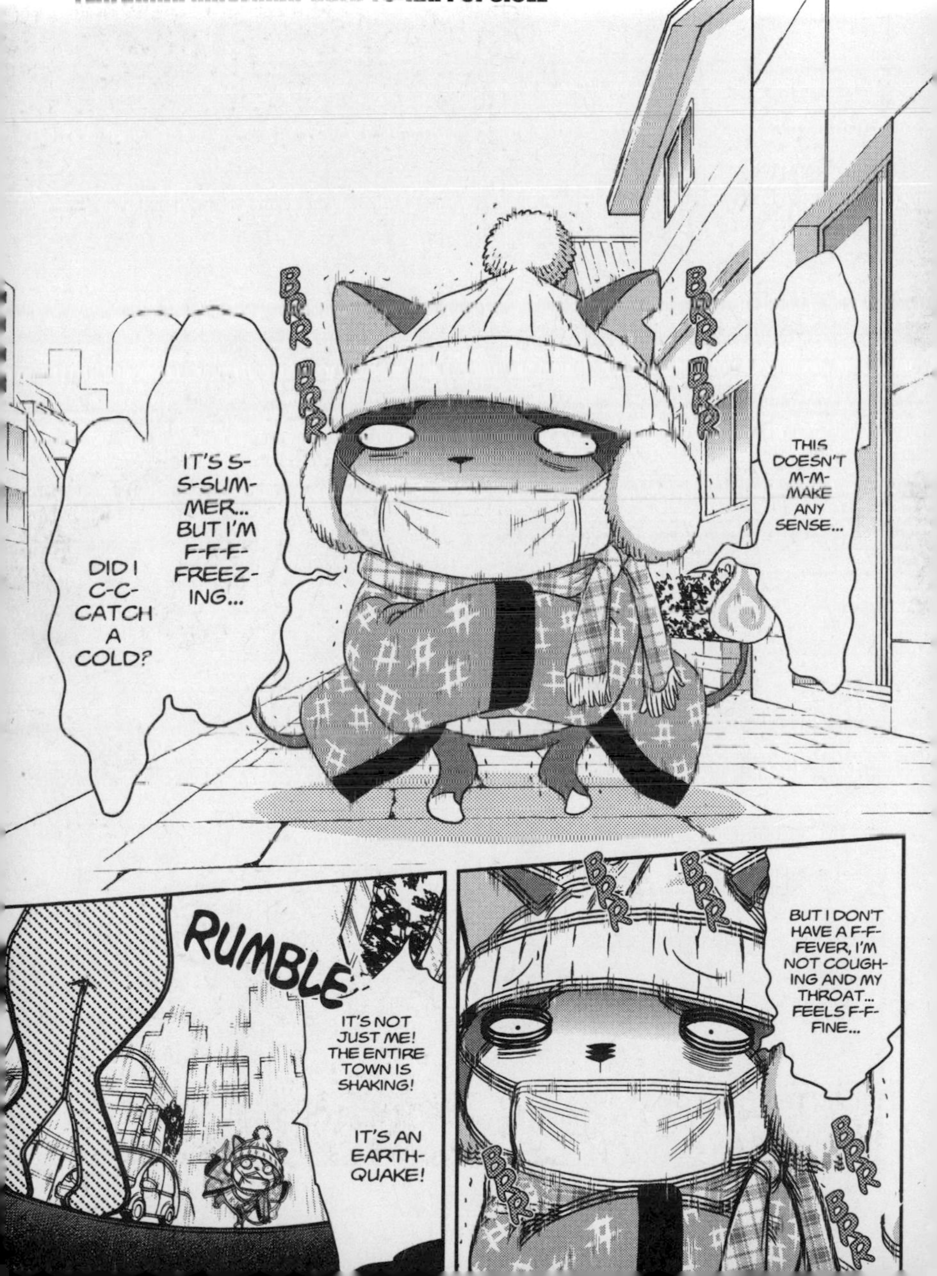
BRR BRR
BRR BRR
THIS DOESN'T M-M-MAKE ANY SENSE...
IT'S S-S-SUMMER... BUT I'M F-F-F-FREEZING...
DID I C-C-CATCH A COLD?
BRR
BRR
BUT I DON'T HAVE A F-F-FEVER, I'M NOT COUGHING AND MY THROAT... FEELS F-F-FINE...
BRR
BRR
BRR
RUMBLE
IT'S NOT JUST ME! THE ENTIRE TOWN IS SHAKING!
IT'S AN EARTHQUAKE!

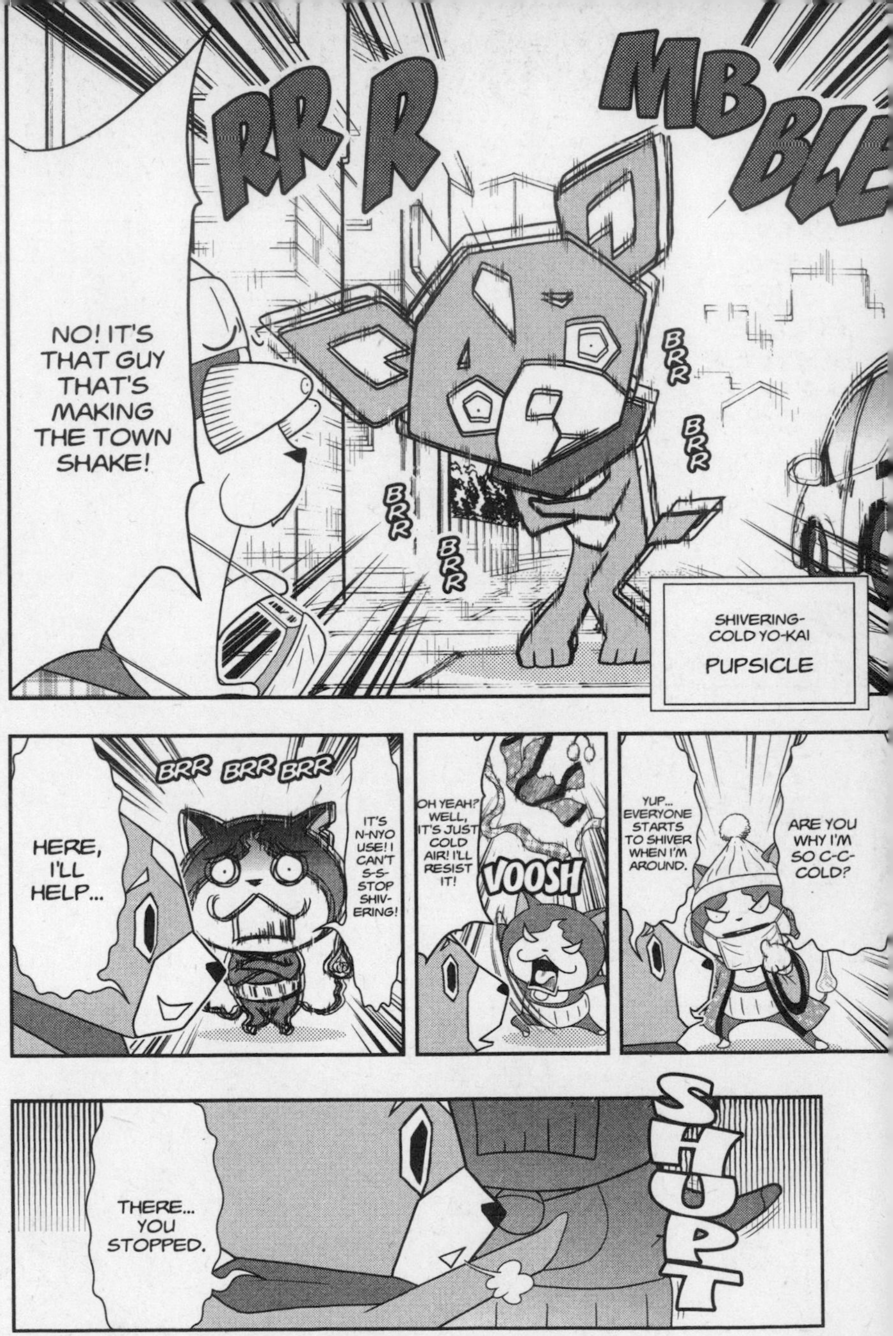
RR R
MB
BLE
SHIVERING-COLD YO-KAI
PUPSICLE
BRR
BRR
BRR
BRR
NO! IT'S THAT GUY THAT'S MAKING THE TOWN SHAKE!
ARE YOU WHY I'M SO C-C-COLD?
YUP... EVERYONE STARTS TO SHIVER WHEN I'M AROUND.
OH YEAH? WELL, IT'S JUST COLD AIR! I'LL RESIST IT!
VOOSH
BRR BRR BRR
IT'S N-NYO USE!! CAN'T S-S-STOP SHIV-ERING!
HERE, I'LL HELP...
SHUPT
THERE... YOU STOPPED.

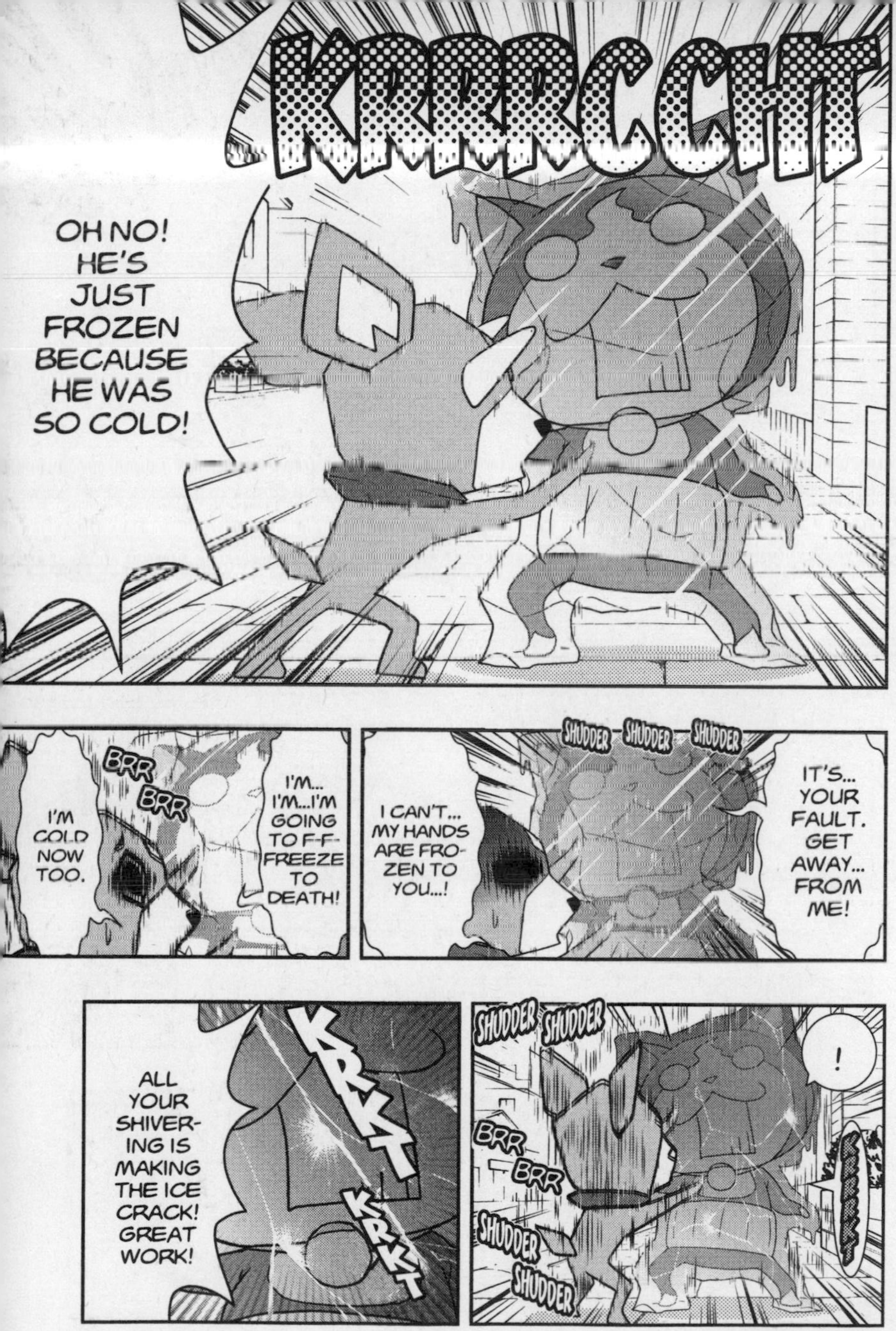
KRRRCCHT
OH NO! HE'S JUST FROZEN BECAUSE HE WAS SO COLD!
SHUDDER SHUDDER SHUDDER
IT'S... YOUR FAULT. GET AWAY... FROM ME!
I CAN'T... MY HANDS ARE FROZEN TO YOU...!
I'M... I'M...I'M GOING TO F-F-FREEZE TO DEATH!
BRR BRR
I'M COLD NOW TOO.
!
SHUDDER SHUDDER
BRR BRR
SHUDDER SHUDDER
KRKT
KRKT
ALL YOUR SHIVERING IS MAKING THE ICE CRACK! GREAT WORK!

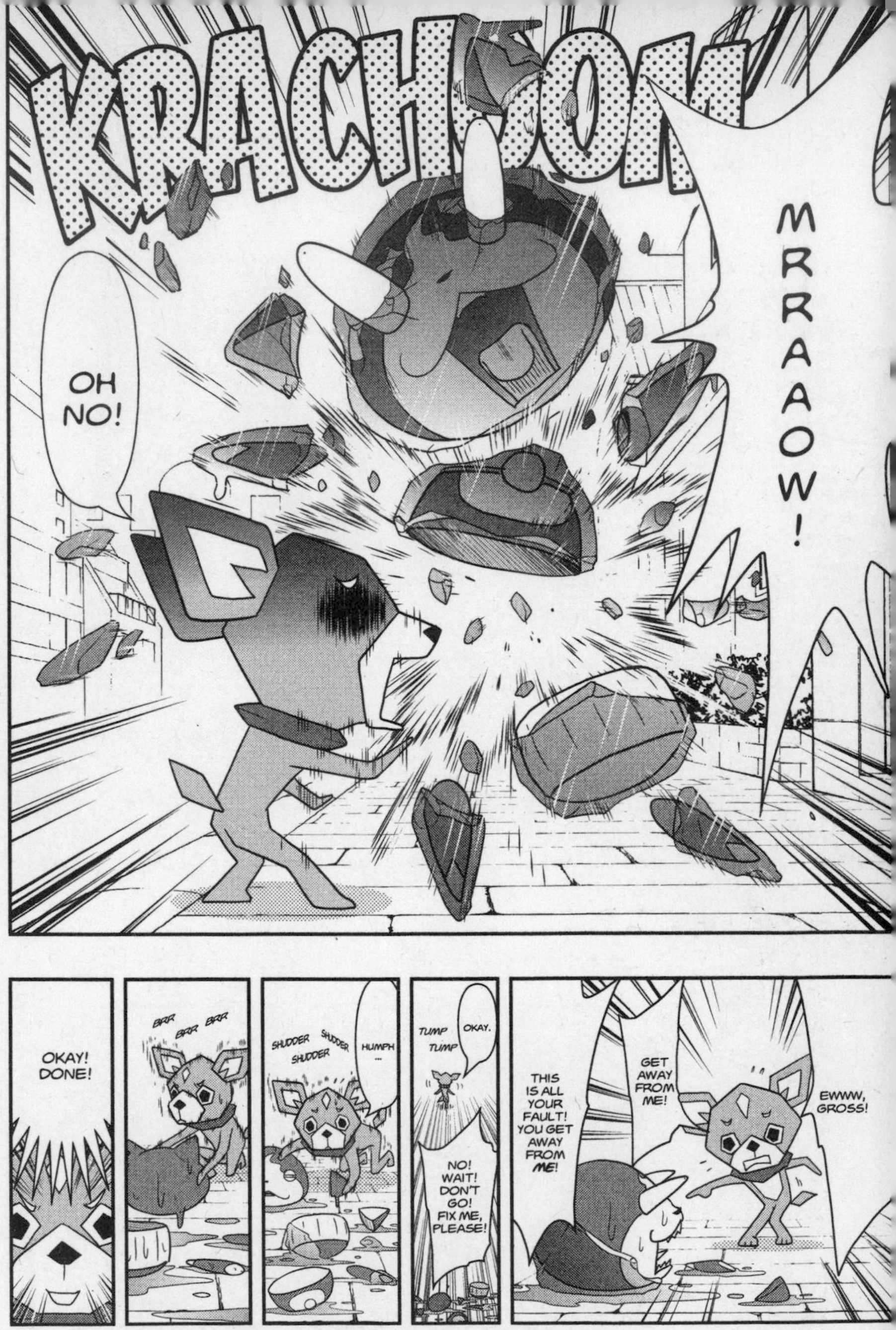
KRACHOOM
MRRAAOW!
OH NO!
EWWW, GROSS!
GET AWAY FROM ME!
THIS IS ALL YOUR FAULT! YOU GET AWAY FROM ME!
OKAY.
TUMP TUMP
NO! WAIT! DON'T GO! FIX ME, PLEASE!
HUMPH ...
SHUDDER SHUDDER SHUDDER
BRR BRR BRR
OKAY! DONE!

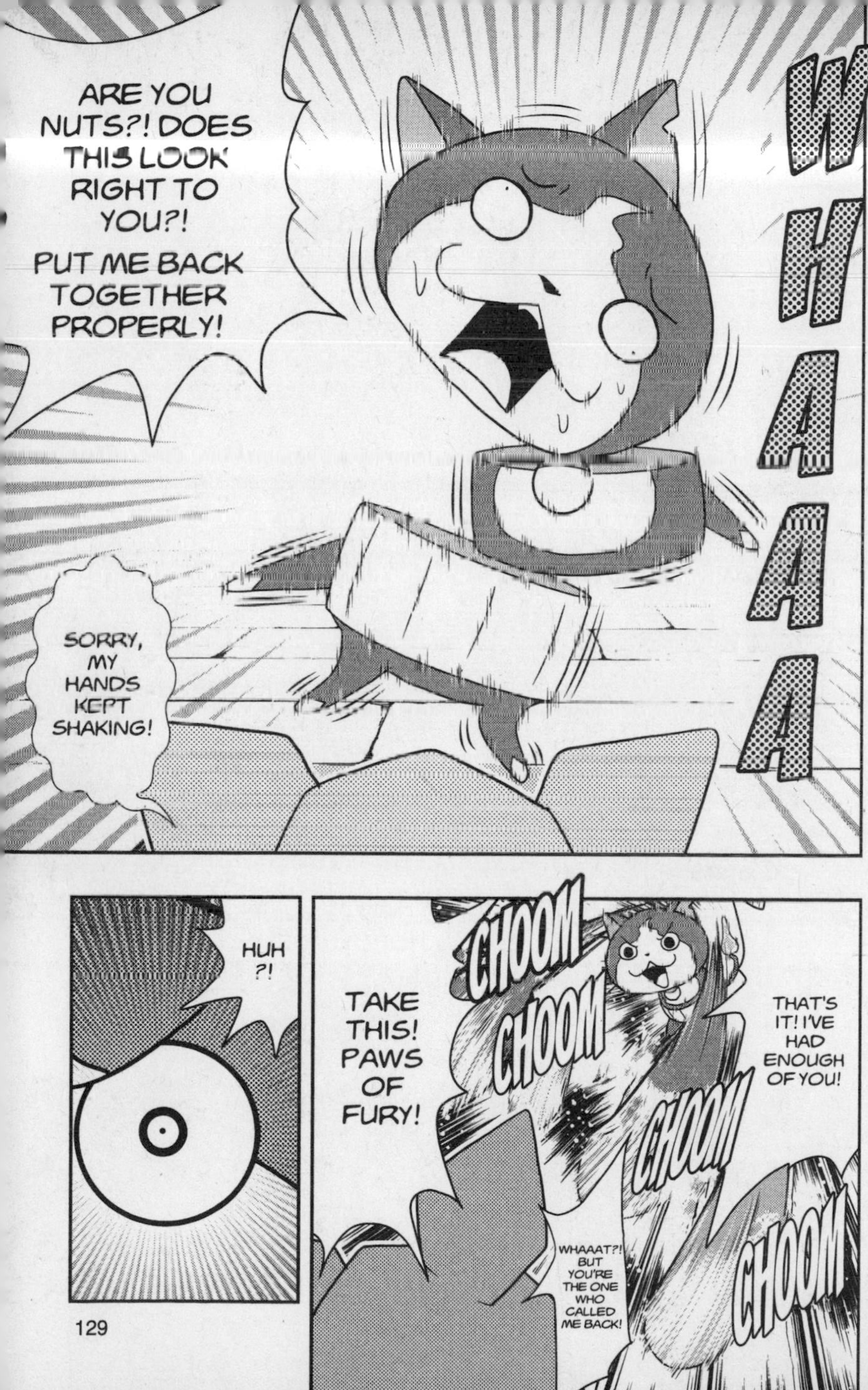
WHAAAA
ARE YOU NUTS?! DOES THIS LOOK RIGHT TO YOU?!
PUT ME BACK TOGETHER PROPERLY!
SORRY, MY HANDS KEPT SHAKING!
THAT'S IT! I'VE HAD ENOUGH OF YOU!
CHOOM
CHOOM
TAKE THIS! PAWS OF FURY!
CHOOM
CHOOM
WHAAAT?! BUT YOU'RE THE ONE WHO CALLED ME BACK!
HUH ?!

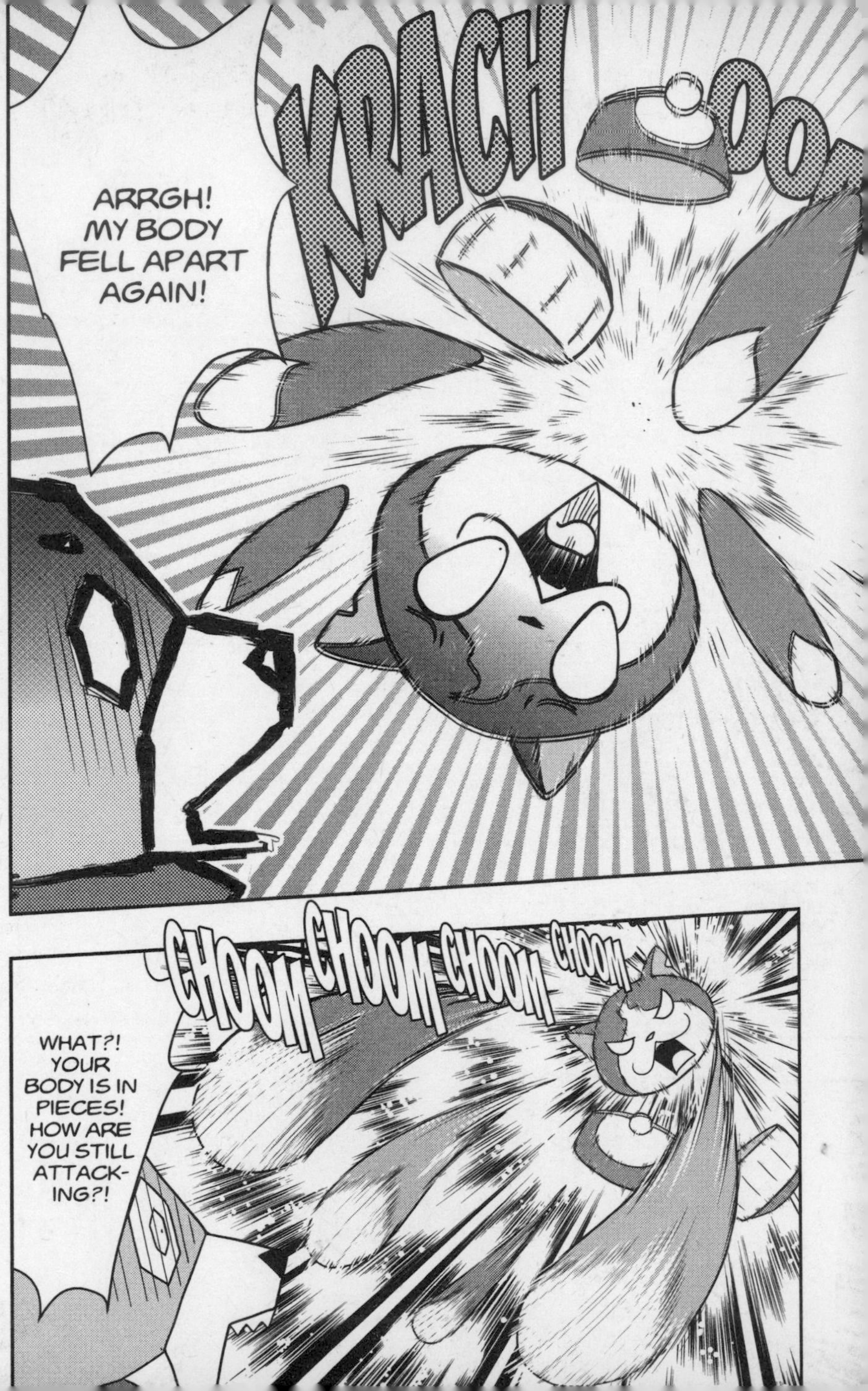
KRACH
ARRGH! MY BODY FELL APART AGAIN!
CHOOM CHOOM CHOOM CHOOM
WHAT?! YOUR BODY IS IN PIECES! HOW ARE YOU STILL ATTACK-ING?!

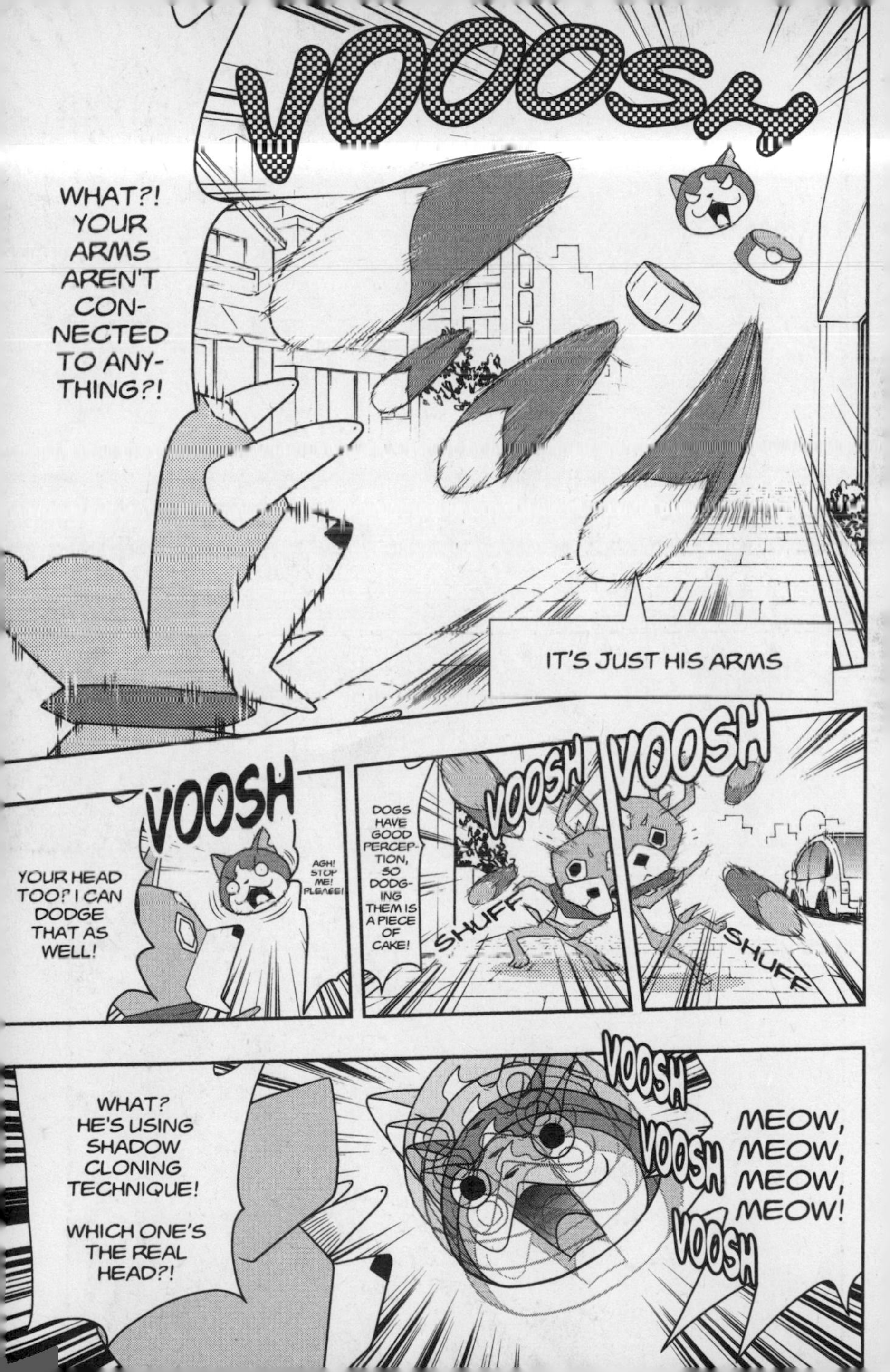
VOOOSH
WHAT?! YOUR ARMS AREN'T CON-NECTED TO ANY-THING?!
IT'S JUST HIS ARMS
VOOSH
YOUR HEAD TOO?! I CAN DODGE THAT AS WELL!
AGH! STOP ME! PLEASE!
VOOSH
DOGS HAVE GOOD PERCEP-TION, SO DODG-ING THEM IS A PIECE OF CAKE!
SHUFF
VOOSH
SHUFF
WHAT? HE'S USING SHADOW CLONING TECHNIQUE!
WHICH ONE'S THE REAL HEAD?!
VOOSH
VOOSH
VOOSH
MEOW, MEOW, MEOW, MEOW!

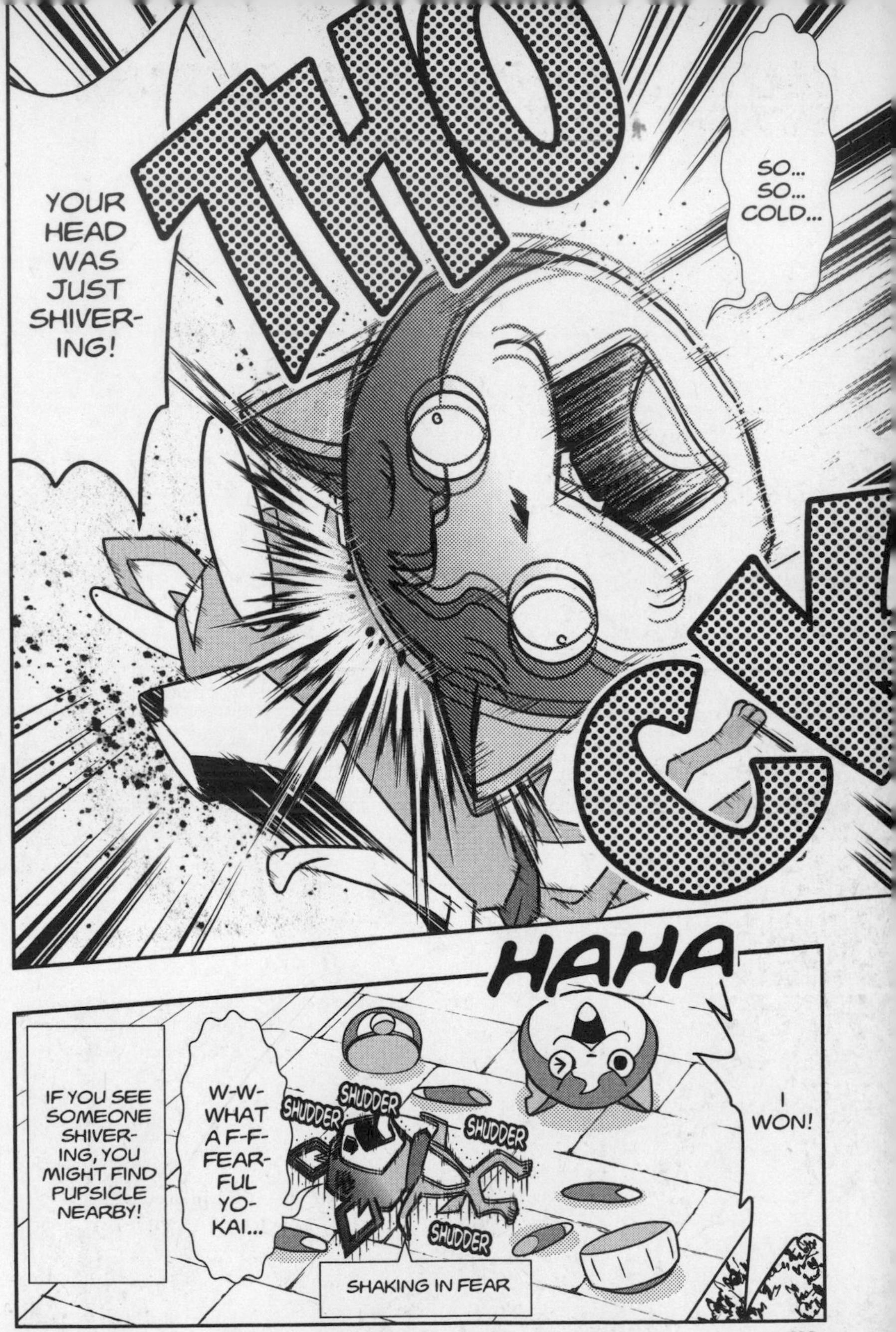
SO... SO... COLD...
THUCK
YOUR HEAD WAS JUST SHIVERING!
HAHA
I WON!
SHUDDER
SHUDDER
SHUDDER
SHUDDER
W-W-WHAT A F-F-FEARFUL YOKAI...
SHAKING IN FEAR
IF YOU SEE SOMEONE SHIVERING, YOU MIGHT FIND PUPSICLE NEARBY!

CHAPTER 53:THE MYSTERIOUS BACKACHE
FEATURING BACKACHE YO-KAI AGON

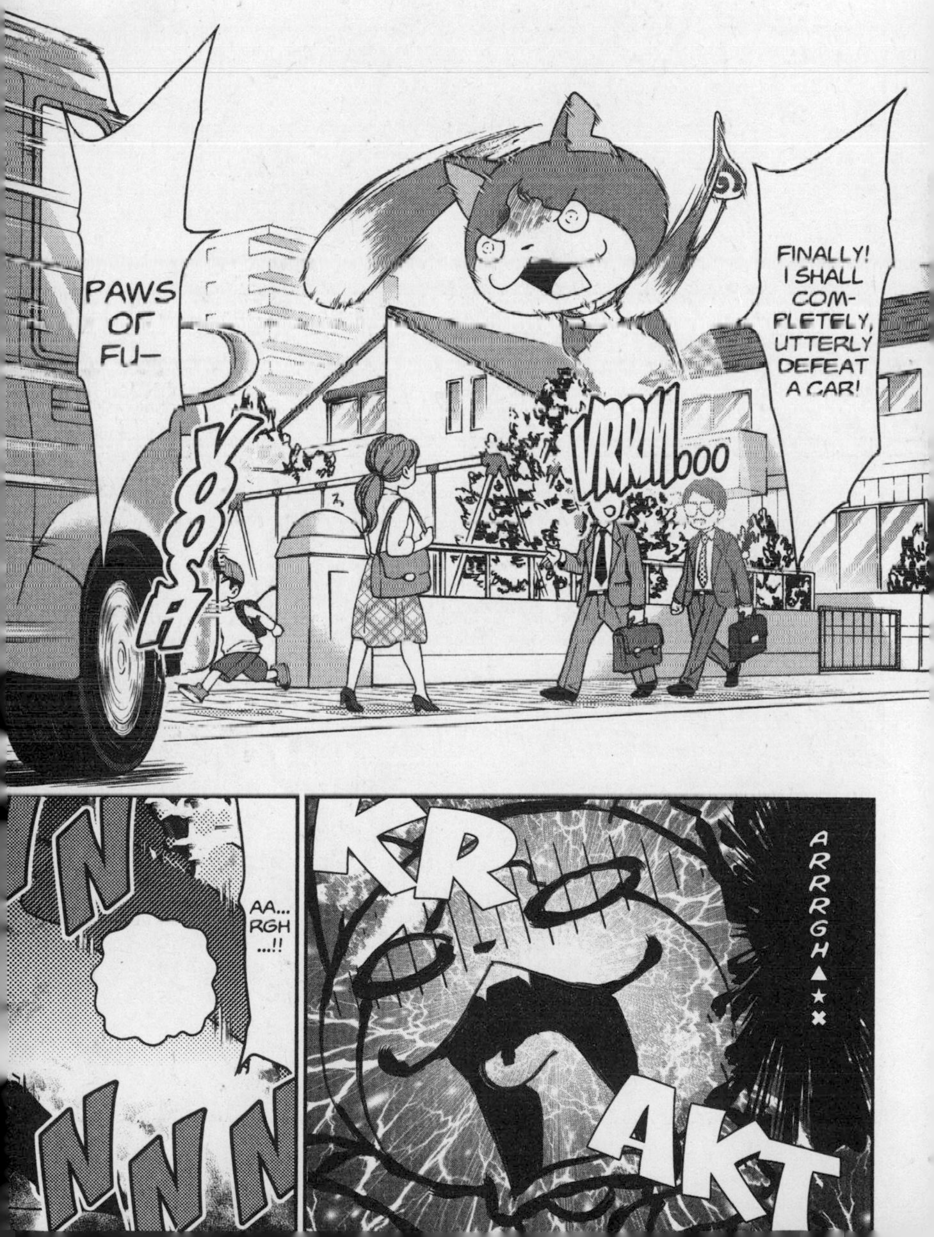
FINALLY! I SHALL COM-PLETELY, UTTERLY DEFEAT A CAR!
VRRMooo
PAWS OF FU—
ARRRGH▲★✖
KR
AKT
AA... RGH ...!!

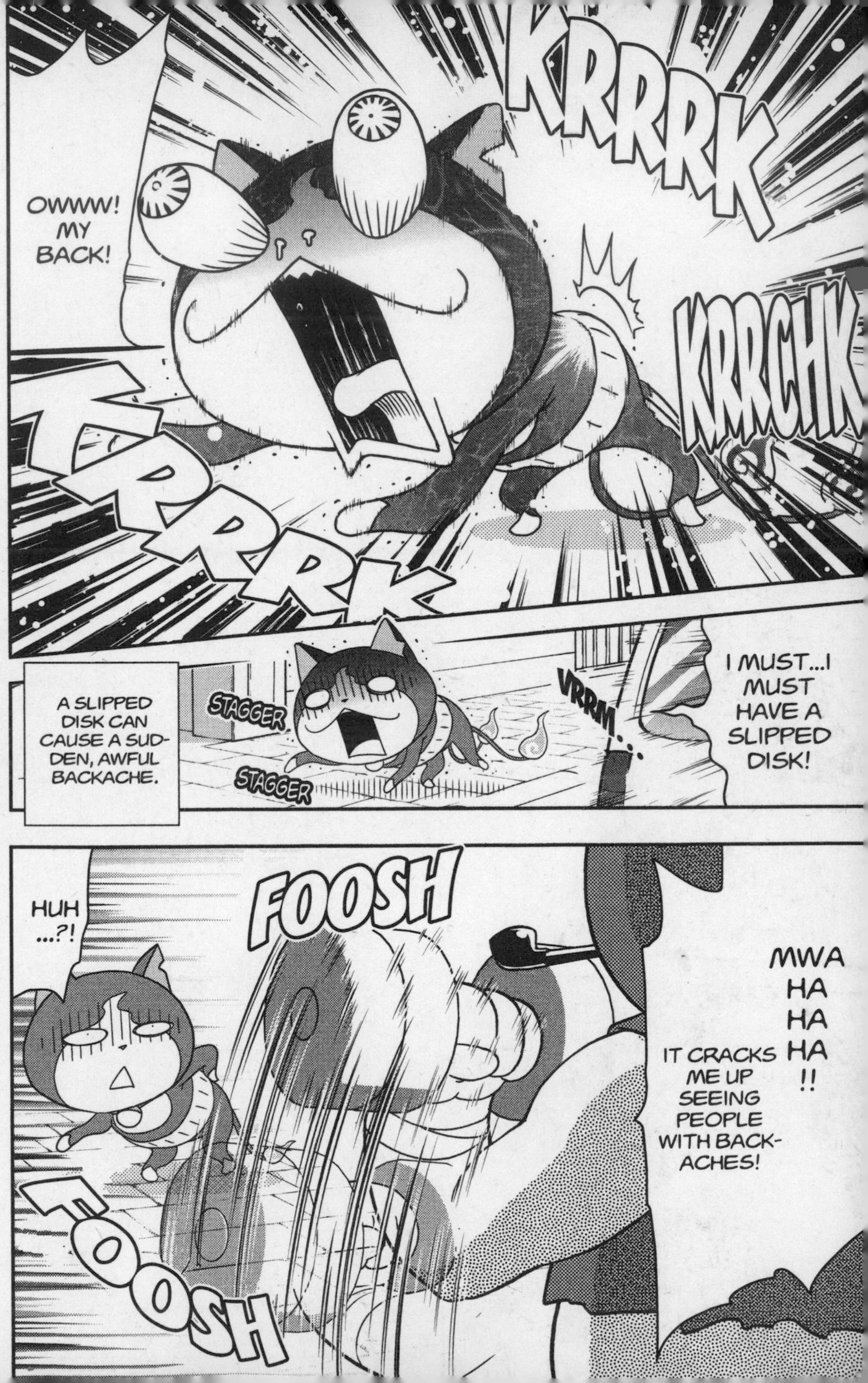
KRRRRK
KRRCHK
OWWW! MY BACK!
VRRRRK
I MUST...I MUST HAVE A SLIPPED DISK!
VRRRM...
STAGGER
STAGGER
A SLIPPED DISK CAN CAUSE A SUDDEN, AWFUL BACKACHE.
MWA HA HA HA !!
IT CRACKS ME UP SEEING PEOPLE WITH BACKACHES!
FOOSH
HUH ...?!
FOOSH

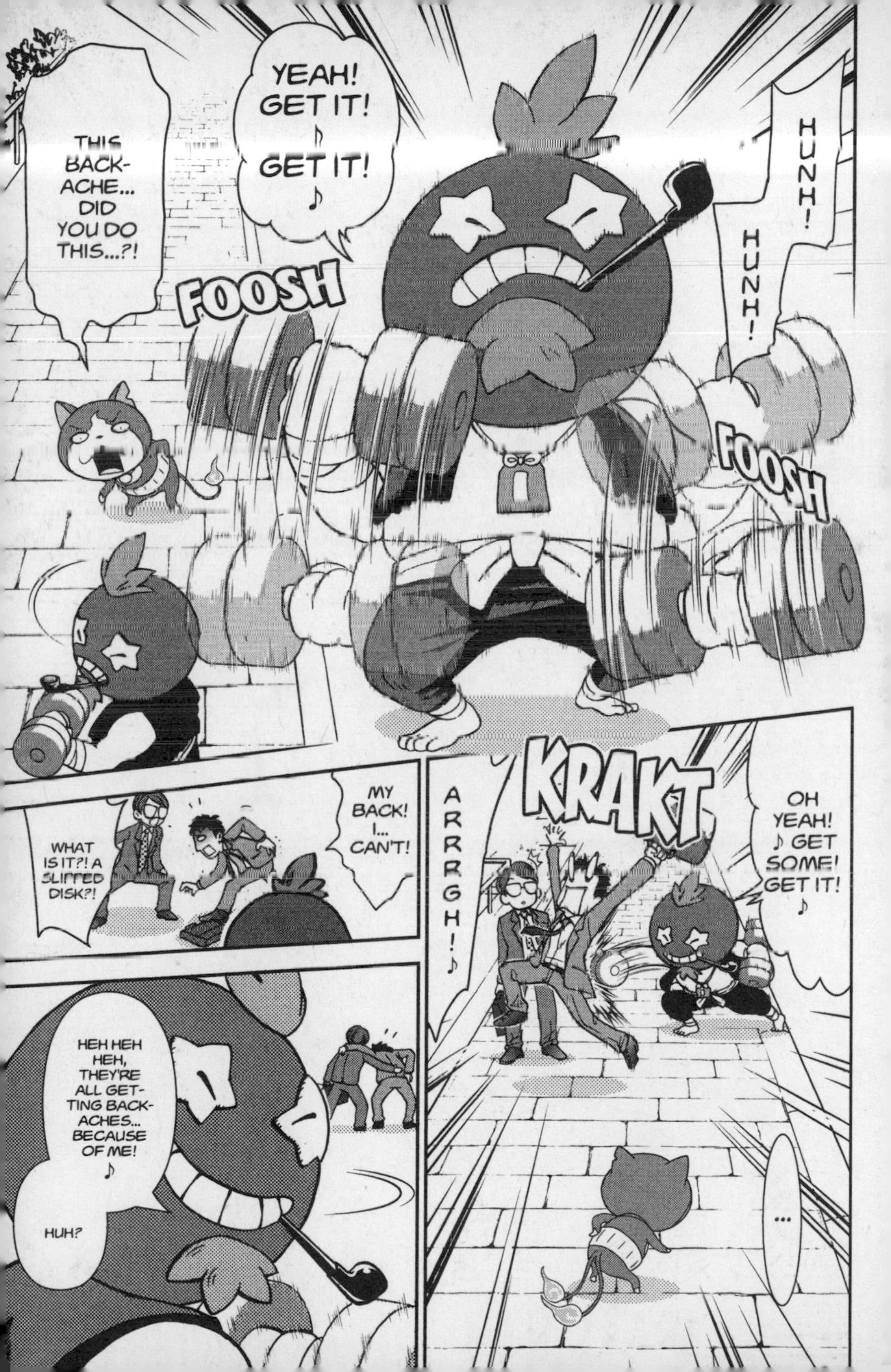

HUNH! HUNH!
YEAH! GET IT! ♪ GET IT! ♪
THIS BACK-ACHE... DID YOU DO THIS...?!
FOOSH
FOOSH
OH YEAH! ♪ GET SOME! GET IT! ♪
KRAKT
ARRRGH!♪
...
MY BACK! I... CAN'T!
WHAT IS IT?! A SLIPPED DISK?!
HEH HEH HEH, THEY'RE ALL GET-TING BACK-ACHES... BECAUSE OF ME! ♪
HUH?

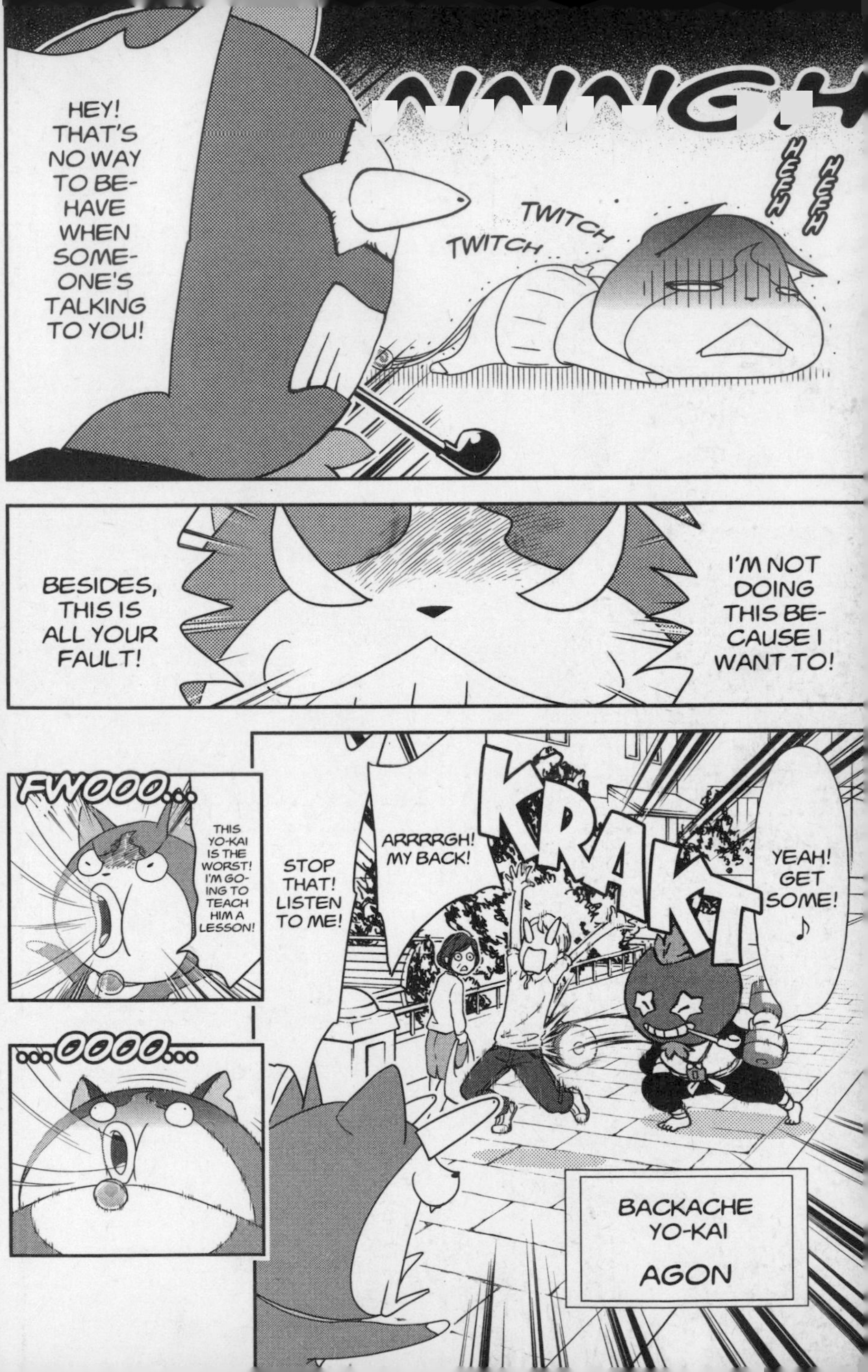

NNNGH
HEEH HEEH
TWITCH
TWITCH
HEY! THAT'S NO WAY TO BE-HAVE WHEN SOME-ONE'S TALKING TO YOU!
I'M NOT DOING THIS BE-CAUSE I WANT TO!
BESIDES, THIS IS ALL YOUR FAULT!
YEAH! GET SOME! ♪
KRAKT
ARRRRGH! MY BACK!
STOP THAT! LISTEN TO ME!
BACKACHE YO-KAI
AGON
FWOOO...
THIS YO-KAI IS THE WORST! I'M GO-ING TO TEACH HIM A LESSON!
...OOOO...

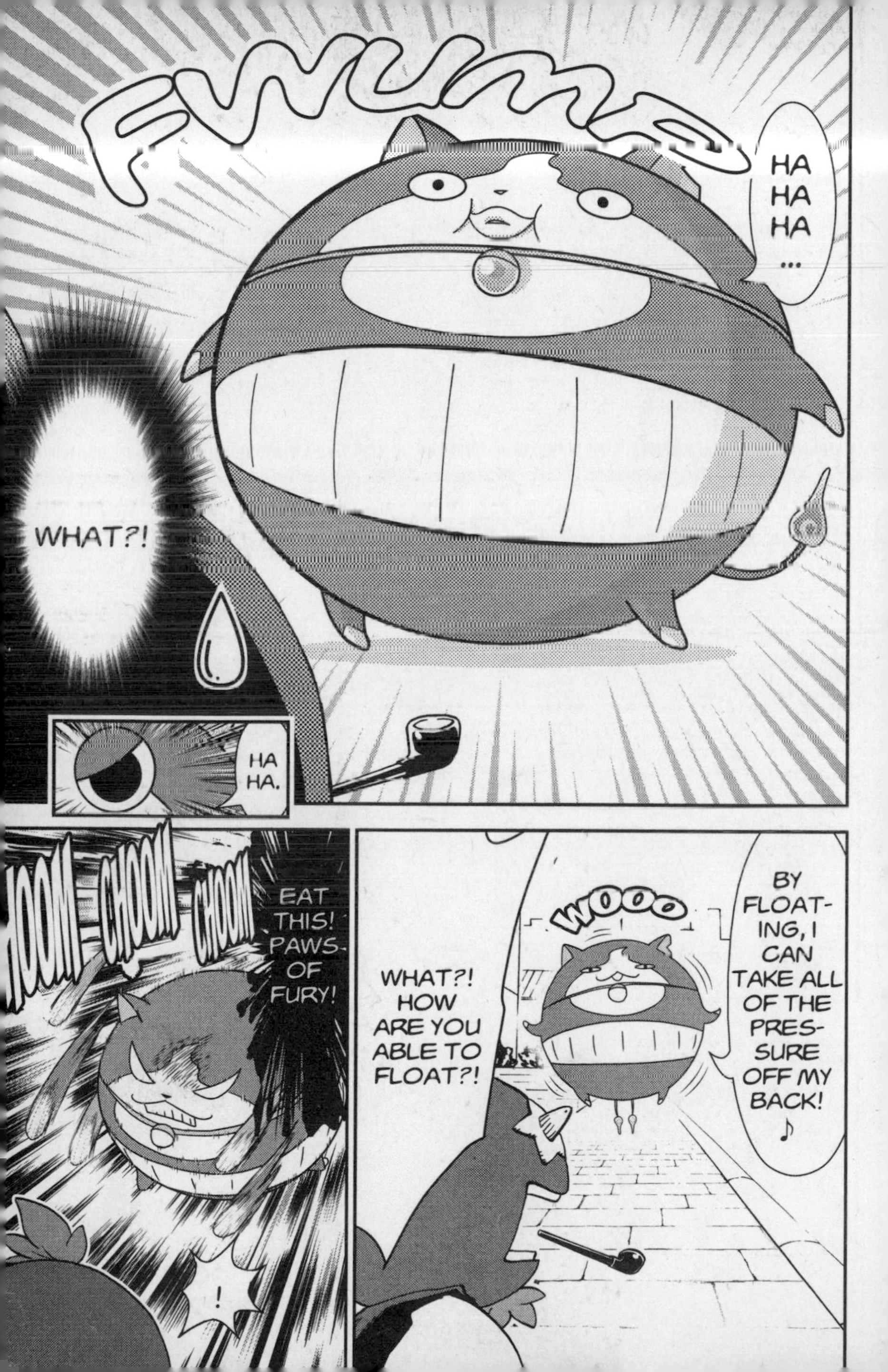
FWUMP
HA HA HA ...
WHAT?!
HA HA.
WOOO
BY FLOAT-ING, I CAN TAKE ALL OF THE PRES-SURE OFF MY BACK! ♪
WHAT?! HOW ARE YOU ABLE TO FLOAT?!
EAT THIS! PAWS-OF FURY!
CHOOM
CHOOM
HOOM
!

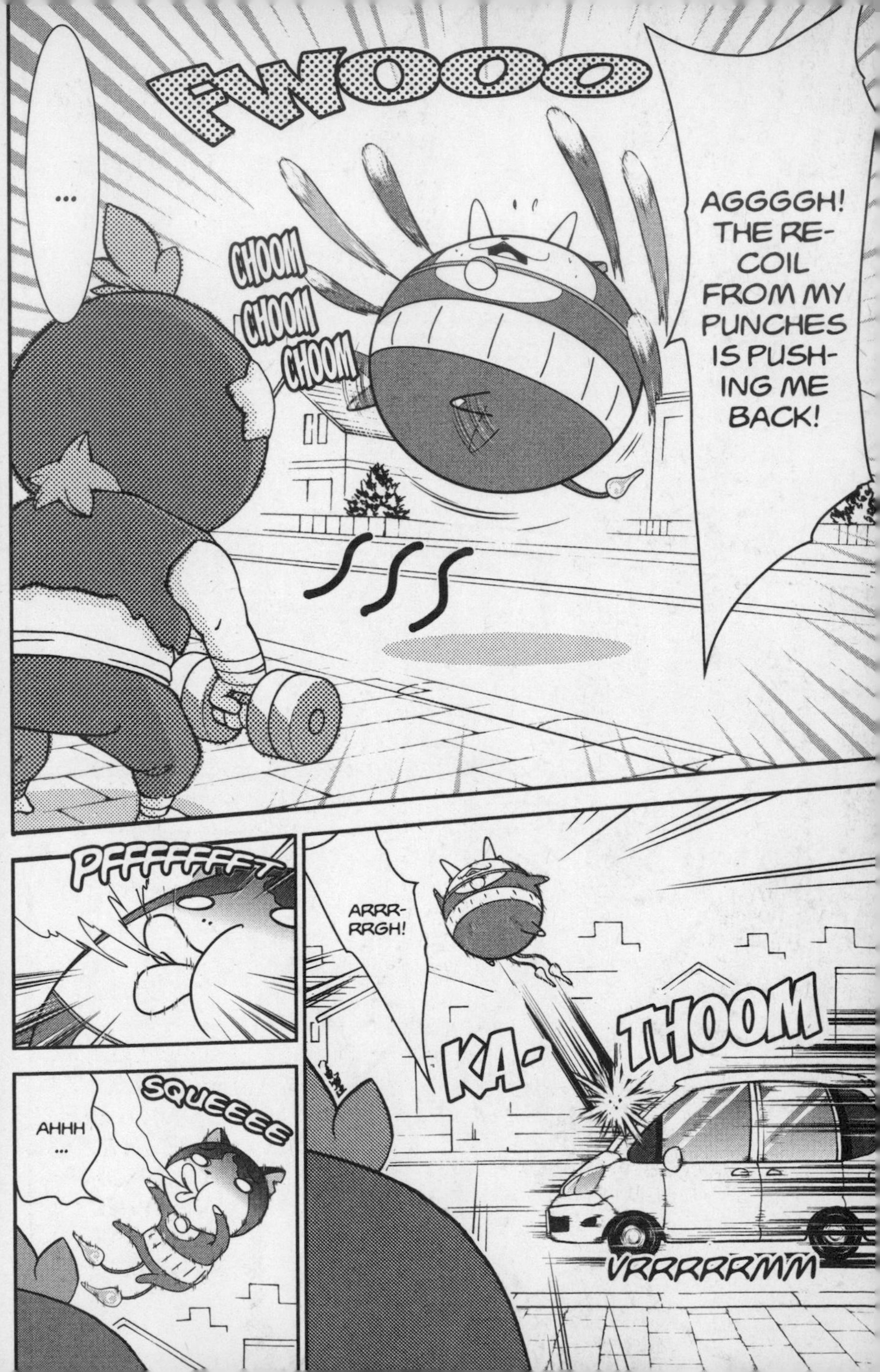
AGGGGH! THE RE-COIL FROM MY PUNCHES IS PUSHING ME BACK!
FWOOOO
CHOOM
CHOOM
CHOOM
...
ARRR-RRGH!
KA-THOOM
VRRRRRRMM
PFFFFFFFT
SQUEEEEE
AHHH ...

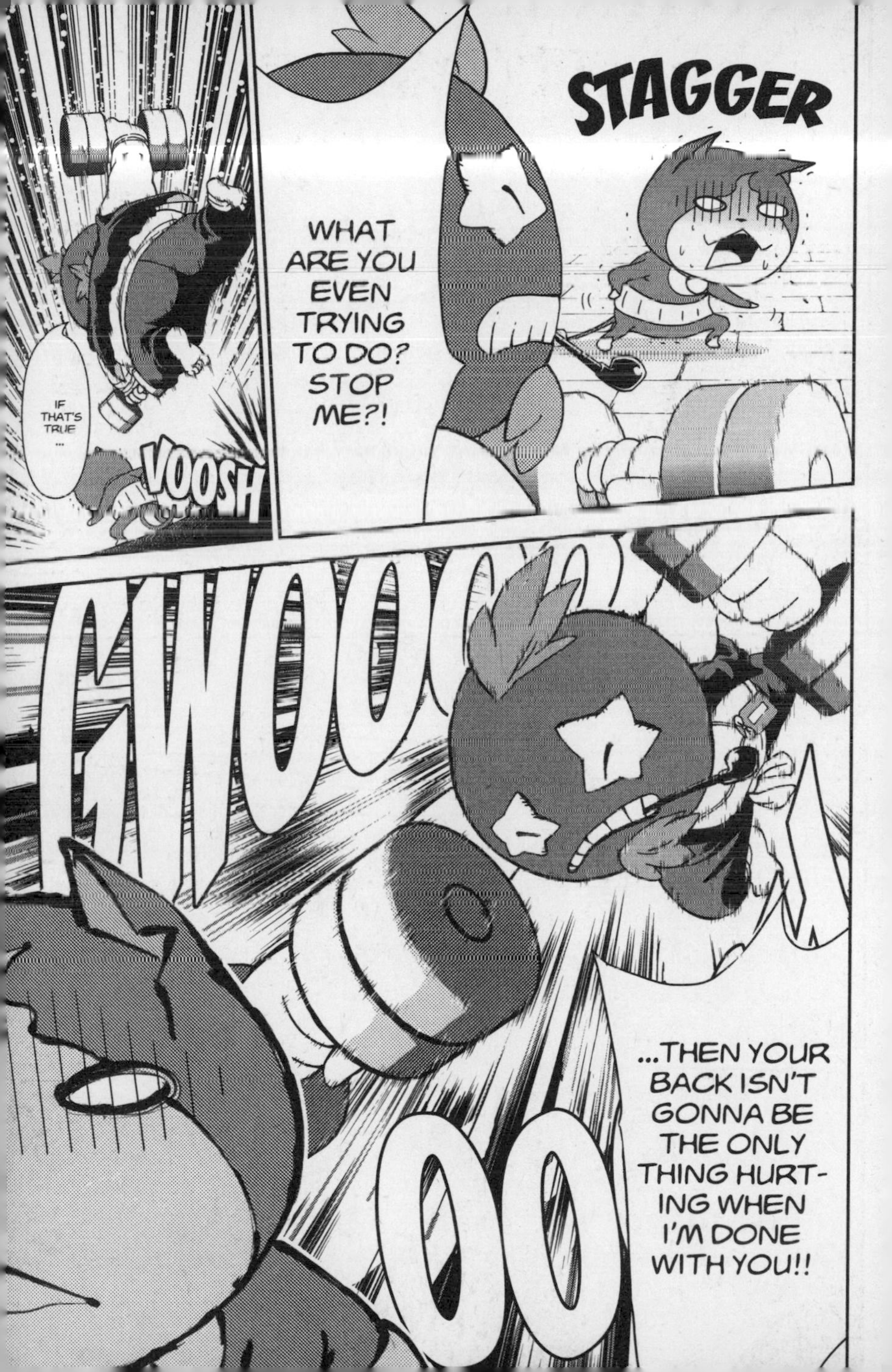
STAGGER
WHAT ARE YOU EVEN TRYING TO DO? STOP ME?!
VOOSH
IF THAT'S TRUE ...
GWOOOOOOO
...THEN YOUR BACK ISN'T GONNA BE THE ONLY THING HURT-ING WHEN I'M DONE WITH YOU!!

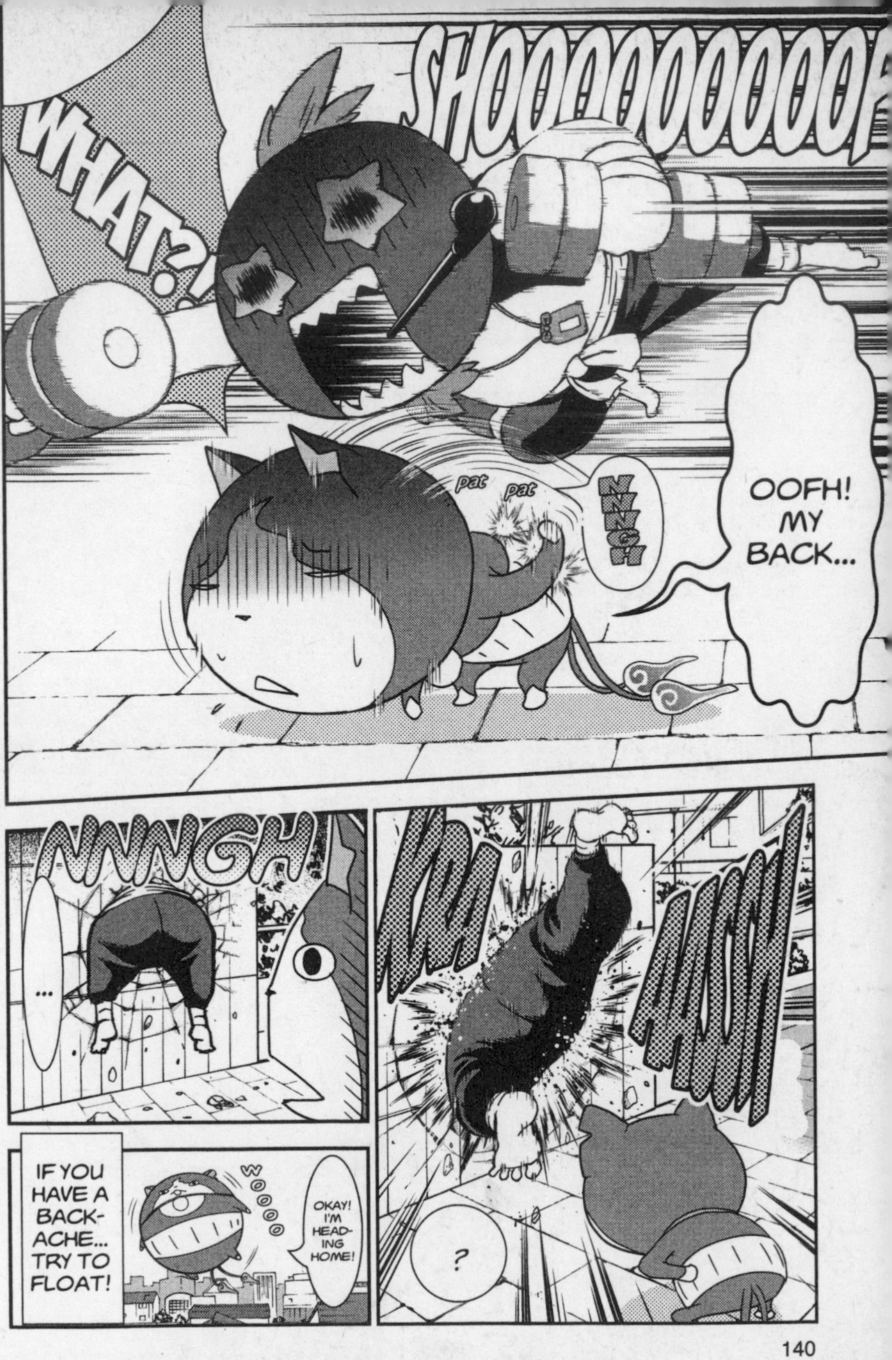
SHOOOOOOOOF
WHAT?!
OOFH! MY BACK...
NNNGH
pat pat
?
NNNGH
...
OKAY! I'M HEADING HOME!
WOOOO
IF YOU HAVE A BACKACHE... TRY TO FLOAT!

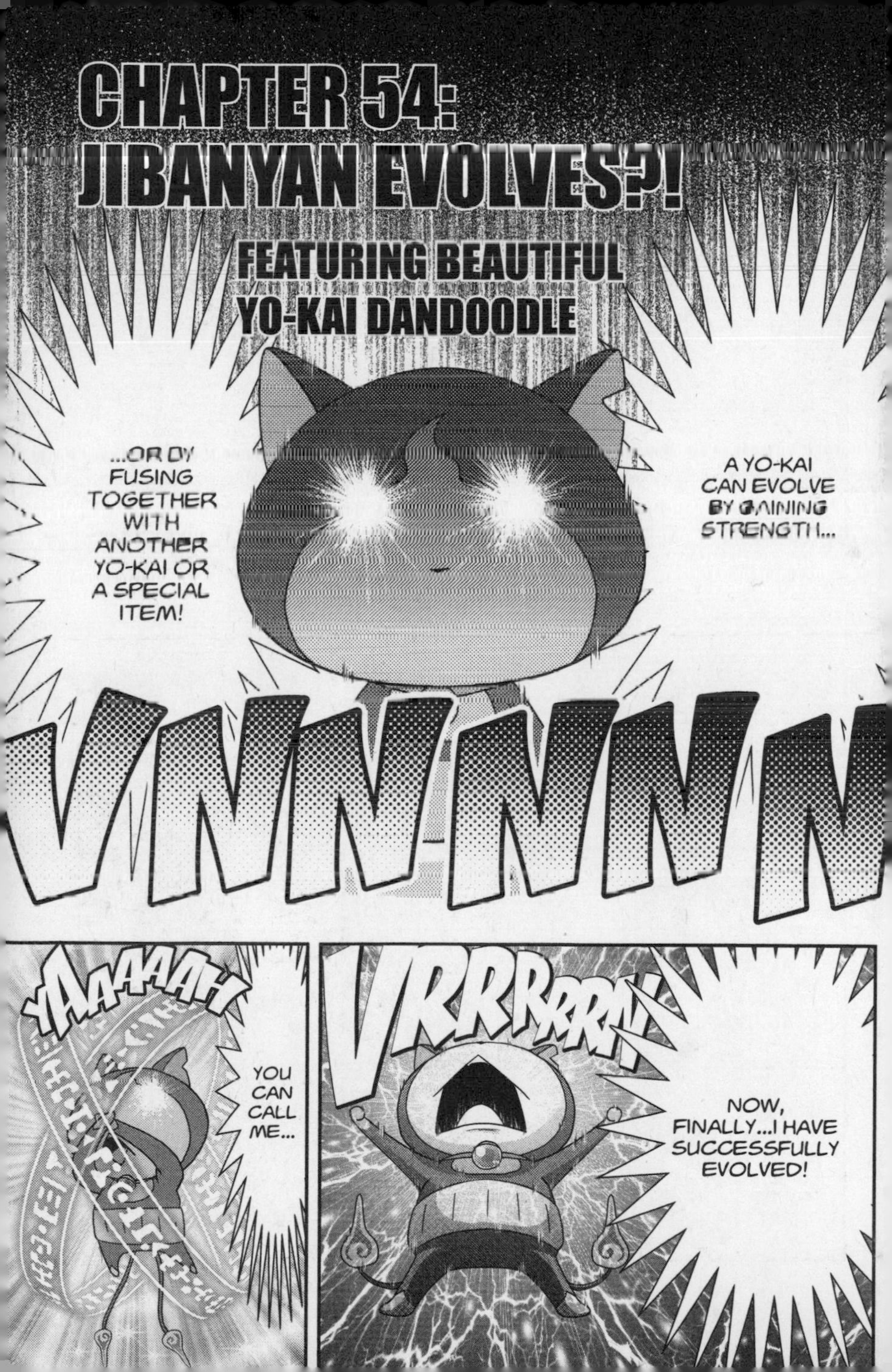
CHAPTER 54:
JIBANYAN EVOLVES?!
FEATURING BEAUTIFUL YO-KAI DANDOODLE
A YO-KAI CAN EVOLVE BY GAINING STRENGTH...
...OR BY FUSING TOGETHER WITH ANOTHER YO-KAI OR A SPECIAL ITEM!
VNNNNNN
VRRRRRN!
NOW, FINALLY...I HAVE SUCCESSFULLY EVOLVED!
YAAAAAH
YOU CAN CALL ME...

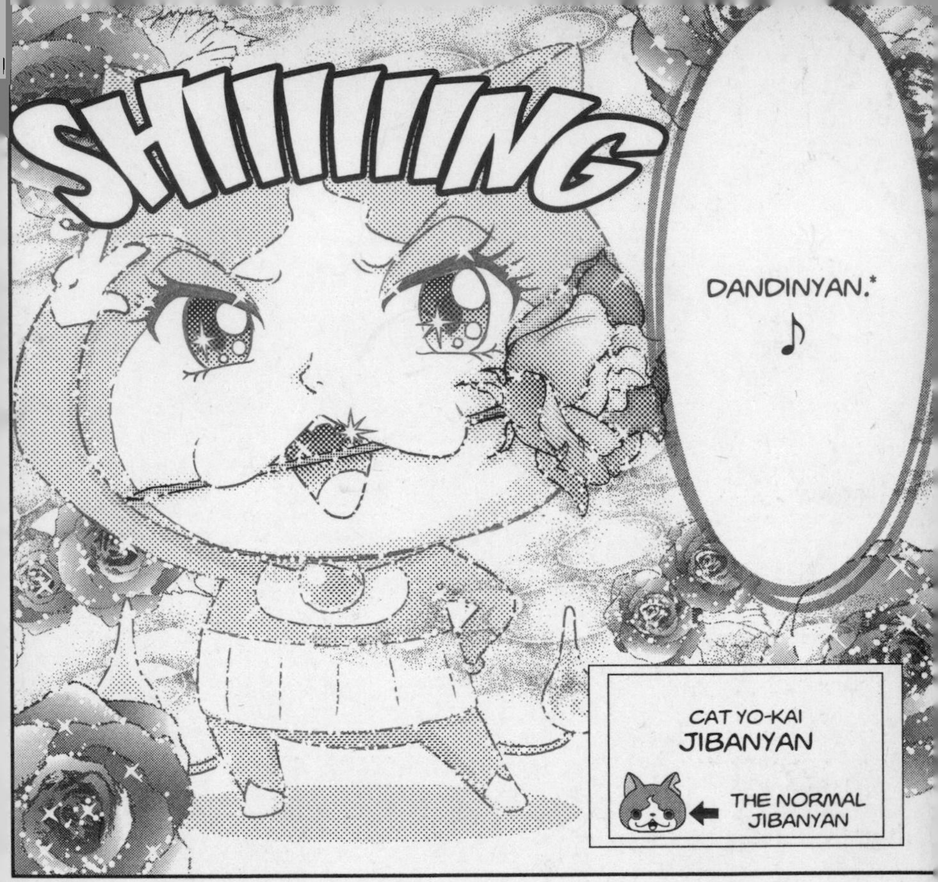
DANDINYAN.* ♪
SHIIIIING
CAT YO-KAI
JIBANYAN
THE NORMAL
JIBANYAN

*HE DOES NOT ACTUALLY APPEAR IN THE GAME.

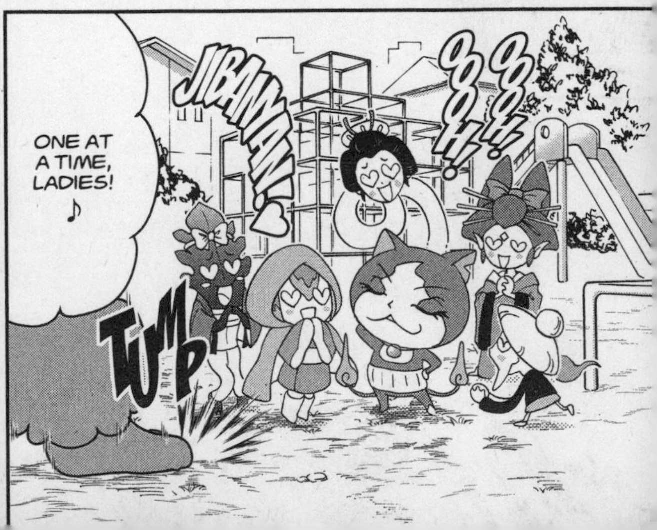
OOOH!!
OOOH!!
JIBANYAN!
ONE AT A TIME, LADIES! ♪
TUMP

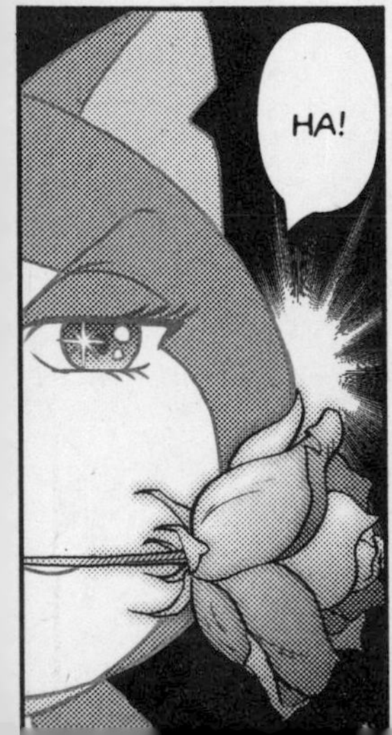
HA!

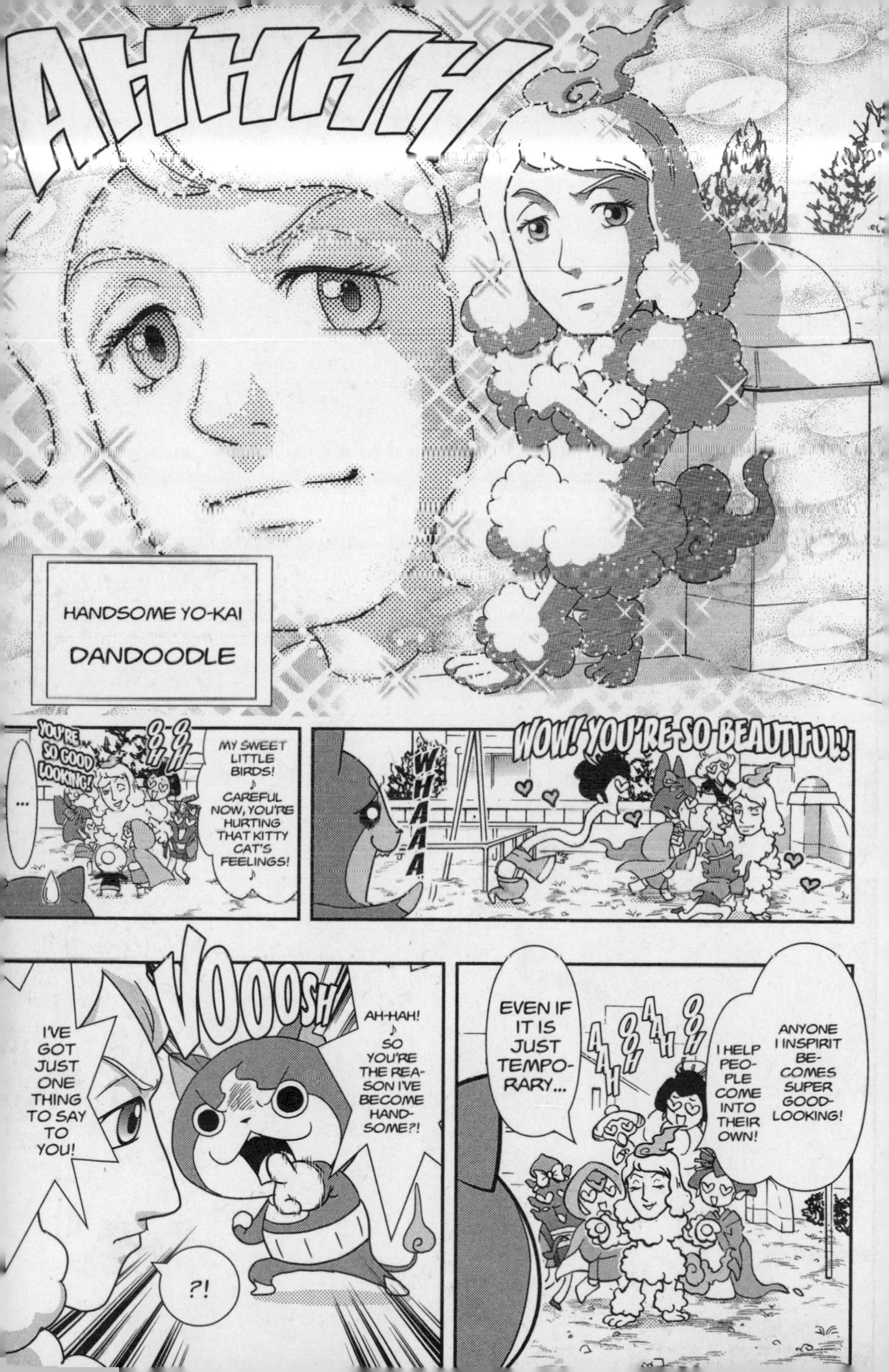
AHHHH
HANDSOME YO-KAI
DANDOODLE
WOW! YOU'RE SO BEAUTIFUL!
WHAAAA
MY SWEET LITTLE BIRDS! ♪ CAREFUL NOW, YOU'RE HURTING THAT KITTY CAT'S FEELINGS! ♪
YOU'RE SO GOOD LOOKING!
...
ANYONE I INSPIRIT BECOMES SUPER GOOD-LOOKING!
I HELP PEOPLE COME INTO THEIR OWN!
EVEN IF IT IS JUST TEMPORARY...
VOOOSH
AH-HAH! ♪ SO YOU'RE THE REASON I'VE BECOME HANDSOME?!
I'VE GOT JUST ONE THING TO SAY TO YOU!
?!

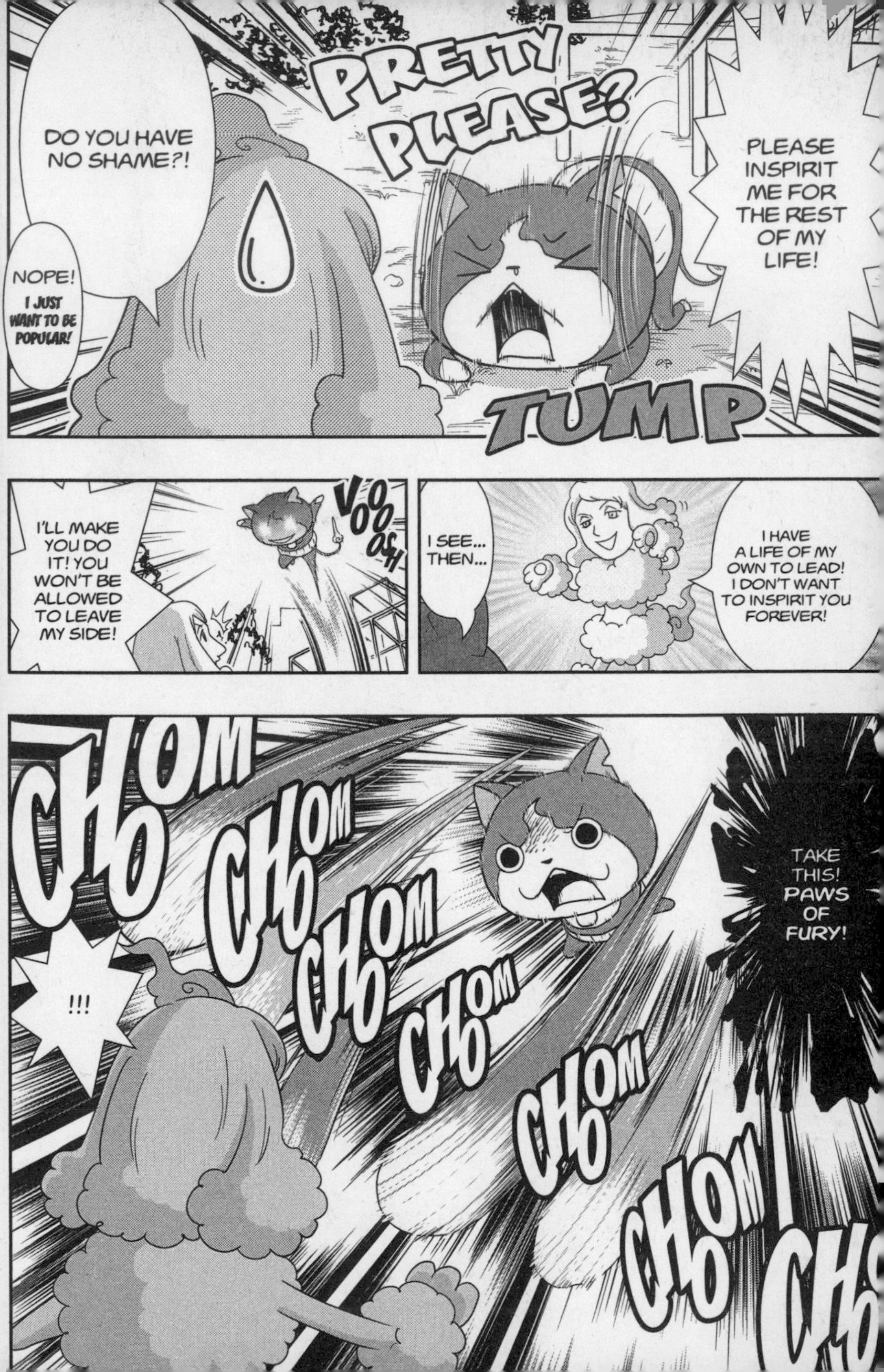
PLEASE INSPIRIT ME FOR THE REST OF MY LIFE!
PRETTY PLEASE?
TUMP
DO YOU HAVE NO SHAME?!
NOPE! I JUST WANT TO BE POPULAR!
I HAVE A LIFE OF MY OWN TO LEAD! I DON'T WANT TO INSPIRIT YOU FOREVER!
I SEE... THEN...
VOOOOSH
I'LL MAKE YOU DO IT! YOU WON'T BE ALLOWED TO LEAVE MY SIDE!
TAKE THIS! PAWS OF FURY!
CHOM
CHOM
CHOM
CHOM
CHOM
CHOM
CHOM
!!!

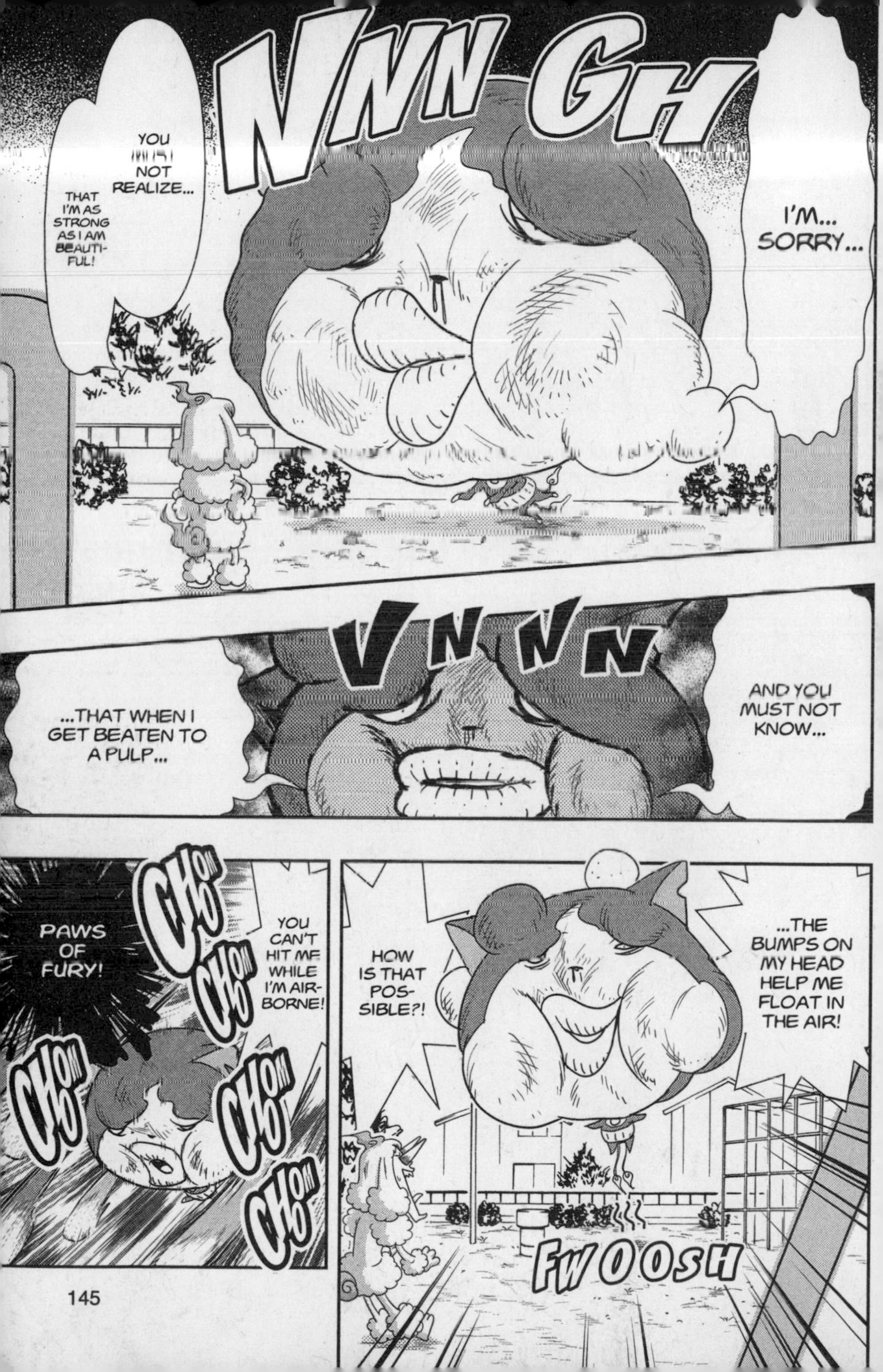
I'M... SORRY...
NNNGH
YOU NOT REALIZE...
THAT I'M AS STRONG AS I AM BEAUTIFUL!
AND YOU MUST NOT KNOW...
VNNNN
...THAT WHEN I GET BEATEN TO A PULP...
...THE BUMPS ON MY HEAD HELP ME FLOAT IN THE AIR!
HOW IS THAT POSSIBLE?!
FWOOSH
YOU CAN'T HIT ME WHILE I'M AIRBORNE!
PAWS OF FURY!
CHOM CHOM CHOM CHOM CHOM

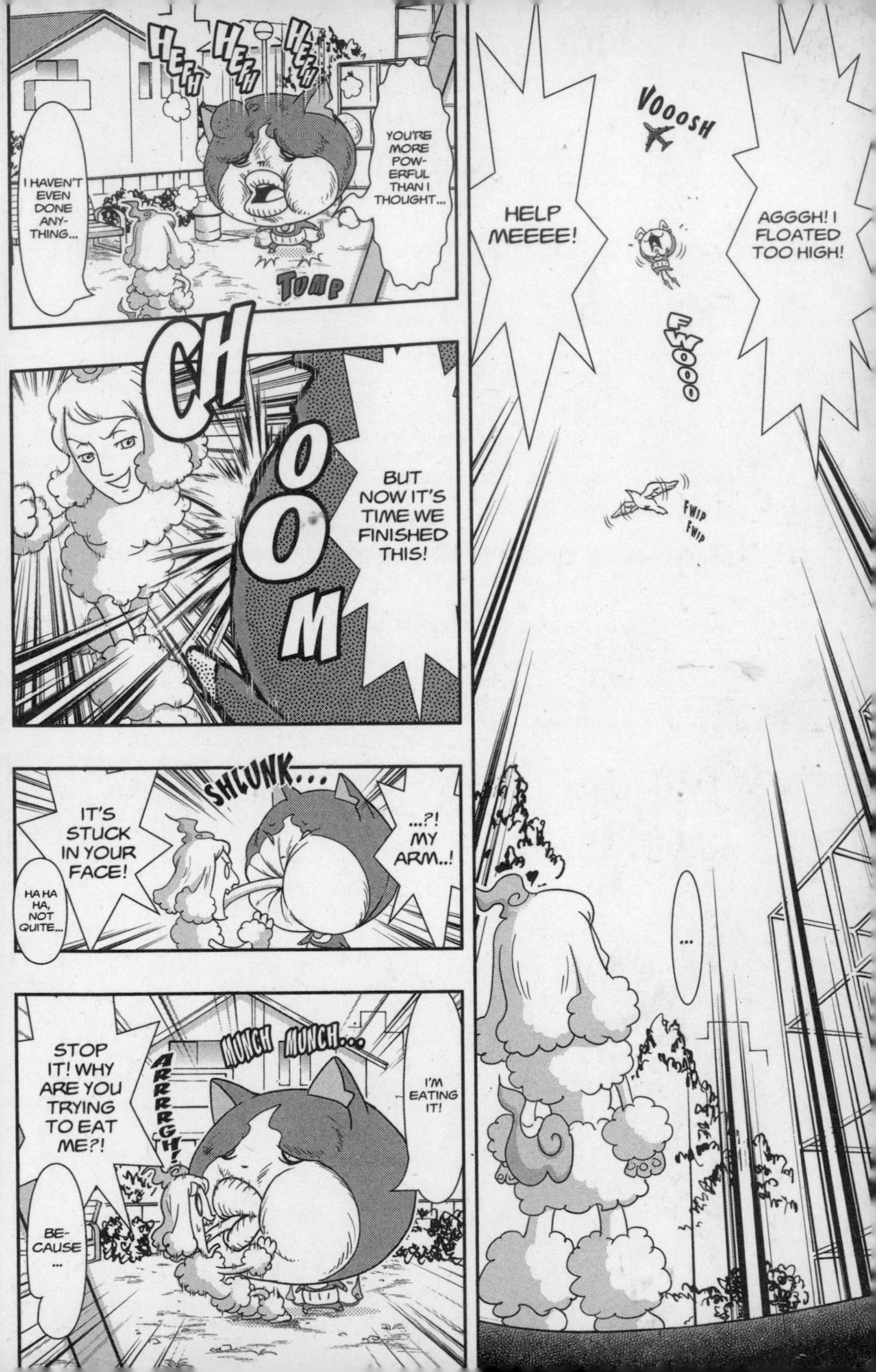
AGGGH! I FLOATED TOO HIGH!
VOOOSH
HELP MEEEE!
FWOOOO
FWIP FWIP
...
HEFH HEFH HEFH
YOU'RE MORE POWERFUL THAN I THOUGHT...
I HAVEN'T EVEN DONE ANYTHING...
TUMP
CHOOOM
BUT NOW IT'S TIME WE FINISHED THIS!
...?! MY ARM..!
SHLUNK...
IT'S STUCK IN YOUR FACE!
HA HA HA, NOT QUITE...
I'M EATING IT!
MUNCH MUNCH...
ARRRRGH!
STOP IT! WHY ARE YOU TRYING TO EAT ME?!
BECAUSE...

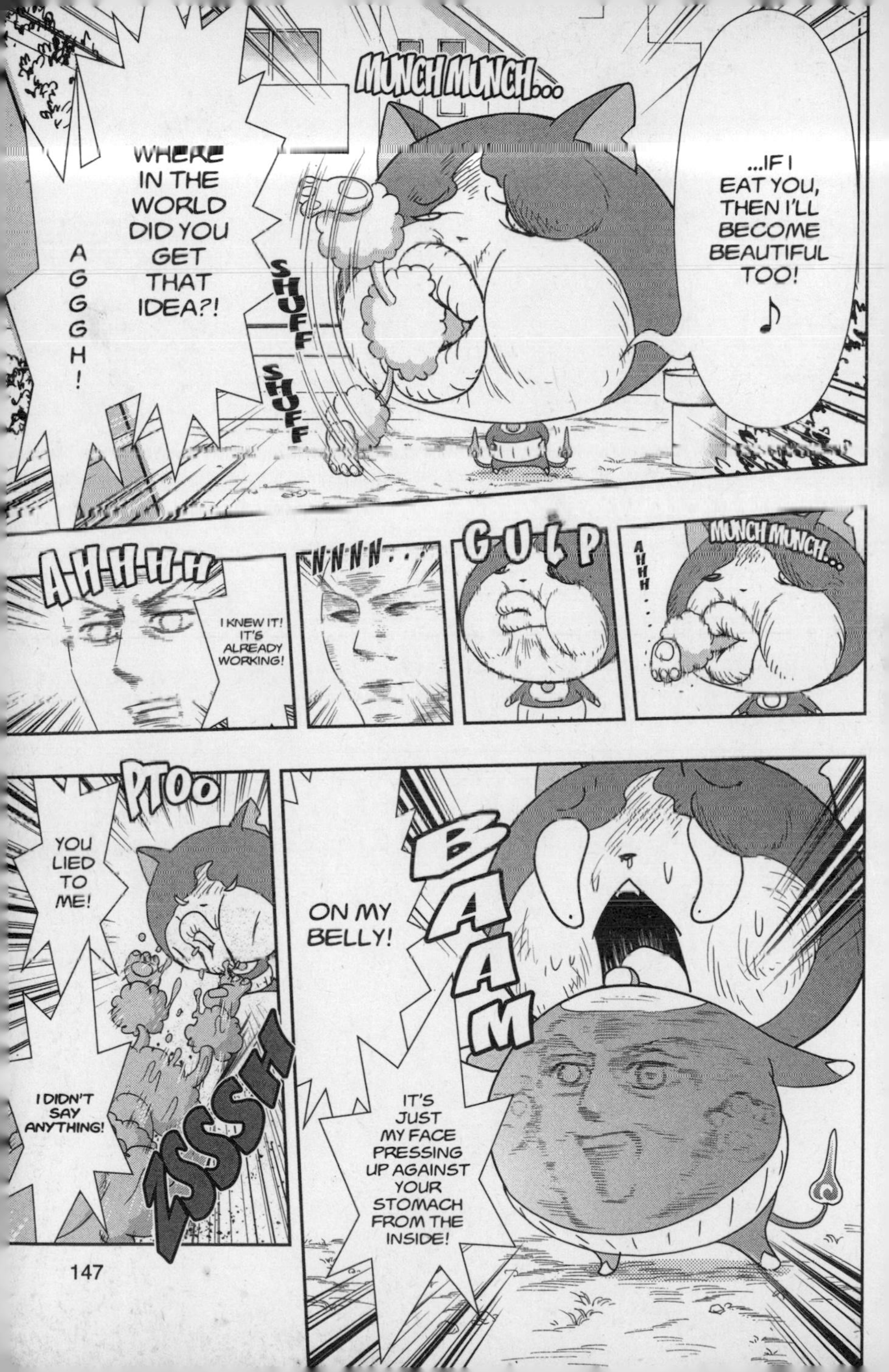

...IF I EAT YOU, THEN I'LL BECOME BEAUTIFUL TOO! ♪
MUNCH MUNCH...
WHERE IN THE WORLD DID YOU GET THAT IDEA?!
SHUFF SHUFF
AGGGH!
MUNCH MUNCH...
AHHH...
GULP
NNNNN...
A-H-H-H-H
I KNEW IT! IT'S ALREADY WORKING!
BAAM
ON MY BELLY!
IT'S JUST MY FACE PRESSING UP AGAINST YOUR STOMACH FROM THE INSIDE!
PTOO
YOU LIED TO ME!
I DIDN'T SAY ANYTHING!
ZSSSH

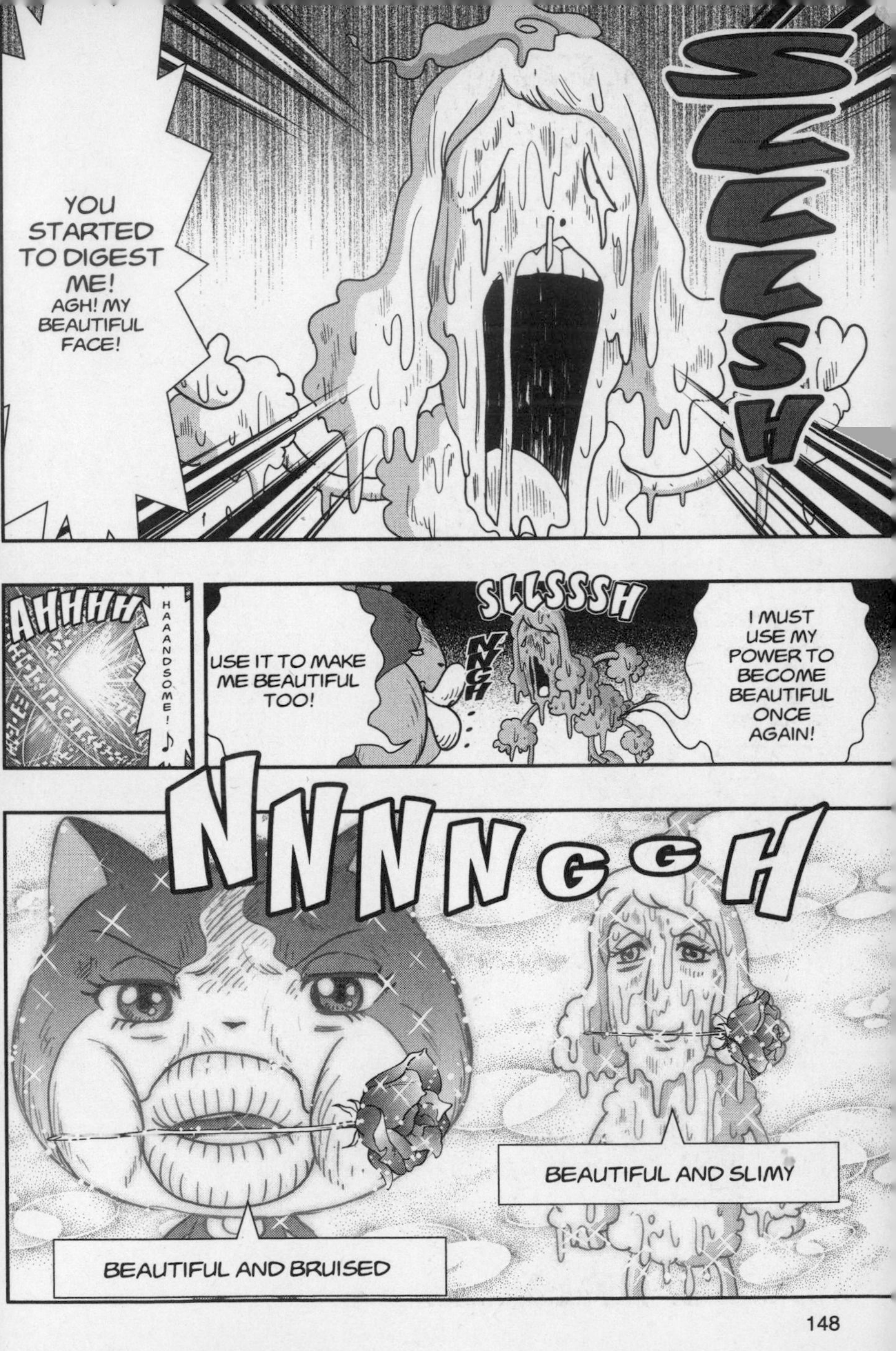
SLLLLSH
YOU STARTED TO DIGEST ME! AGH! MY BEAUTIFUL FACE!
I MUST USE MY POWER TO BECOME BEAUTIFUL ONCE AGAIN!
SLLSSSH
NNGH
USE IT TO MAKE ME BEAUTIFUL TOO!
HAAAANDSOME! ♪
AHHHH
NNNNGGH
BEAUTIFUL AND SLIMY
BEAUTIFUL AND BRUISED

REAL HANDSOME

I WANT TO BECOME A TRULY BEAUTIFUL GUY!
I DON'T LIKE THIS FACE EITHER...
HAAAAANDSOME!
AHHHHH
OH...?
I GUESS THIS IS COOL, BUT...
YOU'RE JUST AN ORDINARY DOG NOW.
SO LAME.

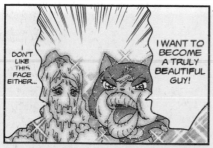

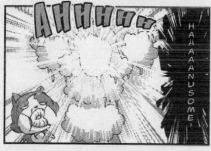

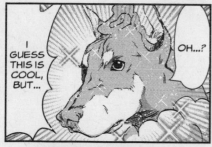

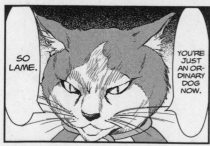

CHAPTER 55: FUNNY FACE A GOGO

FEATURING FUNNY FACE YO-KAI JUMBELINA

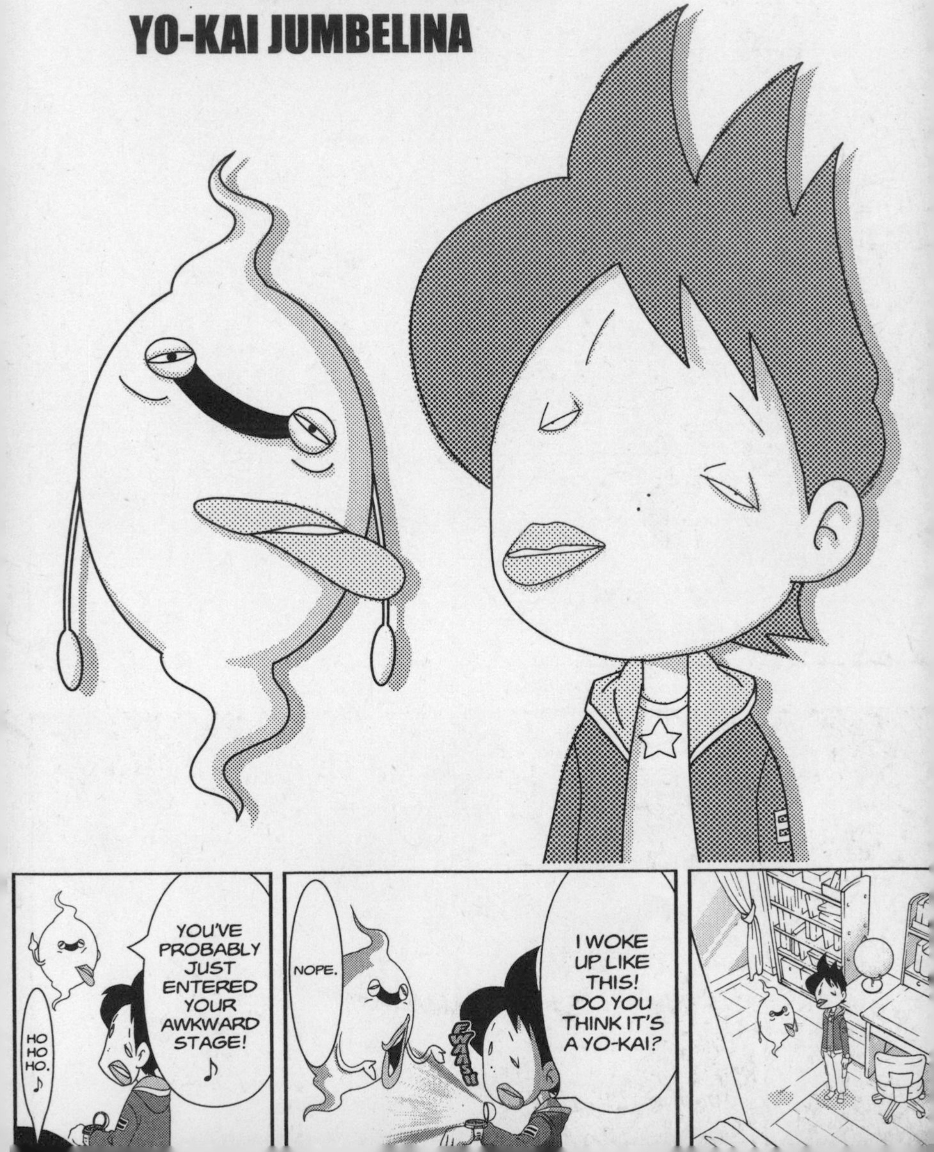
I WOKE UP LIKE THIS! DO YOU THINK IT'S A YO-KAI?
NOPE.
YOU'VE PROBABLY JUST ENTERED YOUR AWKWARD STAGE! ♪
HO HO HO. ♪

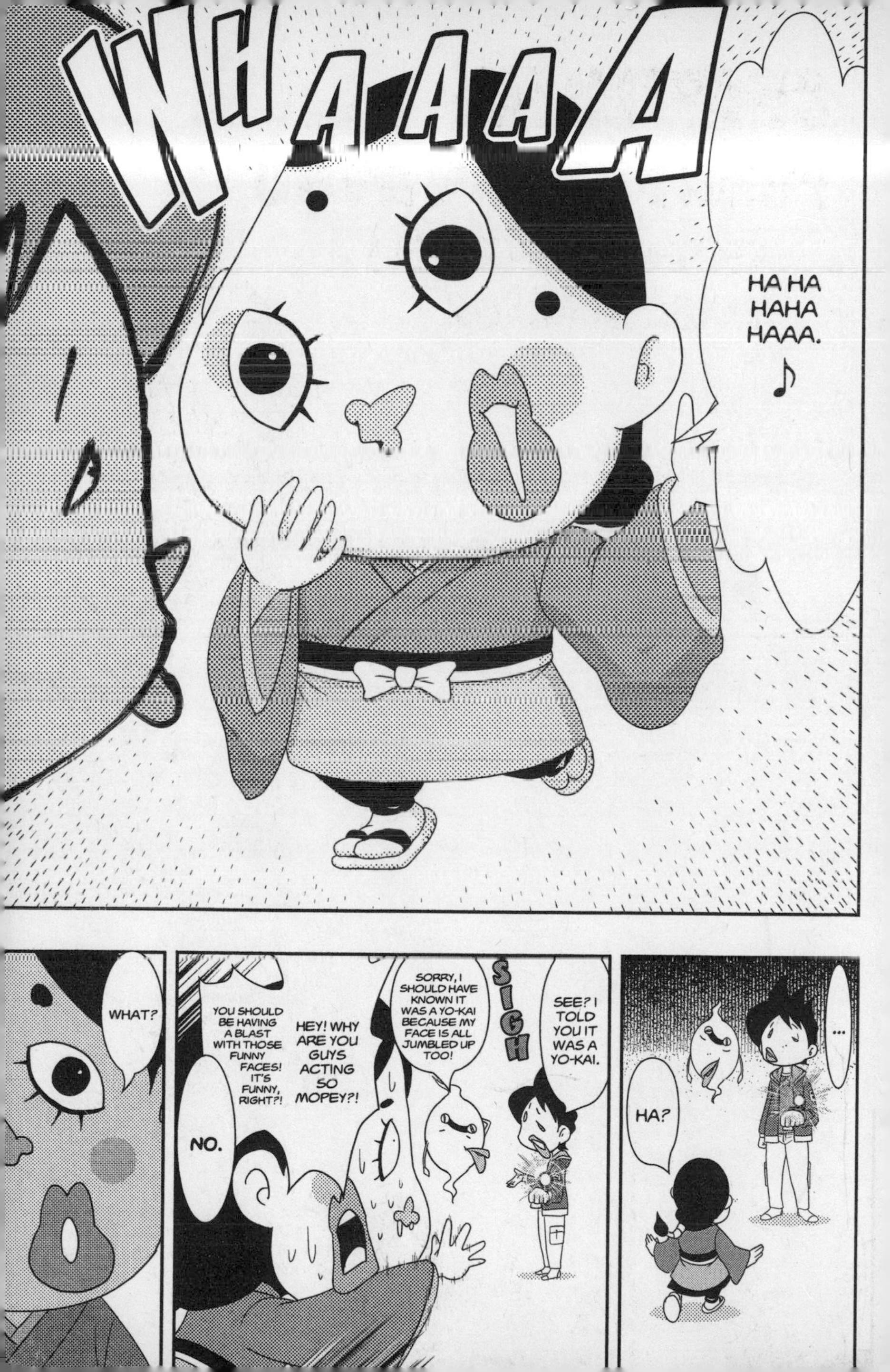
WHAAAAA
HA HA HAHA HAAA. ♪
...
HA?
SEE? I TOLD YOU IT WAS A YO-KAI.
SIGH
SORRY, I SHOULD HAVE KNOWN IT WAS A YO-KAI BECAUSE MY FACE IS ALL JUMBLED UP TOO!
HEY! WHY ARE YOU GUYS ACTING SO MOPEY?!
YOU SHOULD BE HAVING A BLAST WITH THOSE FUNNY FACES! IT'S FUNNY, RIGHT?!
NO.
WHAT?

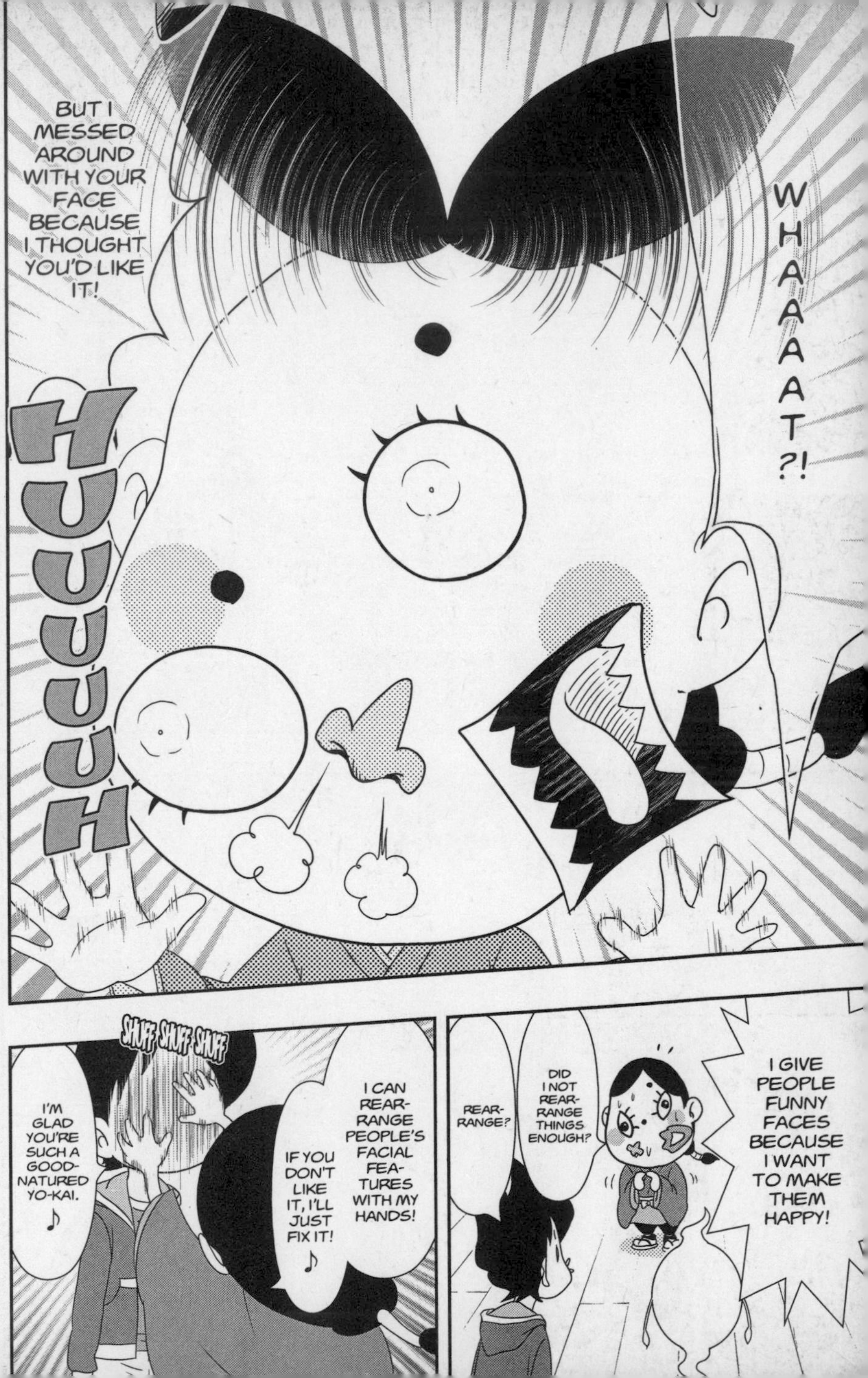
WHAAAAT?!
BUT I MESSED AROUND WITH YOUR FACE BECAUSE I THOUGHT YOU'D LIKE IT!
HUUUUUH
I GIVE PEOPLE FUNNY FACES BECAUSE I WANT TO MAKE THEM HAPPY!
DID I NOT REAR-RANGE THINGS ENOUGH?
REAR-RANGE?
I CAN REAR-RANGE PEOPLE'S FACIAL FEA-TURES WITH MY HANDS!
IF YOU DON'T LIKE IT, I'LL JUST FIX IT! ♪
SHUFF SHUFF SHUFF
I'M GLAD YOU'RE SUCH A GOOD-NATURED YO-KAI. ♪

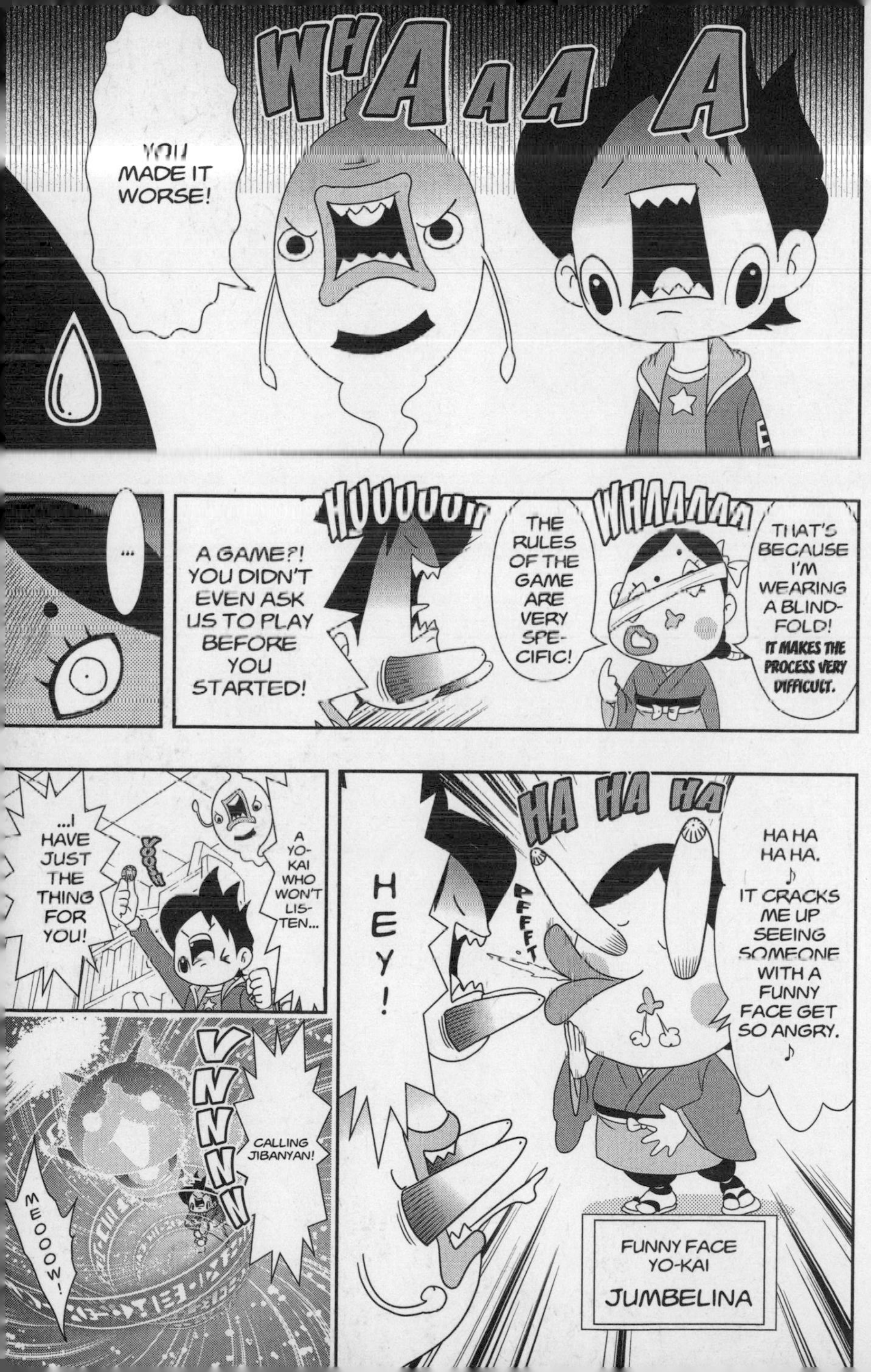
WHAAAA
YOU MADE IT WORSE!
THAT'S BECAUSE I'M WEARING A BLIND-FOLD! IT MAKES THE PROCESS VERY DIFFICULT.
WHAAAAAA
THE RULES OF THE GAME ARE VERY SPE-CIFIC!
HUUUUUH
A GAME?! YOU DIDN'T EVEN ASK US TO PLAY BEFORE YOU STARTED!
...
HA HA HA
HA HA HA HA. ♪ IT CRACKS ME UP SEEING SOMEONE WITH A FUNNY FACE GET SO ANGRY. ♪
PFFFT
HEY!
FUNNY FACE YO-KAI
JUMBELINA
A YO-KAI WHO WON'T LIS-TEN...
...I HAVE JUST THE THING FOR YOU!
VNNNNN
CALLING JIBANYAN!
MEOOOW!

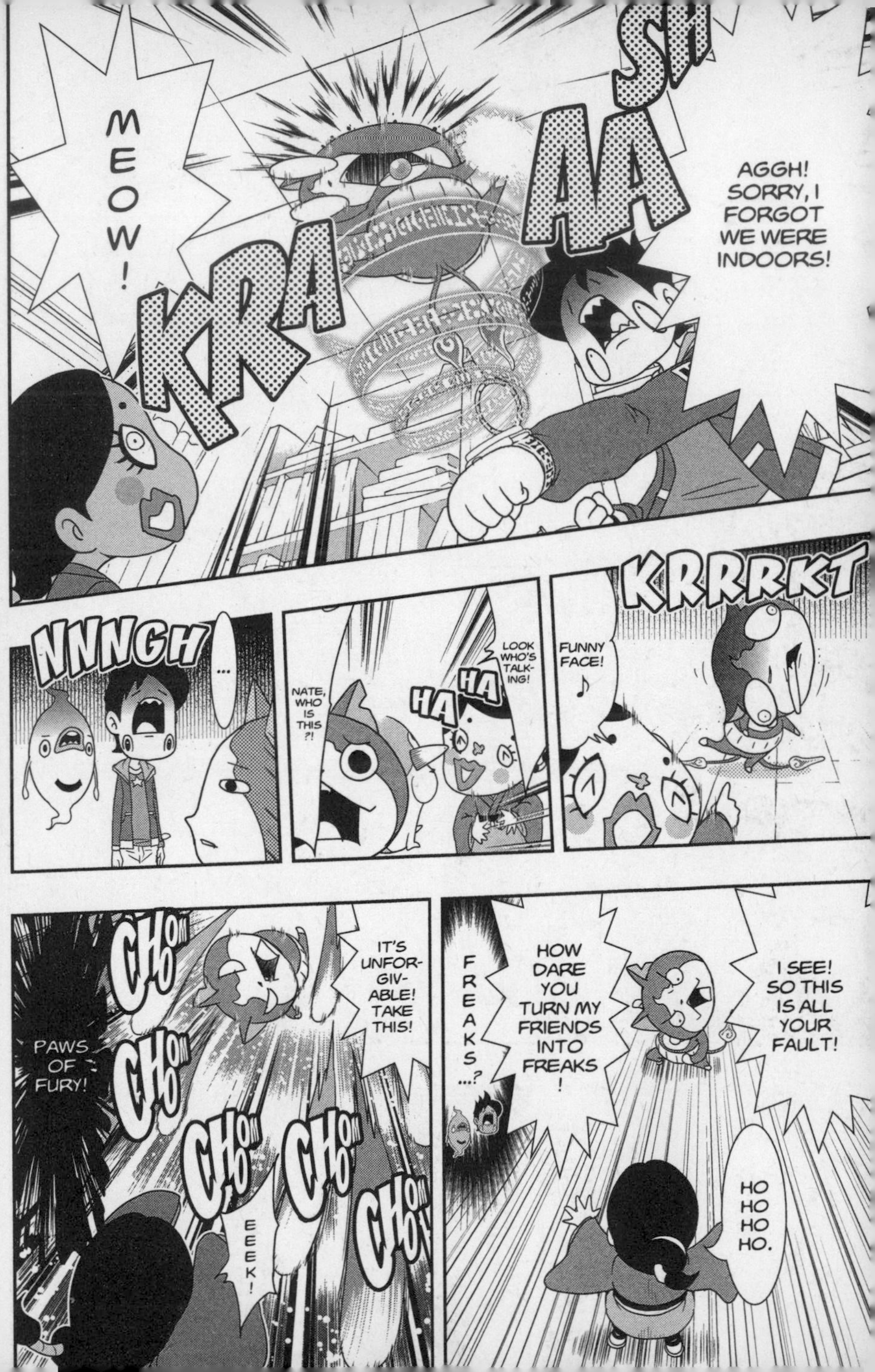
AGGH! SORRY, I FORGOT WE WERE INDOORS!
KRAAASH
MEOW!
KRRRKT
FUNNY FACE! ♪
LOOK WHO'S TALK-ING!
HA HA
NATE, WHO IS THIS?!
...
NNNGH
I SEE! SO THIS IS ALL YOUR FAULT!
HOW DARE YOU TURN MY FRIENDS INTO FREAKS!
HO HO HO HO.
FREAKS...?
IT'S UNFORGIV-ABLE! TAKE THIS!
CHOOM
CHOOM
PAWS OF FURY!
CHOOM
CHOOM
CHOOM
EEEK!

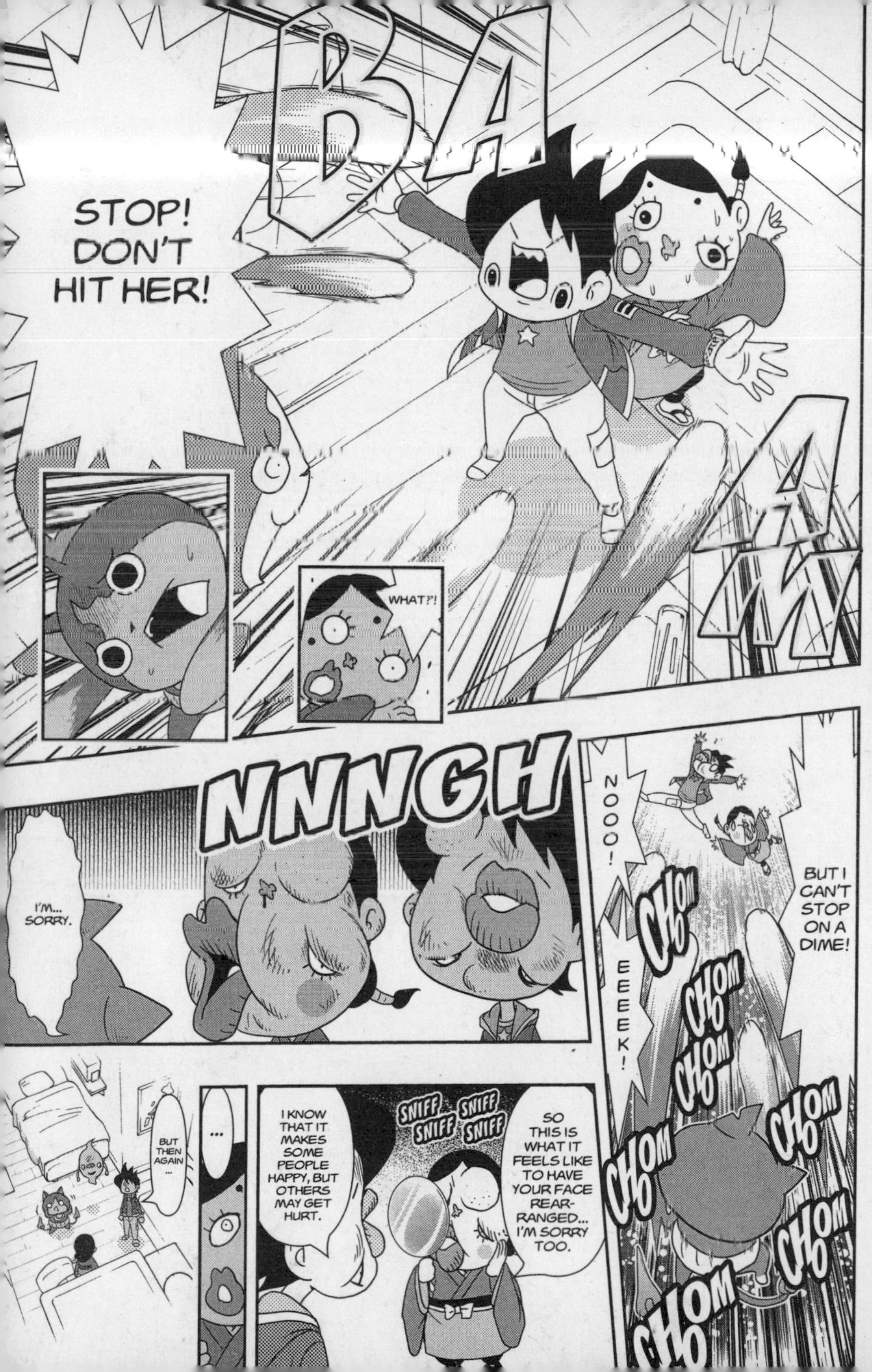
BA
AM
STOP! DON'T HIT HER!
WHAT?!
NOOO!
EEEEK!
BUT I CAN'T STOP ON A DIME!
CHOM
CHOM
CHOM
CHOM
CHOM
CHOM
CHOM
CHOM
NNNGH
I'M... SORRY.
SO THIS IS WHAT IT FEELS LIKE TO HAVE YOUR FACE REAR-RANGED... I'M SORRY TOO.
SNIFF SNIFF
SNIFF SNIFF
I KNOW THAT IT MAKES SOME PEOPLE HAPPY, BUT OTHERS MAY GET HURT.
...
BUT THEN AGAIN...

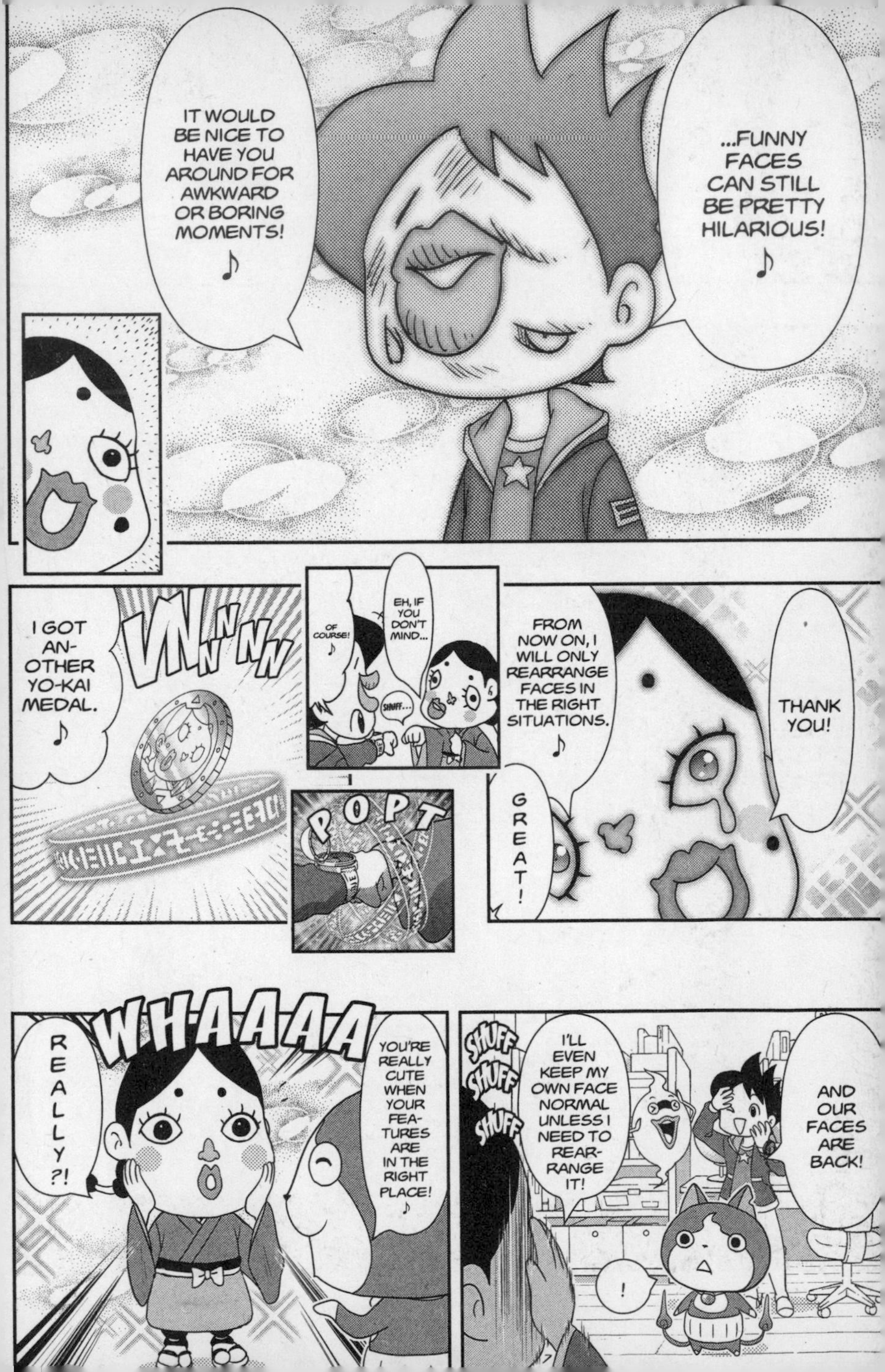
...FUNNY FACES CAN STILL BE PRETTY HILARIOUS! ♪
IT WOULD BE NICE TO HAVE YOU AROUND FOR AWKWARD OR BORING MOMENTS! ♪
THANK YOU!
FROM NOW ON, I WILL ONLY REARRANGE FACES IN THE RIGHT SITUATIONS. ♪
GREAT!
EH, IF YOU DON'T MIND...
OF COURSE! ♪
SHUFF...
POPT
VNNNNNN
I GOT AN-OTHER YO-KAI MEDAL. ♪
AND OUR FACES ARE BACK!
I'LL EVEN KEEP MY OWN FACE NORMAL UNLESS I NEED TO REAR-RANGE IT!
SHUFF SHUFF SHUFF
!
WHAAAAAA
YOU'RE REALLY CUTE WHEN YOUR FEA-TURES ARE IN THE RIGHT PLACE! ♪
REALLY?!

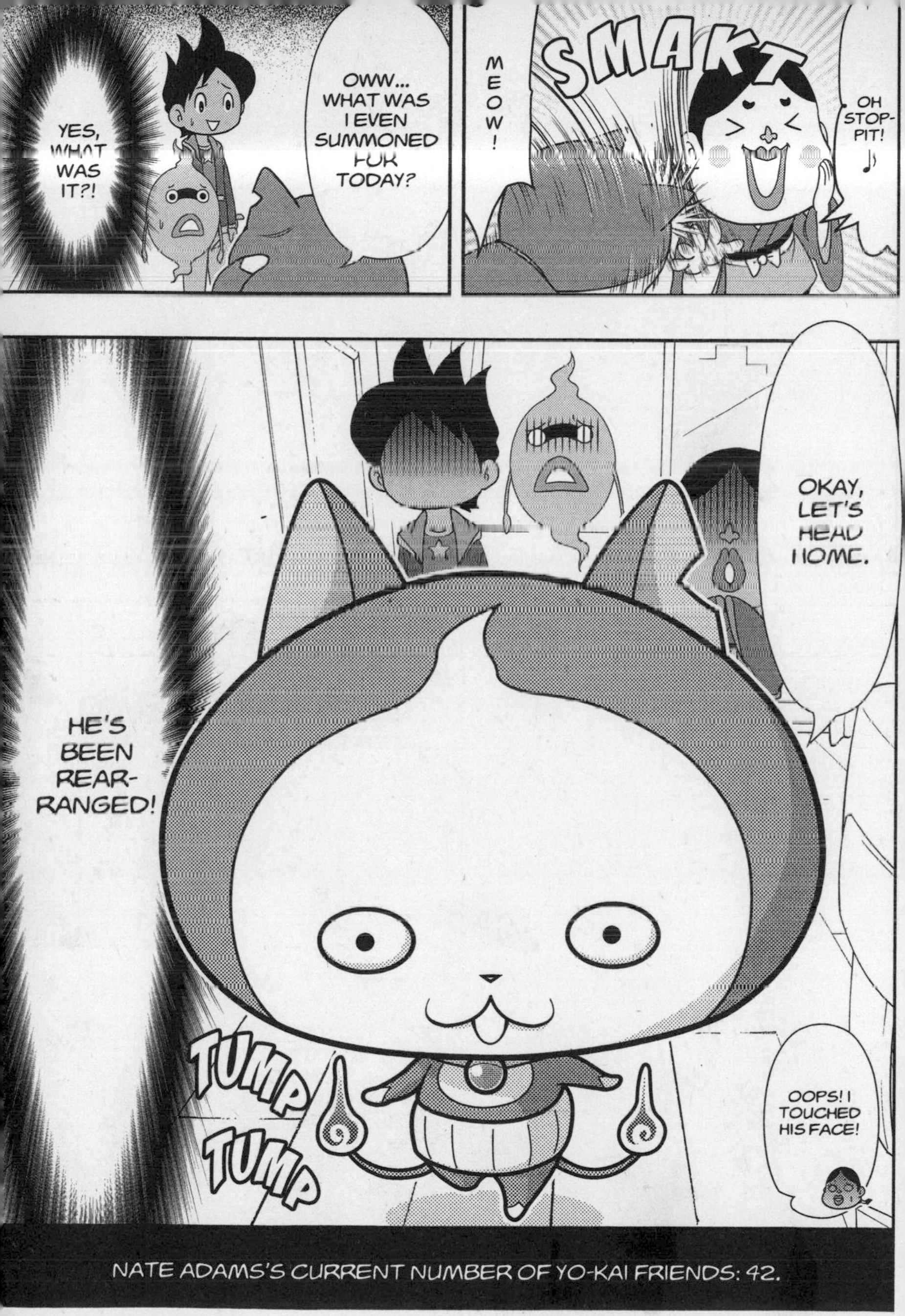
OH STOP-PIT! ♪
SMAKT
MEOW!
OWW... WHAT WAS I EVEN SUMMONED FOR TODAY?
YES, WHAT WAS IT?!
OKAY, LET'S HEAD HOME.
HE'S BEEN REAR-RANGED!
OOPS! I TOUCHED HIS FACE!
TUMP
TUMP
NATE ADAMS'S CURRENT NUMBER OF YO-KAI FRIENDS: 42.

FACE OFF!

KRAKT
HOW DARE YOU REARRANGE MY FACE!!
WHY ARE YOU PUNCHING ME?!
BAAAM
I CAN'T PUNCH LADIES, SO I'M PUNCHING YOU INSTEAD!
THANKS FOR PROTECTING ME!
TWITCH
TWITCH
TWITCH
TWITCH
EH...I DIDN'T... MEAN TO...
LEAVE IT TO ME!
WITCH...
?
FWOOOOSH
PAIN, PAIN... FLY AWAY. ♪
AGGGGH! YOU WIPED MY FACE COMPLETELY OFF!
SHUFF
SHUFF
OOPS...

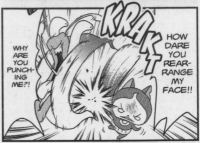

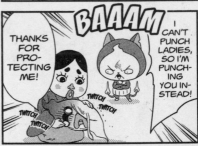

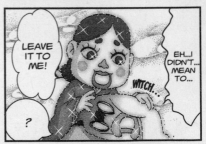

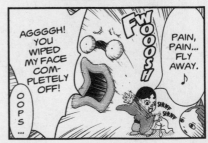

CHAPTER 56: LICK YOUR WOUNDS ♪

FEATURING CURING YO-KAI TONGUS

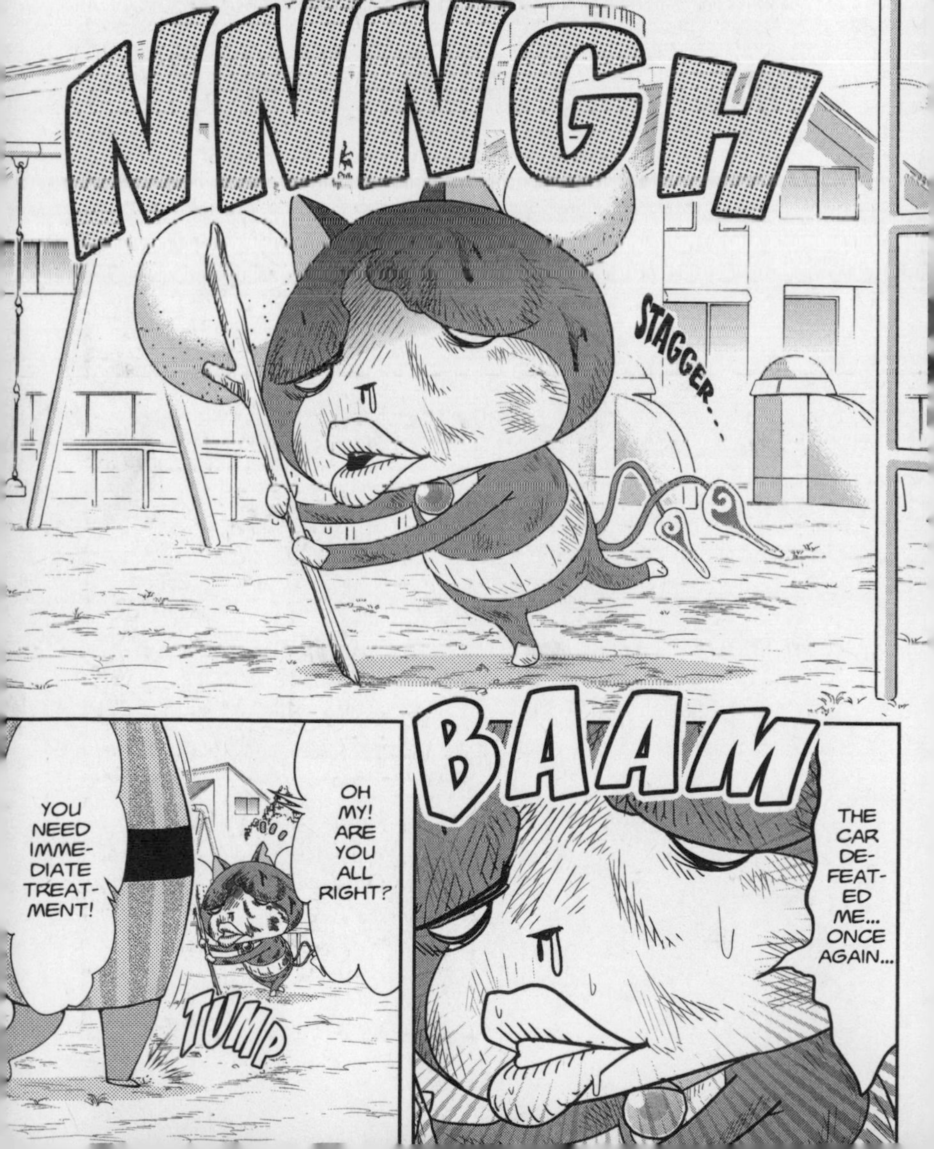
NNNGH
STAGGER...
BAAM
THE CAR DEFEATED ME... ONCE AGAIN...
OH MY! ARE YOU ALL RIGHT?
YOU NEED IMMEDIATE TREATMENT!
TUMP

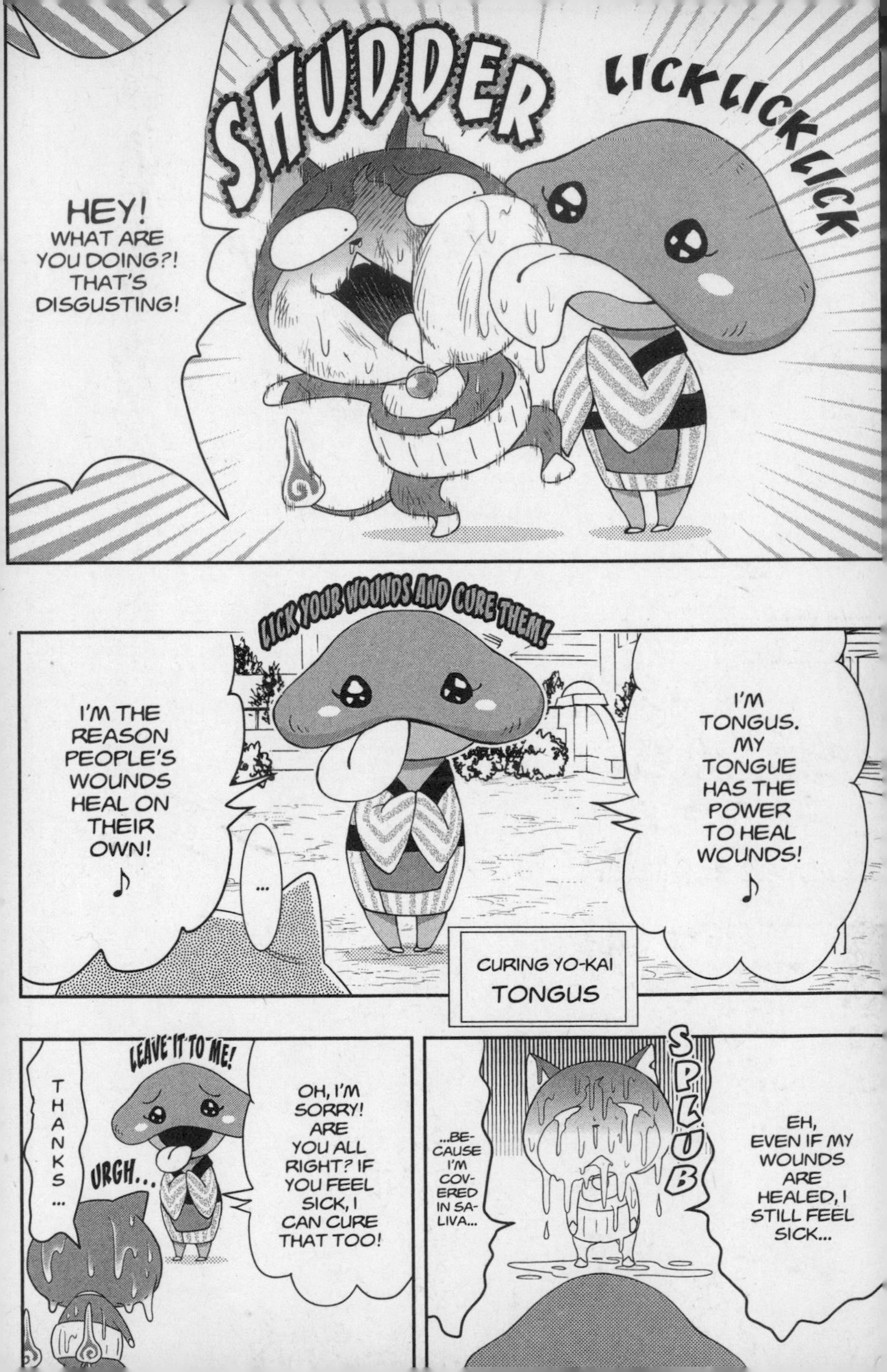

LICK LICK LICK LICK
SHUDDER
HEY! WHAT ARE YOU DOING?! THAT'S DISGUSTING!
LICK YOUR WOUNDS AND CURE THEM!
I'M TONGUS. MY TONGUE HAS THE POWER TO HEAL WOUNDS! ♪
I'M THE REASON PEOPLE'S WOUNDS HEAL ON THEIR OWN! ♪
...
CURING YO-KAI TONGUS
SPLUB
EH, EVEN IF MY WOUNDS ARE HEALED, I STILL FEEL SICK...
...BE-CAUSE I'M COV-ERED IN SA-LIVA...
OH, I'M SORRY! ARE YOU ALL RIGHT? IF YOU FEEL SICK, I CAN CURE THAT TOO!
LEAVE IT TO ME!
URGH...
THANKS...

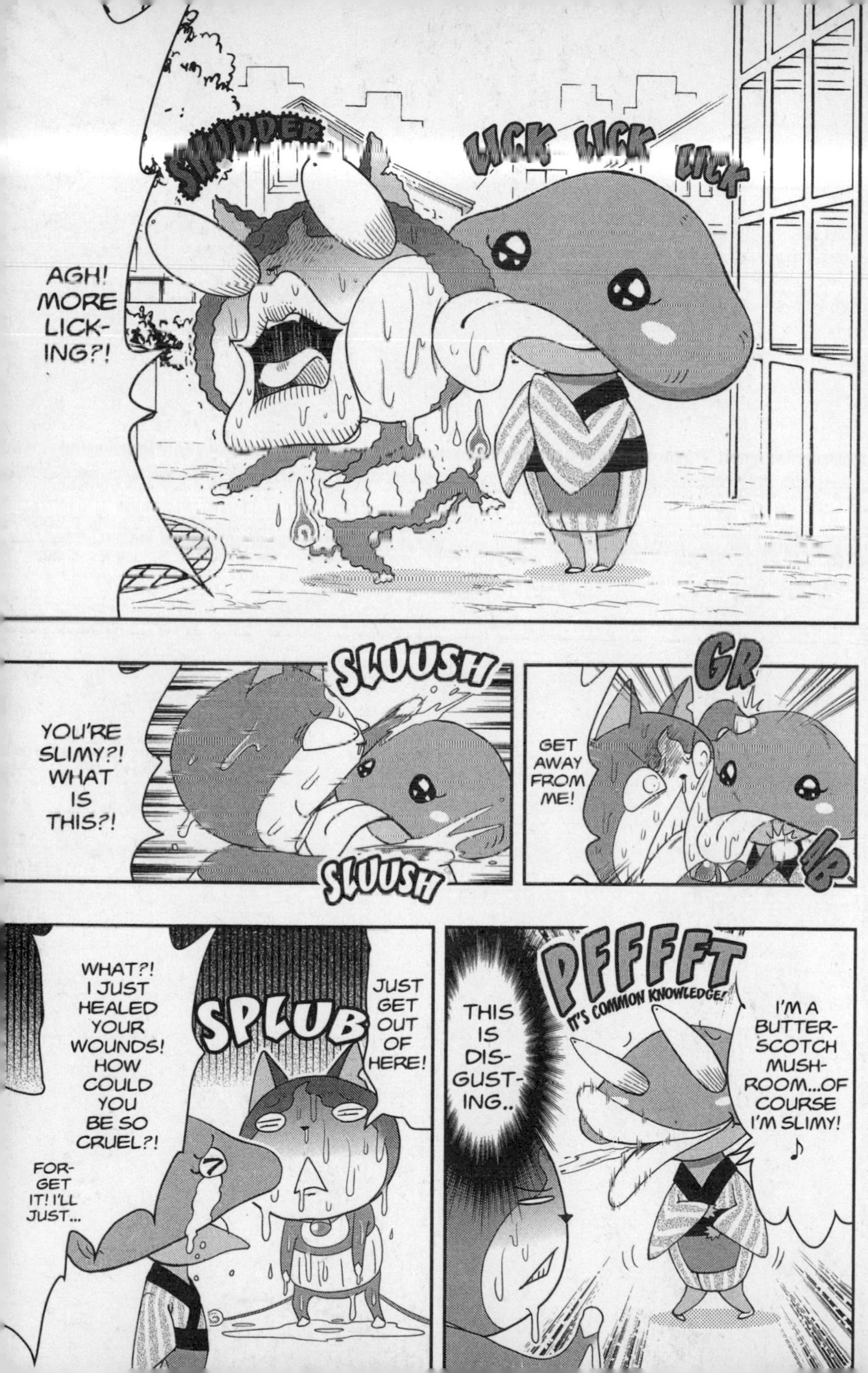
LICK LICK LICK
SHUDDER
AGH! MORE LICKING?!
GR
GET AWAY FROM ME!
SLUUSH
YOU'RE SLIMY?! WHAT IS THIS?!
SLUUSH
PFFFFT
IT'S COMMON KNOWLEDGE!
I'M A BUTTERSCOTCH MUSHROOM...OF COURSE I'M SLIMY! ♪
THIS IS DISGUSTING..
JUST GET OUT OF HERE!
SPLUB
WHAT?! I JUST HEALED YOUR WOUNDS! HOW COULD YOU BE SO CRUEL?!
FORGET IT! I'LL JUST...

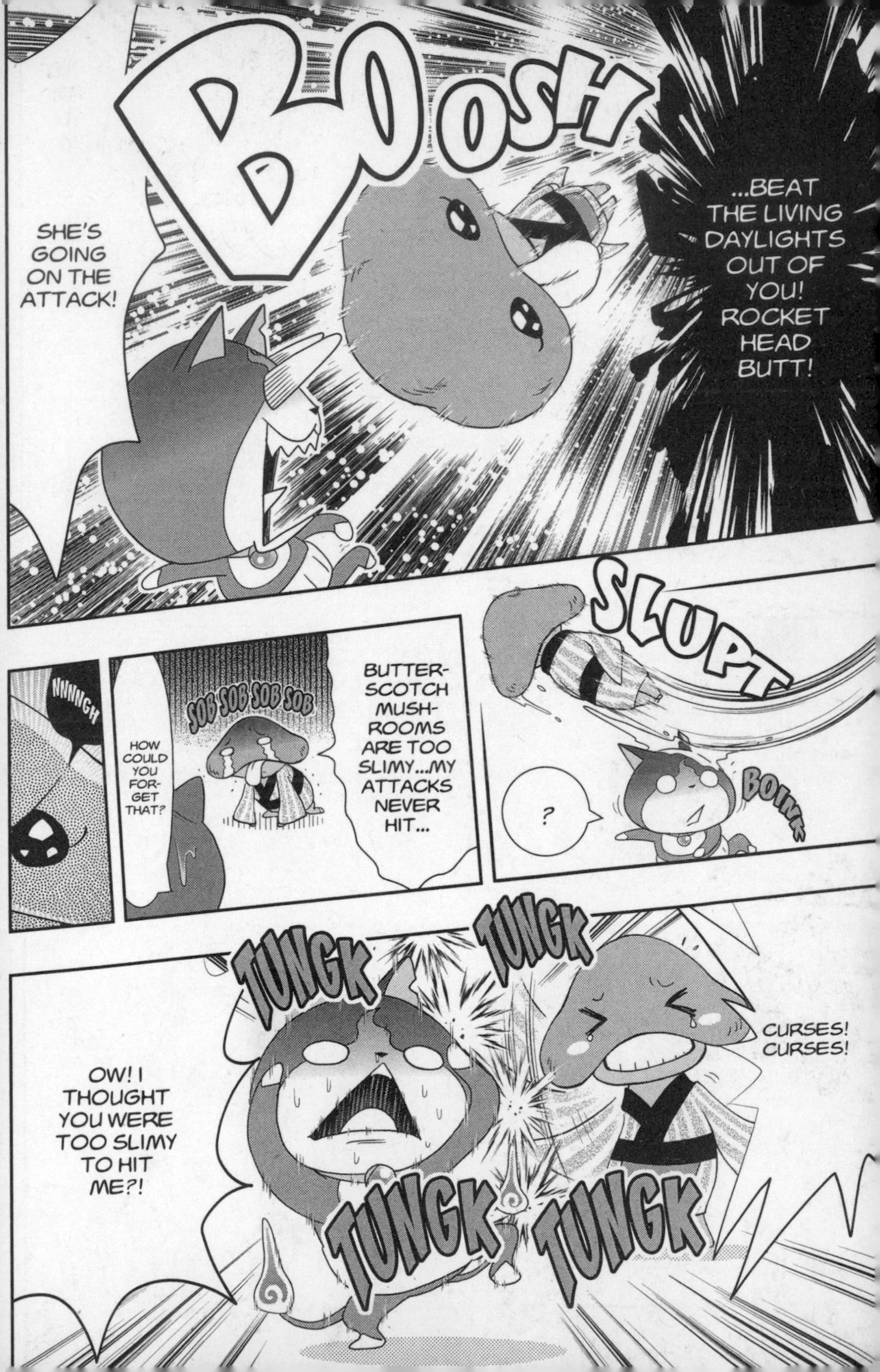
...BEAT THE LIVING DAYLIGHTS OUT OF YOU! ROCKET HEAD BUTT!
BOOSH
SHE'S GOING ON THE ATTACK!
SLUPT
BOINK
?
BUTTER-SCOTCH MUSH-ROOMS ARE TOO SLIMY...MY ATTACKS NEVER HIT...
SOB SOB SOB SOB
HOW COULD YOU FOR-GET THAT?
NNNNGH
TUNGK
TUNGK
CURSES! CURSES!
TUNGK
TUNGK
OW! I THOUGHT YOU WERE TOO SLIMY TO HIT ME?!

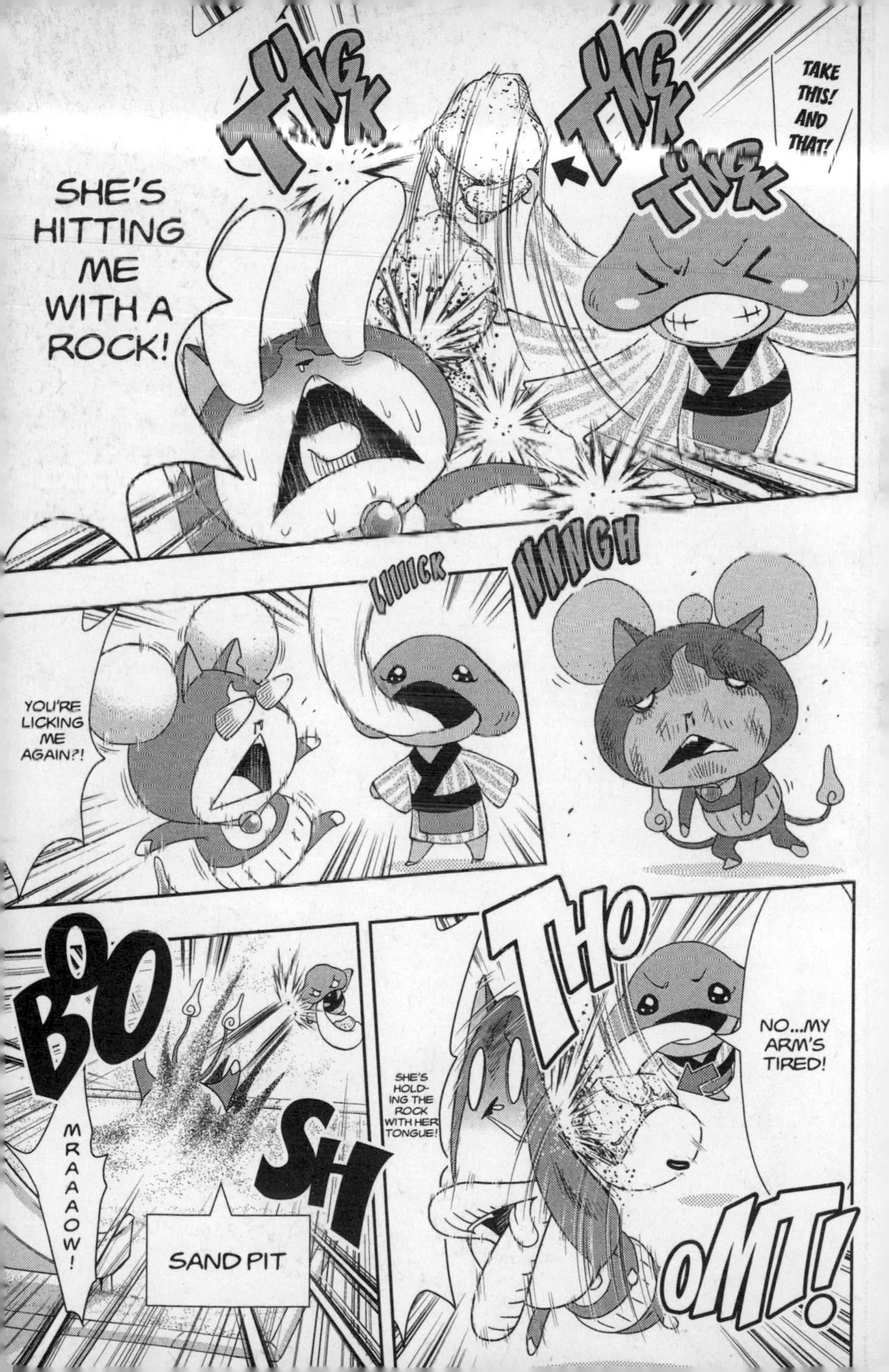
TAKE THIS! AND THAT!
TINGK
TINGK
TINGK
SHE'S HITTING ME WITH A ROCK!
NNNGH
LIIIICK
YOU'RE LICKING ME AGAIN?!
NO...MY ARM'S TIRED!
THO
SHE'S HOLD-ING THE ROCK WITH HER TONGUE!
OMT!
BOO
MRAAAOW!
SH
SAND PIT

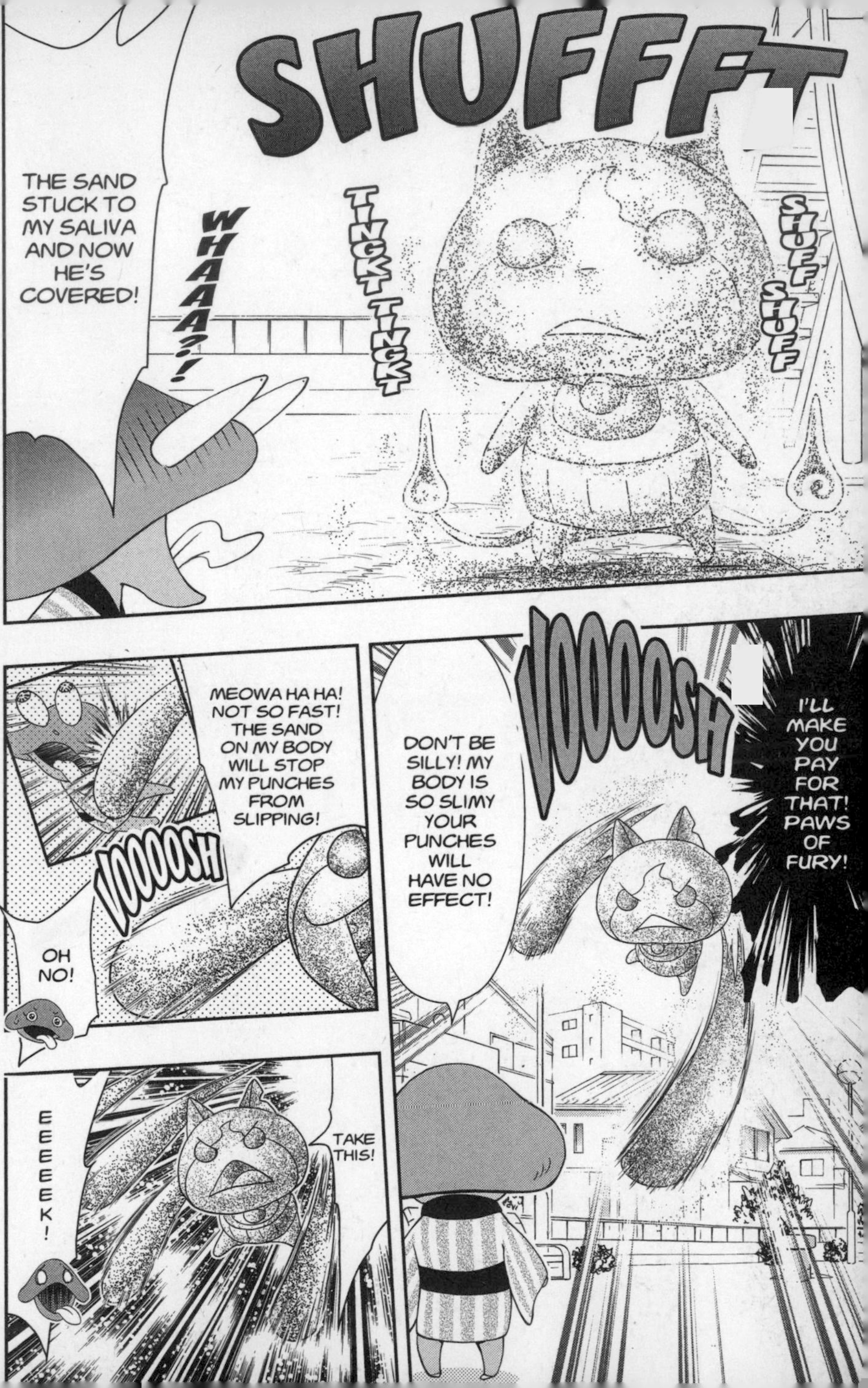
SHUFFFT
SHUFF SHUFF
TINGKT TINGKT
WHAAAA?!
THE SAND STUCK TO MY SALIVA AND NOW HE'S COVERED!
I'LL MAKE YOU PAY FOR THAT! PAWS OF FURY!
VOOOOSH
DON'T BE SILLY! MY BODY IS SO SLIMY YOUR PUNCHES WILL HAVE NO EFFECT!
MEOWA HA HA! NOT SO FAST! THE SAND ON MY BODY WILL STOP MY PUNCHES FROM SLIPPING!
VOOOOSH
OH NO!
TAKE THIS!
EEEEEEK!

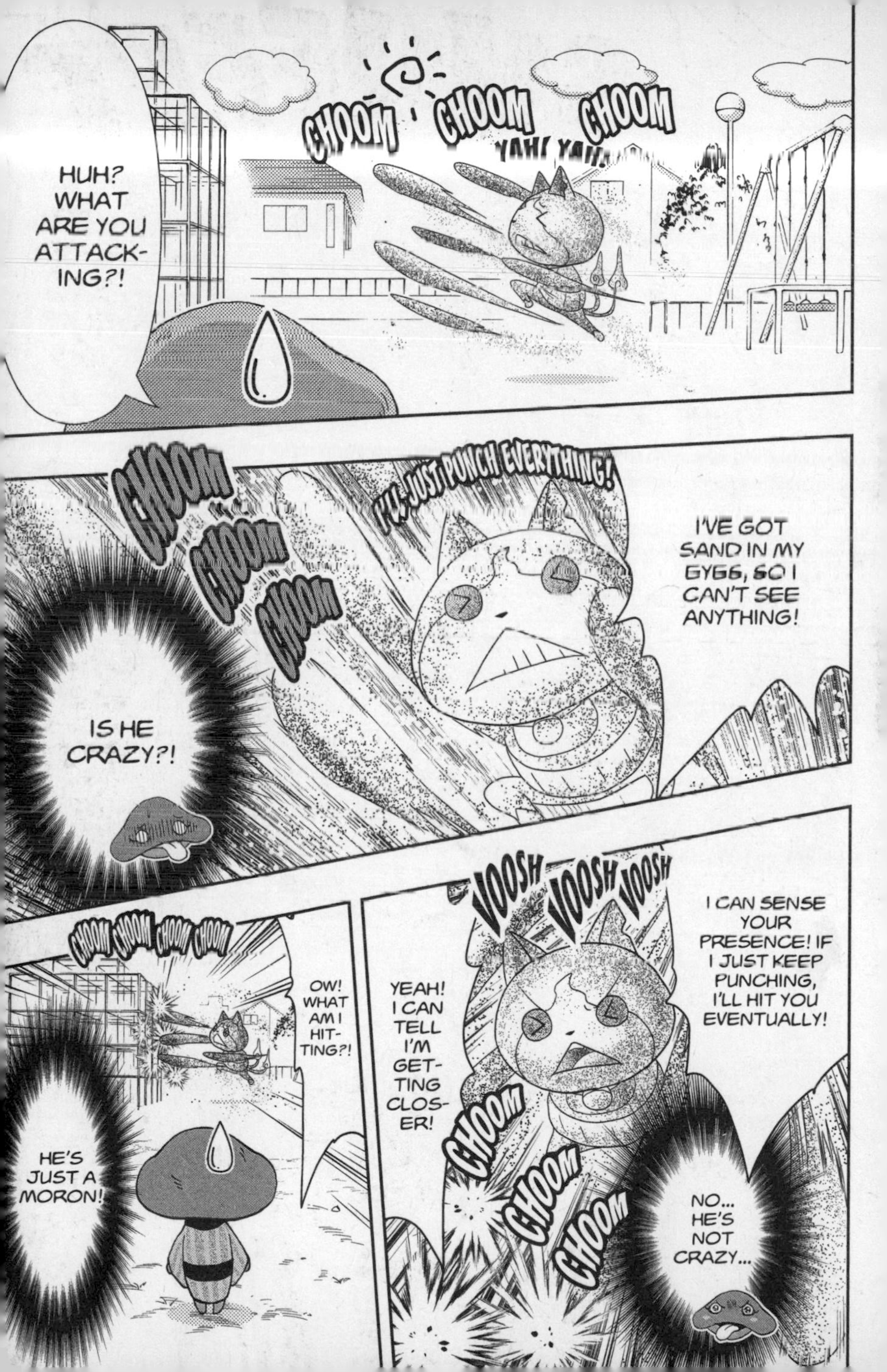
CHOOM CHOOM CHOOM
YAH! YAH!
HUH? WHAT ARE YOU ATTACKING?!
I'VE GOT SAND IN MY EYES, SO I CAN'T SEE ANYTHING!
I'LL JUST PUNCH EVERYTHING!
CHOOM CHOOM CHOOM
IS HE CRAZY?!
I CAN SENSE YOUR PRESENCE! IF I JUST KEEP PUNCHING, I'LL HIT YOU EVENTUALLY!
VOOSH VOOSH VOOSH
YEAH! I CAN TELL I'M GETTING CLOSER!
CHOOM CHOOM CHOOM
NO... HE'S NOT CRAZY...
CHOOM CHOOM CHOOM CHOOM
OW! WHAT AM I HITTING?!
HE'S JUST A MORON!

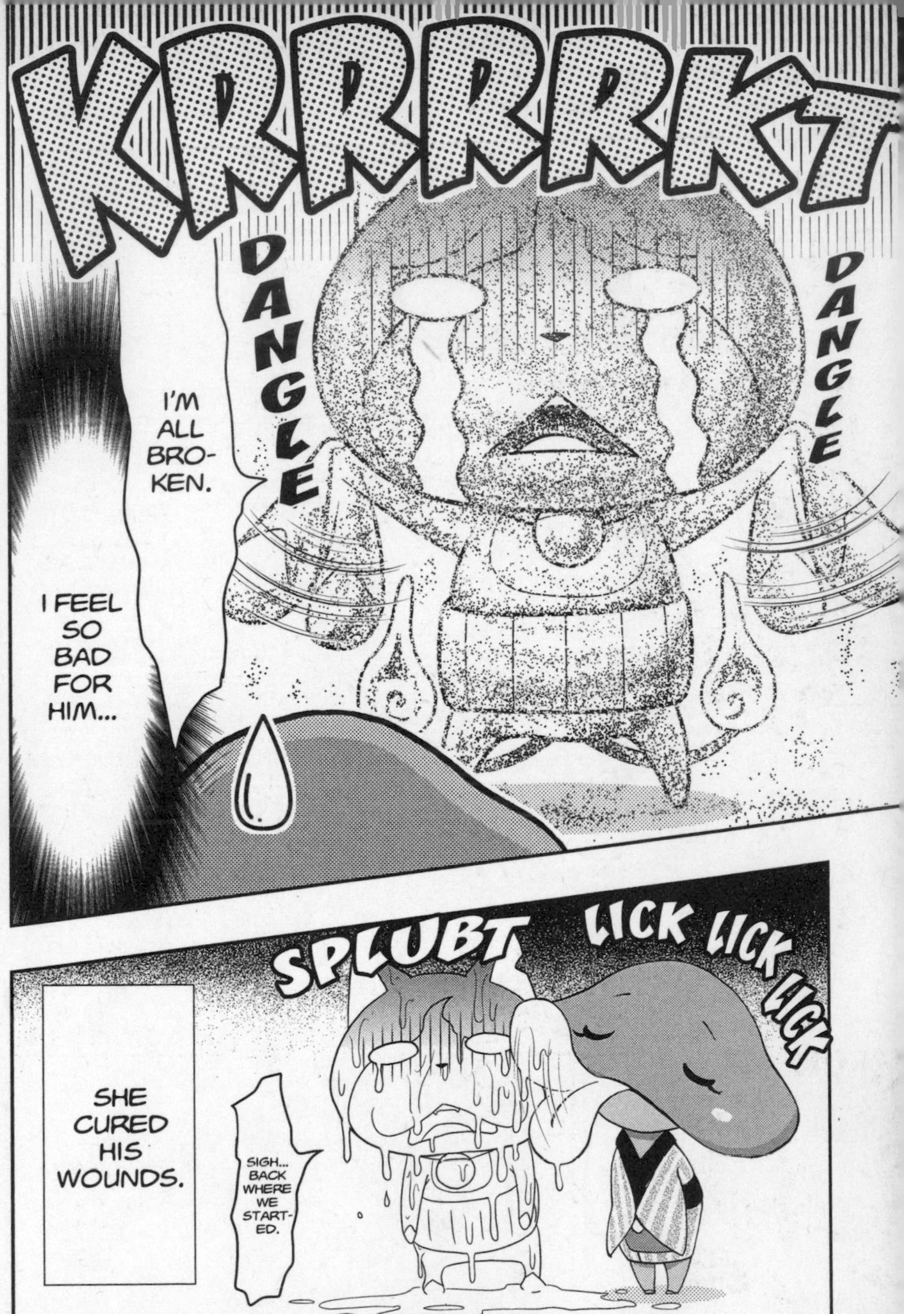
KRRRRKT
DANGLE
DANGLE
I'M ALL BRO-KEN.
I FEEL SO BAD FOR HIM...
LICK LICK LICK
SPLUBT
SIGH... BACK WHERE WE START-ED.
SHE CURED HIS WOUNDS.

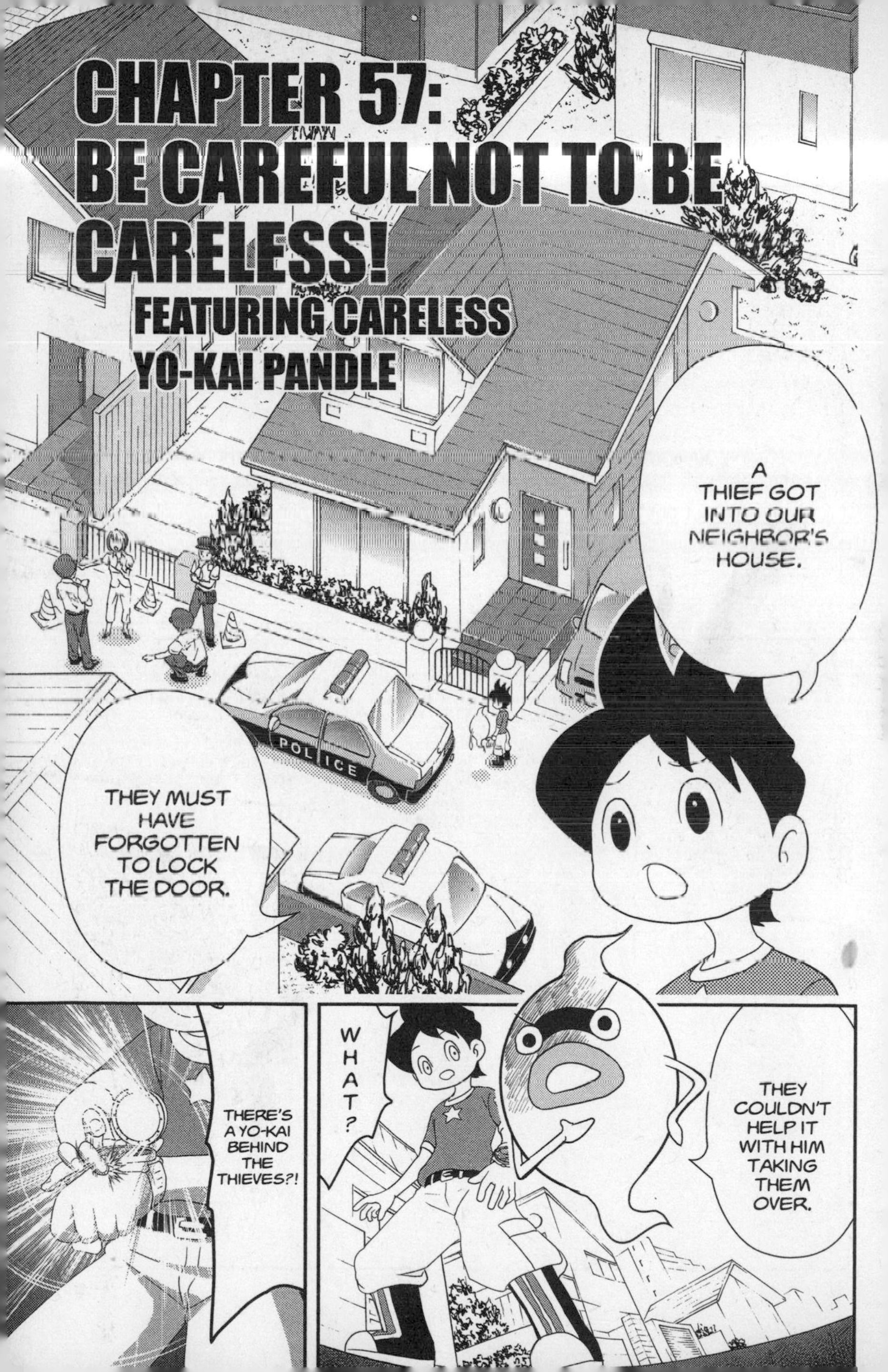
CHAPTER 57: BE CAREFUL NOT TO BE CARELESS!
FEATURING CARELESS YO-KAI PANDLE
A THIEF GOT INTO OUR NEIGHBOR'S HOUSE.
THEY MUST HAVE FORGOTTEN TO LOCK THE DOOR.
POLICE
THEY COULDN'T HELP IT WITH HIM TAKING THEM OVER.
WHAT?
THERE'S A YO-KAI BEHIND THE THIEVES?!

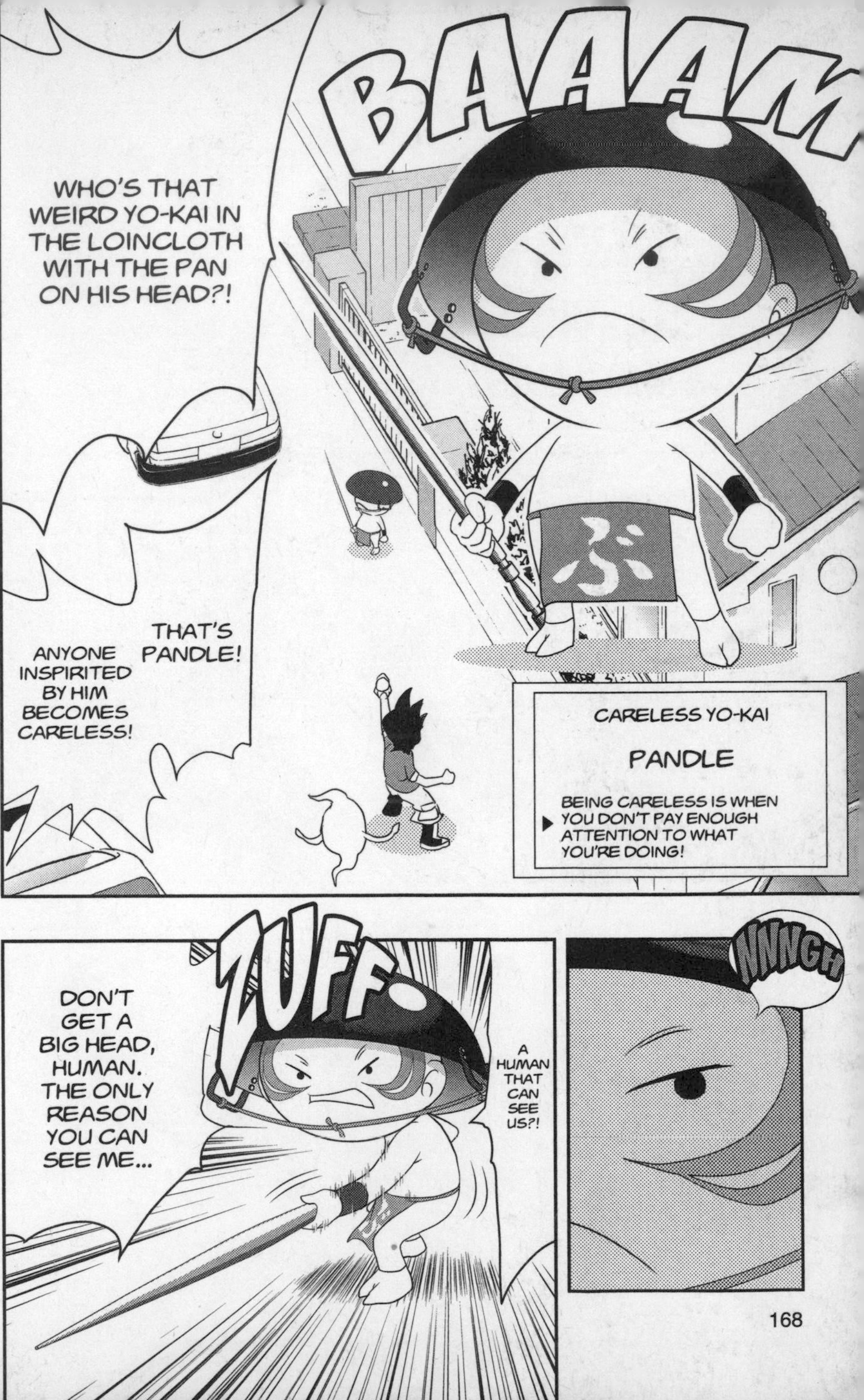
BAAAM
WHO'S THAT WEIRD YO-KAI IN THE LOINCLOTH WITH THE PAN ON HIS HEAD?!
THAT'S PANDLE!
ANYONE INSPIRITED BY HIM BECOMES CARELESS!
CARELESS YO-KAI
PANDLE
▶ BEING CARELESS IS WHEN YOU DON'T PAY ENOUGH ATTENTION TO WHAT YOU'RE DOING!
NNNGH
ZUFF
A HUMAN THAT CAN SEE US?!
DON'T GET A BIG HEAD, HUMAN. THE ONLY REASON YOU CAN SEE ME...

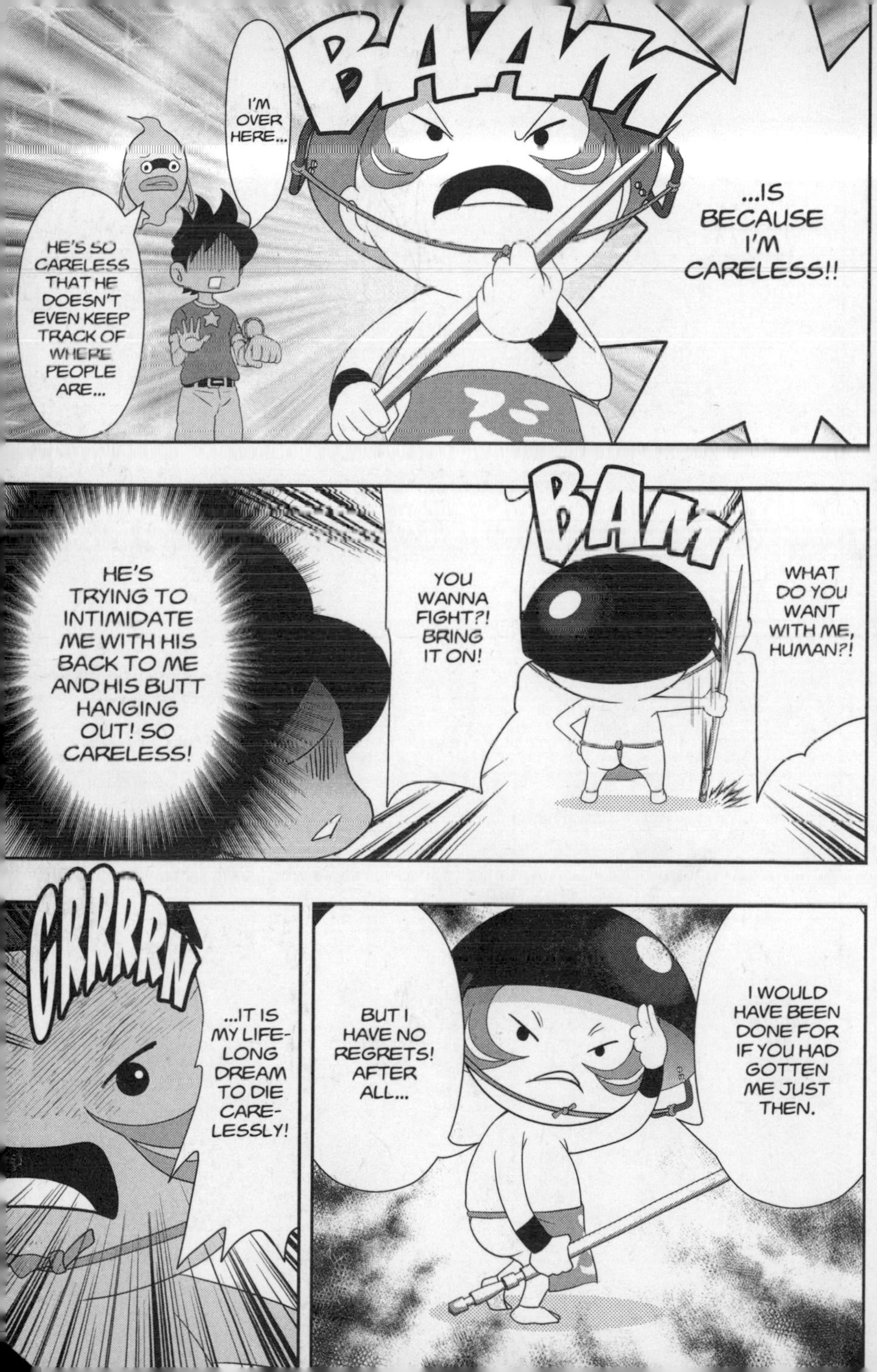
...IS BECAUSE I'M CARELESS!!
BAAM
I'M OVER HERE...
HE'S SO CARELESS THAT HE DOESN'T EVEN KEEP TRACK OF WHERE PEOPLE ARE...
WHAT DO YOU WANT WITH ME, HUMAN?!
BAM
YOU WANNA FIGHT?! BRING IT ON!
HE'S TRYING TO INTIMIDATE ME WITH HIS BACK TO ME AND HIS BUTT HANGING OUT! SO CARELESS!
I WOULD HAVE BEEN DONE FOR IF YOU HAD GOTTEN ME JUST THEN.
BUT I HAVE NO REGRETS! AFTER ALL...
GRRRRN
...IT IS MY LIFE-LONG DREAM TO DIE CARE-LESSLY!

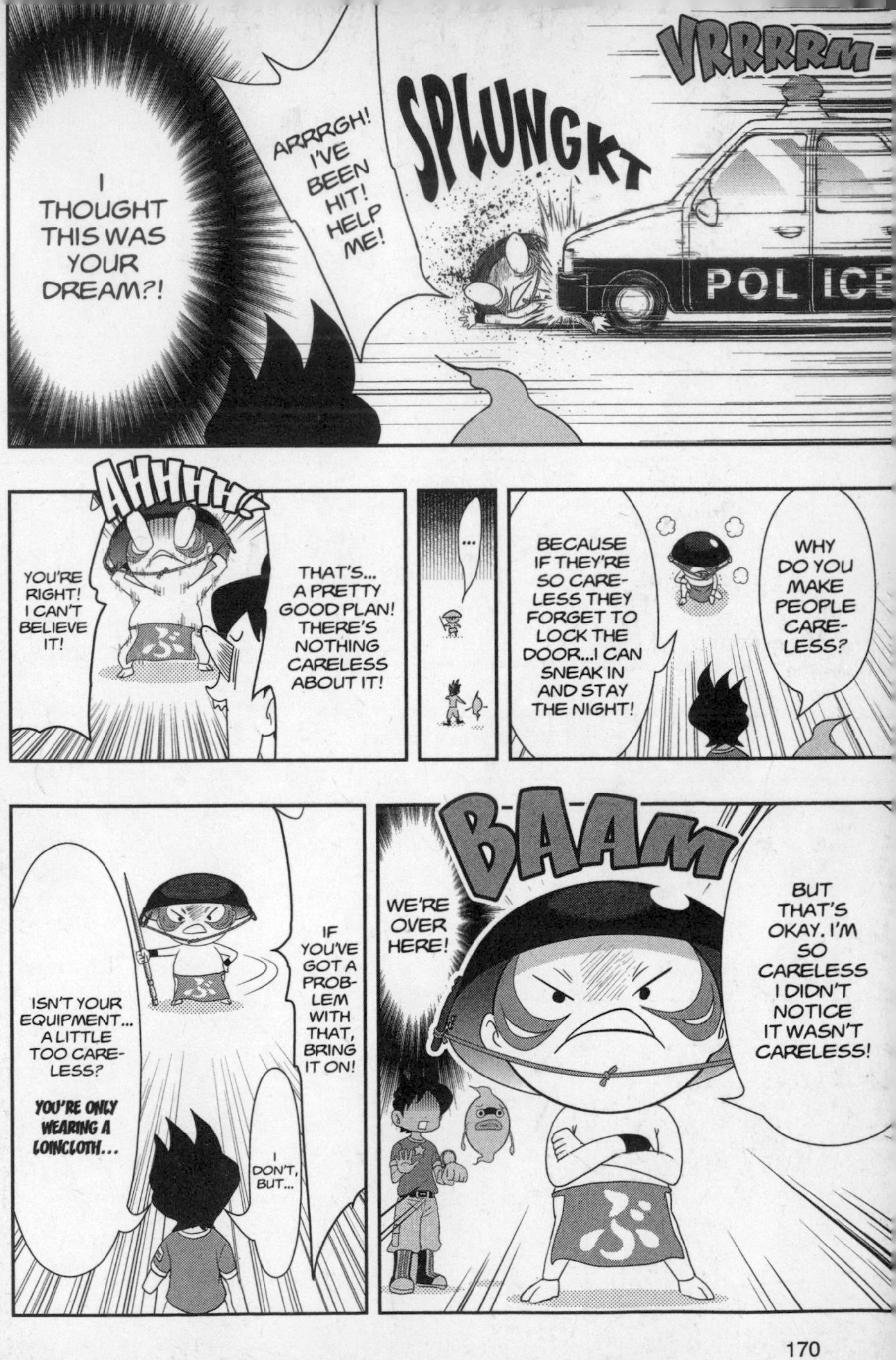
VRRRRM
SPLUNGKT
ARRRGH! I'VE BEEN HIT! HELP ME!
POLICE
I THOUGHT THIS WAS YOUR DREAM?!
WHY DO YOU MAKE PEOPLE CARE-LESS?
BECAUSE IF THEY'RE SO CARE-LESS THEY FORGET TO LOCK THE DOOR...I CAN SNEAK IN AND STAY THE NIGHT!
...
THAT'S... A PRETTY GOOD PLAN! THERE'S NOTHING CARELESS ABOUT IT!
AHHHH!
YOU'RE RIGHT! I CAN'T BELIEVE IT!
BAAM
BUT THAT'S OKAY. I'M SO CARELESS I DIDN'T NOTICE IT WASN'T CARELESS!
WE'RE OVER HERE!
ISN'T YOUR EQUIPMENT... A LITTLE TOO CARE-LESS?
YOU'RE ONLY WEARING A LOINCLOTH...
IF YOU'VE GOT A PROB-LEM WITH THAT, BRING IT ON!
I DON'T, BUT...

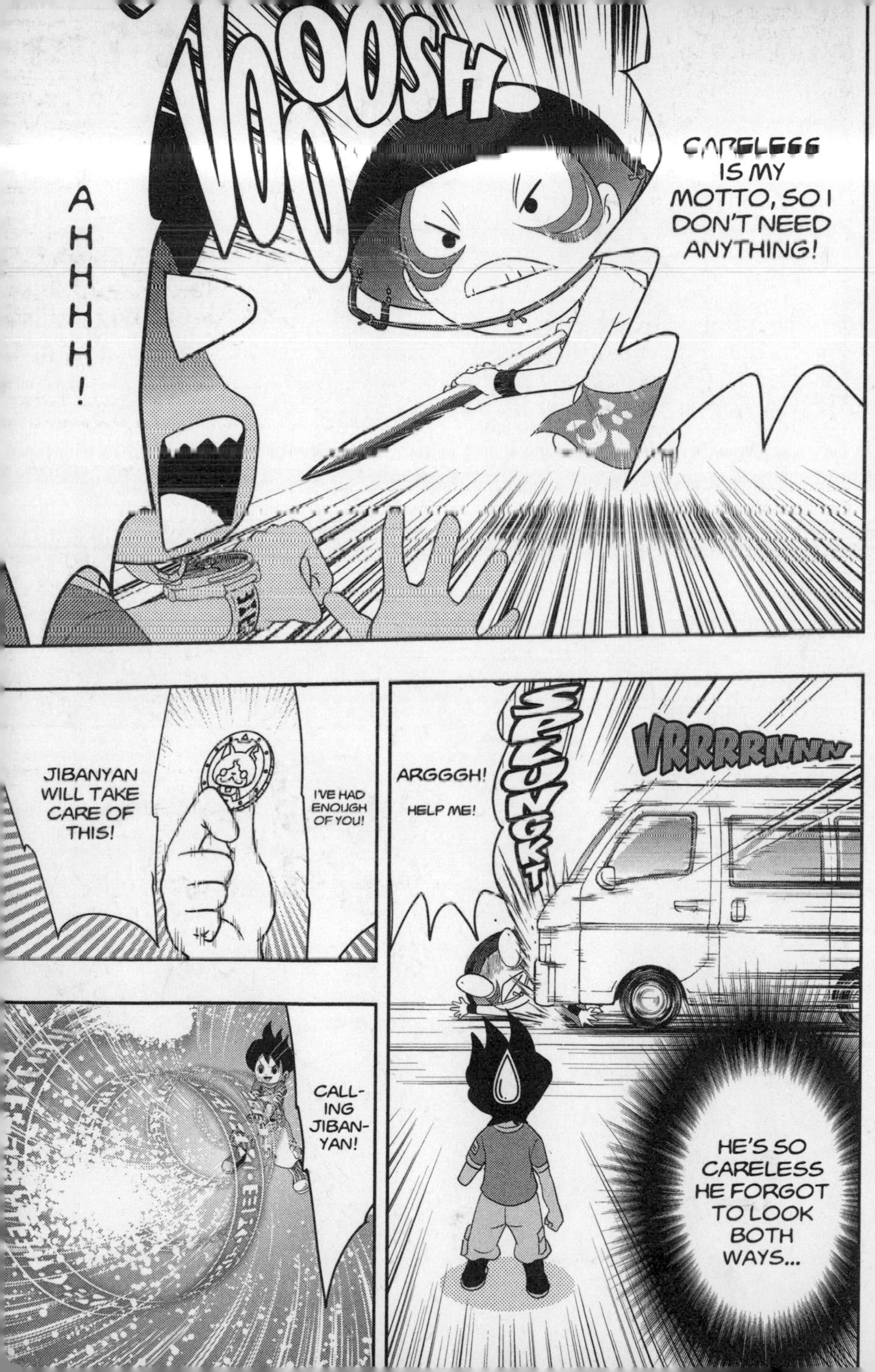

CARELESS IS MY MOTTO, SO I DON'T NEED ANYTHING!
VOOOOSH
AHHHHH!
VRRRRNNNN
SPLUNGKT
ARGGGH!
HELP ME!
HE'S SO CARELESS HE FORGOT TO LOOK BOTH WAYS...
JIBANYAN WILL TAKE CARE OF THIS!
I'VE HAD ENOUGH OF YOU!
CALLING JIBANYAN!

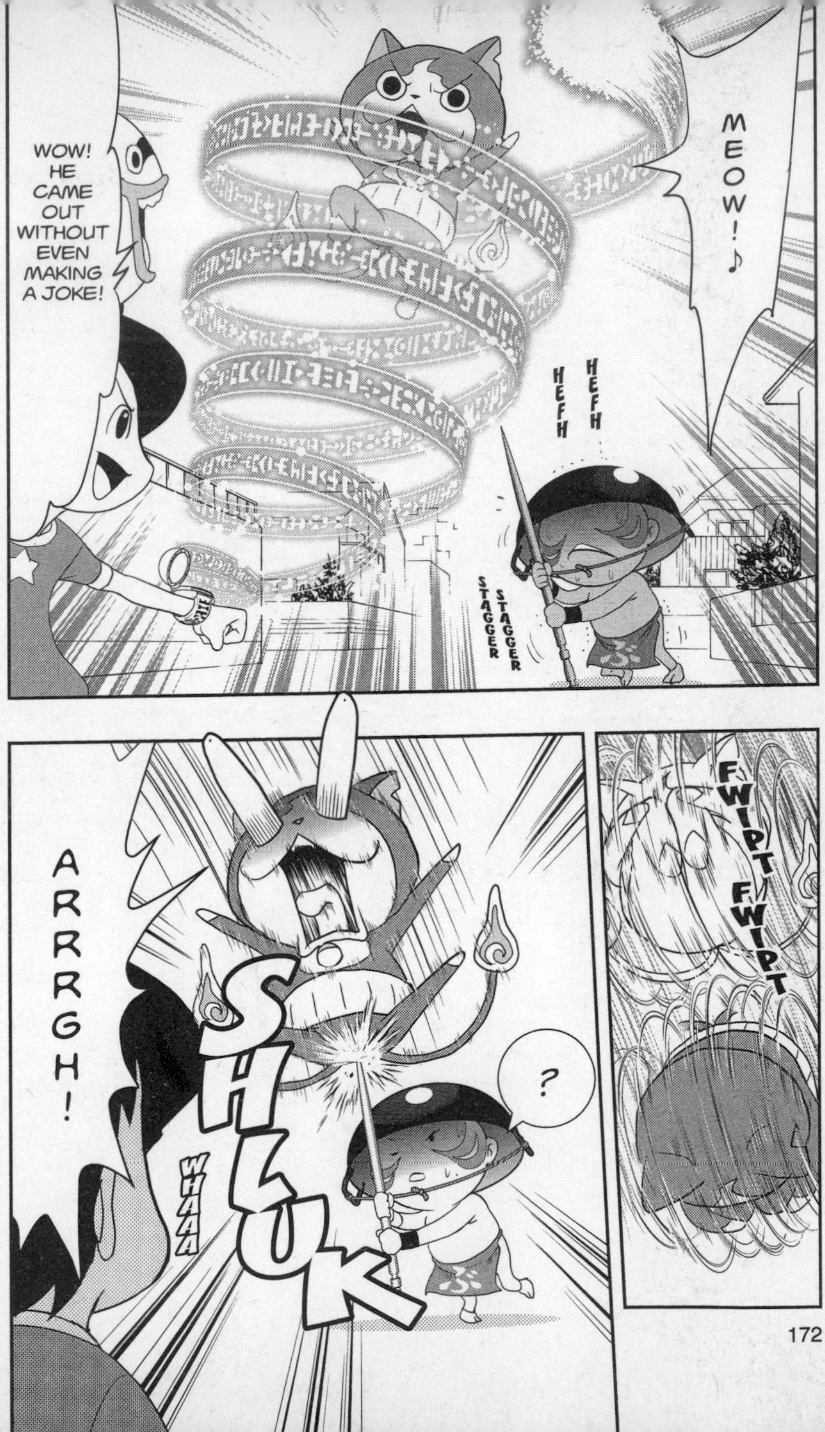
MEOW!♪
HEFH HEFH
STAGGER STAGGER
WOW! HE CAME OUT WITHOUT EVEN MAKING A JOKE!
FWIPT FWIPT
?
ARRRGH!
SHLUK
WHAAA

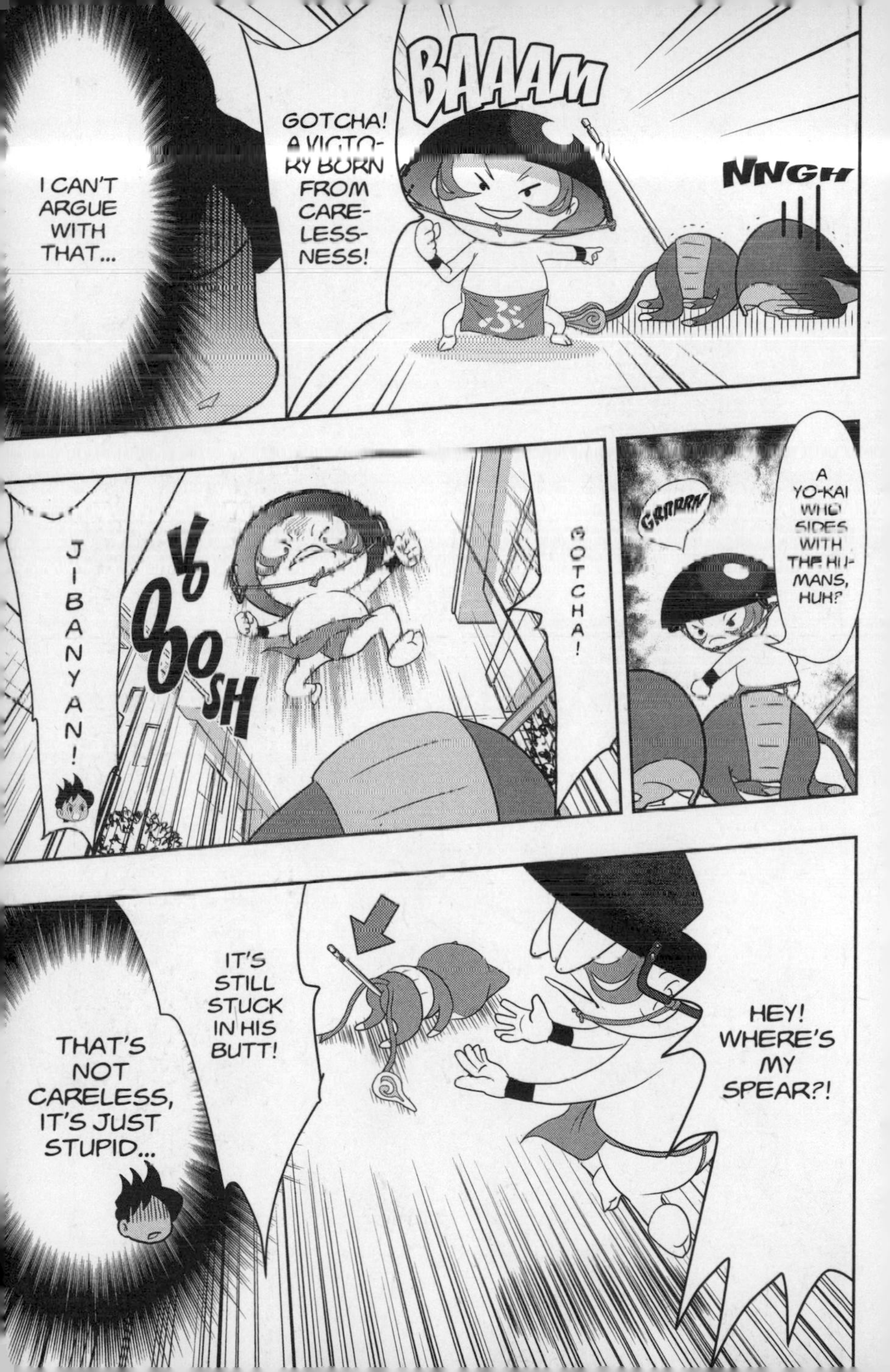
NNGH
BAAAM
GOTCHA! A VICTORY BORN FROM CARELESSNESS!
I CAN'T ARGUE WITH THAT...
GRRRRN
A YO-KAI WHO SIDES WITH THE HUMANS, HUH?
GOTCHA!
VOOOOSH
JIBANYAN!
HEY! WHERE'S MY SPEAR?!
IT'S STILL STUCK IN HIS BUTT!
THAT'S NOT CARELESS, IT'S JUST STUPID...

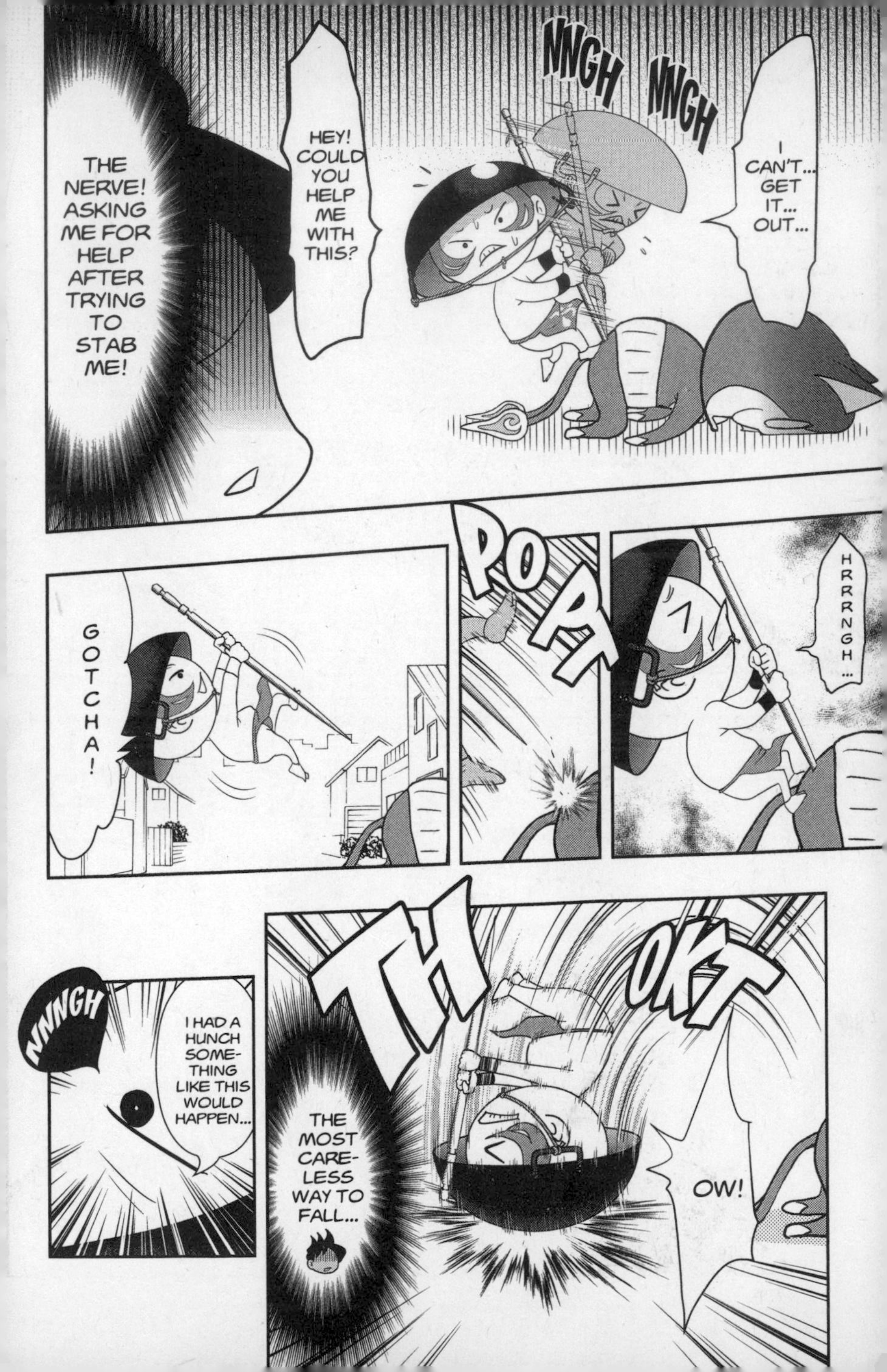
NNGH NNGH
I CAN'T... GET IT... OUT...
HEY! COULD YOU HELP ME WITH THIS?
THE NERVE! ASKING ME FOR HELP AFTER TRYING TO STAB ME!
HRRRNGH...
POP
GOTCHA!
THOK
OW!
THE MOST CARE-LESS WAY TO FALL...
NNNGH
I HAD A HUNCH SOME-THING LIKE THIS WOULD HAPPEN...

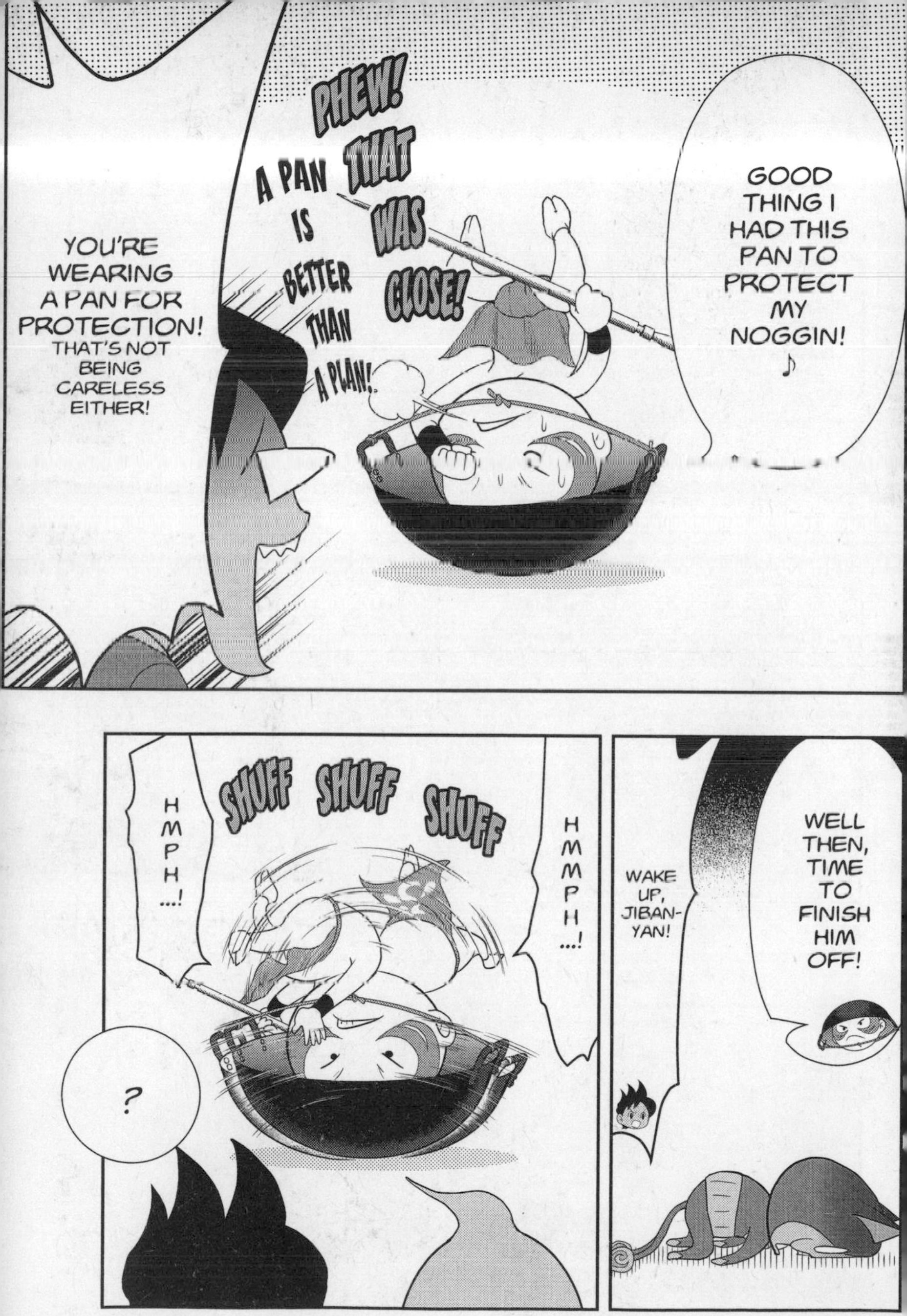
GOOD THING I HAD THIS PAN TO PROTECT MY NOGGIN! ♪
PHEW! THAT WAS CLOSE!
A PAN IS BETTER THAN A PLAN!
YOU'RE WEARING A PAN FOR PROTECTION! THAT'S NOT BEING CARELESS EITHER!
WELL THEN, TIME TO FINISH HIM OFF!
WAKE UP, JIBAN-YAN!
HMMPH...!
SHUFF SHUFF SHUFF
HMPH...!
?

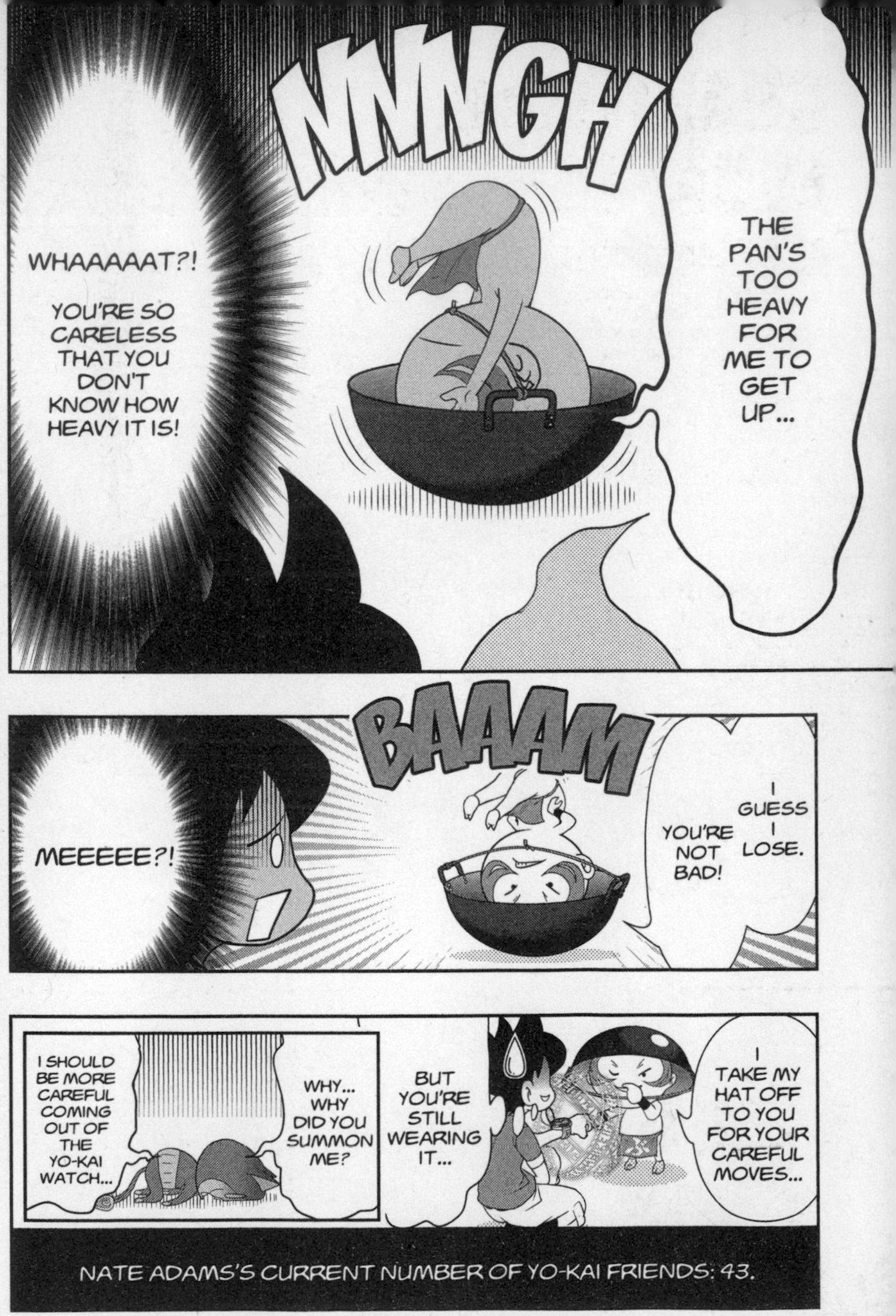
THE PAN'S TOO HEAVY FOR ME TO GET UP...
NNNGH
WHAAAAAT?!
YOU'RE SO CARELESS THAT YOU DON'T KNOW HOW HEAVY IT IS!
BAAAM
I GUESS I LOSE.
YOU'RE NOT BAD!
MEEEEEE?!
I TAKE MY HAT OFF TO YOU FOR YOUR CAREFUL MOVES...
BUT YOU'RE STILL WEARING IT...
WHY... WHY DID YOU SUMMON ME?
I SHOULD BE MORE CAREFUL COMING OUT OF THE YO-KAI WATCH...
NATE ADAMS'S CURRENT NUMBER OF YO-KAI FRIENDS: 43.

CHAPTER 58: ESCAPE THE SWEAT SQUEEZE

FEATURING SWEATY YO-KAI SWELTON

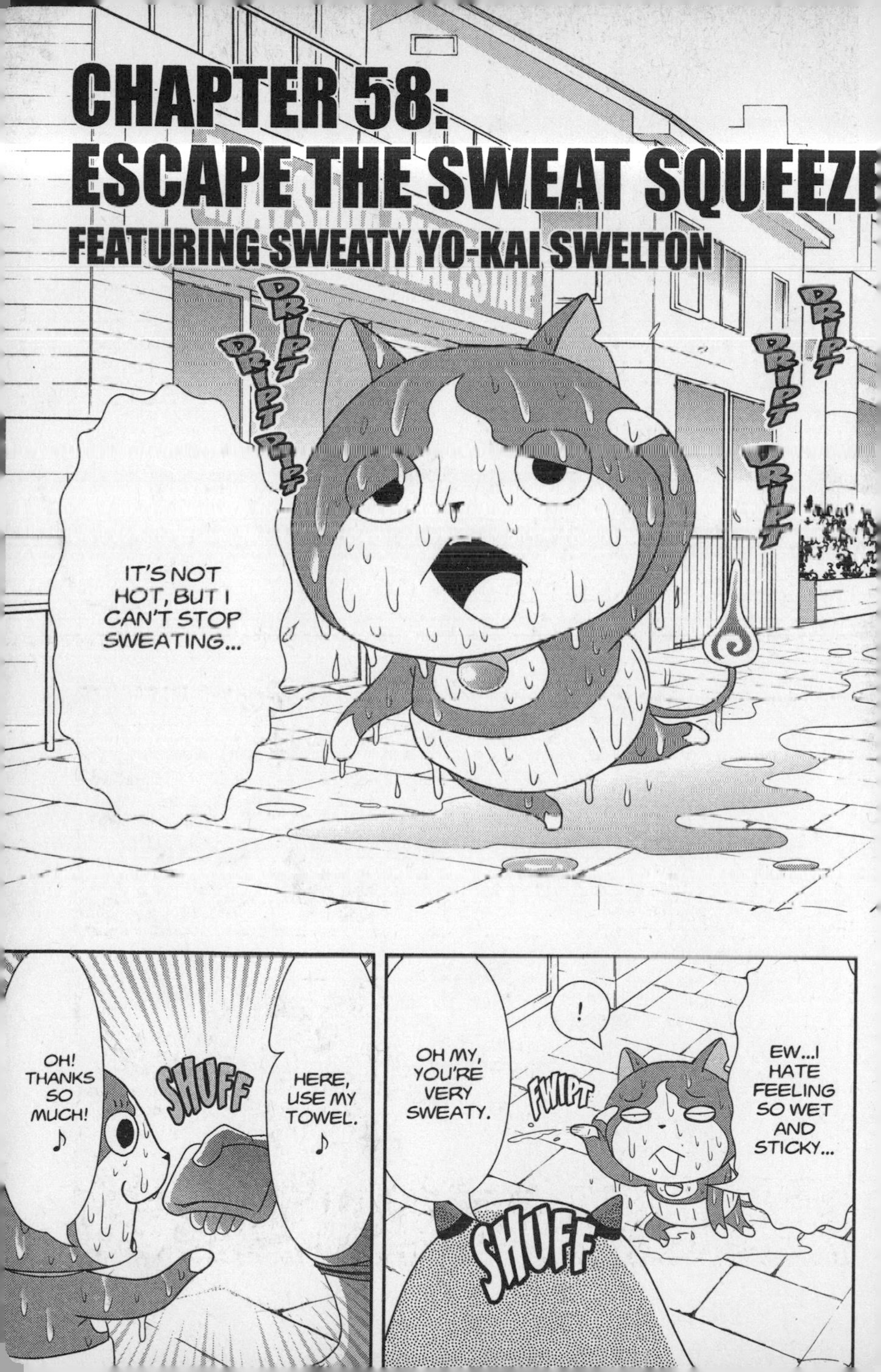
DRIPT
DRIPT
DRIPT
DRIPT
DRIPT
IT'S NOT HOT, BUT I CAN'T STOP SWEATING...
!
EW...I HATE FEELING SO WET AND STICKY...
FWIPT
OH MY, YOU'RE VERY SWEATY.
SHUFF
HERE, USE MY TOWEL. ♪
SHUFF
OH! THANKS SO MUCH! ♪

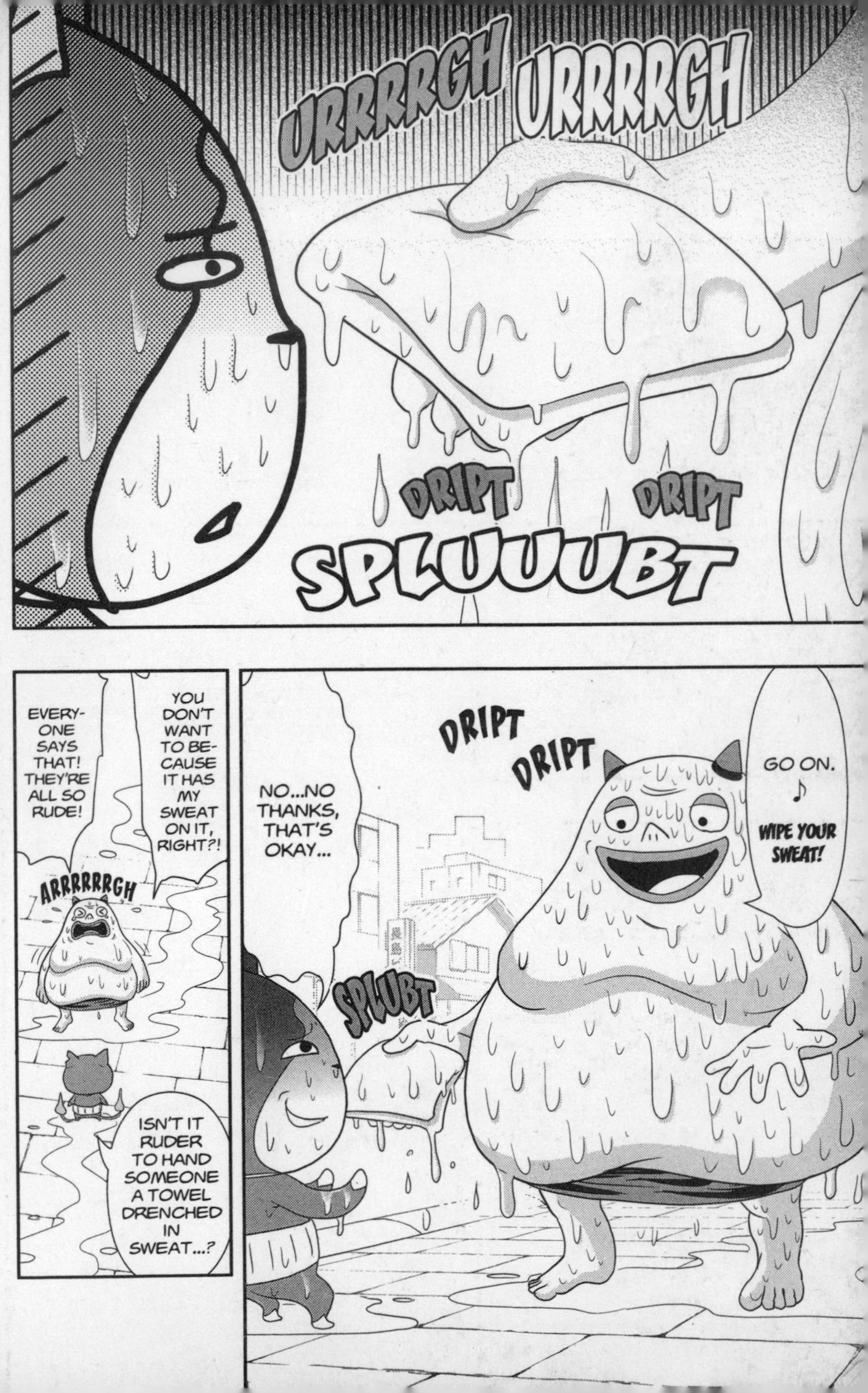
URRRRGH
URRRRGH
DRIPT
DRIPT
SPLUUUBT
GO ON. ♪
WIPE YOUR SWEAT!
DRIPT
DRIPT
NO...NO THANKS, THAT'S OKAY...
SPLUBT
YOU DON'T WANT TO BE-CAUSE IT HAS MY SWEAT ON IT, RIGHT?!
EVERY-ONE SAYS THAT! THEY'RE ALL SO RUDE!
ARRRRRRGH
ISN'T IT RUDER TO HAND SOMEONE A TOWEL DRENCHED IN SWEAT...?

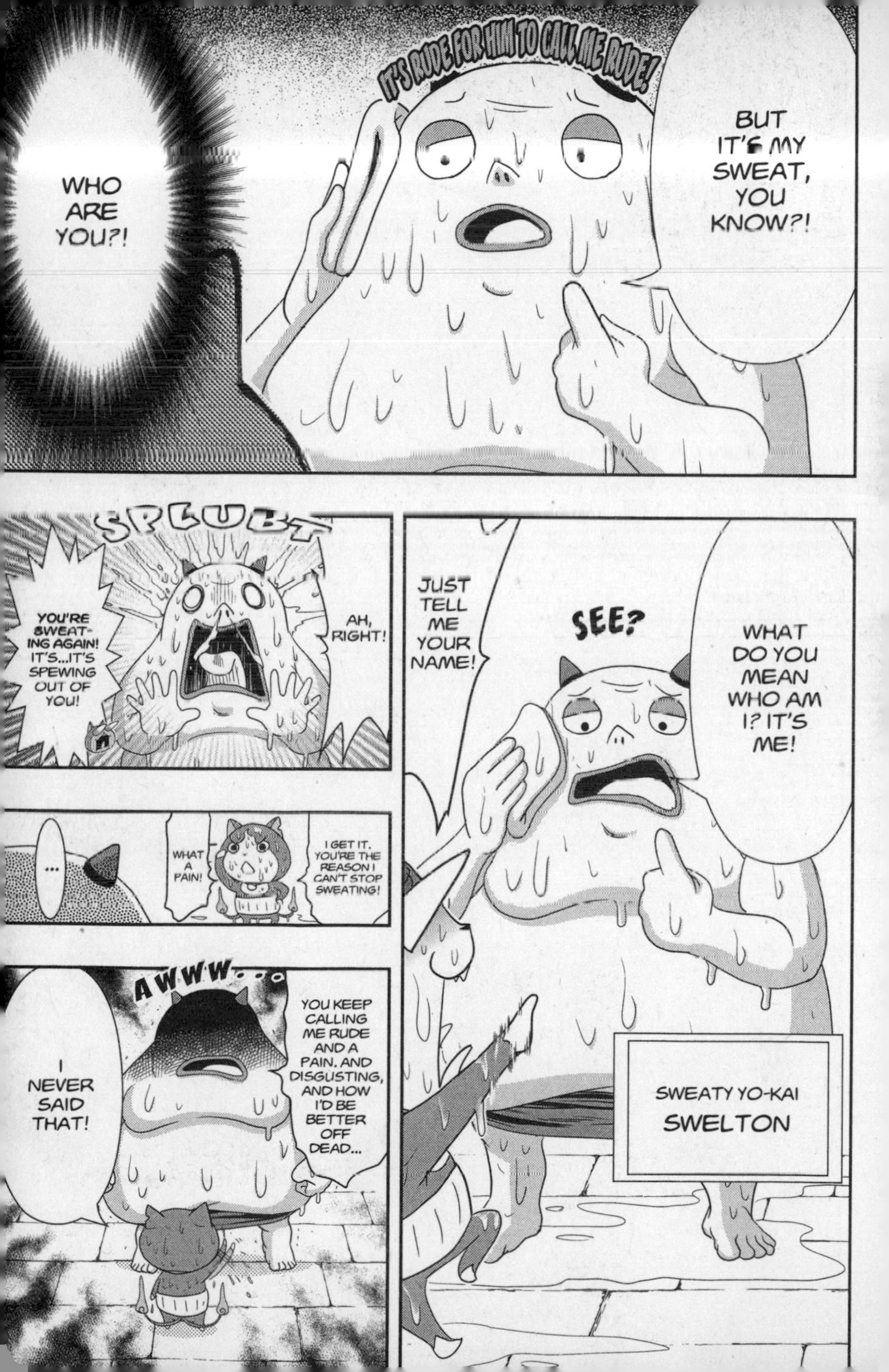
BUT IT'S MY SWEAT, YOU KNOW?!
IT'S RUDE FOR HIM TO CALL ME RUDE!
WHO ARE YOU?!
WHAT DO YOU MEAN WHO AM I? IT'S ME!
SEE?
JUST TELL ME YOUR NAME!
SWEATY YO-KAI SWELTON
SPLUBT
AH, RIGHT!
YOU'RE SWEAT-ING AGAIN! IT'S...IT'S SPEWING OUT OF YOU!
I GET IT. YOU'RE THE REASON I CAN'T STOP SWEATING!
WHAT A PAIN!
...
YOU KEEP CALLING ME RUDE AND A PAIN. AND DISGUSTING, AND HOW I'D BE BETTER OFF DEAD...
AWWW...
I NEVER SAID THAT!

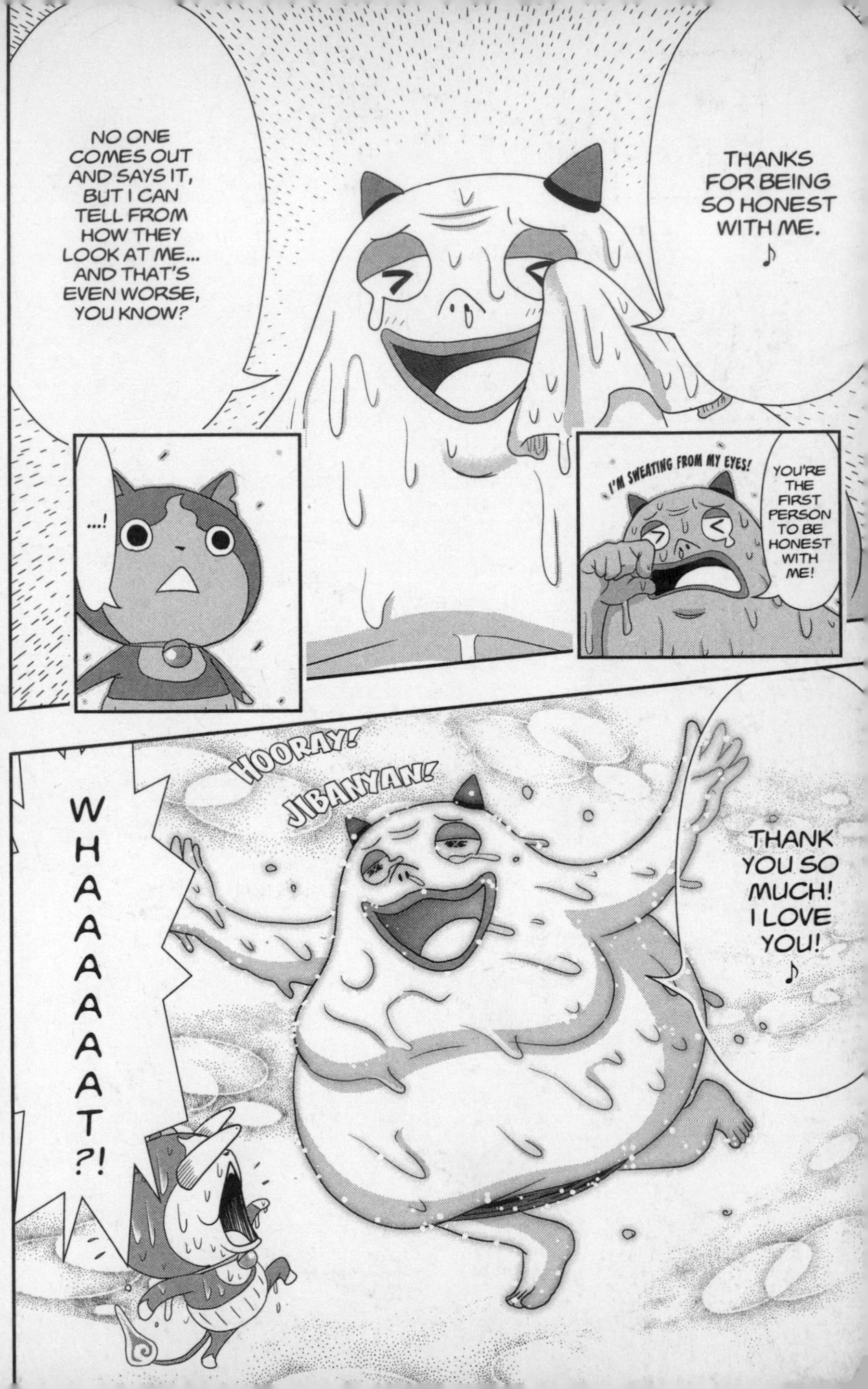
THANKS FOR BEING SO HONEST WITH ME. ♪
NO ONE COMES OUT AND SAYS IT, BUT I CAN TELL FROM HOW THEY LOOK AT ME... AND THAT'S EVEN WORSE, YOU KNOW?
YOU'RE THE FIRST PERSON TO BE HONEST WITH ME!
I'M SWEATING FROM MY EYES!
...!
THANK YOU SO MUCH! I LOVE YOU! ♪
HOORAY!
JIBANYAN!
WHAAAAAAT?!

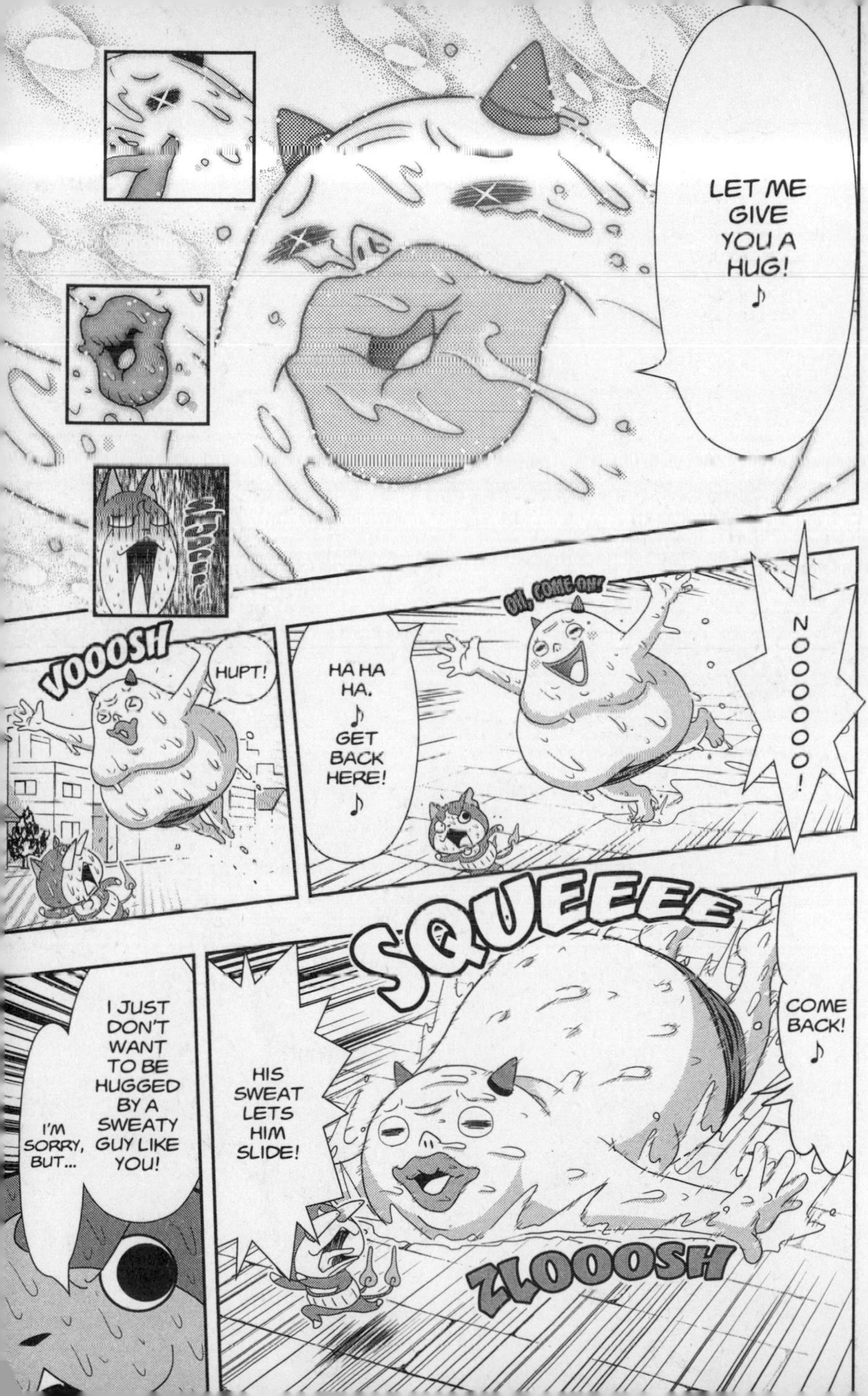
LET ME GIVE YOU A HUG! ♪
NOOOOOOO!
OH, COME ON!
HA HA HA. ♪ GET BACK HERE! ♪
HUPT!
VOOOSH
SQUEEEE
COME BACK! ♪
HIS SWEAT LETS HIM SLIDE!
ZLOOOSH
I JUST DON'T WANT TO BE HUGGED BY A SWEATY GUY LIKE YOU!
I'M SORRY, BUT...

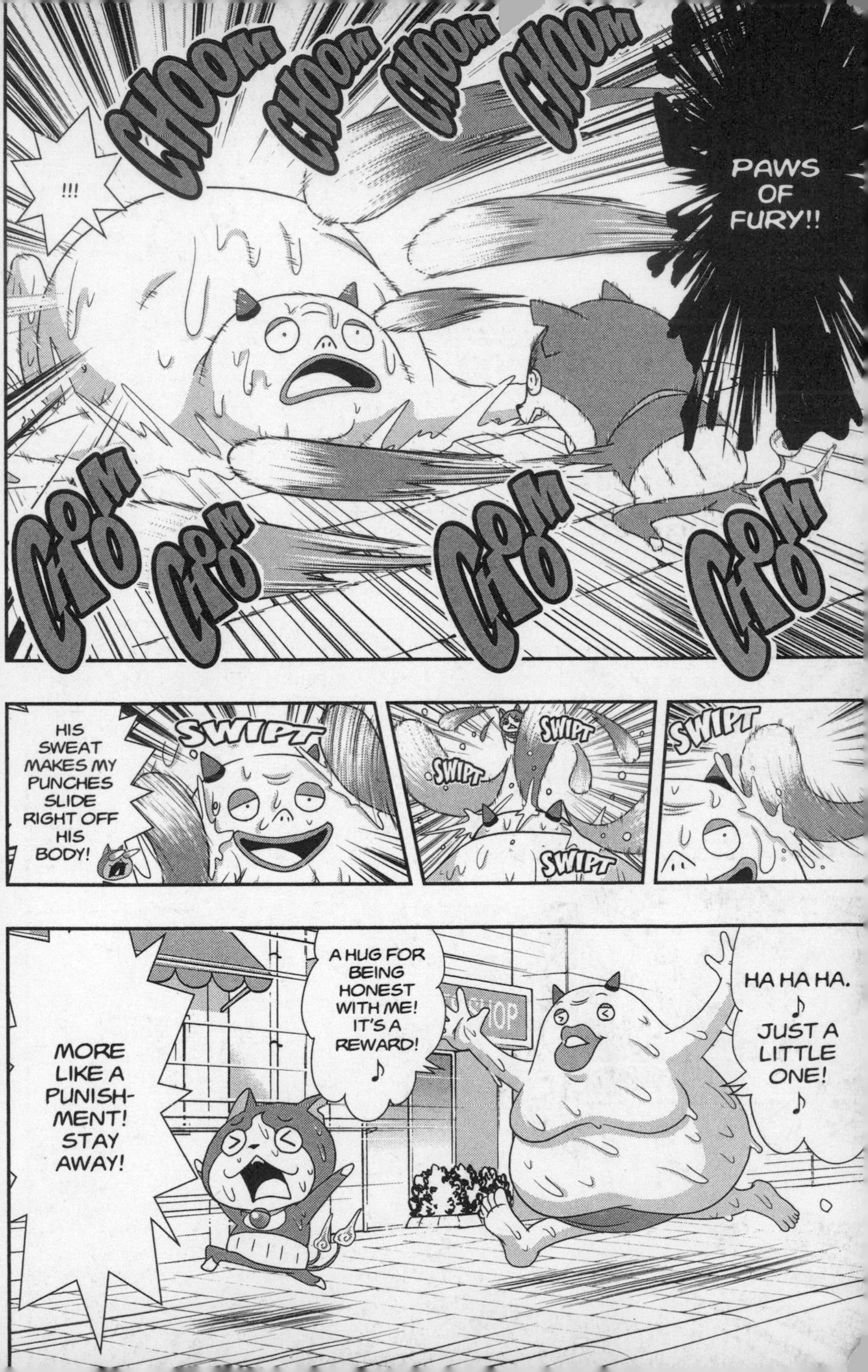
PAWS OF FURY!!
CHOOM CHOOM CHOOM CHOOM
!!!
CHOOM CHOOM CHOOM CHOOM
SWIPT
SWIPT
SWIPT
SWIPT
SWIPT
HIS SWEAT MAKES MY PUNCHES SLIDE RIGHT OFF HIS BODY!
HA HA HA. ♪ JUST A LITTLE ONE! ♪
A HUG FOR BEING HONEST WITH ME! IT'S A REWARD! ♪
SHOP
MORE LIKE A PUNISH-MENT! STAY AWAY!

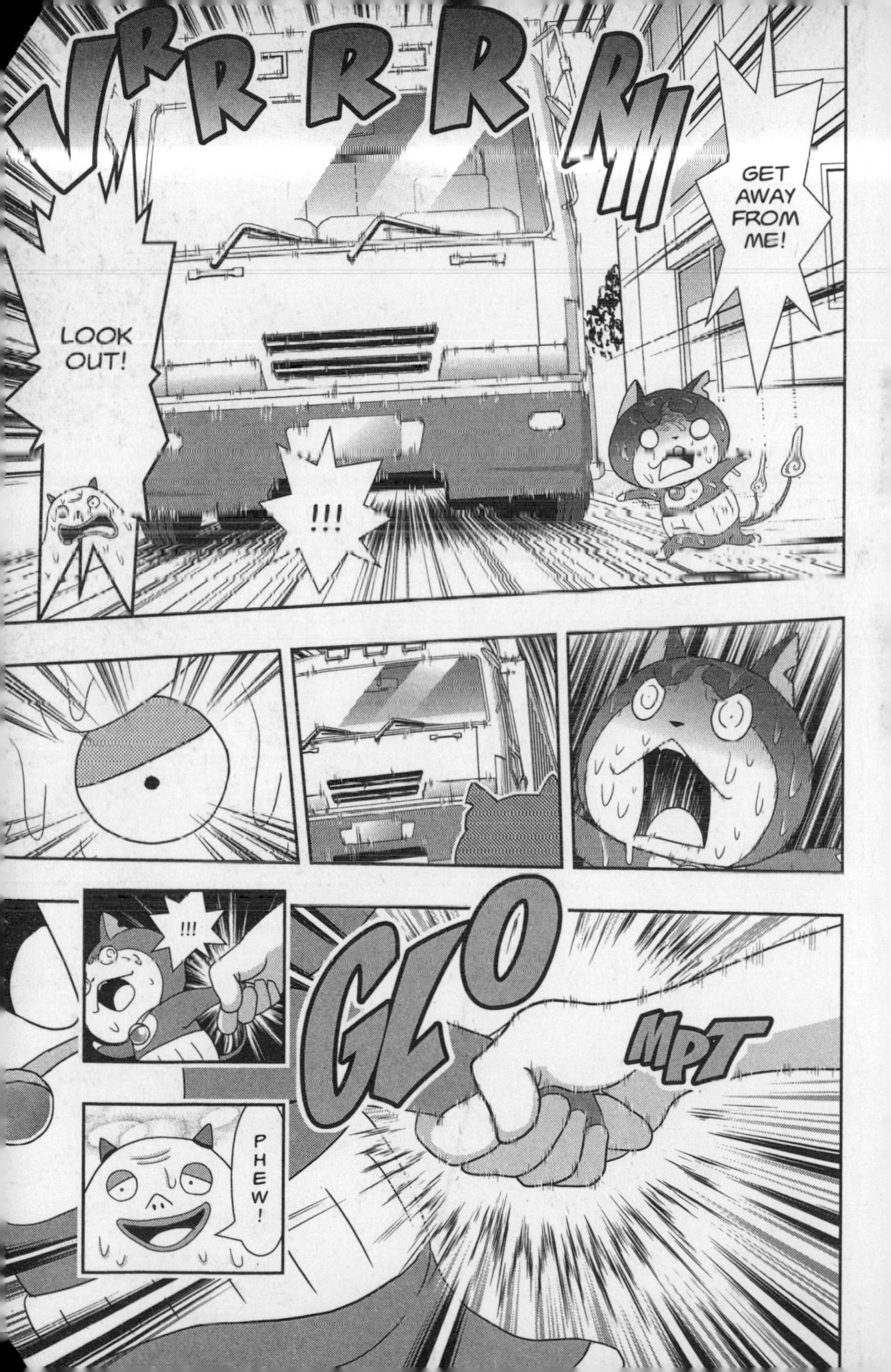
VRRRRRM
GET AWAY FROM ME!
LOOK OUT!
!!!
GLOMPT
!!!
PHEW!

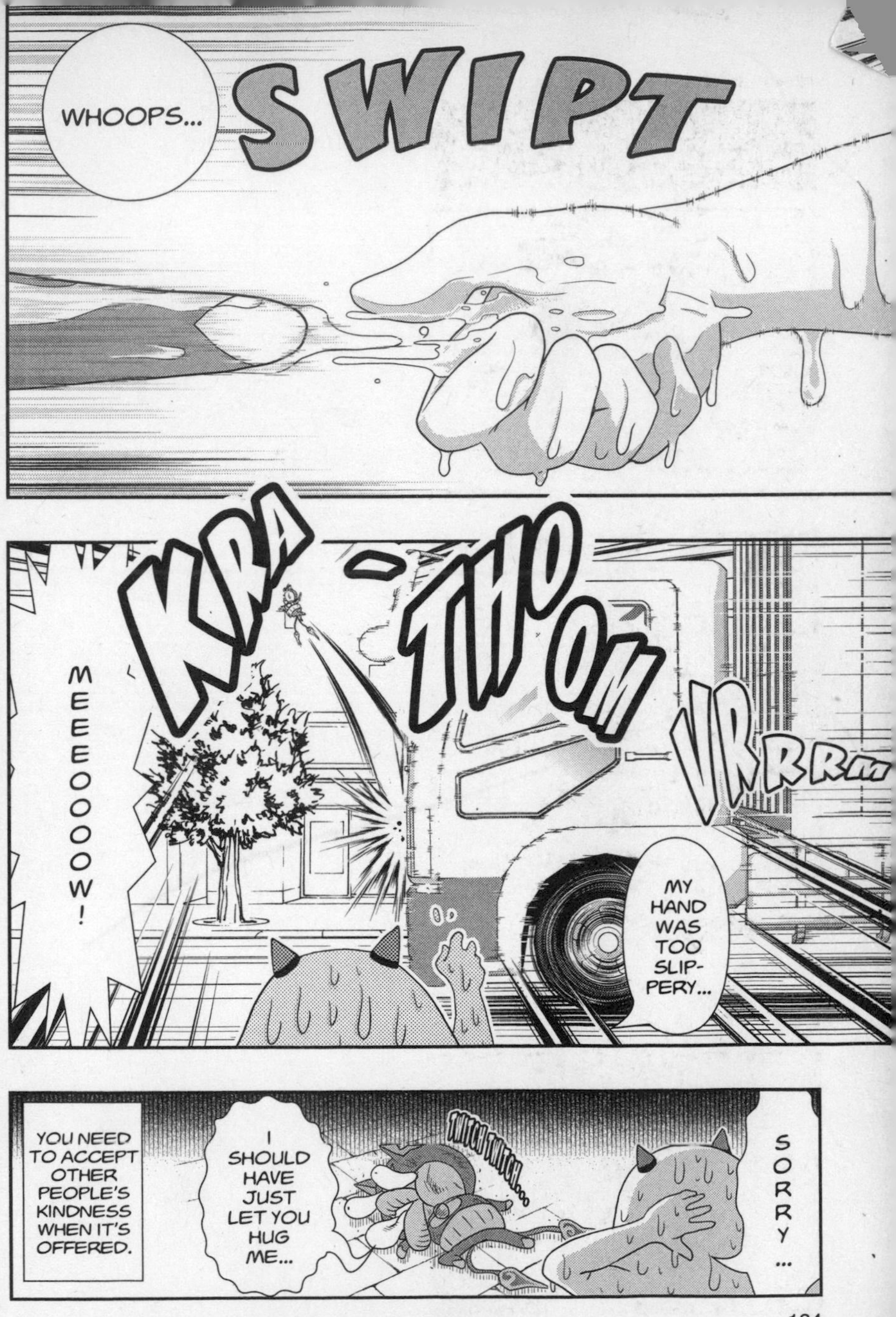
SWIPT
WHOOPS...
VRRRM
MY HAND WAS TOO SLIPPERY...
KRA-THOOM
MEEEOOOOOW!
SORRY...
TWITCH TWITCH...
I SHOULD HAVE JUST LET YOU HUG ME...
YOU NEED TO ACCEPT OTHER PEOPLE'S KINDNESS WHEN IT'S OFFERED.

RINSE & REPEAT

SQUEEE
ARE YOU OKAY?!
I FEEL SO SORRY FOR YOU!
SPLUBT
ARRRGH... SO I GOT HUGGED ANY-WAY...
OH?
VOOSH
SWIPT
MY BODY SLIPPED AWAY BE-CAUSE OF THE SWEAT! HOO-RAY! ♪
ARRRRRRGH
STOP! NO!
FWOOOSH
NO WAY! ♪
CLOMPT CLOMPT CLOMPT
KRA-THOOM
NO! YOU'RE HEADED FOR THE STREET!
NOT AGAIN!

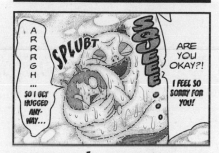

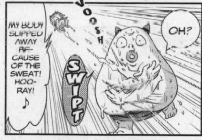

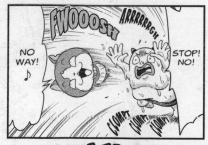

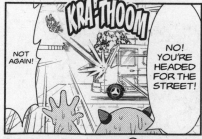

(YO-KAI WATCH VOLUME⑥END / CONTINUED IN VOLUME⑦)

CRACKED WATERMELON

IS IT TRUE THAT IF YOU EAT A WATER-MELON SEED, YOU'LL GROW ONE IN YOUR STOMACH?
IT'S NOT TRUE, BUT EATING WATERMEL-ON DOES MAKE YOU FAST AND STRONG.. LIKE ME!
I'M QUITE AGILE, YOU KNOW. ♪
SHUFF
WATCH THIS. ♪
SHUFF
OOH !!
THUK
OOPS!
KRSHAA
UM...
FUMP

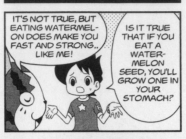

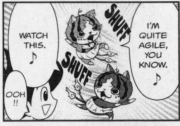

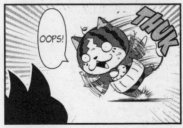

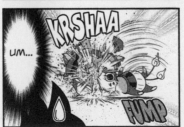

Welcome to the world of Little Battlers eXperience! In the near future, a boy named Van Yamano owns Achilles, a miniaturized robot that battles on command! But Achilles is no ordinary LBX. Hidden inside him is secret data that Van must keep out of the hands of evil at all costs!

All six volumes available now!

DANBALL SENKI
© 2011 Hideaki FUJII / SHOGAKUKAN
©LEVEL-5 Inc.

Little Battlers eXperience

Story and Art by HIDEAKI FUJII

AUTHOR BIO

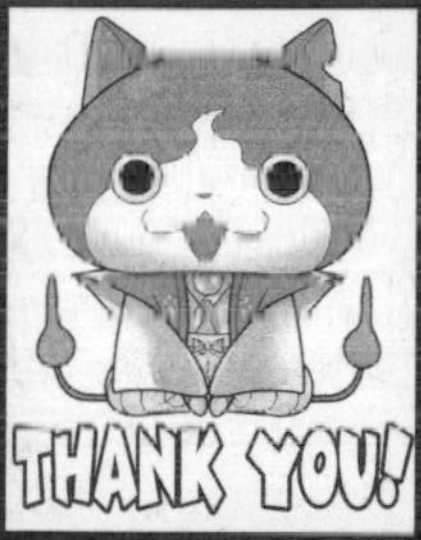
THANK YOU!

Thanks to your support, the *YO-KAI WATCH* manga received the 60th Shogakukan Manga Award. Thank you very much.

—Noriyuki Konishi

Noriyuki Konishi hails from Shimabara City in Nagasaki Prefecture, Japan. He debuted with the one-shot *E-CUFF* in *Monthly Shonen Jump Original* in 1997. He is known for writing manga adaptations of *AM Driver* and *Mushiking: King of the Beetles*, along with *Saiyuki Hiro Go-Kū Den!*, *Chōhenshin Gag Gaiden!! Card Warrior Kamen Riders*, *Go-Go-Go Saiyuki: Shin Gokūden* and more. Konishi was the recipient of the 38th Kodansha manga award in 2014 and the 60th Shogakukan manga award in 2015.

THIS IS THE END OF THIS GRAPHIC NOVEL!

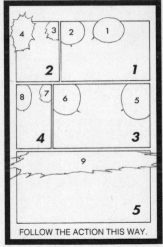

FOLLOW THE ACTION THIS WAY.

To properly enjoy this Perfect Square graphic novel, please turn it around and begin reading from right to left.